MW01095083

COTTON CANDY MASSACRE

Written, Directed, and Produced by
Christopher Robertson

WARNING! THIS BOOK CONTAINS:

Clowns.

Eating disorders.

Like, a lot of clowns.

Explicit violence and gore.

Did I mention there are clowns?

Oh, and scenes of a sexual nature.

It's an 80s movie. You know the drill.

And RUN FOR YOUR LIFE THERE'S MORE FUCKING CLOWNS!!!

ALSO FROM TERRORSCOPE

Virgin Night
My Zombie Sweetheart
The October Society - Season One

Candy Apple Smiles (featured in Blood Rites Horror
Welcome to the Funhouse)

Coming soon...
The October Society - Season Two

REVIEWS

"Chris's writing remains unlike anything in the horror genre, it's mix of humour, heart, and horror being like an assault. Chris has stated that he doesn't view himself as a writer more a storyteller. I would argue that he is and that he's one of the most important voices working in the horror genre today."

- Jamie Stewart, author of The House That Bleeds and Montague's Carnival of Delights and Terror, for Virgin Night.

"Christopher Robertson is writing books that will make any of us who spent hours looking at VHS covers in small dusty video stores smile from cover to cover."

- Damien Casey, author of Pup and The Village of Gil, for Virgin Night.

"This is one of those books that will literally beat you to death with 90's nostalgia (in a good way)."

- Andrew Robert (DarkLit Press), for The October Society - Season One.

"When I say Christopher Robertson has a way with words, I mean he can quite literally pull you into a story and make you see what he does."

- Julia C. Lewis, curiosityboughtthebook.com, for The October Society - Season One.

"Christopher Robertson's new book delves back into the 90s era of kid-friendly horror, taking a leaf or two from RL Stine and Are You Afraid of the Dark. But any ideas of mere homage are quickly dispelled by the author's imagination and writing, which is sharp, poppy and most importantly for this type of book, fun."

- Denver Grenell, author of The Burning Boy and Other Stories, for The October Society - Season One.

"My Zombie Sweetheart is 50s nostalgia, zombie-alien apocalypse and teenage heartbreak put into a blender and set on high. It's fun and sweet until it's not—until it's emotionally wrenching, gore-tastic, cinematically explosive, let's turn this shit up—and I am HERE FOR IT."

- Brittany Johnson, author of Mississippi Blue, for My Zombie Sweetheart.

Heya! Y'all want some toot-tootin' tunes to go with your reading of this here book? Well, golly-gee, hot-dang! Give this here QR Code a scan.

SCAN ME

Don't got no fancy QR scanning thingamajigs? Just head on over to Spotify and search for The Cotton Candy Massacre.

Cotton Candy is my Life!

A Foreword by Damien Casey

"HOLY JUMPED-UP BALD-HEADED JESUS PALAMINA!" Your voice carries all the way through your parents' two-story home. They've worked hard to have such a nice home for your family. At least, that's what they tell you at dinner every night.

Tonight was spaghetti with broccoli sauce instead of tomato.

It looked like pale little green worms someone barfed up.

Why is it so green?

Is this Hi-C?

You send a message to your best friend, "AYYYEEEEEEEEEEE MY CAPS LOCK ISN'T BROKEN I'M JUST STOKED! THE NEW CHRISTOPHER ROBERTSON MOVIE IS PLAYING AT THE THEATER NEXT WEEK!"

The message you get back says, "Hell yuh."

You've both been waiting to see if you would get to see The Cotton Candy Massacre locally. You had to drive across the state to see Virgin Night. Even if that was, like, totes worth it, you don't feel like driving for eight hours again. Still, you're glad you did because that theater was the only one in the state that got special screener shirts for the occasion.

You throw on the soundtrack to My Zombie Sweetheart and look at the posters on your wall. The posters your dad got pissed about because you're ruining the goddamn walls in the "goddamn house they paid loads of goddamn money for!" His words, not yours. Signed 8x10s take up the space in front of your bed; you want to wake up every day and see them. Your prized possession, a Virgin Night poster signed by the actress who played your favorite character, Casey, Jessica Monroe! You couldn't believe she was going to be at that old-time reunion thing. Supposedly she was the lead in the reboot for the franchise. You ordered the older entries when you got home, despite it looking like a bargain bin version of A Nightmare on Elm Street.

Limited edition box set. Wrap around slipcover. New art for each movie with a reverse side showing the original art. You haven't watched the first one yet.

The week drrrraaaaggggssssssssssssss. You watch the entire first season of *The October Society*; when the hell is season two coming out? You watch *Virgin Night* and *My Zombie Sweetheart*. You talk about how Christopher Robertson is making movies for people like you. People who give a shit about real issues in the world. People who want these issues peppered into their entertainment just enough to make you think but not enough to take away from the fun vibe of an over-the-top horror film. You tell them his movies are unlike anything else right now, and you're sure, absolutely sure, that *The Cotton Candy Massacre* is the one that will FINALLY give him the recognition he deserves.

"You haven't seen it yet! Is that the one with the chainsaw guy in leather?" says your pop.

"Different movie! I read the plot!" you argue.

"Plot! The plot is to separate me from a twenty-dollar bill!" he says to you. He hands you the twenty with a wink and says, "I put gas in this morning in case you have to go across state again."

The big day has arrived. You throw on your "Caleb deserved better!" shirt and head to the theater. You see your best friend ordering a jumbo bucket of popcorn and a bag of gummy sharks. Friggin' weirdo is obsessed with sharks, can't even eat popcorn without them.

You talk about how excited you both are. Both of you hoping this feels like the natural continuation of Christopher's style, fun, passionate, honest, and filled with more ooey-gooey than... something really ooey-gooey.

You walk to the counter and order your ticket. The girl working is in spirit; she's painted herself like one of the clowns from the poster. Her name tag reads "Sully."

"This is the first time I've ever met someone named Sully that wasn't huge and covered in blue fur!" you joke.

Sully laughs maniacally and jumps up and down. The joke wasn't THAT funny, but you'll take the pile of cotton candy she hands you for being such a laugh-out-loud side-splitting comedian. Why is it black? You ask. It's chocolate, she tells you. Fair enough.

You feel your feet sticking to the gross floor as you sit down and relax. The coming attractions play. All the trailers are snoozefests about the same garbage. Group goes to place, something supernatural happens in place, all of them look like they were directed by someone who thinks they're the next John Carpenter. YAWN CENTRAL.

The movie starts.

You watch with your jaw open the whole time. He's really outdone himself this time. Everything you've come to love about a Christopher Robertston movie is here, only turned up to twenty-six! You laugh, you cringe, you get emotional over certain characters.

You devour the cotton candy at the same rate your mind devours the movie. Tonight is perfect.

Well, it would be if the booger-dick behind you would just quit snorting sarcastically at everything. Who is this guy? Siskel and Ebert? You turn and ask him that with a mouth full of cotton candy. He stares at you like you're some unhinged maniac. He shuts up, and that's really all that matters.

The movie flies by in a blur after this; you're high on the art of film. The experience is becoming as surreal as an acid trip. Movie mixes reality, and reality mixes with movie until you're positive you can feel all the ooey-gooey covering you from head to toe.

The credits roll, and you look to your friend and announce that *The Cotton Candy Massacre* is Christopher Robertson's best work and that you're going to go buy you both tickets for the next screening. What a ride!

The silly goose doesn't respond because they are clearly still blown away by the film. You ask why they jammed that chunk of plastic in their head like a shark fin; they don't answer.

The annoying guy behind you must have fallen asleep while drinking his cherry slushie. His face is covered in the red mess of spilled drink. You notice no one else is leaving the theater either.

"I'LL GET US ALL TICKETS!" you proclaim as you jump through the doors into the lobby.

Sully is there holding two giant masses of chocolate cotton candy. She hands you one. You both intertwine your fingers as you eat cotton candy. You both hold hands and skip back into the theater for the second showing. You both laugh hysterically as you look at your painted clown faces in a mirror she pulls from her pocket as the opening credits roll.

"The noblest art is that of making others happy."
P.T. Barnum

"We're all pretty bizarre. Some of us are just better at hiding it, that's all."
John Hughes

For Casey.
You're the best.

Chapter One
ONCE UPON A TIME
AT A SLUMBER PARTY

Sometime in the early 80s...

Two girls are up way past their bedtime in a bedroom lined with posters of boy bands and kittens. One taller with jet black hair, the other light, round and bouncy—both lit by the single flashlight the blonde girl holds beneath her chin.

"And then, she goes down to the car; she can't see anything because the lights are so bright, and she can't hear anything because the radio's on. She calls out her boyfriend's name, he doesn't answer, and then she gets close and sees that someone's cut his pecker right off—"

"Ew! Gross!" The dark-haired girl makes a face, but it's an act; it's clear she loves the story.

"And when she goes to scream, she can't... because the man behind her rips her throat out!"

Both girls scream, staring right at one another.

"Then what happens?" The dark-haired girl's eyes sparkle with macabre glee.

"I dunno," the other says. "Mom heard us and made us stop watching."

"Aw," the other girl pouts, and then a wicked smile spreads across her face. "I got one," she says with wicked delight. She climbs off the bed and starts rummaging in her closet. Clothes and shoes fly through the air behind her. "I know it's somewhere in here!" The dark-haired girl holds up a black VHS tape with a blank, torn white label.

"What's that?" the blonde girl asks and scoots across the bed.

The dark-haired girl beckons her friend to follow. "We gotta sneak downstairs and I'll show you."

The stairs and floorboards of the dark-haired girl's house threaten to betray them, but they make it down to the den without detection. Holding the tape like it's radioactive, the dark-haired girl explains, "My dippy stepbrother taped this commercial late one night. It's not supposed to be on anymore."

"Why?"

"You'll see." She loads it into the VCR and hits a series of buttons on the massive TV remote. The room fills with white, static light, blasting both girls in their pajamas into near blindness.

"Hey, kids!" A diminutive clown with lazily applied makeup fills the screen. It's shot on Super 8, and you can barely see the scanlines for the static. Bristly hair pokes through the pancake, and it's not just color distortion making his teeth yellow. "You wanna go bonkers this summer!?" He somehow rolls his eyes in two different directions while a taped audio of kids screaming "Yeah!" plays. "Then come on down to Bonkin's Bonanza! Ay-yup!"

A wooden roller coaster with a painted fiberglass cat face climbs a high-rise; a couple holds each other tight in the front car. There's an awkward and brief cut to a Ferris wheel, carriages shaped like balloons, and it flicks away as the edge of the film burns.

"We got f-f-f-fun rides!"

A dumpy-looking clown in a saggy green business suit stomps along, holding the hands of two children that don't look very happy to be there—the commercial cuts to several more clowns pretending to play instruments to a less than amused crowd.

"Shows and games and everything!"

The shot flicks to a carnivalesque cast standing in front of some entrance gates. A fake rainbow with a giant, leering clown towers over them. At the center of the group stands a short clown, the same one from the start. He has one hand behind the bald strongman to his left and the other behind a beautifully buxom fortune teller to his right. The fortune teller shifts as though she doesn't like where the clown's hand is.

"Come on down to Bonkin's Bonanza this summer, and go bonkers"—the camera zooms into the clown's face though, from the shake, it's obvious the camera operator just ran toward him— "with the carnival that never ends! That's the toot-tootin' truth! Ay-yup!"

"So what?" the blonde girl pouts. "That wasn't scary at all."

"You don't get it? You've never heard of Bonkin's Bonanza?"

"Nu-uh."

"Well," the dark-haired girl's face lights up with ghoulish glee, "it happened back in—"

Summer — 1977.

The sun hangs low, real low, behind some heavy white clouds, cracking the sky like it's grinning. A more whimsical sort might see a giggling face in that, but the man behind the wheel of the big rig hurtling along the highway isn't so inclined.

The truck rattles along an empty highway—

3

"Isn't that always how these things begin? I mean, you don't have a scary story that starts on a Tuesday lunchtime at the mall, after all," the blonde girl's voice-over complains.

"No doy! Anyway, Bonkin's Bonanza was built by Buster B. Bonkin," the dark-haired girl's voice continues. "Clown, carnie and... crime lord!"

Inside the truck, Bob Seger and The Silver Bullet Band sing about how funny the night moves, though the driver ain't listening. He's been on the road too damn long, and his eyes scan ahead for any sign of an upcoming rest stop. The high beams land on a sign of a different kind, though.

"Bonkin's Bonanza — 5 Miles Away!" it reads, but the big white four-fingered gloves wrapping around the edges, not to mention the plastic blue tufts of hair and half a white painted face at the top, gives the driver the shakes. He really needs somewhere to drain the lizard and knowing that he's nearly there has saved him from fishing out another bottle, but clowns... "Clowns, man, fuckin' hate clowns!"

Might as well keep on going, the trucker reckons, but given what he's seen so far, he ain't precisely jumping at getting to his destination anymore.

"Carnival, they said," the driver complains to a faded, torn pin-up postcard of a full-figured redhead pinned to his dash. "Didn't say nothing about some clown hell hole. Oh my Sweet Petunia..."

As the truck pulls up to the front gate, it's met with a massive lit up, flashing rainbow above the entrance with one giant ass fiberglass clown leaning down from above. Neither of its bulging eyes looks the same way, and huge, stubby four-fingered hands reach down towards the gates like they're gonna scoop up some random patrons and shove them into its wide, gawping grin. The clown's legs form the frame for the gate, which sits open, couples and kids flowing each way. The driver's sure glad he doesn't need to go under that Clownzilla and follows the less-colorfully marked lane for deliveries.

It's a pretty straight shot along the side of the park; the fence is high, but here and there, flashing lights flicker above as some ride whirls around.

"Oh, you gotta be fuckin' kiddin' me," the driver moans as he turns towards a rusty-looking warehouse with an employee waving him in. Maybe it's the baggy orange suit or the shoes about half the length of his legs—no, it's the goofy grin on the damn clown's face that makes the driver want to put the pedal down and flatten the thing. The clown gives him the creeps, especially with how bored it looks, so much that the trucker can't take his eyes off it as he backs into the delivery bay, almost going too far and ramping the trailer up onto the platform.

Killing the engine, the driver closes his eyes and takes a deep breath. If he wasn't about ready to burst, he'd sign the load over, get the hell out of there and find a nice, shit- and graffiti-coated rest stop to use rather than set one foot in this bozo-infested hellscape.

The driver opens his eyes, lolls his head to the side, and— "JESUS!" He just about pisses himself at the sight of the clown in the orange jumpsuit right up against his window.

DINK-DINK-DINK, it taps on the window with, thankfully, a regular human-sized hand. It mimes rolling the window down hypnotically. The driver complies and only stares at the clown as it speaks.

"Hey, buddy, you need me to sign that." The clown nods to a clipboard on the dash. The driver reaches for it, never breaking eye contact, even as the clown squiggles his initials somewhere on the paper. "Gonna take us, like, half an hour to get this emptied, might as well stretch your legs." The clown rises to the window, and as it leans in, the driver instinctively moves away. The clown looks around, then uses its hand to shield its mouth as it says, "Stay away from the corn dogs though, trust me."

"O-OK, thanks," the driver manages to say.

The clown in the orange jumpsuit vanishes, and as the driver looks in his mirror, he sees a line of clowns unloading the back of his truck.

"Nope, think I'm gonna stay right here," the driver says and rolls the window up. The freaky accordion music from the park bleeds in, so the driver cranks the radio and tries to drown it out. Closing his eyes, he figures he'll grab a nap before moving on.

So that's why he doesn't hear the disturbance in the cab behind him as something back there stirs. That's why he doesn't see the pale hand, too white to be human, wrap its fingers around the curtain behind him and yank it open. No, the driver doesn't notice a thing till that hand lands on his shoulder and when it does, you better believe you could hear him over all the rides and screams from Bonkin's Bonanza.

BANG-TINK-BANG-TINK-BANG-TINK. Tin signs fly back, each hit with near-perfect precision. The shooter, a handsome Vietnamese man in his mid-twenties, stands aiming the air rifle with the biggest grin on his face.

The carnie getting off his stool to fetch a prize is less amused.

"Oh, Jimmy!" a pretty brunette beside the shooter cheers and throws her arms around him. She plants a kiss on his cheek and points to a stuffed purple bear in a red and white clown suit. "I want that one!" The prize is handed over to her with a grumble, and she hugs it close. Her eyes peer up over the top of the stuffed toy with nothing but love for the man who won it.

Behind the cute couple, the world's oddest one makes their way along the midway. A nearly seven-foot-tall trucker, burly, bearded with his wild hair kept in place with a well-worn hat marches on in a huff, while a man with long hair, a thin, scraggly beard, and a flowing, open silk shirt follows.

"Come on, man, you know I, like, wasn't trying to mess with you—"

"I do not care, Lee! I just do not care!" The big man turns around, faces his friend, for lack of a better word, and points an accusatory finger at him. "A man does not do that to another man when there's—" He stops himself as he looks around warily. The trucker leans in and whispers, "Clowns around here." He shudders at the thought. "The hell were you doing in my truck!"

"Funny story, man, funny story. So you know when you was back in the Bay, and I had those shrooms?"

"Of, course—"

"And you were all," the thin man puts on a macho act, "Lee don't eat those, you don't have any idea what something-something-something man..."

"And?"

"Well, man, I ate them."

"Of course!"

"And I went, like, on this trip, man. I communed. And it took me to places I needed to be, man, like for real."

"Uh-huh, and the place you needed to be was the back of my truck?"

"The Universe sent me there, man."

"Yeah, wanna know what I reckon happened? Your ass got wasted in the back of my truck and you slept for days. The only trip you went on is in your damn Swiss cheese head! The only dang journey was the one my sorry ass inadvertently dragged you on across three goddamn states!" Lee takes a bag of what looks like tree bark out from his pocket and reaches. The trucker slaps his hand. "Not here, goddamnit, Lee!"

"The Universe—"

"Had better send me a sign to a goddamn toilet."

Lee grins and points behind the big man. "She provides, Walker my man, she provides."

"Oh, you gotta be kidding me." Walker turns and spots the sign for the bathroom. A green tin arrow with two stick figures — one in pants, the other a skirt, both with fluffy clown wigs.

"Kn-ock!" a raspy voice calls from outside her tent, and the fortune teller rolls her eyes. She doesn't need her gift to see this coming again. "How's my f-f-f-favorite and f-f-f-fantastically sexy f-f-f-fortune teller doin' tonight?"

The little clown lets himself in. Though he's applied his makeup, Bonko wears a suit with tiny little suspenders holding up his pants. He snaps them for effect.

"It's quiet, Buster, like every weekday. I—"

"Nu-uh! You know that's not my name when I have my f-f-f-face on." Bonko twitches as he stutters. He gestures to his mug, smiling wide enough for the fortune teller to smell moonshine on his breath. It revolts her not just on principle, but that she can tell it's from that bootlegger Williamson in Cherry Lake. "It's Bonko! Ayyup!"

She fakes a smile, even though the little creep's stolen catchphrase makes her want to punch him. "Bonko, it's a quiet night. It'll pick up at the weekend."

"Sounds an awful lot like an excuse, Mari." Bonko waddles over to her and climbs up on the opposite chair. He stares at her across the crystal ball with both hands on the table. "How about you look into that ball of yours? See what happens to employees who don't pull their weight around here? I bet it's f-f-f-fucking enlightening!"

"Bus—Bonko—"

"You know you hafta pay? Ay-yup!"

"Please Bonko, I—"

"One way or another." The clown leers down Mari's top and does nothing to hide his lecherous gaze. "Jesus Christ, those tits are as big as my head! How'd I not notice before?"

He did; he always says this. Every single time the bastard forces Mari to go along with his perverted little games, he makes the same joke. Mari can't tell if he's unoriginal or that lazy, and really, that's the least of her worries. This night though, this time, she's had enough.

"Look at me, Buster—"

"Bonko—"

"Look at me!" Bonko's eyes snap to Mari's, and he finds the fury in them arousing. "I am not sleeping with you ever again. Do you understand?"

"Aw, but I hears ya hubby likes it? Guessin' it's the 'roids? I hears they make a man's wing-dinger shrivel up, an' you know I ain't got that problem," Bonko winks.

"I'm not doing it."

"Okey-dokey-do." Bonko jumps down off the seat, just like that. It's too easy. Mari doesn't trust it.

"That's it?"

"Yeah, no worries, dollface. One of the other skanks around here will do. Oh, wait, did ya think you was special?" Bonko begins to laugh; he wipes away a pretend tear. "Oh, wow, nah toots, I like 'em big titties, but there ain't nothin' special 'bout you 'sides them. That's the toot-tootin' truth!" Bonko waddles towards the entrance. "So just clean out your shit and be gone by the morning."

"You're firing me?"

"Ay-yup! And your big dumb husband too."

"B-but where will we go? Carnival season is nearly over; we put everything we had into this place!"

Bonko pretends to be very interested in the dirt under his fingernails. "You shoulda thought of that before hurtin' my f-f-f-feelings, bitch."

That last insult does it. Even though she has no idea how they'll make ends meet, Mari's had enough. "Fine. I hope you get VD and die, you ugly little shit."

"Halfway there, toots," Bonko says, and Mari throws up in her mouth a little. "Just make sure y'all square up before you leave."

"Square up?"

"Oh yeah." Bonko counts on his stubby little fingers. "You've had your trailer parked on my land for oh, say two months now? That's a helluva lotta rent you owe me. Now. I'm a magnanimous kinda guy, I is. Ay-yup! I don't charge my employees jack shit for parking their rides on my property. But f-f-f-freeloading whores and their tiny-dicked husbands, well they gots ta pay." Bonko rubs his fingers together gleefully. "And that's the toot-tootin' truth."

"How much?" Marianna asks, resignation building within.

Bonko tuts and haws. "'Least a grand."

"You know we don't have anything close to that."

"I also know you got them big old titties, and I wanna nuzzle into them like you was my momma."

"Fine," she relents. "But in your office."

"Nah, your trailer toots." Bonko pulls back the curtain and invites Mari to follow. "'Sides,' I gots to take a monster shit first."

Mari forces the bile back down her throat and follows.

"Nope," Walker shakes his head, "No goddang way."

He stands before three urinals in the men's bathroom. Each shaped like a gaping, slack-jawed clown's mouth with the rest of the face painted on the tiles above.

Never in Walker's life has the man experienced such a paradox before, the urgent need to whizz combined with the complete and utter inability to do so. Even if he was brave enough to whip it out in front of those abominations, Walker knows it would do no good. He feels like one of those painted faces is giving him the thirsty eye, which tears it.

"There is no way in hell." He turns and heads to the single cubicle door. "Oh, Sweet Petunia." He stands in astonishment at the sight of a toilet shaped like an upside down clown, its open mouth the bowl. Walker has seen a great many things on the road, things that don't belong on this earth, things that would cost anyone sleepless nights, but this right here is a thing of pure nightmare fuel. This ceramic monstrosity will be the only toilet in the world that stays clean forever because there's no way in hell he can imagine anyone putting their cheeks anywhere near those clown lips.

"I fuckin' hate clowns!"

Walker decides he'd rather piss his pants, though he settles for a quiet spot somewhere outside on reflection. The restrooms sit on the edge of the midway, and through the fence, Walker spots some trailers. One of them's gotta have a bathroom, right? Beats whipping it out in the open; sure as shit some kid and their folks will happen by, and that's all he needs. So Walker heads over, hoping his gruffness will help him blend in with the rest of the crew.

He passes between two trailers when a loud slap followed by a voice that sounds like it's smoked two hundred cigarettes a day for years calls out, "That's what ya get, ay-yup!" A woman screams in pain, and that brings Walker to a halt.

"All I wanted was a whizz. Just a whizz, God, and what do you do? Y'all send me to a bathroom ripped right from the depths of hell, then shove me into the path of some poor woman getting a smackdown. You know I can't abide that, so why God, why? Why do you got a problem with me taking a freakin' whizz?! Why?!"

Walker steps up to the window, tall enough to see in with just the slightest effort, and the scene laid before his eyes scars his soul. At first, a smile creeps across his face, making that big old beard rustle like a bush full of badgers. On her hands and knees is a woman with two of the most enormous breasts Walker ever did see. Even rounder and more voluptuous than his dear, Sweet Petunia. Then his face fills with sheer, abject horror and disgust as his eyes follow the woman to her rear, to the diminutive clown standing on a footstool behind her, thrusting away with a shit-eating grin on his pancaked face.

A tug-of-war follows on Walker's face. One second it lights up with lustful delight; the next, it droops with pure revulsion. The contrasting sight of such a beautiful woman and a goddamn clown humping away at her breaks Walker's mind for a minute. These two things should not exist simultaneously. Like a pigeon on a bike, it just goes against all natural laws.

"Turn around, toots, I want to f-f-f-finish all over dem titties!" the short ass clown orders, head ticking to the side as he stutters, and Walker's cheeks bubble like a hamster. He swallows his puke as the woman does what the clown says, kneeling in front as he stands on a chair, hands on hips.

"This ain't right," Walker mumbles, and it could apply to his peepin', or the goings-on inside the trailer; it's hard to tell.

The trailer door opens, and a huge man smashes into the room. Nothing but muscle on display above a tiger print banana hammock, he looks at the scene before him with indignant awe.

"Mari!" the strongman yells.

"Chet!" the woman screams.

"I'm cumming," the little clown adds.

For a second, the world freezes; nobody has any clue how to react to a mind-breaking scene of such ridiculously disgusting depravity.

This can't possibly get any more fucked, Walker finds himself thinking.

"There ya go, Chet my boy, I hear yous likes suckin' baby batter off your wife's tatas," the little clown says.

"Mari?" The strongman looks at his wife, confused.

"I didn't want to." Mari can't look at him. "He forced me. Forces all of us—"

"I'll rip you in half!" Chet, the strongman, roars.

"Now wait a minute—" The little clown holds his hands up, only for the strongman to grab him and hurl him across the room like a cannonball. He smashes through the window and lands like a starfish across Walker's dumbfounded face. A second later, he's on the ground, shoved there by Walker, who can't help but stare at the naked clown. For a moment, Walker thinks he has three legs.

"The hell you lookin' at, perv?" the clown spits as he stands up, dusting himself off.

"Bonko!" Chet bellows as he storms down the stairs of his trailer, Mari following close behind, covering herself up.

"Chet, don't do nothin'; you'll only end up in trouble," she begs, but Chet's not listening.

"Bonko, I'm gonna kill you!"

Around the side of the trailer, Bonko turns to Walker. "Ten bucks if you beat the shit out of The Roid Wonder coming our way?" When Walker doesn't answer, Bonko shrugs. "You just lost ten bucks, pal." And the little clown takes off.

As soon as the clown's gone, the strongman appears. "Where is he?!"

Walker's mind is still too broken to form words, but his hand lifts of its own volition and points to where the little naked clown ran. Chet nods thanks and races off that way.

"I fuckin' hate clowns," Walker finally says when they're gone from sight.

14

Screaming erupts across the midway, and not the "Gee isn't this fun?" kind. No, it's the "What the fuck? There's a pint-size naked clown running for his life!" kind.

"Outta the way, f-f-f-fuck bags!" Bonko yells his stumpy little legs carrying him as fast as they can towards the exit.

"Bonko!" Chet roars as he appears at the far end of the midway.

The little man runs, but with a single step, Chet covers more ground than Bonko does with five, and it's not long before the strongman bears down on him, like a semi truck on some roadkill.

"She came on to me!" Bonko insists, but it does him no good. Chet swoops down with one big hand and grabs the little man by the tufts of his blue hair. He lifts the clown up to look him right in the eye. "Would it help if I said I'm sorry?"

Chet sees red and nothing but. He looks around for somewhere to throw the clown. An antique cotton candy machine standing a few feet away catches his eye, the spotty teenager who runs it slowly backing away.

Mari pushes through the newly formed crowd. "Chet! Stop!" she screams.

Pretty sure an ass-kicking is coming either way, and knowing full well he'll just have Chet taken care of later, Bonko decides to stir the pot and get one last dig in. "Come on, man, ain't like I'm the only one 'round here shtooping her. Everyone knows you're into that."

Big mistake. That tears the last of Chet's restraint. He storms over to the cotton candy machine, an archaic monstrosity bearing the legend Zephyr.

"Chet? No!" Mari grabs his arm, tries to pull him back, and Chet elbows free, too caught up in the moment, too

15

lost in his rage to notice as his arm connects with his wife's mouth. She lands on the ground, sobbing, trying to staunch the flow of blood as loose teeth fall into her palm. A couple slip through her fingers, clattering on the cobblestones.

"Oh, this is gonna be tasty," Chet growls.

"W-wait a second now, Chet." Bonko's tone flips. "Think about it! You'll f-f-f-fry for this. Don't!"

Bonko begs for his life as Chet thrusts his little, naked body feet first down into the spinning blades of the cotton candy machine. "You can't do this! I own this place! I own you!" he wails and kicks out as his feet connect with cruel blades that have no business inside the drum. Layers of skin begin to shred, flicking off like layers of an onion, and the well of cotton candy turns from pink to dark red. Blood splatters across the drum, across Chet, across the faces of everyone standing around in shocked awe.

"My blood is in this park!" Bonko yells, irony lost on him, as the blades twang tendons apart, as they shatter his brittle tiny bones. "I'll f-f-f-fucking kill you—" is all he says as Chet pushes him all the way down and the vortex of the blades takes over. Bonko whirls in circles; it's the wildest ride in the park, spitting insults and spatter over everyone in sight. Bits of skin and bone fly free as his arms wave in the air like one of those inflatable tube men stuck on a record player. One slab of pasty meat hits a young girl in the face, while a chip of bone gets one boy in the eye, blinding him for life.

Walker stumbles through the crowd and stands beside his friend. Lee reaches into his bag of shrooms and lifts one to his mouth, uncertain if the carnie carnage before him is real or not. "Far out, man."

"You will not believe what I just saw," Walker says, then a piece of skull, complete with skin and a little tuft of blue hair, smacks him in the chest, sticking to his shirt. He stares at it, broken inside, and says nothing. Nothing until an EMT, a half hour later, shines a flashlight in Walker's eyes and asks his name. He doesn't say it; no, all Walker says is, "I fuckin' hate clowns..."

"That didn't happen," the blonde girl states, more hopeful than certain.

"It did! I kid you not," the dark-haired girl teases. They're back in the bedroom, sheets over their heads making them look like two mismatched chattering ghosts. "And you know what?"

"What?"

"I heard from my stepbrother, who heard from his friend, who heard from his older sister who went to college, that Bonkin's Bonanza is still out there. They never tore it down even after it closed, and if you go there, you can still see the blood on the ground where Bonko died."

"Shut. Up."

"It's true." The dark-haired girl's head snaps to the side. "You hear that?"

"Shut up!" The blonde pulls her hands to her mouth, eyes going wide.

"Is that... ohmygodlookitsbonko!" She points across the room, and the second the blonde girl looks away, the dark-haired girl pounces on her, covering her friend with the bedsheet.

There are screams of terror, then joy, that give way to fits of laughter as the two of them roll around together. Eventually, they tire, falling asleep tangled together in a mess of sheets and limbs.

In time the flashlight dies, plunging the room into darkness.

Chapter Two
ROUSTING ABOUT
AT THE CARNIVAL OF CRIME

A few years later...

The screech of rusted metal on concrete comes first, then a vertical crack in the dark appears. Barely a sliver, but it cuts like a laser.

"Come on, put your backs into it," someone yells outside, her voice deep and commanding, with just the right balance of implied threat and the conviction to act on it.

"Tryin', boss," another voice assures. He grunts and mumbles as he tugs at the door, but the crack only widens an inch.

"Try harder! We open in—" The rust holding the hinges tight crumbles. The door sails open fast and hard. At first, the light is blinding; the two figures beyond the threshold are indistinguishable silhouettes against brilliant daylight. One tall, broad at the top though they narrow to a stiletto sharpness on the way down. The other barely reaches the chest of the first; he's stick-thin and moves with a stooping shuffle. "—a week..." Her voice trails off.

A sea of dust motes cavort through the beam of light, the first to breach the storeroom in a decade at least.

"Oh my god, it's really still here." She walks into the gloom and yells, "Find the damn light, will ya?" Her heels clack and echo as she approaches a sliver of light that lands on faded, flaking red paint. The corner of some hulking, old machine peeks out from beneath a stained dust sheet.

Overhead the light clunks to life as a voice yells out redundantly, "Found it, boss," bathing the room in a weak yellow glow.

Much of the storage shed is of little note. Dirty sheets cover spare ride carriages, boxes of mechanical parts, and several metal shelves lining the walls and holding little save for about ten years' worth of dust. The only thing of note, and all that interests the boss, stands alone.

"They said it was destroyed, but oh, I knew better." She takes the edge of the sheet and whips it away, setting free a tide of dust. Sharp, shark-like eyes, attentive beneath slicked back hair, glint as they explore an antique, freestanding cotton candy machine. She runs a manicured finger along the surface, gently, as though stroking the thigh of a lover. A line clears in the dust, revealing cherry wood with scattered dark stains. The drum rests with a fine layer of fuzz, dark streaks, and patches faintly visible beneath.

"Whatcha found, boss?" a voice from behind asks as a carnie with long hair and mutton chops comes over, dusting himself off. He'd be taller if he didn't hold himself in a persistent hunch.

"Reese, oh my dear little Reesy, this right here is the machine that killed Bonko the Clown."

"Shit." Reese leans in to inspect the drum. "No way, is that—"

"Blood? Yes," the boss says with delight. "Yeah, it's still stained with the blood of Bonko." She draws in a deep breath, as though savoring the musty air. "You smell that?"

Reese takes a whiff. "Dust? Woodworm?"

"Money," the boss corrects him. "That, my dear Reese, is the scent of cold hard cash. Smells a little bit like blood, doesn't it?"

"Ruth—"

"Oh yes." Ruth moves her palms through the air as though framing a picture. "Folks will come for miles to see this thing. They'll pay even more to eat sweet cotton candy spun from it." She clears a spot near the edge, wiping the dust away with her hand. "We'll put a plaque commemorating it right here."

Clouds of black smoke announce the approach of a rattling little purple VW Beetle before it rounds the corner. You can see it all the way from the gates to Bonkin's Bonanza, where the leering Clownzilla still stands guard over the entrance. A decade or so of weather and disrepair hasn't done anything to soften the thing's grotesque grandeur; patches of moss even make it look like it's lost some teeth.

The driver of the Beetle spots it through the crystals and dreamcatchers hanging from her mirror, and the clown's massive, fiberglass grin triggers foul memories. She questions why she's doing this, why she's come back to Bonkin's Bonanza after all these years.

That woman, the one with the too-wide grin and beady shark eyes, found her working out of a flea market by an outlet mall just outside Redcastle.

Cut to: the big woman as she sits down, grinning with cheeks like two juicy apples. "Two bucks for your fortune," Marianna the Magnificent says, chewing some gum, barely even bothering with the faux European accent these days.

"How about I tell yours, instead?" Ruth's ready to burst, but she puts two notes down on the table and slides them over to Mari all the same. "It's got you getting out of this trash heap and heading up your own attraction again, your own tent, the whole damn thing."

"Yeah?" Mari's only got about two months left on her lease for this spot, and she's been considering not renewing. It turns out folks who shop in these kinds of malls don't want to hear how disappointing the rest of their life's going to be. "What we talkin', 'cause I ain't doin' no more topless fortune tellin'—"

"I've been looking for you, Marianna." Ruth's face lights up. "THE Marianna!"

"Listen—"

"You are her, right? From Bonkin's?" Ruth places an old, faded and torn flyer from the park's heyday on the table. It shows a gorgeous, exotic woman leaning alluringly over a table draped in purple cloth The crystal ball moved conveniently aside to let her cleavage take center stage. The woman in this run-down, sickly fluorescent rat-trap bears a striking resemblance to the one on the flyer, but only if you look for it. On paper, she's gregarious, thrusting herself into life with shameless aplomb; the one across from Ruth hides from the world behind shapeless folds of silk and lace.

"Nah, hun, that ain't me, so why don'tcha take your money an—" Mari attempts to slide the two bucks back when Ruth slams one hand down on top of her hands. Looking up, Mari watches her reach into her suit jacket pocket. Great, she figures, I'm about to get popped in a flea market; how didn't I see that one coming?

"That chain around your neck, your late husband gave you that. I saw it on the Channel Five Special." Ruth slides her hand back out and places a stack of cash on the table. Mari's jaw drops, and so does her gum, vanishing somewhere down her cleavage. She doesn't even care. Not when she's looking at more money than she's seen in the last six months. "That's five hundred dollars, Mari, and that's a signing bonus. We can discuss your rates later."

"You, uh, I mean, w-where? Where's the job?"

Ruth leans back in her seat, folding her fingers together. She doesn't need to answer; Mari knows from that grin on her face, from the fat stack she's offering. "Oh, no. No freakin' way, nu-uh, no."

The woman just cradles her fingers and smirks till Mari pulls a face, somewhere between disgust and resignation, and drags the pile of cash across the table.

Cut to: Bonkin's new owner as she marches down the central midway, moving quickly for a woman in outlandishly high Manolo Blahniks.

Reese has trouble keeping up; his inverted right foot makes it easier to move in an almost sideways shuffle. Busy workers make sure to stay out of her way, causing Reese to duck and weave between them as he struggles to match her pace.

"You sure this is a good idea, Ruth? Ain't this all a bit, y'know, tacky?"

Ruth stops to give Reese a once-over, flicking her eyes from his lank, greasy shoulder-length hair to his bristly and uneven mutton chops. She doesn't have to say anything; the insult is implied. Her eyes then land on a painter, about to start work on some signage. "No!" Ruth storms over. "No, no, no! Just what do you think you're doing with that?" She points to an open tin of primer.

"Gotta do an undercoat, Ma'am, before—"

"I said restore. Re. Store! Not"—Ruth waves her hand dismissively—"desecrate and slather! I want as

23

much of the original Bonkin's Bonanza preserved as possible."

"So..."

"So clean it, fix it, and leave it. Understand?"

"Yeah—I mean yes, ma'am," the painter gulps and puts the lid back on the primer.

Ruth turns and looks around the midway, trying to figure something out. She takes a few steps towards the middle and stops, looking down at the once brightly painted, now sun-damaged and weed-cracked cobblestones. At a glance, it would appear as though a spiral pattern had once been painted there. Only it's too uneven and random for even the carefully calculated off-kilter designs that litter Bonkin's Bonanza.

"Here," Ruth states as though standing on the site of some great historical significance. "This is where it happened." She closes her eyes and listens—almost hearing the screams, the grinding of bone and metal, the curses spouted by the clown as he was torn to pieces by the whirling blades of a cotton candy machine designed by a twisted maniac. She can almost taste the historical cocktail of carnage and cruelty.

"Ruth, I gotta be honest, I don't know about this. Are folks really gonna come back here after, you know?"

"Do you know how much Bonnie and Clyde's car cost?"

"Well, they stole it, so—"

"Don't get smart with me, Reese; it doesn't suit you," Ruth growls. "Back then, it was worth maybe four hundred dollars, if that. A hundred and twelve bullet holes later, Charles Stanley bought the thing for over three thousand. Now, Reese, I know you're not good at math, but that's nearly ten times what it would've cost off the lot. Skip to the fifties, and Stanley sells it for fourteen and a half grand! Second-hand cars don't often appreciate in value, y'know. Then, just last month, the thing sold for a quarter mil!"

Reese scratches his head. "You sayin' that cotton candy machine could be worth—"

"I'm saying—and try your best to follow me here, Reese—that people are sick. They're demented, perverted little fucks who love sex, violence, and death. Especially when it's all mixed together. Shit, you should know that better than anyone. Bonkin's Bonanza has all that and more." Ruth rubs her hands together, excited. "Oh sure, we'll get the uptight church types from Cherry Lake kicking up a stink, but they won't matter when folks will pay through the nose."

"Yeah—"

"Think about it." Ruth marches on, leading Reese farther along the midway. Workers buzz around, fixing up old rides and installing new ones. Ruth wades through the hubbub like a pharaoh. "Why do folks come to these places in the first place?"

"For fun?"

"For danger! For the taste of it. They ride the coaster, shriek in the house of horrors, and cuddle at the top of the big wheel because it's a safe, more or less, dose of what scares them shitless." Ruth gestures to the work going on around them. "I'll build it, and they'll come, oh how they'll come." Forming one hand into a fist, she adds, "There's a sicko born every minute. Time was they paid their buck to gander at freaks like you. These days they wanna cozy up with Bundy and Ramirez. I'm gonna give them what their little black hearts desire. Let them rub up against a real-life monster, not just some doofus in a rubber mask. And they'll love me for it!"

The two of them stop before what appears to have once been a grand mansion, older than everything else in the carnival combined, half torn down, with a striking striped Big Top grafted onto the old brickwork, like two buildings fused by some mad science experiment. Workers and engineers carry in gear, machinery, and things that look like animatronic puppets.

"This right here will be my masterpiece." Ruth's eyes wander the building with wonder, seeing something that's not there—yet.

"Yeah, but kids—"

"Love this shit just as much as their folks. Who do you think kept the legend of Bonko the Clown alive for the last ten years? Long after the TV specials aired? Oh, they tell stories of this place, and you better believe they're gonna lie to their daddies and steal cash from their mommas' purses to come here."

"Ms. Hardstack," a man in work overalls interrupts as he approaches, "there's a delivery you gotta sign for—"

"I'm sure you can." Ruth's too lost, a million dreams of what the carnival can be dancing through her head.

"No, ma'am, sorry, but they said it's gotta be you. Something about live—"

"Why didn't you say so!" Ruth interrupts and grabs the poor man by the shoulders. She's so excited it looks like she could eat him. "It's here! It's here! What a day this is!"

Ruth marches off, full speed, black eyes glinting with frenzied excitement.

"The hell did she buy?" Reese asks the worker.

"I dunno," he replies, "but whatever it is sure sounds angry."

Chapter Three
BREAKFAST AT CANDY'S

One week later...

Split-screen:

On the left, sunlight streams through gossamer curtains, bouncing off a New Kids on the Block poster and landing on the face of a girl with puffy red eyes. Her blonde hair, all shaggy like a Motley Crue groupie, doesn't look like it's seen a brush in a while. Pouty lips mumble in her sleep, making her ever so slightly chubby cheeks tremble as she chews on a finger. There are wadded up tissues all around her, and she hugs a stuffed raccoon tightly to her chest.

On the right, a shirtless and athletically lean guy lies awake with one hand behind his head, staring up, his intense green eyes staring at nothing whatsoever. His hair effortlessly parts curtains that fan out across his pillow as he bites his lip, lost in thought.

In both scenes, an alarm goes off.

The girl wakes slowly, and the second her eyes land on the clock, she bursts into tears; the boy turns gradually to his clock radio and slaps it. In tandem, both sit up. The boy's feet reach his floor, strewn with dirty laundry; the girl's short legs dangle two inches from the floor. They both make their way to their separate ensuite bathrooms. The boy does some arm stretches and cracks his neck; the girl wipes her eyes with her pajama sleeve.

Lights come on in each bathroom.

The boy's is bare except for a few Playboy centerfolds pinned to the back of the door. Jennifer Lyn Jackson's curls float around her open shirt, and the boy winks at her through the reflection. He pours some mouthwash in his mouth and gargles it while flexing his muscles, nodding with approval at the definition.

A square of lightbulbs come on around a Hollywood-style mirror in the girl's bathroom, complete with a cursive pink neon word—*Candy*—at the top. She looks at her shaggy dog reflection and sobs again.

The boy looks down at his sink and spits, then his eyes land on the top of his wastebasket. There's a Polaroid sitting on a pile of bunched up, crusty tissues. He reaches down and takes it, his hands trembling slightly. It shows him with his arms around the girl on the left. He's behind her and rests his chin on her shoulder as she reaches out, holding the Polaroid camera at arm's length. Her smile is so genuine he feels his heart break even before he reads the caption: Candy & Rocky Forever.

The girl slumps to the floor, landing on a pink fuzzy bath mat. A similar Polaroid sits in two halves on the tiles, split right between the two teens. On one half, her lips are pouted in a kiss, and on the other, he smiles with genuine, adoring surprise.

Candy reaches for the half with Rocky; he drops to his knees, a flood of tears running down his pretty-boy face. She scowls, small round face fierce as an angry kitten and tosses the torn picture of the boy into the toilet. She flushes, and as the boy's photo swirls, she trembles, biting her finger; Rocky rolls onto his side and cries like a baby till the split moves, giving way to Candy on her own.

Candy comes out of her bathroom, eyes raw but, for the moment, dry. Her entire tiny little body shudders even as she considers getting dressed and doesn't know where she'll find the energy for it. All she wants to do is crawl back into bed and sleep until she feels nothing.

Then a song kicks off on the radio. Vince Neil sings about a guy they call Dr. Feelgood. Candy finds her toes tapping along to the music, but it's the image the song brings to mind that does more to beat back the misery than the music itself.

Cut to: some outdoor party, kids holding plastic cups around a bonfire.

"Oh shit, this is my jam!" a girl screams at the top of her voice, more than a little drunk, shoving aside two kids making out by the fire as she heads towards Candy. "Bitch, get off your adorably tiny booty and dance with me," the tall girl demands, firelight dancing in her silver septum piercing. Dark, dyed hair spills across her face and she flicks it through the air, headbanging.

Candy feels Rocky's fingers tighten on her, ever so slightly, before he makes an effort to let go and her friend pulls her right into a twirl. "Just remember to give me my girl back after, 'kay, Leigh?" he jokes.

"She's my girl now," Leigh fires back and sticks her tongue out.

The girls dance by the firelight, feeling the noise so much it lingers till this day.

It's a good memory, despite Rocky being part of it, because of Leigh. Her best friend. Thanks to a simple memory of good times and great jams, Candy finds the strength to put on some clothes and face her first day flying solo.

Curled up on the floor in his bathroom, Rocky finally stops crying. It didn't hit him till he saw that photo. She's gone; she's really gone.

When Candy dumped him over the phone last night, he thought maybe she was just pissed at something; she wasn't making much sense, and even if they were split for good, so what? It's not like there aren't any other girls out there. Like Kat Munroe, for one. Not like there was anything special about Candy.

Except there was—is. Candy, the tiny girl with the massive heart, made Rocky want to be a better guy. She was the girl he ran to.

"Yeah, why'd you go and fuck it all up then?" he says, grabbing a fistful of his tousled curtains. They stay upright, oily and unwashed, even after he uses the same hand to slap some sense into himself. "Alright, none of this feelin' sorry for yourself shit, get your ass in gear and get her back."

Rocky takes a sniff of his underarm and winces; a generous dose of Axe body spray isn't gonna cut it, so he heads for the shower. He does all right cleaning up, till Kim Carnes comes on the radio singing about this girl with Bettie Davis Eyes, and suddenly Rocky's not in his bathroom anymore.

Cut to: the winter formal, his first actual date with Candy. She looks like she should be on a cake; she's so tiny, the dress so big at the bottom. They're slow dancing, and even though the hall's packed, they're the only two people there. Even Candy's shadow, and best friend Leigh, telling her date to keep his hands off her butt, though not quite so politely, doesn't spoil the mood.

A football-shaped phone trilling cuts into Rocky's shower/crying time, and he grabs a towel on his way to answer it.

"Candy!?" he asks, way too desperate.

"Ohh, yeah, big boy, it's me, Candy, just callin' to see if you want some more this sweetness," the voice on the other end jokes in a falsetto.

"Go take a run and jump, Cliff; that's not cool," Rocky snaps.

"Woah, dude! You forget to take your chill pill this morning?" Cliff says. "You've seen it then?"

"Seen what? No, man, never mind. Listen." Rocky puts the phone to his chest and thinks of the best way to phrase this without making himself sound and feel like a complete and utter loser. "Candy and I are splits."

"You too, huh?"

"Whaddya mean?"

"Leigh left me a message on the answering machine, and I quote, 'dumping my limp-dicked ass'."

"Shit."

"Fuckin' sister's still laughing." Cliff yells to someone else in his house, "Quit it, Stacey, or I'm gonna microwave your Barbies! Man, what the hell? Is it like national dump a dude day or somethin'?"

"Hey, I didn't say I got dumped."

"Rocky, c'mon. I mean, c'mon."

"I'm serious, bro, I—"

"OK, dude, I'm gonna stop you there. You gotta look at your car."

"Huh?" Rocky pads over to his window. "What's wrong with"—He pulls some of the Venetian blinds down and drops the phone—"Shit!"

"I tried to warn you. Rocky? You there, dude?" Cliff's voice comes through the discarded phone as Rocky's footsteps race down the stairs.

31

Candy feels her spirits lift as she comes down the stairs to the smell of fresh coffee and toast. She's not told her parents yet about her breakup and doesn't know if she will. A quiet, regular morning with Mom and Dad sounds just about right.

"Mornin'," Candy calls out as she rounds the corner at the bottom of the stairs and finds herself in an empty kitchen. "Oh." They've already left for work, Candy realizes, and a twitch of loneliness yanks at her heart.

Cereal and dried marshmallows clink into a clear bowl as Candy pours herself some Lucky Charms, doing her best not to look at the crumpled letters with different college letterheads in the trash. It's the only box left in the pantry, and she wants something sweet and sugary, even if the cheery cartoon on the front reminds her of how Rocky once asked, slightly drunk but deadpan serious, if she was an actual leprechaun.

"I mean, you're cute like one; leprechauns are cute, right? You're cute." He asked for her number not long after. In my defense, Candy tells herself, he is hot. A total sleaze, but undeniably a gorgeous one.

Candy disappears into a puffy armchair, legs up and crossed as she flicks the TV remote.

"Are you feeling more and more disconnected as the world—"

"Nope." Candy changes the channel. "It's too early for that freaky lake cult stuff," she moans and lands on the news. A man with silver hair and a jet black mustache, the disparity strikingly unsettling to Candy, stands in front of a line of people pushed up along a fence.

"Thanks, Gail. I'm here outside the gates to Bonkin's Bonanza. Once the sight of a brutal murder, it stands on the verge of a grand reopening. Now, as you can see"— The camera pans up to show the massive fake clown that forms the front gate, fences still shut tight between the monster's legs as it leans over a rainbow down toward the waiting crowd—"the new owners have kept the name and that's not all, Gail. I'm told they fully intend to embrace the bloody history of Buster B. Bonkin, aka Bonko the Clown, and we at Channel Five News will be given the first look later on today when the gates of Bonkin's Bonanza open once again. This is Brock Hauser. Back to you, Gail."

Brock stands still, smiling for an awkwardly long time before a woman's voice cuts in. "Thanks, Brock." The feed switches back to the studio, with a well-made up woman in a dress so red it leaves after images on Candy's TV. "For more about the infamous Bonko the Clown, don't miss Channel Five's award-winning expose, Blood and Greasepaint: The Crimes of Buster. B. Bonkin, tonight at nine. In other news..."

Candy tunes out the rest. She's lost in memories of Leigh telling her about Bonko, ghost stories whispered beneath bedsheets and over the brim of flashlights at slumber parties. She'd wanted to go to Bonkin's Bonanza, of course, even before there was talk of it reopening. Leigh's obsessed with carnivals and creepy stuff, so Bonkin's is like Halloween at Christmas for her. Number one of Leigh's list of messed-up places she wants to visit.

They'd gotten as far as driving most of the way there, one time, Candy, Leigh, Rocky, and Cliff, but when Candy wanted to turn back, Rocky and Cliff didn't put up much of an argument.

There's something wrong if clowns don't unsettle you, Candy always thought. Nobody likes them. But Leigh, well, Candy recalls when a clown tried to give her a flower balloon at the state fair, and Leigh decked him.

Till just now, Candy didn't get it. Leigh hates the things with a passion, yet she can't keep away. Just like how she wishes Rocky would drop dead and also that he were here right now, wrapping his arms around her.

That thought sends Candy right back into a pity spiral, and in seconds she's got tears in her Lucky Charms. It doesn't last long as the whole house, no, the entire street, rumbles at the ratcheting up guitar riffs, bass, and drums of a very familiar rock song. Candy smiles as the voice of Gene Simmons wails, "Mhm, yeah-ha," and her shoulders bop involuntarily along with the "do do do do-do do-do do-do do do!"

Rocky stands in his driveway in just a towel, staring in open-mouthed horror at the desecration before him.

"Hey, kid, put on some pants," an older neighbor demands, hanging out of his station wagon. He pulls into a drive a few doors down. Several older ladies, power walking in armbands and legwarmers, giggle and wave. Rocky ignores both; the defilement of his baby wounds him almost as, if not more, deeply than the loss of Candy.

Another teenage boy, this one dressed in blue jeans with his hands tucked into the pockets of a matching denim jacket, walks up the drive and stands next to Rocky. He brushes the fringe feathered, shaggy hair out of his face. "I tried to warn you, dude."

"The... the 'Cuda... how could she..."

"Yeah." Cliff puts a hand on Rocky's shoulder. "Hell hath no, shit, what is it again?"

A younger girl, around eleven, with a face full of sneering braces, passes by leisurely on her bike. "Hey Rocky," she sings, winks, and wiggles her pinky at Cliff.

"Stacey, I swear to God!" Cliff warns her, and the girl flips him the bird as she peddles on.

"The 'Cuda." Rocky's still in shock as he stumbles towards the car. Once his father's, now Rocky's. Once a beautiful and beloved 1971 Plymouth Hemi 'Cuda, now a trashed disaster. Rocky's hand trembles as he places it on the hood, comforting the car as though it were a dog at the vet. "What did she do to you?"

"It's probably not as bad as it looks," Cliff says, and Rocky slowly turns, eyes burning with fury. "Sorry," Cliff winces.

On the hood of the 'Cuda, scratched deep into the lime green paint, a short yet very girthy penis with the balls made into little feet says with a little speech bubble, "Hi! I'm Rocky and I'm a cheating Cocky!"

"That'll buff out," Cliff tries to comfort his friend.

Rocky wanders around the side, looking in the window to see the interior almost entirely coated with flour and crushed eggs.

"Good valet. Take care of that, no problemo," Cliff offers with a wave of his hand.

Rocky reaches for and tries to pull free a piece of paper stuck to the side of his car. He can't get that piece free, nor any of the identical copies plastered to the vehicle. The same image over and over, times a hundred: a photocopied Polaroid of Rocky facing the camera and a girl with red hair, who clearly isn't Candy, arms around him—lips inches from his.

"Yeah, don't know how you unring that bell." Cliff scratches his shaggy head.

Rocky takes another step forward, and his towel comes away.

"Dude," Cliff calls out, but Rocky's lost in the shock of what's become of his car. What's become of his life.

The same neighbor who just demanded Rocky put on some pants marches across the lawns between the houses. His comb-over bounces loose with each angry stride, and he clutches a crumpled piece of paper in his fist. He walks right up to Rocky and slams the sheet against the teenager's chest. "Find some pants, get them on, and keep it in them!" he demands and stomps back the way he came. "Kids these days!"

Rocky takes the paper in hand; it's the same image that's glued to his car. The same one that's scattered up and down the street like flyers promoting a touring carnival.

Cut to: a black Chevette Hatch ripping down a quiet suburban street, blasting KISS at full volume, driven by a tall and aggressively pretty (in a "go fuck yourself kind of way") girl with lip and septum piercings.

"Tonight, I wanna give it all to you," she sings along with Gene Simmons, slightly off-key, but she doesn't look like she cares. Her ringed fingers, poking out from handmade and out-of-season fingerless gloves, tap the wheel to the beat. She pulls the car up to a quiet house, hitting the brakes and making them squeal. The engine, and more importantly, the radio, stay on as she climbs out her window, resting her butt on the edge. The horn blares for a moment, but she needn't have bothered; the front door opens and Candy steps out, biting her knuckles to hide her smirk while shaking her head.

"I was made for lovin' you," Leigh shouts. "Baby, you were made for lovin' me." She taps her chest and then makes a heart with her hands, throwing the shape at Candy.

"Do you know what time it is, Leigh?" Candy asks, barely able to contain the smile that always accompanies Leigh's brash brand of fun.

"Yeah, bitch, time you got off that cute little butt of yours and stop feeling sorry for yourself! It's carnival time!"

Chapter Four
PAINT A SMILE ON THAT FACE

The hungry wail of three almost identical brats makes the girl drop her bag, professional quality makeup brushes and paints scattering to the floor of her room. Not a single piece of furniture matches, and each looks a decade or two shy of new. The contents of her bag just might be worth more than everything in there—flushed, round-cheeked girl included.

"Shit," she curses and panics. In her haste to pick up the brushes, she stands on one, freezing in a wince as the plastic handle cracks under her sneaker. "No," she whimpers, pulling her foot back. Her eyes land on the shattered brush, and she grimaces. "No."

"Sully!" The bedroom door flies open, not so much as a courtesy knock. The man on the other side, hair receding so far it's gone from his head entirely and forming colonies across his shoulders, growls the girl's name again. "Sully!"

"What!" Sully snaps.

"You need to get your ass out here and help with these dang kids."

"I can't, Pa. I got work today."

"I don't," Sully's father burps, "give two shits. Your momma got a migraine—"

"Momma's always got a migraine. 'Specially after she's up all night drinkin'."

"You watch your mouth," Sully's father threatens with a single, hairy finger. "That's your momma you're sassin'."

"I gotta get ready for work!"

"Where you workin', you need all that?" He waves at Sully's kit dismissively.

"I'm paintin' faces at Bonkin's—"

"Bonk-what? That a strip club? You on the pole, girl?" her father asks.

"What? No! God, no, Pa!"

"Good, I don't need the boys sayin' they saw your tatas and whatnot," he scoffs. "Like anyone would pay for that."

Sully doesn't like the way her father talks about her body. She likes the way he looks at it even less, and he's been doing a hell of a lot of that since she turned eighteen. This job at Bonkin's Bonanza doesn't pay much, and it's just for two days a week, but Sully hopes— no, she knows—once people see how good her work is, maybe she can move into full time—get the hell out of her parents' house, and the whole damn town while she's at it.

"Jesus Christ, Pa! Go get Milly to help. They're her kids!"

"You better pull your weight around here," her father warns, "or you're out on your ass." He slams the door behind him, making the cracked mirror hanging next to it threaten to fall.

Sully waits till his footsteps quake down the hall before she allows herself the privilege of pity. It's just a little sob, no tears; she can't ruin the makeup she's already applied—no time to fix it, after all. So Sully shrugs and

39

shakes it off, then works on the girl in the cracked mirror, painting a fake smile on her face.

It's no good, though. Sully's hand trembles and she gets the line wrong. The sight of the girl in the mirror with the skewered liner pisses her off. Sully stares at her in disgust till the reflection smirks. And it speaks:

WHATCHA LOOKIN' AT, YA STUPID GOOBER?

"Stop it." Sully's face twitches as her eyes water.

JUST A STOOOOPID, FAT LITTLE GOOBER. AIN'TCHA?

"Please stop." Sully clenches her eyes shut and when she opens them, the twisted sneer in the broken glass is gone. It's a relief, but she still can't hold the pencil steady and throws it down with a frustrated groan.

Caving in, Sully stomps to the broken dresser, rattles a stuck handle, and pulls a drawer open. She hesitates before reaching in and taking a candy bar from her stash. Ripping the wrapper off, Sully holds it before her, then turns to the girl in the mirror. She watches with shame in her eyes as she stuffs it in her mouth. Then another, and another till the shake in her hand subsides. She drops to the floor, back to the wall, and tries not to listen to the girl in the mirror.

Rocky slumps down on a sofa, legs wide apart, with just the towel wrapped around him.

"Dude." Cliff obscures the view between Rocky's legs with his hand, averting his gaze. "Maybe that old-timer has a point? Pants?"

"The hell am I gonna do?" Rocky ignores the suggestion, both hands tugging his parted curtains up into devil horns.

"Start goin' steady with Kat Munroe?" Cliff shrugs, and the fury from Rocky's stare makes him regret it. "Shit, dude." Cliff takes a seat next to his friend. "You're asking the wrong guy. Remember, I too am a card-carrying member of the Dear John club."

"Yeah, man, sorry." Rocky wipes his eyes and pats his friend's back. "So, what did you do?"

"Hell, if I can figure it out. I mean, who doesn't want a piece of this?" Cliff jokes and flexes some nonexistent arm muscles.

"Better call a vet, bro."

"Yeah? Why?"

"'Cause those swans really are sick," Rocky says with a sincerity that immediately crumbles as Cliff starts to chuckle. In seconds both boys are laughing like goons.

"Look at it this way, dude, 'least you 'n' Candy, y'know." Cliff winks, clicks his tongue, and mimes humping someone doggy-style. "Only time I whipped my pecker out, Leigh just laughed."

Rocky howls with laughter, his face and chest turning bright red.

"Wow, dude, just wow," Cliff sulks. "I'm glad my disappointing sex life can bring you some joy in your hour of need. Seriously."

"I know," Rocky sniggers. "It's just, man." And his laughter instantly transitions into sobbing. "The hell is wrong with me? I don't care about that shit. I miss the way she can't say the word video right. Or how she's such a sore winner at every damn game. What do you call that?"

"Love," Cliff nods, mouth pulled into a pained smile. "That's love. I think, anyway."

"Yeah." Rocky takes a corner of his towel and uses it to dry his eyes.

"Dude, come on, stop rubbing it in!" Cliff jokes, and when it doesn't get a laugh, he adds, "Anything I can do to help put a smile back on that face?"

"Yeah!" a shrill voice calls from the window behind them. "Get your tinky-winky out; that'll give him a laugh!"

"Stacey!" Cliff jumps to his feet and races to the front door. "I'm gonna take that bike and park it in your butt!"

That, funnily enough, does the trick, and Rocky cracks a smile.

"Cheer up, bitch," Leigh says as her shitty car threatens to have a heart attack on the road. Candy seemed happy enough when she got in the car, but as the tunes turned mellow, the mood, and Candy, soured.

"Leigh... What's wrong with me?" Candy asks as she plays with her fingers.

"The hell you mean, homegirl?"

"I mean, there has to be a reason Rocky—"

"Nope, no, no fuckin' way is that on you. It ain't your fault Rock-For-Brains couldn't keep his paws off another chick!"

"Maybe... if I looked more... never mind." Turning, putting smile on for her friend, Candy lies. "I'm good."

"Naw, girl, you're fuckin' schweet!" Leigh elbows Candy. She looks over Candy's outfit, slouchy, near-transparent, off-the-shoulder t-shirt, bright pink vest, and shorts. Just something she threw together in a second, and yet she looks great. Leigh, for a second, wishes she could look as effortlessly adorable as her best

42

friend instead of what she's decided to call the prettyful hobo look. "You're looking choice, I'm looking fine—"

"As always."

"As always! Bitch!" Leigh blows her a kiss. "And we're going to Bonkin's fuckin' Bonanza! Woo!"

"Yeah..." Candy slips back into a solemn silence as she watches the trees whip past.

Leigh can't think of what else to say, so she just blurts out, "I broke up with Cliff, too."

"What!?" Candy snaps back around. "Why didn't you say? What happened?"

"You think I'm gonna keep dating that clown after his"—Leigh puts on a faux macho accent—"brother from another mother"—and back to normal—"stepped out on my best friend!? Hells to the fuck no!"

Candy smiles and wipes away a little tear—one not shed in sadness for once. "You didn't have to do that."

"Yeah," Leigh says and flashes back to when she and Candy were about eight.

Cut to: eight-year-old Leigh kicks seven shades of shit out of a tree in a far too sunny graveyard. It doesn't make any sense for it to be such a nice day, not when they're burying her mother. Eight-year-old Candy approaches. At her touch, Leigh breaks down and falls into Candy's arms, sobbing. Candy strokes her friend's hair and bites back her own tears.

"Why?" Leigh sobs. "Why her, too? Why does everyone leave me!?"

"I'll never leave you," eight-year-old Candy promises as she puts her forehead to Leigh's. She repeats the words, ones they'll say to one another countless times over the years: "It's you and me, Candy and Leigh, together forever, you'll see."

It works a little. Leigh feels the black clouds in her heart clear just enough to see that there can be daylight again someday. Things aren't quite as scary when you've got someone who loves you by your side, after all.

Cut to: back to the car, Candy's words echoing through Leigh's head as they rest against her chest, carved into the locket she keeps tucked under her safety pinned to-shit Joan Jett t-shirt. "Yeah," she says, "I did," and before it gets too real, Leigh thinks up something to lighten the mood. "Here, take the wheel," Leigh says without waiting for Candy to react, and she ducks down to search the floor of her car.

"Leigh!" Candy leans over her friend's back, grabbing the wheel as the car veers to the left. A quick turn, and the car jerks back into the lane.

"I know it's down here somewhere. Just hold it." Leigh scatters a pile of open and empty cassette tapes as she searches. One box lands, face-up, and Candy's too busy trying to see over Leigh to notice the label reads *For Candy,* with a purple love heart around her name.

"I can't see over the wheel!"

Leigh sniggers, bordering on full laughter.

"It's not funny!"

"Blame Clark. Most of these are his."

"Cheeuh! I've seen your room—"

"Got it!" Leigh jerks back up, and Candy slips back to her seat as Leigh takes the wheel in one hand, brandishing a tape with the other.

"What's that?"

"The answer to the funk you're slipping into." Leigh slams the tape into the deck and hits play. Cyndi Lauper fills the car, warbling about showing your true colors. "Shit, wrong side." Leigh ejects the tape and flips it around. A few seconds later, a drum and guitar kick off and Leigh sings along, "*On the floor of Tokyo—*"

"Yeah!" Candy cheers and starts to dance in her seat, waving her little arms in the air. "*When there's no one else in sight.*"

"*In the crowded lonely night,*" Leigh picks up, more rebel yell than in tune.

"*Well, I wait so long.*" Candy takes her turn.

"*For my love vibration,*" Leigh goes and mimes playing with herself, sending Candy into clapping hysterics.

Then, together, they sing, "*And I'm dancing with myself! Oh-oh dancing with myself, oh-oh dancing with myself!*" as the car chugs past a road sign: Bonkin's Bonanza 5 Miles Ay-Yup!

Sully, flustered, comes out of her room and hefts her bag on her shoulder as she hurries down the hall. She reaches an open lounge kitchen, and the screaming intensifies like you would not believe.

Three toddlers, all in dirty onesies; the only difference is a bow on the middle one. They sit screeching like hungry baby birds in a playpen nest of half-broken toys. Neither the kids' mother nor their grandfather is anywhere to be seen—that is, till he plods into the room buttoning up his gas station work shirt.

"Where's Milly?" Sully asks, and her father shrugs.

"Don't look like she came home last night," he says and clears his throat into a dishtowel. It comes away sticky and brown. He tosses it back onto the worktop without a thought.

"So they've just been there all night?"

Sully's father shrugs again.

"Wait, you're working?"

45

"They always said you was a sharp one." Sully's father taps his head condescendingly.

"I need the car to get to work."

"Tough titties."

"Come on, Pa! Can you give me a lift at least?"

"I could." And he shrugs again. "But who's gonna look after these kids?"

"Momma—"

"Got a migraine." Sully's father points a warning finger at her. "Don't you go wake her now!"

"I got work too, Pa!"

"Paintin' faces ain't no job, Sully," her father scoffs. "You think you're gonna make a livin' drawin' whiskers on snot-nosed brats? 'Bout time you got your head outta your ass, girl."

"I'm a makeup artist," Sully mutters to herself. She feels the tears well up, and the doubts with them.

NO, YOU'RE NOT. YOU'RE WORTHLESS, YOU'RE JUST A STUPID FAT LITTLE GOOBER, AREN'T YOU...

"Heeeeey," a voice sings from the back door, cutting through Sully's intrusive thoughts and demanding everyone's attention. Both Sully and her father turn to see a stick-thin girl in Daisy Dukes and a frayed cropped vest with strappy heels suspended between fingers over her shoulders. "You guys are up early!"

"Jesus, Milly, have you been out all night?" Sully can smell weed and Jack Daniels from across the kitchen.

"No." She giggles the suggestion off, takes one step into the kitchen, staggers, and crashes to the floor.

46

Out of breath and half-dead, Cliff drops to a lean against Rocky's open bedroom door. "She," he pants, "got away."

"Never shoulda quit the team, bro," Rocky teases. He's put a pair of boxer shorts on, but that's it.

"Ha"—breath—"ha. So, plan? Wanna drive down to Cherry Lake and pick up some of those church cuties?"

"Gotta get her back." Rocky ignores the suggestion and stares at the few clean clothes he has left.

"Dude, let it go. They're gone, and you think Candy's sitting at home just waiting for you to show up with a boombox or something?"

"Whatever, bro, you can go do some Dirty Dancing with the Churchies. I'm gonna find a way to make it up to her." Rocky pulls a cropped sports jersey over his head; it stops just above his smooth navel. "How's this look?"

"Like Freddy's comin' for ya, dude. No. Just no."

Rocky takes it off, tossing it aside, and continues his rummage.

"You're really jonesing for her, huh?"

"I love her, bro," Rocky's voice warbles. "I love her, and I fucked up. Big time. I need to try."

"Shit." Cliff comes into the room. "If we're doing this, then we're doing it right." Cliff pushes Rocky aside and looks through the closet. He takes out a pale green shirt, black tie, and dark brown leather jacket. "Here, get these on."

"A tie?" Rocky takes the clothes, confused. "We're not going to church, bro—"

"Just shut that pretty mouth and get dressed," Cliff sighs. Rocky does as he says, though as he buttons the collar of his shirt, Cliff butts in, "No, leave that, totally, let the tie hang loose." Cliff steps back to take in his handiwork. "Perfection." Rocky stands there with the jacket on, the top two shirt buttons undone, and the tie hanging low. Oh, and still in just his boxers below the belt.

"I need pants," Rocky points out.

"No, you don't," a voice says from the hall with a giggle.

"Stacey!" Cliff spins around, rolls over Rocky's bed, and races after his little sister. He manages to catch her this time, halfway down the hall, and he scoops her up into his arms.

"Let go!" she protests, legs kicking in impossible directions as Cliff hefts her off the ground.

"Sure, no problem," Cliff says and lifts her up over the railing, dangling Stacey over the drop-down to the first floor below. "Here good for ya, dweeb?"

"No!" Stacey protests. "Don't you dare, or I'll tell Mom!"

"Hard to tell Mom when you're in a million bits!"

"Come on, bro," Rocky says, coming along the hall now with dark, ripped jeans and Adidas hightops on. "Leave her, and let's go find the girls."

"You're looking for Candy and Leigh!? I know where they are," Stacey pleads.

"Bull. Shit." Cliff says.

"I'll tell Mom you swore—" Stacey shrieks as Cliff raises her towards the drop again. "OK! I won't! I won't!"

"Start talkin'," Cliff warns her.

"I saw Leigh's car heading out of town! I swear!"

"Shit," Rocky curses and kicks his heel.

"I know where they're going," Stacey promises. "Take me with you guys, and I'll tell you!"

"How about," Cliff lifts her again, "no!"

48

"Wait," Rocky interrupts and nods for Cliff to let Stacey down. Once the girl has her feet back on solid ground, Rocky leans down so he's eye to eye with her.

"Stacey, it would mean a lot to me if you'd tell me." Rocky gives her a smile and brushes aside his hair just to emphasize his eyes. "Pretty please?"

Stacey blushes and giggles, "OK, Rocky. I think they're going to the carnival. Leigh said—"

"Shit, yeah," Cliff snaps his fingers. "Makes sense. Leigh's obsessed with that place."

"Your car good to go?"

"Aw, yeah, dude," Cliff holds his fist out to bump. "Cliff!"

Rocky bumps it and chants "Rocky," and together they shout, "To the edge! Boom!"

The two boys head down the stairs, and Stacey stomps her feet. "Hey!" she shouts. "You said you'd take me with you!"

"Uh, no, we didn't," Cliff points out.

"Sorry, kid." Rocky waves.

"Not! Fair!" Stacey fumes as the boys head off.

"Oh Jesus, Leigh, it's huge," Candy sighs as Leigh's car emerges from the off-road and they see the massive line of people waiting to get into Bonkin's Bonanza. "This is insane. We're never getting in!"

"Ye of little faith," Leigh smirks. "Don't you worry your pretty little head."

After they find somewhere to park, Leigh marches alongside the line, head held high and oblivious to the occasional glare from the crowd, all pushed up together along the fence. Candy follows a few steps behind, very much feeling the accusatory stares. She bites on her knuckle to hide the nerves while trying to keep up with Leigh's longer-legged pace.

"Leigh, where are you going?" Candy asks, worried. "The line's back that way."

"Yeah, the loser line," Leigh scoffs.

"Hey!" a person in the crowd protests; a few others sneer, and Leigh just marches on.

"I told you, bitch, I got this," Leigh insists, and Candy follows along, nervously avoiding meeting the eyes of anyone in line.

Leigh smirks when they near the front as her eyes land on a boy zipped up inside a neon orange sleeping bag, dozing on a stool. Only his face pokes out; he looks like a slug with spectacles on. "Yo! Clark!" Leigh yells and waves. "Thanks for saving our spot, dude!"

"Oh no." Candy stops dead. Leigh can't seriously expect her to skip the line? All those people, it's just wrong, she can't— ·

Clark jerks awake as Leigh leans over the barrier and puts her hand down on his shoulder. "I wasn't, Mom, I swear!" he protests, still half asleep, and smacks his lips as he blinks. "Leigh?" A beaten, dog-eared paperback slips to the ground, though neither Leigh nor Clark notice.

"Jesus, Clark, keep your perverted dreams to yourself." Leigh lifts one leg over the barrier, then the other, bringing her cherry red Docs down onto the ground while resting her butt against the railing.

"Um, excuse me," the man in line after Clark protests.

"You said you'd be here first thing!" Clark says, shrugging out of his sleeping bag.

"Yeah, but I say a lot of things," Leigh points out as she looks back at Candy—the tiny girl stands back from the line, still chewing her knuckle, even as Leigh urges

50

her to come over and join them. Eventually, she shuffles over, though it's more all the eyes on her than Leigh's urging that does the trick. She can't climb the barrier, so Candy ducks under it instead. Stooping slightly to pull it off, she picks up Clark's book. Its cover's faded and creased, with half the title torn off, but she can make out the artwork: a fearsome pirate woman, her back to another, swords at the ready facing off against frightening shapes leering from a thick jungle.

"Excuse me?" The man behind Clark puts his hands on his hips and stares.

"Hey Clark," Candy waves with her fingers. "Here's your book."

"'Hi, Candy," he says back with an awkward smile. "Thanks." He takes the paperback, somewhat embarrassed she saw him with it.

"What's this trash you're reading?" Leigh swipes it before Clark can shove it in his bag. "Lemme guess— Buxom Warrior Babes of Battleword?"

"Um, no, it's about pirates, and 'least I can read!" Clark snatches for the book, but Leigh holds it high.

"She's kinda cool looking," Leigh admits and bops Clark on the head with the book before she returns it.

"How did you let Leigh talk you into this? Have you been here all night?"

"Yeah, no, I mean, it's cool. I was gonna anyway so—"

"Excuse! Me!" The man behind them raises his voice.

"No," Leigh rolls her head, "excuse me!" She holds her palm to the guy and gives him the once over. "The hell is your problem, Stu?"

"My problem, wait, my name's not Stu—"

51

"Dude, you look like a Stu if ever I saw one." Leigh laughs while Candy makes herself even smaller, and Clark pretends to be interested in his shoes.

"I do not!"

"He looks like a Stu, right?" Leigh asks the woman behind Not Stu, and she kinda nods. "See?"

"Look, fuck this, you cut! No cuts!"

"Moi?" Leigh touches her chest with both ringed hands and feigns innocence—well as close to it as she can. "I didn't cut. My brother here was saving our spot."

"That's not fair," Not Stu complains.

"Life's not fair, Stu. Deal with it!"

"I—my name's not Stu!"

"Look, it's about to open. Just let it go, man," someone in line behind Stu says.

"Yeah, man, it's cool with me if two hotties wanna cut in."

Leigh smirks.

"No!" Not Stu insists. "No, it's not fair!" As some security guards reach the gate and begin unlocking heavy iron chains, Not Stu pipes up even more. "She skipped the line!" They ignore him. "This bitch skipped the line!"

"Woah!" Leigh acts like the insult takes her back, and one guard approaches. The line in front of them begins to move. "Woah, woah, woah! Watch the b-word, dude. Misogynist much?" She flips Not Stu the bird discreetly, which sets him right off.

Leigh puts her arm around Candy. "Come on, bitch, let's go."

"You, goddamn—I'll—"

"Cut that shit right now," a big, broad and bearded guard warns Not Stu, "or I'll kick your ass outta here like that." He snaps his fingers, and it sounds like thunder.

"Thanks, Mack." Leigh winks at the security guard.

"Gotcha, Leigh." Mack tips his head.

"You know her! Oh, that's it, I'm gonna have words with your boss," Not Stu threatens as Mack wades through the line towards him.

Leigh waves with her fingers, "buh-bye," as the line in front of them begins to move, and she heads toward the ticket booth.

"And you, oh you goddamn whore!" Not Stu yells as he's dragged away. "You can suck my fucking dick!"

"You sure about that?" Leigh yells without looking back. "Might bite the little thing off." She laughs as Clark buys their tickets and the gates of Bonkin's Bonanza open for the first time in more than ten years.

Chapter Five

WELCOME TO BONKIN'S BONANZA!

"Fuck," Ruth growls, "fuck-fuck-fuck, don't stop, you dirty little monkey!" She tosses her head back, eyes shut tight, the top of Reese's head just about visible between her parted, muscular legs. Her fist tightens around the handle of a black leather bullwhip that's wrapped around Reese's neck. He earns some cherry pie while Warrant sings about something not altogether different from two prominent wall-mounted speakers.

They're in an office, ornate and surprisingly classy, with a huge picture window occupying the back wall behind a desk. Ruth reclines on a plush red leather loveseat below a vast framed portrait of Buster B. Bonkin in full clown regalia, ironically taller than the man himself was.

She grits her teeth and smushes Reese's head with her thighs as she looks upon the portrait. Her eyes flick to the side, to framed photos of the old Bonkin's Bonanza cast, to Marianna the Magnificent in her low-cut, frilly dress. The last woman Bonko— "Shit! That's it! There!" Ruth screams, her thighs tremble, and Reese is almost crushed between them.

Reese emerges from below, pushing himself up onto his knees. His face slick and wet, mutton chops plastered to his face, he looks for something to clean up with, and

Ruth just pushes him off the loveseat, letting him remove the whip from his neck.

"Time to get to work, monkey boy," she says as she pulls up her pants. "What time is it, anyway?"

"'Bout," Reese glances at his watch, "shit, it's gone ten."

"Fuck." She shoves Resse to the door. "Wash the pussy out of your mouth. We got natives to greet!"

"Shiiiiit," Cliff whistles as he and Rocky lay eyes on the line, waiting to get in. It's moving slowly but still trails around the fence. "I guess we just find somewhere to park—"

"There!" Rocky causes Cliff to slam the brake. "There she is!" He points through the windshield to the front of the line, where the unmistakably mismatched duo of Candy and Leigh stand at the feet of some fucked up giant clown. Clark's trying to pay while rolling up his sleeping bag, hair a bedheaded riot.

The sight of Candy fills Rocky's heart with a rush of hope and dread; just knowing she exists makes him feel like there's still a shot for him, despite all evidence to the contrary. He feels almost instantly sick with fluttering nerves; it's a new sensation—a terrible one he wouldn't suppress even if he could. No matter how painful, it's still Candy, and she's still in his heart.

"How'd they get to the front of the line?" Cliff wonders aloud.

"Doesn't matter," Rocky says, "but we can't wait. Fuck knows where they'll be by the time we get in." Rocky's eyes land on the sign for the service road. "Follow that," he orders.

"You sure, dude?"

"Most definitely," Rocky smiles. "We're not waiting around like a bunch of chumps. Let's go."

"Get your ass in gear before you make me late," Sully's father demands as he pulls the handbrake on his truck. The heap lurches to a sudden stop, and it's a good thing Sully clutches her bag like it means the world to her. "Don't let the door hit you on your fat ass, might break it."

"Gee, thanks, Pa," Sully says.

"I'm talkin' 'bout the door," he explains, though Sully knows. She wrestles with the door handle, rattling it till the passenger door jerks open. Mismatched red and blue Docs land in the dust as Sully slides out, leggings roughly the same color but tucked into them, and a tutu-like miniskirt follows.

"Can you pick me up after closing tonight?"

"You fuckin' kiddin' me!? You have any idea what traffic's gonna be like when this shit hole lets out? You can walk your fat ass down to the rest stop if you want a lift." That's nearly five miles Sully thinks, after a whole day of work. "Might do it some good," her father chuckles.

"Thanks—" Sully tries to say, and her father cuts her off with a rev of the engine.

"Shut the damn door. I gotta go."

Sully does what he says and stands there as the truck kicks up dust. She coughs, turns, and makes her way towards the staff gate when something begins to gnaw at her. Like eyes upon her, someone hidden, watching. Sully looks around and just misses the heads of two boys as they duck beneath the dash of a parked car. Weird, she thinks, but shrugs it off and makes her way to work.

"You think she saw us?" Cliff whispers, head wedged between the door and wheel of his car.

"I dunno," Rocky says softly back, almost in the footwell of the passenger side. "Wasn't that the weird art chick from school? Fuck, what was her name?"

"Sully, I think," Cliff offers. "She's kinda cute, you know..."

"Bro, you've just been dumped. Don't you think you outta try and fix things with Leigh?"

"I'm just sayin'! 'Sides, didn't she have a crush on you?" Cliff winks.

"Go fuck yourself."

The boys go quiet for a moment as Rocky scans the fence for any way in.

"Hey Rocky," Cliff says

"Yeah?" Rocky hisses.

"Why are we whispering?" Cliff asks.

"I dunno," Rocky says, and they both risk a look. They watch as Sully holds a badge to a security guard at the back gate, and then the metal fence opens electronically.

"That's some security they got. You sure about this, dude?" Cliff asks.

"Not like we got any choice," Rocky states.

"Guess not," Cliff relents. "Let's do this, then."

Rocky nods and the two of them get out of the car. As they wander along the nearly ten-foot-tall fence that circles the park, checking for loose boards or cracks, the trunk of Cliff's car clicks open all on its own.

"Oh my God, this place is frick'n hellacious." Leigh spins around all giddy, like it was Christmas morning or something.

"Looks kinda..." Candy trails off, not able to think of anything polite to say.

"Grody." Clark has no compunctions when it comes to his stepsister. "Let's find a locker so I can stash my stuff."

"You're grody, four-eyes!" Leigh gasps like a five-year-old who just spotted some elves and a jolly fat man in red getting off a sleigh. "Check it!"

There's the usual office, hospitality, and dime locker storage to their left, but along the walls, there's a whole banner line of vintage advertisements for performers and acts. Leigh races past one for Reese, The Monkey Boy—a hunched over kid around ten with a full face of scraggly hair—to a hanging tapestry nearly twice her size showcasing a huge man in tiger-print underpants lifting a massive weight with just his pinky and a wink.

"It's him, Chet Redwood." Leigh strokes the tapestry, completely ignoring the *No Touching* sign. "Dude fed Buster B. Bonkin to a cotton candy machine like he was making margaritas."

"Gross." Candy raises an eyebrow. "Wait, how though? That's not even—"

"Clark! You brought the camera?" Leigh yells, ignoring the question.

"Yeah, I mean, you told me to."

"Well, whip that bitch out and take our photo," Leigh orders and waves Candy over.

"What should we do?" Candy flips between cute poses, pouting and giggling. Leigh watches her for a second, a genuine smile on her face. It's good to see the girl having fun again after what just happened. "Oh! I got it. Leigh, do what he's doing." Candy points to the banner of Chet.

58

"'Kay," Leigh says with a slightly embarrassed snort. She sniggers as she adopts a similar single bicep pose as Chet's image, side-on with one knee up and her right arm curled. "What are you doing?"

"Two secs." Candy looks around then races over to grab an empty bottle crate sitting just inside the locker room. She drags it over and leaves it on the ground in line with Leigh's flexed arm. "OK." She hops up onto the crate and still has to go on her tiptoes to get her face above Leigh's arm. Folding both hands under her chin, Candy leans her head towards Leigh and adopts a butter wouldn't melt smile, eyes rolled to her friend. The scent of Candy's hair fills Leigh's nose. "Cut the crate out of the picture, 'kay Clark?"

He doesn't answer. Clark's eyes are drawn to a girl hurrying the wrong way, moving against the crowd flowing up the midway. The intensity of her scowl and pace doesn't match her cute round features, made all the softer with her long cropped hair. It's her, he says to himself, the art chick from school. The one he never had the nerve to speak to, she's—

"Earth to Clark!" Leigh interrupts Clark's daydream. "Hurry up and take the photo, ya dork!"

"S-sorry." Clark gives an overeager thumbs up. "I got it." Then he puts himself in a silly-looking braced squat as he lines up the shot.

"Say creepy-fucking-murder-clown!" Leigh hisses through her posed smile as the flash fires.

"You're late." Sully's boss, an older woman with short silver hair, taps the painted watch on her wrist, and though it's kinda funny, Sully doesn't laugh.

The park's just opened, and already the playpens, sandboxes, and ball pits of Small Wood are alive with chaos and high-pitched squeals. Gaggles of wild kids assault a man in a raccoon costume wearing a t-shirt that reads "Rowdy the Raccoon."

Sully dumps her bag at her station, one of three inside the face painting tent, and begins to unload her kit, starting with a banana-shaped pencil case.

"Sorry, I'm so sorry I—"

"Sully," her boss says, painting whiskers on her face.

"It's just my pa, and my sister and her kids, and—" The totality of the morning comes crashing down on Sully, all her father's insults and the general oppressive shittiness of her life at home. It hits harder with some distance—when she's not wallowing in the mire.

"Sully!" her boss snaps. "Quit it." Sully snaps to, nodding her head more to convince herself than affirm what her boss is saying. "Look, go clean yourself up, get your face sorted."

"OK," Sully wipes away a tear, "OK," but she just stands there.

Her boss comes over, puts a hand on Sully's shoulder, and says, "You've got talent, kid, but that's only going to get you so far. You want to do this for real? Right?"

"Y-yeah," Sully sniffs. "Yeah," she repeats, firmer.

"Then let me tell you, you'll have to deal with so many bastards and bitches you'll want to go all Buster B. Bonkin on them. The trick is not letting them know they get to you, got it?"

Sully nods.

"You can't just paint a smile on your face, kid; you need to make them believe it's real. Even when most of the time, it won't be. See, I don't give two shits what's going on in that head of yours. You're on my time now. Cry on your lunch break if you have to."

"I'll be good. I can do it," Sully promises and doesn't convince anyone at all.

"You better, and if you think I'm being harsh, just wait till you meet MY boss."

She heads to the bathroom, rubbing her eyes with the back of her hand, fake flying elephants bobbing up and down beside her.

The scent of Candy Alley hits Sully as she pushes through the crowd. Fried sugar, malted caramel: the air is sticky with it. It would be so easy to call it quits, right? Give up and stuff her face till all she feels is full. A hazelnut-dipped churro's so much more appealing than putting up with that harpy back there. Maybe just—no!

Candy will make her feel good for the moment, but she needs this job—needs out of this damn town. There'll be time for frozen bananas and mini-donuts dipped in choclate later

She pushes on past Candy Alley, feeling the sweats come on, through yellow and red doors into a garishly-tiled bathroom and goes straight for the mirror.

Sully doesn't like the girl she sees reflected back at her. She's short, pudgy, with stupid hair and lips that always make her look like she's scowling. Nevertheless, she says to her, "You got this."

NO, YOU DON'T, the girl in the mirror says. **YOU'RE JUST A FAT LITTLE GOOBER WHO CAN'T DO SHIT.**

Sully shakes her head and tries to deny what the other girl says.

YES, the other Sully growls; *YOU KNOW YOU ARE. FATTY-FAT GOOBER-GOBBLER!*

"No," Sully protests and breaks down again.

"There's no way, dude. We've been 'round half the park and nothing," Cliff complains and kicks a can onto the road. "Startin' to think we might as well just get in line."

"You remember what Coach said when we were up against Cherry High in the regionals last year?" Rocky crouches by the fence, inspecting a loose board only to find wire mesh on the other side.

"Get those pants off, boys! It's wrestlin' in the showers time!" Cliff mocks in a gruff voice.

"If you can't beat 'em head-on"—Rocky steps back and looks up at the fence—"go over their heads."

"Wait, was that the time you faked a sprain for like three weeks just to fuck with their heads?"

"Yep." Rocky's eyes wander along the fence to the gate, to the security guard in the booth on the other side. "They figured I wasn't a threat, so they wasted their best runner."

"And how does faking a limp get us over a ten-foot wall?" Cliff doesn't see the relevance of Rocky's story.

"We don't need to go over," Rocky smirks. "We're gonna walk right in through the gate."

"Rocky, dude," Cliff says, "like Coach said, I love the balls on ya, kid, but I don't see how this doesn't end up with us in jail."

"Come on, lemme show you." Rocky creeps along the fence to the gate, and Cliff follows. As they approach,

Rocky urges Cliff to listen with a hand gesture. "What do you hear?"

"Screaming, circus music, kids crying," Cliff shrugs. "My life ticking away?" Rocky puts a finger to his lips then points towards the gate. Straining to listen, Cliff thinks he gets it. "Hair metal?"

"Right. Every time we passed near the gate, I could hear the guard listening to that shit, and you know what we passed back there?"

Cliff shrugs.

"There's one car parked over there covered in stickers for KISS, Whitesnake," Rocky explains. "I'm thinking we fuck with his car. He'll come running, and is he gonna bother to lock the gate behind him on the way?"

"Rocky, you sick puppy, I love you. What do you need me to do?"

"Get behind that dumpster and be ready to move fast; when that weird art chick went through, it looked like it closed fast. Wedge it open for me."

"Gotcha." Cliff gives Rocky a fist bump. "Boom!"

"What about me?" a little voice asks from behind, and Cliff shrieks.

"They're really going for the whole clown thing, aren't they?" Clark pushes his glasses up with a finger as a tall, thin clown waves at the three of them from some junk food stalls to their right. He hops from foot to foot, trying to get their attention, while displaying a tray of candy packets strapped to his waist.

"He's freaking me out." Candy shudders. "I mean, who'd want to be a clown?"

"Y'know what they used to call the carnies who sell junk food?" Leigh's eyes light up with wicked joy, a devilish smile spreading across her face.

63

"Why do I feel like I don't wanna know?" Candy bites down on her knuckle.

"They called them—" Leigh lunges in and goes for Candy's side as she yells, "Candy Butchers!"

"No!" Candy shrieks and squeals at Leigh's touch. "Don't! No!"

"They're coming for you, Candy." Leigh does her best *Night of the Living Dead* voice, and Candy's face turns pink, giggling till she snorts.

"No fair! Stop!" Candy protests and tries to escape Leigh's clutches.

"He's gonna chop you up and sell you to the kids," Leigh continues to tease, lifting Candy up from behind and spinning her around as her short legs kick wildly. They have that much fun; they're oblivious to anyone around them till the two girls crash right into the large woman in a crimson and black suit marching past.

"Ohmygod," Candy yelps, and the shock lets her escape Leigh's grasp. "I'm so sorry!"

For a second, a cold fury washes over the big woman's face, her eyes flaring below slicked-back hair, and then it passes. She flashes the girls and Clark a shark-toothed smile. "Nonsense. No harm done, and I'm glad you kids are enjoying my carnival."

"No shit," Leigh nods approvingly. "You bought this place?"

"Oh yes." The big woman straightens her blazer. "Ruth Hardstack." She offers her hand and Leigh shakes it.

"Even though, you know, all the murders?" Clark asks.

"Especially with all the murders!" Ruth spreads her arms wide, motioning to the currently closed big top, the games alley, and garbage joints.

"Badass," Leigh adds. "And, like, we're totally sorry for kicking you."

"Again, no harm done. Now, young lady, what's your name?"

"Leigh." She tilts her head towards the other two. "This is my BFF Candy and my step-dork, Clark."

"Hiya!" Candy chirps.

"I'm not a dork," Clark protests dorkishly.

Ruth doesn't seem all that interested in the other two. "You strike me as a young woman with an eye for the macabre, would I be right?" she asks Leigh.

"If that means everything fucked up and stabby, then yeah. Big time!" Leigh smiles.

"Then you, my dear, absolutely must visit The House of Bonko Murder Ride," Ruth grins.

"Oh, I'm gonna get married there. Where is it?"

"Why, just beside the Big Top, my dear." Ruth puts a hand on Leigh's shoulder. "Tours begin after lunch, and I'll tell the boys there to put you and your friends on the VIP list." Ruth claps her hands. "Now, to business. Have fun, kids!" She marches on with a backward wave.

"I dunno if I wanna go there," Candy grimaces while Leigh's eyes fill with morbid glee.

"Stacey, I'm gonna lock you in Dingo's crate again when we get home! How did you get here!?" Cliff growls at his little sister.

"Guys, keep it down!" Rocky urges.

"Hid in the truck, nyah." Stacey sticks her tongue out, and Cliff tries to grab it between his fingers.

"Well go back and wait in it!" Cliff orders.

"Nope." Stacey crosses her arms and shakes her head, side-ponytail swishing.

"Stacey—what are you doing?"

The little girl's eyes water as though she turned a tap on behind them, and she begins to sniff. Her cheeks start to flush, and her lips tremble.

"Don't you dare," Cliff warns.

Stacey pulls in some short, sharp breaths and rocks on her heels. She's a second away from wailing when Cliff relents.

"OK! Fine!"

Stacey instantly recovers, a big gap-toothed smile on her face.

"Shit," Cliff says to Rocky, "sorry, dude."

"No, it's OK. Actually, I think she can help." Rocky nods. "Yeah, this'll work."

Stacey absolutely beams at the very idea of helping Rocky out.

A couple of minutes later, Rocky kneels by the metalhead's car and gives Cliff a thumbs up. He shoots one back, then turns to his sister. "Don't mess this up, or I'll tell Rocky you wrote his name on the bathroom mirror in Mom's lipstick."

"You wouldn't dare." Stacey is, for once, at a loss.

"Try me, dweeb. Now get to it." Cliff shoves his little sister gently. Her sneakers scuffle, then she catches her momentum as she moves towards the gate.

Pulling in one big breath, Stacey screams, "Mister! Mister!" She races towards the fence. "Somebody's trying to steal a car over there!"

The metalhead guard sighs as he gets off his seat. He hitches his belt on the way to the fence.

"He's gonna steal it!"

Pressing his face against the gate, the metalhead guard can just about see Rocky's back as he pretends he's jimmying the lock.

"Motherfucker!" the guard yells and hits the button for the lock, pushing through without giving Stacey a second glance. As soon as he passes the dumpster, Cliff slips out and blocks the gate from shutting. For a second, he thinks about letting it close and locking Stacey out, but the kid's already ahead of him, ducking between his legs.

"Get the fuck away from my car," the metalhead huffs and puffs. He's already out of breath before he's even halfway to Rocky. Making sure to keep his face turned, just in case, Rocky bolts, leading the guard around the back of a sheet metal storage shed.

"Come…shit…oh, fuck…back here!" The guard slows to heavy plodding steps, while Rocky's not even close to breaking a sweat.

He leaves the metalhead guard leaning against the back of the shed, holding his side, and casually jogs over to his waiting friend. "Nice work." Rocky fist bumps Cliff as he comes through the gate and then offers Stacey a high-five as the metal clangs behind them. She gleefully accepts.

"Woo! What are we gonna ride first?" Stacey wonders.

"We aren't gonna do shit." Cliff rummages through his pocket. "Here" He holds out some cash. "Go ride the kiddie coaster; we men have men stuff to do."

"Aww! No fair," Stacey pouts but takes the money anyway. She stomps her feet as the boys walk on.

"Hey!" someone yells, and the three turn to see a muscle-bound security guard who makes the last one look like a puppy. "What are you kids doing back here?" his twitching beard demands to know. The tag on his shirt reads "Mack."

"Fuck," Cliff says.

"Shit," Rocky adds.

"I saw them climb the fence, mister! They snuck in," Stacey jeers and makes a face at Cliff.

Mack barrels towards them, picking up speed like a semi-truck, and the boys run for it.

"I'll get you for this, Stacey," Cliff warns as he goes. The kid just counts her cash as Mack thunders past her.

Chapter Six
A DARK AND MYSTERIOUS FATE

"It's not funny, you guys!" Candy stomps her feet, on the verge of tears.

"I mean, it's pretty fuckin' funny," Leigh sniggers as she and Clark stand on the other side of a short fence from the tiny, scowling blondie. Screams whip past above them as the Wild Cat Coaster rattles along the track. Feels like they're rubbing it in. Just to the side of Candy, there's a sign—"You must be this tall to ride"—and the arrow's about an inch higher than the top of Candy's head.

Leigh and Clark move up a few steps as riders depart the parked cars. "Hey, Clark, toss her the camera; she can get our photo before we ride."

Clark doesn't do it; he figures Leigh's just joking, but he wouldn't be so cruel to Candy even if she wasn't.

"Whatever." Candy hefts herself up onto the railing. "I hope you bump your big stupid head on the damn thing!"

"I'm sorry, what was that?" Leigh mimes like she's deaf. "I can't hear you over all the screams of pure, thrilling joy! Later, bitch!"

"No fair." Candy sulks back down and glances at the sign again. "Stupid thing." She kicks some dirt at it.

The disappointment cracks open a door that's been held closed with frayed string all morning. It sucks getting left out, sure, but what sucks more is the swirling internal vertigo that hits when Candy's eyes land on a couple racing to join the back of the line. The boy lifts his arm and the girl slips in, and watching them click together like jigsaw pieces makes Candy feel like she's missing a piece of her own. A bitterness overcomes her; she nervously nibbles her knuckles and bites down hard enough to pierce the skin—Candy doesn't care. Right now, she welcomes the pain; it's a damn sight better than what's going on within. She finds herself wanting to warn the girl that her boyfriend will probably cheat on her too; worse, she almost hopes he does so that she's not—

"It's not just ride bringing you misery, is it darling?" A thick accent cuts through Candy's dark thoughts, almost as though it can read them. The voice sounds indistinguishably foreign, from some Eastern European country that doesn't exist anymore. Candy looks across to a purple tent, decorated with stars and moons, at a stunning and well-proportioned woman draped in sheets of dark blue and purple silks leaning against the railing outside, a cigarette dangling between two lace-gloved fingers. "Come, dear, let me tell your fortune," the woman says and puts the cigarette out against a no smoking sign. She disappears back inside the tent with a clatter of beads and the clinging of chimes.

With nothing better to do than eat away at herself; Candy follows.

"I wanna be a Ghostbuster!" a kid demands, causing a face painter to pause with a look of sheer puzzlement.

"Um, they just look like regular people," the face painter says and looks to his colleagues for help.

70

"Ghostbuster! Ghostbuster! Ghostbuster!" the kid chants.

Halfway through turning a particularly dumb-looking boy into a turtle, Sully raises a shaky finger. "I, uh, think I know what to do?"

"There ya go, kid; Sully the Clown's gotcha," the other painter offers and sends the kid her way. The turtle boy jumps down from his seat and runs around, making plane noises with his arms out.

"Looky-me, I'm a flying turtle!"

Sully giggles, and the suddenly clear sight of her makes the wannabe Ghostbuster kid pause for a second. Maybe it's the painted-on red smile or the blue inverted teardrop eyes—it's a bold look, and the kid's not the only one who's noticed. Sully's boss wouldn't think this is the same girl who just about had a breakdown less than an hour ago. Sully seems more herself this way. Like this is her true face.

"Come on," she pats the empty seat. "Or are you... afraid?"

"I ain't 'fraid of no ghosts!" the kid declares and bounces up onto the chair.

Sully gets to work; she only needs red, white, and little black to recreate the Ghostbuster symbol, the spook's hands on the kid's cheeks while the shocked little ghostie face covers one eye.

"Whatcha think?" Sully holds a rainbow-colored hand mirror for the kid to see their face and watches as it fills with joy. "Who ya gonna call?"

"Ghostbusters!" The kid leaps off their seat and struts around. "Ghostbusters! Ghostbusters!"

"Nice work." Sully's boss shoots her a thumbs up, and the clown girl beams—for about three seconds.

71

"He-ey, Sis!" Sully turns to see Milly, pretty much in the same clothes she stumbled home in, though she's swapped the stripper heels for basic flip-flops. The triplets pull against harnesses. Over by the entrance to the face-painting tent, a tall man with a handlebar mustache, a worn Skidd's Bay Sharks baseball cap on his head, drinks from a poorly disguised beer can. "Do me a favor?" Milly asks, and Sully knows precisely what that'll be.

GOOOOOOBER, the voice inside her head croaks.

"How is he still on us!?" Rocky yells as he and Cliff dart between parked trailers.

"I dunno," Cliff gasps for breath, "but I can't keep goin', dude. I'm gonna die."

"Never shoulda quit—"

"Dude! I swear, we get away from the goddamn Terminator, and I'll run laps with you at 6 a.m. every day, but right now we gotta think of somethin' fast!"

"We gotta split up." Rocky scans for a landmark, and his eyes land on a giant red and white canopy high above the fence. "You see that huge tent thing?"

"Big Top," Cliff huffs. "Yeah, dude?"

"I'll meet you there. Ready?"

"No—"

"Break," Rocky yells, shoving Cliff to the left, into a gap between two trailers. Cliff slams against a wall and can't hear anything over the pounding of his heart besides Mack's approaching boots. He looks around for somewhere to hide and tries the nearest door. Luck's on his side, it seems, and Cliff slips inside just as Mack passes—the trailer almost rattling.

"Phew," Cliff breathes easy. For a second.

72

"The fuck you doin' here?" a guy with lank long hair and scraggly mutton chops demands.

Cut to: Candy pushes her way into a tent that smells of incense, the kind they burn at the record store Leigh takes her to in Redcastle, only Candy can't detect any undercurrents of weed. Either all the crying blocked her nose, or this woman genuinely likes the stuff.

"Come, dear, sit," the woman gestures, and Candy thinks that her accent's changed a little. She does what the woman says, pulling out a high-backed wooden chair and sitting on the plush purple cushion. Her feet dangle an inch from the floor. "I am Marianna The Magnificent." The woman's green eyes sparkle against her tanned skin, though Candy notices that her tan doesn't continue all the way down her neck.

"Candy," she shrugs and fights the urge to chew on her knuckle again. She knows it makes her look like a child, but she can't help it. Marianna's beauty, her proportions, trigger Candy's self-critical neurosis. She has curves in all the right places, while Candy has them in the wrong ones—at least, that's how she sees herself. No wonder Rocky went for a girl like Kat Munroe.

"Boy trouble?" Marianna pushes her ruffled sleeves up, exposing forearms covered in lace and astrological jewelry.

Candy stares, stunned.

"Don't have to be psychic to see that, my dear. Is written all over your face."

"Am I that obvious?" Candy sulks.

Marianna smiles. "Pretty thing like you, of course, you're magnet for boys and boys, I know all too well, nothing but trouble." She smiles. "And I saw way you were staring at sweet young couple in line."

73

Candy blushes.

With the subtlest flick of her wrist and a dart of her eyes, Marianna draws Candy's attention to a small silver plate on the table beside the crystal ball.

"Oh." Candy reaches into the pocket of her shorts. "Sorry," she says and puts some money down on the plate. "Is that—"

"That'll do fine." Marianna takes the plate and slips it below the table. While her hands are out of sight, the overhead light dims, and the crystal ball comes to light. The walls of the tent fill with slowly rotating stars and moons. "Do you wish to know of past, present, or future, dear?"

"Why would anyone wanna know their past?" Candy asks, confused. "I mean, it's already happened."

"True, and yet we carry with us as though very much alive, very much present. There's lot you can learn from past, dear."

"OK then, what do you see about my past?"

Marianna waves her hands over the ball, fingers moving as though plucking on invisible strings, tapping into the tapestry of fate. "I see a bond, a sister, but no blood. She means great deal to you."

"That's gotta be Leigh," Candy says and figures Marianna must have seen them together before she and Clark went on the Wild Cat—an easy guess.

"And you mean great deal to Leigh, yes." Marianna's face changes for a second, as though seeing something surprising with her closed eyes. A smirk twitches across her face.

"What is it?" Candy leans in.

"The future, but you asked about your past, dear."

"No fair," Candy sulks.

"Tell me about Leigh?"

"She's the best," Candy says.

"That is statement, opinion, not what I asked."

"I don't get you."

"You admire her, yes," Marianna says and Candy nods in response. "Why?"

"I, I mean, she's like the total opposite of me."

"How so?"

"She's strong. I mean, she broke up with her boyfriend too, and she's out there having a good time while I feel like I'm two seconds away from crying all the time. I keep pretending I'm OK, but—" Candy buries her face in her hands as the tears flow. "I'm sorry. I'm so sorry!"

Marianna hands a silk handkerchief over. "Is OK, dear. Past is often painful."

Candy takes it and wipes her eyes.

"Some of us let tears flow. Others hide suffering behind mask of joy." The thought almost makes Marianna break character, recalling the faux indifference she wore as Bonko exploited and degraded her.

"She's way tougher than me. Like, back when we were in junior high—"

Cut to: The phone in Candy's bedroom rings. Candy's at her desk, doing some homework, and her pencil clatters on the desk as she makes a run for the phone. She picks up the handset and doesn't even get a word in before Leigh's voice screams, "911, Candy, get your tiny butt over here yesterday!" down the line.

Jump to: Candy standing at Leigh's bedroom door as it opens. Her eyes go wide at the sight that greets her. "Leigh, what did you do!?"

"It's not as bad as it looks." Leigh stands with a towel held to her nose, most of it soaked in blood. "The stupid magazine made it sound easy." Leigh removes the towel and shows Candy a silver half-hoop piercing jammed into one nostril. "Don't laugh!"

Candy doesn't even think about it; she leads Leigh over to a bed surrounded by posters of Joan Jett and sits her down. "I'm just gonna..." Candy reaches out to touch the piercing, and Leigh flinches even before she makes contact.

"Fuck, it hurts!" Leigh curses.

"Why didn't you wait till the weekend? My mom could have driven us to Redcastle to get it done."

Leigh shrugs. "Didn't want to be a burden."

Candy stares at Leigh like she's stupid. "You're not a burden, Leigh. I dunno what to do: pull it out or push it through?"

"It's gonna hurt like a bitch either way, right?"

"Oh, for sure," Candy grimaces.

"You sure you got enough muscle in those tiny arms to get it through?"

Candy glares, looking to Leigh like the world's most adorably angry kitten. It makes her forget about the pain for a second. "Try me," the girl says, and Leigh smirks despite the pain it causes.

"Through," Leigh nods, and as Candy takes hold of the hoop, she grimaces. "Oh, this is gonna suck."

"It'll be over in a minute," Candy reassures her, examining where the hoop has started to go through.

"Such a loser," Leigh says, a tremor in her voice. "When you gonna realize that and ditch my butt too?"

"You're not a loser." Candy picks up the towel with her free hand and dabs away some blood. "And I'm not ditching you. Remember, it's you and me."

"Candy and Leigh."

"Together forever, you'll see." Candy meets Leigh's eyes and offers her a warm smile. It does nothing to lift Leigh's spirits.

"Don't make promises you can't keep, shorty," Leigh scoffs.

"I don't," Candy promises. "Anyway, you lose any more blood, and it's you leaving, in an ambulance. Seriously, Leigh, you coulda really hurt yourself."

"Shit," Leigh shrugs, "they took my Mom and my Dad from me. What else I got lose?"

"Me," Candy says and drives the hoop all the way through Leigh's septum.

"FUCK!" Leigh howls as Candy backs away, wincing. Leigh's whole body tenses up; she makes fists and shudders. For a moment, Candy thinks Leigh's about to explode, until she begins to sob. Leigh rocks with each cry, her face turning red around tightly clenched eyes.

"Oh, Leigh!" Candy scrambles across the bed on her knees till she reaches and wraps her arms around her friend's shoulders. Leigh leans in, tapping the side of her head against Candy's forehead. Candy places a hand on Leigh's face, turning her so they're forehead to forehead, eye to eye. She smiles at Leigh, whose lips quiver, and a tear flows. "It's OK, don't cry."

"Shove it, narbo." Leigh playfully pushes Candy away. "I'm not crying." She touches her now fully pierced septum. "Just a single bitch tear, is all."

Cut to: Marianna's tent, Candy's face glowing with affection as she talks. "Nothing scares her. I was a total baby when Leigh did my belly button, and she just does her nose herself!"

"She didn't, though, did she?" Marianna points out. "You were there."

"I don't follow." Candy stares.

"I have no doubt your friend Leigh is fierce and bold as you say, but I suspect that is armor. She lost both parents, yes?"

"Yeah, like I said," Candy nods.

"Sometimes, dear, wounded animal bears teeth not because it's strong but because it knows it is not. It takes particular will to face a cruel world so boldly as your friend does, but it takes another kind altogether to set aside yourself and come running to friend's aid at second's notice."

"What are you saying?"

"That you, Candy, are not as weak as you think. You have strength to put others first. This, as fate would have it, may not be in your best interest, however."

"Wait, what did you see in my future?"

Marianna shakes a finger. "You paid for insight into past, dear, and future is, at best, murky."

"Tell me!" Candy reaches into her pocket for more money.

"It's time you were back with friends, dear." Marianna gestures to the door. "They're looking for you."

"How do you—"

Leigh's voice cuts through the serenity of the tent, rising above the distant din of rattling wood and frenzied screams. "Has anyone seen my daughter? She's missing! About four foot eight, blonde hair, answers to Candy?"

Candy turns back, but Marianna's already gone. "Where..."

"Please!" Leigh calls out. "Candy, Momma's worried!"

Chapter Seven
RUNNIN' DOWN A RABBIT HOLE

"Where'd you go, you little shit?" Mack yells. He's sure he saw the skinny bastard go this way, and now there's no sign of him. He's gotta be hiding somewhere. "Look, shit-bird, I got places to be, so if you get your scrawny ass out here, we'll call it quits. Deal?"

Cut to: inside a trailer, to Rocky catching his breath with his back against the door as the runner's high hits. All the adrenaline coursing through his blood washes over the predicament he finds himself in. Like always, Rocky's gone fast, gone hard, and done got himself in trouble. This time backed into a corner, an alcove of trailers, with no way out.

"Hey! Shit-bird!" Mack yells from outside. Rocky can't help but admire that for a muscle-bound goon, this guy sure can move. "Last chance," Mack warns. "Fine, you asked for it."

Rocky hears a different trailer door slam open and figures he has about a minute till Mack works his way to this one—plenty of time to find somewhere to hide or sneak out a back window. Then the toilet flushes.

"Oh..." Rocky's grin vanishes. The lock on the bathroom door clicks, and tendrils of steam pour out as the door opens. A woman steps out, a towel pressed to her body, drying herself. It's about three seconds before she sees Rocky standing there, frozen. Rocky flashes his best smile and gives her the pretty boy eyes. Another second, and the woman screams—Rocky can feel Mack's boots pounding towards the door.

"Sorry about this," he shrugs and pushes past to the back of the trailer.

The door flies open, and Mack ducks in as it slams against the wall. "Where is he!?" Mack's yell frightens the woman, and she drops her towel. He tries not to look and sees everything. "Sor—" he tries to say, and she shuts him up with a glass-cracking screech.

Rocky can't get the window open in the bedroom, but he lucks out with a skylight over the bed. He's almost through it when Mack, red in the face, barges into the room and takes a swipe. He misses, and Rocky scrambles to the roof. Mack doesn't even think about trying to get his bulk through that small hatch and charges back outside to head the little bastard off.

Rocky's on the roof of the trailer when Mack comes out; the big guy slows now, a confident smirk making his beard shuffle. Despite their thickness, he somehow manages to fold his arms and nods to Rocky. "Gotcha now, kid. Nowhere to run."

"Would you believe me if I said this was all a big misunderstanding?" Rocky offers.

"Sure," Mack waves it off like he's happy to forgive and forget.

"Yeah?" Rocky's dubious.

"Of course. Why don't you explain to my buddies here though?" Mack kisses his tattooed knuckles. "They're a might confused."

"How about I give you and your friends something for your time, and we call it a day?"

"Oh kid, I'm gonna take your wallet anyway; the ass-kicking's on the house."

"Bitchin'." Rocky looks towards the carnival. It's not that far to the inner fence, and if he could just make the jumps, he could be there in seconds. Yeah, Rocky nods; let's Super Mario Bros. this shit.

"Gotta come down at some point, kid."

"See, that's where you're wrong," Rocky says and goes for it like he just caught a gold star. He jumps from one trailer to the next, landing with a hollow thud on the tin roof.

Mack saunters over and stands below this one. He glances to the next, then up to Rocky. "Nice jump, kid, but you ain't making that one."

"Sure I am." Rocky winks. "Just need a bathroom break first." Rocky leaps, not to the next trailer but to a chemical toilet stationed between them. It's a small landing, and Rocky almost overshoots it but manages to land in a crouch. He's about to cross the rest of the gap to the next trailer when everything starts to shake. Mack, gripping both sides of the toilet, rattles it, nearly sending Rocky flying. That gives him an idea, and he uses the momentum of the rocking toilet to launch himself to the far-side trailer. Suddenly much lighter, Mack pulls the chemical toilet harder than he needs to; it begins to topple towards him as the door flies open—as the contents of the bowl sail through the air like clumpy brown soup that's been left out of the fridge for three days.

"Shit," Mack curses.

"Shit." Rocky winces, and the open cubicle falls on Mack, entombing him in something so foul it makes Rocky want to gag all the way across the yard. "Sorry," Rocky grimaces as furious fists batter the inside of the toppled toilet. He jumps to the next trailer, then over the fence without looking back.

Rocky lands behind a family of four, startling them all. "Morning, folks," he says with a flash of that pretty boy smile and saunters on. He looks around, spotting the tip of the Big Top over a sign for Small Wood, and fixes his jacket before he heads that way. He should have bought Cliff enough time to get away, and now that the adrenaline is wearing off, he feels that same sinking sensation that's been haunting him all morning again. He knows each step is one more without Candy in his life, and the longer this takes, the further she gets from him. He needs to get her back, he needs—

"You little shit!" The voice rages from behind, and Rocky turns to see Mack, covered in brown splotches, at the threshold of a gate to the backyard. Rocky doesn't have time to snicker at the irony; he just runs. Mack comes, hard; he's really pissed off now and, track star he may be, not even Rocky can keep going forever—not to mention he's never gonna find Candy if he's on the run all day. No, Rocky's gotta lose him, preferably five minutes ago.

Mack can move, but is he agile? Rocky gambles on—no.

Taking a sharp turn, he cuts across rainbow-painted cobblestones into Small Wood then leaps clear across a low fence; it's nothing compared to the hurdles he's used to, and neither is the tiny train carrying kids slowly around some shrubs and a small pond. He jumps both those and the opposite fence once across, cutting right through Small Wood and out into Candy Alley—the name above the food stalls makes his heart feel like it's hit a brick wall.

"Outta the way!" Mack barrels across the train tracks behind Rocky, the faces of those nearby twisting in disgust.

"Fuck me, is the guy a Terminator or somethin?" Rocky's eyes meet a little kid who starts to cry at the swearing. A scowling mother marches over, and with Mack on his tail, Rocky's got no choice. Though he'd rather not, he heads into Candy Alley, nearly knocking over a harried, mustached dad carrying a tray full of milkshakes. He manages to keep the shakes together, but his glasses slide to the tip of his nose, making it hard to see.

"Watch it!"

"Sorry!" Rocky yells as he ducks around a corner, weaving between crowds of people waiting to buy popcorn and hot dogs.

"Move it," Mack yells, and, still spinning, not to mention half-blind, the dad with the shakes can't get out of the way. Mack collides with him, crushing the tray and splattering flat against the man, sending them both to the ground in a tangle of limbs and cold, clumpy milkshakes. At least the chocolate and strawberry masks the other stink Mack's covered in—well, almost.

Rising to his feet and wiping the gunk from his eyes, Mack roars like a royally pissed off bear covered in a sticky shit-shake.

Rocky looks this way and that and figures no matter where he runs, Mack's got a decent chance of spotting him as soon as he gets out of Candy Alley. Need to lay low for a bit, Rocky realizes, and so he slides over the counter of what looks to be an empty donut shack. He wedges himself down under the counter and goes flush against the wall just as Mack storms past. He's feeling pretty good, all things considered, outsmarting Carnie Arnie and side-stepping a hell of a beating.

"Rocky," someone says, and the smirk vanishes from his face as he looks up to see a redhead dressed in a lacy white dress. A large plastic clock dangles from her neck, and two bunny ears sit above cute round glasses. She holds a box labeled Alice's Donut Hole. "What are you doing here?"

The look Rocky gives her says, "Oh shit," but the only word that comes out of his dry mouth is, "Kat?"

"Please!" Leigh begs every passing stranger who does their best not to meet her eye. "My little girl's missing! She's about this high." Leigh leans down and holds her palm around her thigh. "Candy! Come, come get your juice box!" Leigh walks backward, hands clasped to her mouth, and doesn't notice the clown behind her till she backs right into his bowling ball gut. "Hey." Leigh gets ready to say something nasty when she turns and gets an eyeful of the surliest, dirtiest clown. Stained white t-shirt, red suspenders holding up patched suit trousers with a face that's all-white pancake save for a red spot on the nose. There are flecks of makeup in his beard and brushed back long hair. It looks like he's selling balloons, since he has a handful of them at the end of an upheld tattooed arm, but who's gonna buy them when he's making it look like they're filled with cigarette ash and syphilis?

"Watch it, kid," Hobo the Clown grunts, the cigarette in his mouth bouncing with each word, the ash catching on his belly outcrop.

It's not often something makes Leigh shut her mouth, but here it is. Her lips turn into something halfway between a snarl and a sneer, equal parts indignation and revulsion rising within. Leigh holds that same look of contempt and disgust as the clown walks off, flicking his cigarette on the ground.

"Fuuuuuuck, that's one warped ass clown," Leigh shudders. "Bet he has a van with free candy painted on the side, only the Es are backward, and there's a yellow-stained mattress in the back."

"You're sick," Clark points out.

"Soaked in the tears of kids whose faces grace milk cartons all across the state." Leigh ignores him.

"How come you're so scared of clowns?" Clark asks, feasting into a bag of mini-donuts.

"How come you're such a dork?" Leigh helps herself to one of Clark's donuts without asking. "Some questions were never meant to be answered." She munches.

"Seriously, it doesn't make any sense to me. You hate the things, but here you are."

"And you hate worms, but that doesn't stop you from playing with that one between your legs. In your room, the bathroom, the freakin' den—"

"You swore you'd never tell!"

"Point is." Leigh takes another donut. "Ask a stupid question, get a stupid answer."

"There's no such thing as a stupid question," Clark insists.

"Just stupid people," Leigh smirks. "I know."

"Not what I was gonna say—"

"Hey, guys," Candy chirps as she runs over. "Oh, donuts!" Clark's shoulders slump as he offers Candy the last one, and she takes it. "Did somebody say something about a juice box?"

"I'm working!" Sully protests, though it's obvious the idea is a foreign concept to Milly. She looks around, hoping she's not making a scene again. "I can't, Milly."

"Please! When it opens, Nevill wants to go on the Wild Cat and the murder house thingie," Milly pleads.

"So? Go. I can't look after them, Milly. I'm working!"

"Look, you're painting whiskers on kids' faces. Like, it's not fixin' a car, or somethin', Sully. Quit being such a goober."

GOOBER!

"I can't—"

FATTY-FAT GOOBER!

"Babe," Nevill snorts from the entrance, "let's book."

Milly looks from her boyfriend to Sully and decides to give her sister no choice. "Here." She thrusts the lead from the triplets' harness towards Sully and skips back over to Nevill.

"Milly!"

"Thank-you-byeeeeee!" Milly waves and walks into Nevill's waiting arms; the two of them are gone before Sully really processes what's happened.

Now she's left with her nephews and niece, Tyler, Trixie, and Tommy, while the line of kids waiting for their faces to be painted grows.

Tyler takes a brush from Sully's desk and jams it so far up his nose he begins to cry. That sets the other two off, and no amount of Sully shushing them gets them to quiet. "Come on, shhh, come on, please!"

The three of them start a chain reaction all around the tent. Younger children, babies in pushchairs: all of them start wailing one by one, till the entire tent is filled with nothing but a chaotic choir of ear-piercing warbles that threaten to shatter the sanity of everyone over the age of five.

The only thing that breaks through the cacophony is a single, shrill word. "Sully!"

Sully can feel the eyes of her boss on her neck before she turns. And she can hear the words leave her lips before they're even formed. "Get your kit and go; you're fired."

"The heck are you doing here, Rocky?" Kat smiles as though the boy hiding under her counter is there just to surprise her. She puts the box down and suddenly feels incredibly self-conscious in her white rabbit costume. Tucking a few loose strands of her red hair behind her ear, Kat blushes as she teases, "If you wanted to see me again, you could have just called."

"I didn't know you worked here," Rocky says. "Look, I'll explain later, but I'm in trouble. Can I hide here?"

"Rocky, I—"

"Hey." Mack slams his palms down on the counter, about three inches above Rocky's head. Rocky's eyes widen, and he holds his breath. "You seen a skinny ass kid with stupid hair and a leather jacket run through here?"

Kat's eyes flicker below for a second and land on Rocky's. They silently plead for her to keep quiet.

"Y-yeah," she says, and Rocky silently screams. "Yeah, I saw someone like that running off towards the High Dive."

"Damn." Mack slaps the counter, making both Rocky and Kat jump. "Fucker thinks he can get away. Oh I'm gonna rip him in two." Mack peels off but, just to be safe, Rocky holds his breath for a good twenty seconds.

"He's gone," Kat says and then kneels down to Rocky's level. She gives him a cute smile that goes all the way to her pale green eyes. "What did you do to make Jeff so mad?"

"Jeff?" Rocky crawls out of his hideaway. "I thought his badge said Mack?"

"Oh," Kat giggles, "that's a nickname. I heard he beat this one guy up so bad the paramedics said he looked like a Mack Truck hit him." She shrugs. "Guess it stuck."

Rocky gulps as he gets to his feet and thinks about how this day can't get any worse. Of course, that's when he hears them.

"Well, buy enough for everyone next time! Jesus, Clark, think about others for once!? Urgh!" Leigh moans.

"Very funny," Clark complains.

"I'll buy them, my treat." Candy tries to make peace, and then her smile vanishes as the three of them arrive at Alice's Donut Hole, and her eyes land on Rocky and Kat, inches apart, the two of them flushed and looking hella compromised.

"Candy..." Rocky doesn't know what else to say. All he's thought about is finding her, fixing things, while never giving much thought to how he might do that. Thinking things through to the end isn't really Rocky's strong suit.

Kat's smile begins to slip away as she realizes Rocky was never there to see her at all; of course, he wasn't, but she wanted to believe so, and therefore she did.

"I-" Rocky begins to say and falls short as Candy's eyes flit between him and Kat. Her world collapses for a second time at the sight of them. It makes her sick, the thought of another girl's lips on his, and the very idea that bothers her so much even after they've broken up makes Candy hate how weak she is, how enthralled she is by this worthless, cheating idiot.

"I can explain," Rocky pleads and moves away from Kat.

"Don't—" Leigh begins.

"Don't!" Candy yells, cutting her friend off. "Don't bother!" She looks to Kat. "I hope he cheats on you one day, too." And she runs away.

"Candy! No!" Rocky slides across the counter and goes to follow, but Clark's in his way.

"I didn't—" Kat tries to protest, the whole situation entirely confusing her.

"Zip it, floppy ears," Leigh warns her, and Kat shrinks away.

"Move it, poindexter." Rocky shoves Clark aside and follows on Candy's heels. "Candy, look, will you just let me explain? I swear—" He catches up and puts a hand on Candy's shoulder, then feels one on his own a second later. Rocky's spun around and looks up to meet Leigh's eyes. "Back off, Leigh," he warns.

"Or what, Rock-For Brains?" She pokes him in the chest. "You'll hit me? Do it, like to see you try."

"I'm not gonna hit a girl," he says and tries to move her hand. Leigh shoves him, sending Rocky down into the dirt. "The fuck!"

"Stay down." She points right at him, and when Rocky makes to stand back up, Leigh readies to boot him.

"No," Candy protests and gets between them. "No, please don't," she says to Leigh, then turns to look over her shoulder at Rocky. "He's not worth it. Let's go."

Candy walks on without giving Rocky another look. It pains her to do so; the traitorous heart beneath her chest beats for him like no other, and Candy wishes so badly it wouldn't while wanting nothing more than to turn around, look into those pretty eyes that make time stop, and let the world melt with him.

Clark shuffles by next, doing all he can to avoid contact with Rocky while Leigh remains over him, fire and fury burning behind her eyes.

"Come near her again, and I'll put you in the hospital," Leigh promises and feigns a kick at Rocky. He flinches; this makes her smile, and she leaves him there in the dirt, where he belongs, staring up at a perfectly blue sky.

Chapter Eight

CARN-EVIL CROSSROAD

Tink-tink-tink

Fade to: Ruth tapping on a wall of blue glass, the window into a vast aquarium Nothing responds to the sound.

"Reese! Get your monkey ass over here." Ruth squints through the murky water but can't see far. "Reese!"

"S-sorry, boss." Reese hobbles over, dragging his club foot so fast it catches on one of the aquarium's pump cables, and he goes flat to the ground. Ruth snickers, and that's about as much help as she offers. "I'm OK," Reese states, even though Ruth never asked, and then joins her at the window. "You called?"

"What's wrong with this picture?"

"Um, it's a fish tank, boss."

"First"—Ruth whacks Resse across the back of his head—"it's an aquarium. A fish tank's where you keep those diseased little goldfish the natives waste their cash trying to win. Second"—she whacks him again—"I know what it is! It's what's inside, or should be, that's the matter."

"Oh." Reese rubs the sore spots on the back of his head. "Yeah, the pump failed, and nobody noticed, so it nearly died—"

"What!?"

Reese ducks, but no swing comes this time.

"It's OK! We still had the other tank. It's all good."

Ruth smiles, disconcertingly, and fixes the lapels of Reese's cut-off denim jacket. "It's all good," she nods, then pulls Reese in close, up off his feet and right to her face. "It's all good, is it!?"

"Y-yeah!"

"We are twenty minutes from showtime, the star attraction is missing, and you didn't think to tell me!?"

"I'm sorry! I'll—"

"You'll get it back in there; that's what you'll do, won't you, Monkey Boy?"

"Yeah, boss, of course!"

Ruth releases him. "See that you do." She fixes her suit. "Or you'll be its next meal." Ruth composes herself and then leaves to prepare for the first tour.

Rocky drops down onto a bench along the side of the main throughway, the Big Top entrance to his right, Candy Alley to his left, and sighs. He covers the back of his head with his hands, grips his hair, and tries to find a way to reconcile just how badly he's fucked everything up.

There's something so surreal about the whole situation, sitting on a colorful bench in the middle of a carnival, calliope music in the air, and people dressed as clowns walking around. It feels like something he saw in an old movie this one time, something about a person not realizing they were dead as they wandered around town. That's how he feels, like the walking dead, and the whole thing must have broken his mind because when Rocky looks up, he sees Cliff, only he's wearing a blue cap with a stuffed hot dog glued to it. There's another

92

guy in a hot dog hat ahead of Cliff who turns and looks over his shoulder, calling back.

"Keep up, kid," the guy says. His shirt reads Willie's Wiener Wagon, and so do the boxes Cliff's carrying.

Rocky mouths, "The fuck," and rises to his feet as Cliff follows the other guy across the throughway towards the food stalls.

Cut to: inside Willie's Wiener Wagon, the other guy shows Cliff how to heat the dogs. "It's easy, kid." He loads them onto the rack with a greasy pair of tongs. "See?"

Cliff nods, using overt eagerness to mask how out of his depth he is.

"Yeah..." Ding-ding-ding, the bell on the counter goes. "Look, why don't you take the orders, and I'll get things going back here."

"Sure," Cliff nods and heads to the front of the shack.

He fiddles with the shutter and rolls it up. "Willie's Wiener Wagon, how can—oh, shit."

"What's up, kid?"

"Nothing," Cliff says, then yells back, louder, "Nothing!" He turns to face his customer, a little girl holding a balloon shaped into some kind of rodent. She smiles a firestarter grin, and her side ponytail bounces. "Can I help you?" he gulps.

"Yeah." Stacey goes up on her tiptoes. "Willie," she snickers and wiggles her pinky, "do you have any dinky dogs?"

Cliff glances to ensure his new boss won't catch him and then swipes for Stacey's shirt. "I'm gonna shove that balloon down your throat, then pop you like a zit."

"That's not good customer service," Stacey pouts. "I wonder what your boss would think?"

"Stacey, I swear—" Cliff cuts himself off as Rocky walks up to the counter, staring in stupefied shock. "Rocky?" Cliff takes in the dirt on his friend's jeans and shirt. "The hell happened to you, dude?"

"I'm gonna tell Mom you swore—"

"And I'm gonna tell Mom you're a bi—"

"What's going on?" the boss asks as he approaches. "There a problem here?"

"Yeah," Cliff yells. "Yeah, there's a problem!" He grabs his cap, yanks it off his head, and tosses it to the ground. "You can stick this job and this whole wiener shack up your ass! I quit!" Cliff hops up onto the counter, swivels around, and jumps down on the other side. He storms away, and, in utter bewilderment, Rocky and Stacey follow.

"Well, that was dramatic," Rocky points out when he and Stacey catch up with Cliff.

"Had to sell it," Cliff shrugs. "Always wanted to quit a job like that."

"Somebody'd have to give you one first," Stacey smirks.

"The only job you'll ever get is as a toilet brush," Cliff says right to her face. She scowls, in bitter silence, biding her time.

"Bro, have I got a story to tell you."

"Yeah." Cliff slaps his friend on the shoulder. "Me too, dude. I kid you not. First though, who's hungry?" he asks, then takes three hot dogs wrapped in foil from inside his jacket with a wink.

"Just slow down!" Leigh yells as she chases after Candy. A joke half forms in her head, something about little legs taking her surprisingly far, but even Leigh knows this isn't the time for that. "Candy!" People all around stare; things are long past a scene, not that Leigh cares all that much, but she doesn't want all these strangers thinking shit about her Candy.

Clark follows behind Leigh, feeling even more out of place and useless. He just sort of hovers there, not sure he's part of this situation, but wanting to help out all the same.

Eventually, Candy gets tired of running from her feelings and decides to take them out on a bin shaped like a pot-bellied clown holding its mouth open. It barely rattles, even when Candy gives it all the force she can.

Leigh has to bite back the urge to snicker. The whole scene would be adorably hilarious if her best friend's heart weren't in a worse state than the scraps of junk food stuffed into that trash-eating clown-bin hybrid from hell.

"Go to hell, Rocky!" Candy swings another kick. "Go chase Kat down her little rabbit hole! See if I care!"

That does it; Leigh can't hold back the laughter at that one. She tries, oh how she tries, with hands over her mouth, but the more she fights the urge to laugh, the harder the giggles come through. Her face flushes and then she can't hold it anymore—the laughter comes, and Leigh doubles over, howling.

Candy snaps to Leigh—eyes sharp with anger under a bedraggled blonde fringe. Maybe if she wasn't already in hysterics, Leigh could have held back, but Candy's stare hits Leigh like a kitten rudely awoken from a nap. It's too cute.

"I-I-I-I'm—" Leigh tries to control herself and can't. "It's just, little rabbit hole!"

Candy scowls, then smirks, and a second later, the giggles rise in her too. Before she knows it, she's laughing at her accidental innuendo. It's short-lived, though, just a pressure release, venting pent-up stress, and the grief asserts dominance once more. Her rage spent, Candy collapses in on herself, pulled into the black hole of heartbreak again.

Leigh goes to her, lowers herself, and takes Candy into her arms.

"I still love him!" Candy sobs, and the thought of that cuts Leigh deep. "Why do I still love him!?"

"I dunno." Leigh pats Candy's hair, running her fingers through it. "I mean, I didn't get it in the first place, so—"

"I know," Candy snorts. "Sometimes I think you only got with Cliff just so we could all hang out."

"Candy." Leigh doesn't know what to say to that—mainly because it's true.

"God, I'm such a loser!" Candy cries.

"Um, can I say something?" Clark shuffles his feet off to the side. Leigh genuinely forgot he was even there. Both girls say nothing, so he figures he's good to go. "I'm not the kind of boy girls cry over. Or even think about—"

"No, Clark—" Candy tries to protest.

"It's OK; I'm not looking for pity or nothin'. I'm OK with it. Leigh says I'll be rolling in it when I'm some rich super-nerd, so there's that."

"It's true," Leigh shrugs.

"I'm the kinda boy who has a crush on someone for years and never even thinks of talking to them."

"Clark, I keep telling you, I'm technically your sister!"

"So to do what Rocky did, to play with the hearts of two girls like that, and act like he's the victim—he's not worth it. Candy, you deserve better than someone who'll make you cry over them. And take it from a real loser. You're not one."

"Thanks, Clark," Candy says and wipes away a tear. "That's very sweet, and you're not a loser!"

"Yeah," Leigh adds, "much as it pains me to admit. Get your butt in here!" She opens her arms and makes space for Clark to join the group hug. This awkward, silent moment of vulnerability puts Leigh on edge, so she thinks of something to say to break it. "Well, hasn't this been a fantabulous day?"

"What's next?" Candy asks. She looks at one of the park clowns in polka-dot shorts, string vest, and bowler hat, twisting balloons into vaguely animal-like shapes for a group of kids.

"Maybe the clowns turn all Cujo and start trying to bite everyone," Leigh shudders.

"Why do you love this place so much if clowns freak you out? I mean, nobody likes clowns, but I'm surprised you haven't punched one yet."

"That's not true. I've already put one clown in the dirt so far." It takes Candy a second to realize she means Rocky, which brings a smile to her face. "What time is it, anyway?"

"Just gone one." Clark checks his Casio calculator watch.

A dramatic fanfare blasts from speakers across the throughway, as if on cue. Candy, Clark, and Leigh turn as fireworks blast in the air over the fused mansion and Big Top at the center. The doors to a balcony open all on their own, and a figure emerges from the darkness within. Tall, broad at the top, and sharply angular on the way down. Even from a distance, Ruth's black and red suit seems garish, but there's something up with her face—it's too hard to see at this distance, to be sure, but she looks... paler.

"Ladies and gentlemen," Ruth's voice booms across the carnival, "The House of Bonko... is open!"

"Woah." Clark pushes his glasses up his nose.

"We're not going in there." Candy shivers.

"Aw hell yes, we are." Leigh's already three steps on the way. "Nothin' like a good scare to make you forget how shitty things are. C'mon!" Leigh holds her hand out for Candy, and, somewhat reluctantly, she takes it.

"Clark?" Candy says as the three of them head towards the dark ride. "Don't be so hard on yourself."

"What do you mean?" Clark asks.

"There's a perfect girl out there for you, Clark; you just haven't met her yet."

Clark blushes and smiles sheepishly as the three of them head to The House of Bonko.

Cut to: Sully sitting down on a bench by the edge of the Small Wood Soft Play. Her right arm trembles; she's not aware of this. She's not aware of much right now. Inside her head, Sully's staring down the inevitability of never leaving home, never being more than a live-in babysitter for her sister, a caretaker for her alcoholic mother, and her father...

A plastic ball clunks against her head, breaking Sully out of her downward spiral. She looks up and spots the triplets tittering. One of them threw it—probably Tyler; he has another one in his hand ready to go, and he's shooting her that look, the same one the brat's grandfather has. The "what you gonna do about it" look.

EVEN A KINDERGARTENER KNOWS YOU'RE A LOSER.

"Shut up," Sully whispers.

JUST A DUMB GOOBER, NO JOB, NO NOTHIN'.

"Shut. Up." Sully's voice rises, earning her sideways glances from nearby parents.

Tyler pulls back, a big smirk on his face, snot running down to his lip, and readies to hurl another ball at Sully. In her head, he throws it, only for Sully to catch it. She stands, marches over, and holds it right in his smarmy face, tells him off for misbehaving, and drags the three of them out of the ball pit. After that, she tracks down Milly and her boyfriend of the week, hands the reigns to her kids back, and fucks off outta town for good.

In reality, she sits there, one arm quivering, as the ball plonks off her painted-on smile—the voice inside snickers

LOSER. LOSER, FATTY-FAT, LOSER.

It sings, and Sully finds that she doesn't exactly disagree.

"I can't believe you pulled the 'it's my first day' excuse," Rocky says.

"I can't believe you Ferris Buellered the Terminator, dude. You know if he ever catches you"—Cliff's point is muffled with grunts as he crams his hot dog into his mouth—"it's been nice knowing ya." He sits between Rocky and Stacey on a bench. His best friend holds his head in his hands while his little sister works away at her hot dog, a goofy smile on her face.

"The Mack Truck is the least of my concerns, bro," Rocky sulks. "What are the odds Kat works here and that I hide in her stall? Then Candy, Jesus man, what do you call that?"

99

"Kismet?"

Rocky only glares in response.

"Look, dude, I'm just saying, from where I'm sitting, I'd love a hottie like Kat crushing on me right about now. Ladies aren't exactly lining up to climb this Cliff, y'know."

"That's 'cause you got a tiny wiener," Stacey jumps in.

"I'm gonna cut that stupid ponytail off while you're asleep, Stacey!" Cliff says right to her face.

"'Least my hair will grow back!" She sticks a sticky tongue out at her brother. "You'll always have a tiny pecker!"

Rocky snorts. "She's not wrong, bro."

"Aw, come on, not you, too!?" Cliff feigns outrage. The truth is he'd take all the abuse in the world if it helps cheer his friend up. "So what's the plan now, dude?"

"I wanna ride the Wild Cat! Oh, and the spook house! And, and, and—"

"The only thing you're riding is my foot all the way home, Stacey!" Cliff turns back to Rocky. "Think we should get outta here before Mack finds you again?"

Rocky thinks about it for a moment. "I can't give up, bro; I just can't. I love her."

"I love you, Rocky," Stacey sighs sweetly, and the boys ignore her.

Cliff sighs. "OK." He stands and offers Rocky his hand. "We ain't getting anywhere sitting on our butts, though, so let's move." Rocky takes his friend's hand and stands, the two of them locked together like brothers in arms.

"Thanks, bro," Rocky says.

"Always, dude," Cliff nods, then the two of them stand there like they're posing for the cover of some dumb buddy action comedy movie. "Uh, where we going?"

"I—" Rocky's about to say he doesn't know when a fanfare blasts through the air. As they follow the sound around the Mirror Maze, their eyes land on the Big Top Mansion, at the tall woman on the balcony on the second floor, and a familiar trio making their way towards the attraction.

"Woah, look at the line already!" Clark says as he approaches The House of Bonko with Candy and Leigh. The entrance to the ride's through the mansion's front, though the line trails all the way along the Big Top.

"Guess everyone wants a piece of Bonko, huh?" Leigh adds.

"Don't you guys think it's weird they're making such a big deal out of him? I mean, he was a real bad guy." Candy rubs her shoulders.

"People love sex and violence," Leigh shrugs.

"People are just messed up." Candy eyes the line. "I don't want to wait in that line; come on, we'll come back when it calms down."

"Ah, but you're forgetting," Leigh holds her finger up, "we're VIPs!" Leigh runs over to the booth and wraps on the glass. She represses the urge to shudder when a droopy balding clown turns to face her. "Yo, name's Leigh, and I was told I'd be on," she fake coughs, "the list."

The balding clown doesn't say anything; it just looks down at something below the window, nods, and then opens the exit gate. He ushers Leigh on, and she turns to the others, beckoning them to follow. Clark follows, no bother, but Candy drags her feet while putting her knuckle in her mouth. She can't help but feel that going into this house will be a big mistake.

As the three of them make their way to the door via the exit path, someone in line takes exception. "Goddamnit!" Not-Stu yells. "Not again!"

At the entrance, Leigh jumps to attention. "Three VIPs for the tour, if you please!"

"Yeah, just a second," the worker says and ignores her cheeky grin. He lifts a velvet rope and lets the first two in line join them—a too-thin girl in a frayed vest and a man wrapped in denim and the scent of Budweiser. The worker does a quick headcount and then looks to a colleague holding three fingers. Turning back to the line, the worker calls out, "Any trios or singles?"

Somewhere at the back, a hand shoots up. "We're a trio!"

Leigh scowls; there's something irritatingly familiar about the voice, but it's hard to tell over all the chatter and spooky music pumping out of the speakers hidden around the house. Only when the trio comes into sight, when the workers let them through the gate, does she realize who they are.

"Aw, fuck," Leigh says as Cliff, Rocky, and Stacey make their way to the front. Behind her, the doors to The House of Bonko creak open.

Chapter Nine
HOUSE OF A THOUSAND GIGGLES

They pass through the doors into a vast hall that looks like someone loaded a cannon with circus paint and blasted bad taste everywhere. There's no wall the same color, or even in scale, and the group's sneakers scuff on uneven zig-zagging tiles.

"Well, shit." Leigh twirls in wide-eyed wonder at the chaotic, carnivalesque splendor.

"Welcome!" Ruth's voice booms off the walls as she stands on the floor above, arms spread wide. As all eyes turn to her, the doors slam closed, making each of them jump as the lock clicks.

Leigh feels Candy grab her arm and squeeze in close, and she tenses up, instinctively, ready to put herself between Candy and whatever's coming their way.

There's a twisting, spiraling staircase leading up to the balcony, flanked on either side with garishly painted elephants mounted by diminutive clown riders.

All eyes are on Ruth as she descends. It's not the sheer size of her presence or the striking ringmaster ensemble she's squeezed into—a black and red striped bodysuit with a large and very full, open chest area featuring delicate golden tassels that swish with each step. Nor is it the matching long-sleeved and embroidered red jacket, knee-high leather boots, close-weaved fishnet stockings, or even the black leather bullwhip coiled on her round hip. No, it's her face that leaves them all stunned.

Crumbly white pancake, deep black sunken diamond eyes, and a too-red, too-thin smile that curls up sharply across her cheekbones—it's frightening and familiar at the same time. None of them have to look far to figure out where they've seen this face before; it stares at them from dozens of framed paintings scattered across the wall, off-kilter and uneven. It's the face of Bonko the Clown.

"Welcome," Ruth repeats, "one and all, to the House of a Thousand Giggles! Come this way, and prepare yourselves to find out the true story of Buster B. Bonkin." And she leads the way to the back of the hall, towards the only open door. One with a bold sign in colored lightbulbs which reads "Murder Ride" above it.

"Do you think that means we'll get murdered on the ride?" Cliff jokes in the back.

"Here's hoping," Leigh mumbles and follows Ruth, dragging Candy along, with Clark following.

"Damn," Nevill can't help but say as his eyes watch Ruth go, earning him a smack.

"Baby!" Milly complains, but Nevill shrugs it off and throws his arm around her bony shoulder. Wouldn't mind giving that ass a honk, he thinks, and this time keeps the thought to himself.

Rocky, sensing his moment, makes for Candy, only to be blocked by Leigh putting herself between them.

"Get out of my way," Rocky demands.

"Make me." Leigh cracks her knuckles. Clark, sweating a little, joins her.

"I just wanna talk to her," Rocky pleads.

"She doesn't want to talk to you," Leigh insists.

"It's OK, Leigh." Candy comes through between her friends. "Let him say what he's got to say." She folds her arms and looks him dead in the eye.

"Candy, I, uh." Rocky runs his hand through his hair.

"Yeah, see, that's not gonna work anymore, Rocky. You can't just stand there looking pretty and think I'm gonna come running back; acting bashful isn't an apology."

"I'm sorry—"

"No, you're sorry you got caught!"

"That's not—look, I didn't mean it, OK? It was an accident—"

"Accident!" Candy laughs. "You just fell on her lips, huh? You buying this, Leigh?"

"Happens all the time," Leigh says, deadpan. "Can't count the number of people I've Frenched on accident."

"Face it," Candy pokes Rocky in the chest, "you're about as fake as this whole stupid carnival. So why don't you go chase Kat down her little rabbit hole? She's dying to have you, after all!"

Candy storms off while Leigh shrugs, "Couldn't have said it better myself," then follows.

"Shit," Rocky curses, "this isn't gonna work."

"Maybe you need to think about—" Cliff offers, and Rocky doesn't listen.

"I need to get her alone; can't do anything with her fucking bodyguard there." Rocky turns to Cliff. "You got any ideas?" he asks as they head into the ride.

"Yeah, I think I do," Cliff says as his eyes land on the four two-seater carriages waiting for them. Milly and Nevill are already climbing into the first one; she giggles as Nevill takes the opportunity to squeeze her butt. They hold their arms up as the safety bars come down while Candy and Leigh wait for the train to move up. Kneeling

105

to meet Stacey's eye, Cliff begs, "I need you to scream and cry like somebody just ran over your Barbies with a lawnmower."

"Yeah," Stacey pouts, "and if I don't?"

"Then I'm gonna run over your Barbies with a lawnmower!"

"Nu-huh!" Stacey shakes her head.

"What do you mean, nu-huh!?"

"Sweeten the deal," Stacey demands.

"Damnit." Cliff looks to Rocky's desperate, pretty face, then across to the train as the bars on carriage two lift. "What do you want!?"

"Um, lemme think..."

"Stacey!"

"I want you to have a tea party with me."

"That's it!? Deal!" Cliff sticks his hand out.

"In full costume. And I want to do your makeup!"

"What?" Cliff gulps.

"Cliff, please," Rocky pleads.

"Damnit, fine. Deal!" Cliff groans. "Now scream!"

Stacey gives Cliff her trademark firestarter grin and then instantly transitions into a wail of sheer agony. It pierces the air and ears of everyone, causing all eyes to turn to her. All except Candy as she takes her seat in the second carriage.

In the chaos and confusion, Rocky makes his move. He dashes across the platform, slipping around Leigh, and slides into the seat beside Candy.

"Wait!" she protests as the bars come down, locking in place. "What the hell, Rocky!" she protests and then yelps as the carriage rocks to life. They're carried into the dark together before she can say anything else.

Split-screen: Milly with Nevill; she's excitedly hugging Nevill's bicep while he looks around, chewing gum and acting like he doesn't care. Candy and Rocky's carriage clatters through glow in the dark framed doors, she as far to one side as she can get, while Rocky pleads across the gulf between them.

Next: Leigh and Clark's carriage jerks along the rails— he's looking around with quiet wonder while Leigh tries, in vain, to lean over and see what's going on in Candy's car; Cliff and Stacey come in last, with her bouncing on her seat while Cliff drums his fingers on the bar, hoping Rocky's doing OK.

"Look—" Rocky tries to say, and the carts all bump to a halt. It's pitch dark, and for a second, he thinks it's gotta have broken down, before all four carriages spin ninety degrees to the right in tandem.

Split-screen: Milly leans in, sure she sees something in the dark, a faint outline of a shape; Candy bites down on her knuckle, hiding behind her fist.

HA-HA! A round, clown face springs out of the darkness towards the carriages.

Split-screen: Milly yelps in terrified delight, cuddling into Nevill as he pretends not to have jumped himself; Candy jumps into Rocky's arms and for a second, she forgets everything else. He's so stunned he doesn't think to react, even if it feels like it's the first time his heart's beat since they broke up. She pushes away half a second later, disgusted at herself.

The larger-than-life clown face dangles before them, spotlit from below, making the two tufts of horn-like blue hair on either side of the otherwise bald head cast a devil-like shadow behind. It bounces on coiled metal, like an overgrown jack-in-the-box as scratchy circus music picks up, accompanied by children singing something incomprehensible.

Split-screen: Leigh shudders as she says, "This is FUCKED"; Stacey bounces as she says, "This is AWESOME!"

"Bonko the Clown!" a voice booms from speakers built into the carriages and mounted in the shadows. "AKA Buster B. Bonkin, the Infamous Murder Clown of Clear Lake County, The Strange State Slasher. You think you know the story? Think again. Come, join us, and delve into the true horror of Buster B. Bonkin!"

All four carriages flick forward and clunk along as dozens of idiosyncratic giggles fill the dark behind them. After clattering through a set of double doors, they stop with a quick spin to the left. Everyone's on edge this time, and even so, most jump as several overhead lights clunk on, unveiling a wholesome yet unnerving tableau. Several child-like mannequins move in basic, robotic patterns, pushing toy cars and waving dolls.

"Although the oldest of the Bonkin children, Buster was born with a rare genetic condition, stunting his growth. His younger siblings all outgrew him and would tease Buster relentlessly." Another light comes on, showing a small child-sized automaton at the back with the wrinkled, sour face of an older man.

Several disembodied voices—taunts and jeers—play over one another, each rising in pitch till the riders have to cover their ears, till everything plunges into silent darkness at once.

"The fire was considered an accident," the recording states, and the scene relights with a flickering red and orange glow that casts dancing, panicked shadows.

Flash-cut: flickering grainy black and white footage of a young Buster's smiling face, shadows from a match's flame dancing across it.

Intense child-like screams and pleas for help come from all around; they sound unnervingly realistic. "Given what we know now about Buster B. Bonkin, who's to say..."

The carts all spin in a half-circle, with no warning, tossing their passengers around as the display behind them goes dark once more, the sound of laughter just barely detectable below the final wails of agony. More joyful music pipes up as the next scene begins—a tin puppet circus with little cut-outs performing various acts all at once.

"Buster found work in the one place he could: the circus. He joined the famous Achilles Maze Travelling Show." A small cut-out of a much more cheerful Bonko pops up and hops along, waving at the audience.

Split-screen: Milly coos, "Aw, ain't he cute!"; Leigh shakes her head. "Still nope!"

"Till tragedy struck..." One of the cut-out puppets, shaped like an elegant woman, climbs the highwire and dances along the rope only to fall—the sound of bones snapping cracks all around.

Flash-cut: grainy newsreel footage of the real acrobat as she lies broken in an impossible shape amongst the sand and blood. Somewhere backstage, watching, Bonko smirks.

The four carriages resume their journey; this time, the recording accompanies them through the dark.

"Not much is known about the years between his time with Achilles Maze and the opening of Bonkin's Bonanza."

The cars all stop, and above them, a panoramic, backlit sepia photo of the old carnival comes to life with the sounds of elephants and children's laughter.

"Bonko, as he preferred to be known, established the carnival on his father's land—after the man's tragic demise, of course—and made sure to employ as many former carnival, circus, and freak show workers as possible."

An old-time radio broadcast cuts in. "Tragic news about the fire in Woodvale; we'll update when more information is available. Now, for something lighter, we have here one Buster B. Bonkin—"

"Bonko!" a chirpy voice corrects.

"—Bonko, who's opening a brand new year-round carnival out in"—static conceals the location—"and he promises it's the most authentic carnival experience of all time. Is that right?"

"Ay-yup!" Bonko giggles. "It's a f-f-f-fun and safe place for all the f-f-f-family! That's the toot-tootin' truth!

Split-screen: Nevill furiously pushes two fingers of one hand through a hole made with the other while miming "f-f-f-fuck"; Rocky looks at Candy, who does her best to ignore him.

"And is it true you're mainly hiring former and current carnival folk?"

"Ay-yup! That's right! It's my dream to build a home for all the f-f-f-freaks like me!"

The recording fizzles away as the narrator returns. "A dream, or perhaps, a nightmare..." The backlight changes and flickers like lightning, with the devil-like silhouette of Bonko flashing in between blasts.

As the cars move along once more, Rocky takes another shot. "Listen, can you at least let me say I'm sorry?" Candy pretends to be very interested in the side

110

of their carriage. "I know what I did was wrong. I shouldn't have let her kiss me—"

"Seriously!? Let her!?" Candy turns to him, her face alive with a fury her tiny frame can barely contain. "I've seen the photo, Rocky. Did you let her drive you both out to the Kissing Creek, or was that an accident too?"

"I was just giving her a ride home—"

"Oh, I'm sure you were giving her a ride!"

"Look, jeez, I fucked up, OK!? I'm an asshole, but it's not like you're Miss Goddamn Innocent!"

"Oh, really? And how is this my fault!?"

"Look, the shit you did to my car? That's thousands of dollars to fix, Candy. That's not cool."

"I didn't touch your precious car and if I did, I would have burnt it to the ground. It makes me sick thinking about what we did in there!"

That stabs Rocky to the core. Desecrating the 'Cuda is one thing, but the memories they made in the backseat—they were truly special to Rocky. He doesn't know what to say to that, slumping down in his seat as the cars arrive at the next scene.

"In the Summer of 1977, Bonko the Clown met his demise at the hands of Chet Redwood." The lights come on and—

Split-screen: all eight riders at once, each of them in stunned, shocked awe.

A model of a cotton candy machine stands in the middle. An animatronic version of Chet lifts and lowers a disemboweled Bonko in and out of the drum.

Screams of agony rip from the speakers, accompanied by shocked gasps and calls for help. Small jets of red-dyed water squirt from the machine, lightly splattering the eight of them.

"After his death, many of Bonko's crimes came to light."

The cars move again, along a corridor with lit frames coming to life as they pass. They showcase news clippings covering armed robberies and multiple missing persons. "Suspected of at least two dozen murders, no evidence could be found tying Bonko directly to the crimes. Nothing concrete, anyway. That is, till investigators uncovered how Bonko disposed of the bodies..."

All four cars arrive at a flat, blank wall. The passengers stir nervously, wondering what will happen as an electric shutter begins to rise. All of their faces are lit with a strange, blue glow as they stare into a vast aquarium. Something stirs inside; bubbles race and plants wave.

Split-screen: all eight of them lean forward, trying to make out what lurks in the murk. Tiny jets of something red squirt into the water against the glass. They turn to wisp-like vapor, and all eight riders hold on for dear life as the seats rocket towards the glass—

BOOM!

Something bashes into the window. Screams of joy and terror follow. A second later, it swims past, almost casually gloating about its jump scare. It's about three meters of pure terror—an angry as hell bull shark with one eye.

The recording laughs, "Don't worry, kids, it can't hurt you. Unless you'd like a dip?" It laughs again. "No one ever found the bodies because Bonko fed his victims and anyone who crossed him to his favorite pet—Bruce the Bull Shark. Bonkin's Bonanza proudly presents THE Bruce, brought back home from the private zoo he found his way to... Say, he looks hungry—" The shutters drop the train into darkness again. "Feeding time!"

"How much d'you think a shark costs, baby?" Milly asks as she and Nevill disembark the ride. He just shrugs in response.

Candy jumps out of her car as soon as the bar lifts; she shoves it up and it bounces back as Rocky tries to follow, clunking him on the head.

Leigh and Clark clamber out next and move to flank Candy as they head into the next room, while Cliff and Stacey head over to help Rocky up.

The group winds through a twisting, off-kilter corridor full of mind-bending optical illusions and trick compositions.

"Candy, wait!" Rocky comes running along the corridor, the ringing in his head not helping with the disorienting layout, and he runs into one of the walls.

"How many times can I say it? We're over! Done!" Candy yells without looking back.

"Take a hint, loser!" Leigh adds.

"Oh, fuck off, Leigh, you goddman bitch!" Rocky snaps. That stops everyone in their tracks, even Milly and Nevill, who both wish they had some popcorn right about now.

"Fuck you say!?" Leigh steps to him, standing an inch taller; she looks down into his pretty-boy eyes and dares him to repeat it.

"I know it was you who fucked with my car. Don't think I'm gonna let that slide."

"Anytime, little man," Leigh smirks, "anytime."

"Just make sure your step-narc's there to snap this one too," Rocky dares her.

"What's that supposed to mean!?"

"Oh, sure, like it was a coincidence he was there to take a photo of me 'n' Kat, huh?"

"That wasn't me," Clark protests and Leigh holds her arm out to stop him. "How would I even know you'd be there?"

"That's an excellent question." Things begin to rattle around in Rocky's head, making a hazy kind of sense.

"I got this," Leigh says to her stepbrother, then turns back to Rocky. "Read the room, loser. Let her go!" She turns, puts her arm around Candy, and walks her towards the exit, pushing past Milly and Nevill.

They emerge into a rear courtyard, and for a moment, the sight before them puts all the drama to rest. An antique cotton candy machine sits in the middle, circled with black velvet ropes.

"Is that…?" Leigh asks, a gleefully macabre smile on her face.

"I hope not." Candy bites her knuckle.

"Ohmygawd!" Milly screeches and leaps down the stairs, racing over to the machine. "Baby, look! It says this is the machine that killed Bonky!"

"Far out," Nevill says as he approaches his girl.

"That's right!" Ruth booms, appearing seemingly from nowhere. "The very same cotton candy machine that killed Buster B. Bonkin!" She stands behind the machine and leans on it carefully. The device comes to life with a flick of a switch, spinning sugar threads into a sickly sweet whirlwind. "Who wants a taste?"

"That story is bogus," Nevill snorts. "Ain't no way one of those things can kill a man. They don't even got sharp blades or nothin'."

"Ah, but that's where you're wrong." Ruth gestures to some raised lettering, scrawled in some form of archaic cursive. "This is," she reads, "a Zephyr!"

114

"What's a zebra got to do with cotton candy?" Milly squints.

"The Zephyrs," Ruth ignores Milly's stupidity, "were designed in the 1930s by a surgeon of ill repute. Suspected of heinous crimes, including, but not limited to, cannibalism, this surgeon had a taste for lamb."

"Oh, yum!" Milly smiles.

"She means kids." Leigh rolls her eyes.

"Indeed, and this surgeon designed this machine so that anyone reaching into the drum would get a nasty surprise... Discontinued!" Ruth makes Milly jump. "Then banned outright; many a child lost a finger, many a carnie a hand."

"Yeah, so how come Bonko got one?" Nevill asks.

Ruth just smiles for a moment. "Buster collected objects of iniquity, and for a price, so can you." Ruth raises a clear plastic bag with the face of Bonko printed on it. "Ten dollars for a bag of Bonko's Cotton Candy. Those who've dared to taste it say it's sweeter than blood!" Ruth grins, and the crowd falls into silence.

"Please, baby, please!" Milly begs. "Please get me some." She plays with the bottom of her tank top. "I'll do that thing you like if you do." She gives him the eyes and plays with her foot.

"I'll take a bag!" Nevill declares.

"Yay! Make it two! We should get Sully somethin' for babysitting!"

Nevill shrugs and hands over two sawbucks. Ruth takes a stick and scoops some cotton candy up, pushing it into the bag. The spun sugar goes dark, almost blood red, then turns jet black in seconds.

"Oh, wow," Leigh says, coming over and looking at the bags in Ruth's hand. "How does it do that?"

Ruth's eyes flicker, almost as though she is surprised. "Magic, my dear," she winks. "Care to taste history?"

"I wish! I'm broke!" Leigh looks over her shoulder to Candy, then to Clark.

"Let's just go," Candy says and she heads towards the exit. Leigh's disappointed but follows all the same.

"How did you know?" Rocky barges out of the house, raising his hands in wonder. "Just right place, right time? Or did you put her up to it?"

Leigh stops dead. She has nothing to say about that, mainly because Rocky's sudden astuteness stuns her.

"Leigh?" Candy asks, the silence incriminating.

"Kat seemed to think I was on the market; wonder where she got that idea?"

"I—" Leigh turns to Candy. "Look, I only wanted to show you what kind of a guy he really is."

"No, Leigh, no," Candy's voice warbles.

"Some friend you got there," Rocky shouts.

"Candy, I was just trying—"

"No, Leigh." Candy bites her hand as her eyes water. "No."

Leigh's heart shatters as her stomach turns; this was the last thing she wanted. She always knew Rocky was no good, that there was no way an all-star track and field hero like him was going to college after the summer and not be drowning in groupies wanting a piece of him. No way was he gonna keep it in his pants until mid-term when Candy could visit. This was for the best, right? Like a Band-Aid that needs to come off? So why does she feel like a fucking monster?

"Candy, I..." is all Leigh can say as her best friend, the person she loves most in the world, looks at her with nothing but despondent devastation in her eyes. She watches, helpless, as Candy runs for the exit.

116

Rocky struts over, stands beside Leigh, and says with nothing but contempt, "Read the room, loser. Let her go."

"I'll fucking end you!" Leigh snarls. She spins on her heels and pushes Rocky to the ground, going with him. The two of them roll around in the dirt as the rest of them look on, stunned. Ruth takes a radio from her jacket and calls for security, then heads over to try and break up the fight.

Moments later, two security guards race in through the backdoor. They wrestle Leigh and Rocky apart, lifting them to their feet. Rocky swings wildly. "Let me go!"

"Not happening, shit-bird," the guard holding Rocky states, and the boy freezes; his eyes widen as he looks up to see the smiling, bearded face of Mack grinning at him. "Hi."

"Fuck," Rocky curses, and Leigh spits at him from across the courtyard. The guards drag them away, out through the exit, and in all the chaos, no one spots Stacey, scooping a wad of cotton candy up and shoving it into her pocket.

Chapter Ten

I HATE MYSELF FOR LOVING HIM

Cut to: a live feed from Channel Five News, outside The House of Bonko. Brock Hauser combs his silver hair and eyebrows, not aware that he's currently on air.

"Huh?" Brock asks and touches the mic in his ear. "Why didn't you—" He fixes his jacket, stands straight, then puts on his newsreader face with a gleaming, white smile. "Gooooood afternoon folks, this is Brock Hauser with Channel Five News, live from the newly-reopened Bonkin's Bonanza, and"—Brock gestures to his left; the camera pans to show a busy throughway and a line snaking around outside the house—"it's safe to say it's been a success!" The camera centers on Brock once more as he continues. "The star attraction, which you can see behind me, The House of Bonko promises to be the world's first"—Brock squints, obviously reading something off-camera—"true crime murder ride? Really? I mean, of course! And I want you all at home to join me, Brock Hauser, as I brave The House of Bonko in just a few moments, but—"

A clattering commotion off-camera interrupts him. The shot races around, the crowds and stalls a blur, till it lands on the source of the uproar. Two security guards back out of a gate around the side of The House of

Bonko, each of them restraining a teenager as best they can.

One guard, who looks like his muscles have muscles, holds a handsome young man in a brown leather jacket kicking out at a girl in torn tartan jeans and a slashed, safety-pinned Joan Jett tank top. The camera zooms in, and the mic is just able to pick up the yelling.

"I'm gonna **BLEEP** you up, Pretty Boy!" the punk girl screams.

"Anytime **BLEEP**, any **BLEEP**-ing time, you Goddamn **BLEEP**!" the pretty boy snaps back.

The punk girl thrusts her head back, cracking the guard carrying her in the nose, and she slips free as he reaches up to staunch the gushing blood. She swings for the pretty boy, but the guard holding him uses his side to block her.

"Come on, Mack," she yells, "let me get the **BLEEP**-er once!"

"Back off, Leigh," the security guard warns her.

"Yeah, **BLEEP**," the pretty boy spits, "back the **BLEEP** off."

The punk girl roars and claws at the pretty boy as two more security guards rush over, both of them grabbing an arm and dragging her away.

Brock pushes his way back in front of the camera, shooting an accusatory look at the camera operator for daring to cut him out of the shot.

"Well folks, it looks like those two have had a bit too much sugar. This is Brock Hauser, live from Bonkin's Bonanza, signing off." He holds the smile till he thinks the feed is cut and then mutters, "Hopefully those **BLEEP**-wits at the studio were quick with the

BLEEP-ing button." He looks off-camera and tuts. "**BLEEP**-ing animals." Brock holds a finger to his ear, and his face turns white as he listens to something only he can hear. He looks right into the camera. "**BLEEP**."

Candy sits on a bench across from a massive rotating circle of caged fiberglass hot air balloon baskets with the words "'Round the World" flashing across the middle.

There's a barbecue van just by the entrance, filling the air with rich, smoky sweetness. The big, bald lead chef fist bumps another carnie, a scrawny guy with fuzzy sideburns, who hands over a bag of that black cotton candy.

Candy stares at it all without taking in anything. She's a million miles away, inside, and she's just about gnawed through the skin of her knuckles.

A family of three, the mustached father covered in milkshake stains, squeeze in together for a photo at a cut-out stand featuring four oddly shaped, faceless clown bodies. When the camera flashes, Candy sees a different picture in her head, the one where the boy she loves kisses a pretty redhead with nerdy librarian glasses.

The carnival sounds wash over Candy and she doesn't notice as someone sits down beside her. She doesn't hear them speak and only snaps back to reality when they place a delicate, pale hand on her arm. She jumps, a little yelp escaping her lips, and then Candy's eyes land on Kat's gentle smile.

"Hey, Candy," Kat says, those two simple words solemn with guilt.

"Kat," Candy says, acting polite enough, but she'd rather not be.

"So, I'm probably the last person in the world you wanna talk to right now." Kat plays with the hem of her lace dress.

"Honestly," Candy laughs, and some tension releases, "till a few minutes ago, yeah. Now, not so sure."

"Oh," Kat bites her lip. "Um, is everything OK? No, sorry, stupid Kat, of course, it's not. I mean, has something happened?"

"Yeah," Candy kicks her feet an inch from the ground, "you could say that." She looks back to Kat.

"Does it help if I say I'm sorry?"

"Kat." Candy shakes her head. "I'm just so sick of pretty promises from pretty mouths that mean pretty much nothing."

"I see." Kat hangs her head and Candy feels an odd sense of pity. It makes her feel like trash for snapping.

"You thought Rocky and I broke up, right?"

"Yeah." Kat can't bring herself to meet Candy's eyes. "Yeah."

"Would you have kissed him even if you didn't?"

"I want to say no," Kat takes a deep breath, "but I can't."

Candy nods, shaking a tear from her cheek. "Leigh spread the rumor about us. She wanted to show me what he was really like." Candy shakes her head, biting back the urge to ugly cry. "I guess she was right."

"If I could take it back, I would," Kat offers.

"Who kissed who?" Candy pulls her hand away from her mouth, shaping a fist, trying to make herself strong.

Kat takes a moment to answer, unsure if she should. "I kissed him."

"Did he kiss you back?"

"Candy—"

"Did he kiss you back!?"

121

Kat nods. "But only for a bit! He pushed me away!"

"Oh, awesome." Candys shakes her head and looks to the sky, to the big wheel of balloons that looms over them. "That makes it all better, right?"

"He stopped me—"

"I can't believe you're sitting here defending him."

"I'm not—"

"Yeah! You are! Did you break into his car? The' Cuda." Candy does a bad impression of Rocky. "Did you drive down to the creek?"

"No... I thought you guys broke up, so I asked him for a lift. I told him the fastest way home was through Kissing Creek. I... tried to make a move in the car, then he got out. I thought maybe he was just nervous, so I went after him, I—"

"You love him, don't you?" Candy stares right at Kat and dares the other girl to meet her eye. Kat gathers her strength and does.

"Yeah," Kat says, her voice breaking. "I can't help it."

"Me neither," Candy relents. "I hate myself for loving him!"

"It's you he loves, Candy." Kat puts her hand on Candy's. "It hurts me so bad to say that. I've been crushing on him since fifth grade."

"Really?" Candy raises an eyebrow. "Even with the bowl cut?"

"Especially with the bowl cut."

Kat lets out a single giggle. A moment of silence passes between both girls, then one by one, they teeter towards tittering and before either of them knows it, they're laughing together in the shade of the big wheel.

"Stop! Please, stop!" Sully yells as she chases after Tyler, who runs wild, while Tommy picks his nose and Trixie plays with dirt.

Parents of other children stare on, disapproving, as though their children wouldn't ever consider being so disobedient. Sully's on the verge of tears, her hair messed up like a drunk bird made a nest; the face she painted on just a few hours ago has melted. It sags, running down her cheeks in greasy smears. "Please!"

Tyler climbs up onto a picnic table, thankfully vacant, but his mischievous eyes are on the next one, and the ugly sneer he gives Sully tells her exactly what he's got in mind.

"Get down from there right now," Sully whimpers. She meant it as a command, but it comes out a meek plea, and all it does is fuel Tyler's willfully disobedient streak. He leaps to the table and kicks over a cup of soda, splattering a suburban dad about to bite down on a Willie's Wiener Dog. His shock doesn't have time to turn to outrage before Tyler gives the rest of the table the boot, making two smaller kids cry and cling to their mother. The woman turns to Sully, indignation and condemnation radiating from her gaping mouth and flared nose.

Tyler leaps to the following table, laughing as he kicks more overpriced junk food, stomping on unopened chip packets just to listen to them pop. More eyes turn to Sully and she can hear them muttering, denouncing her.

"Can't control her kids."

"Terrible mother.

"Trailer trash wh—"

"They're not my kids," Sully sobs and sinks to a squat. She covers her face with her hands, hoping that she can somehow shut the world out. "Not my kids, not my kids," she chants, and it helps to drown out some of the murmurs spreading across this little corner of Small Wood, but not the voice from within.

YOU'RE SUCH A LOSER, SULLY, her inner thoughts say. *SUCH AN UGLY, FAT LOSER.*

"No," Sully heaves, "no."

FATTY-FAT GOOBER-GOBBLER, FATTY-FAT—

"Momma!" Tyler's scream cuts through, and Sully jerks her head up. Tyler leaps from one table into the open arms of his mother, who shrieks and spins the pint-sized terrorist around. The other two triplets waddle up to their mother, and Sully finds herself thankful for Milly's arrival. The distraction and escape from the stares of all those parents are enough to make her forget, for a moment, that Milly's lack of responsibility got her fired. It was Milly's fault, though—

YOU WOULD HAVE FAILED ANYWAY, the voice says. *MILLY'S JUST AN EXCUSE.*

That doesn't have the effect the inner voice thinks it will have; instead of beating Sully down, it adds a little fire to her—enough to get her off her ass and across the picnic park.

"Sully! Ohmygod! Like, you shoulda seen it. There was these puppets and a freakin' shark! Then this punk chick tried to punch this preppy boy. It was wild, wasn't it, baby!?"

Nevill chews his gum and nods along.

"We got you some cotton candy!" Milly holds out a clear plastic bag emblazoned with the face of Bonko the

Clown, filled with a spindly black substance more akin to fungus than spun sugar.

"I want some! I want some!" all three triplets chirp at once. They bounce up and down, going for the bag like baby birds at feeding time.

"What's up, sis?" Milly finally notices that Sully's just standing there, her right arm quivering.

"I got fired." Sully stares at her sister as she says it, but she's really looking into her own bleak future.

"Shit!" Milly gets all dramatic. "What did you do?"

"What did I do..." Sully giggles, a nervous titter, earning her several wary glances. "What did I do?"

Sully lunges for Milly, hands around her sister's neck in seconds. "It was your damn kids who got me fired, while you were off fucking around with your boyfriend of the week!"

"Sully!" Milly manages to protest. Her face turns red, her lips blue.

"Your brats cost me the only shot I had at getting out of this fleapit town, and now I've got nothing. Nothing!"

"Sully!" Milly's voice cuts through, and Sully's back, standing before her sister. She looks at her hands; they shake, and not from nerves this time. It felt so real this time...

YOU'RE A MONSTER, SULLY, the voice chuckles.

"Sully? What happened?" Milly gives her a look that says *I can't be bothered with your weirdo wiggin' out.*

"Nothing." The words escape Sully's dry lisp like a raspy breath. "Nothing," she says louder and then snatches the bag of cotton candy from her sister. Hugging it to her chest, Sully runs off to find somewhere private to cry and eat through her depression.

"Shit," Milly curses. "Baby, look after the kids for a minute? I gotta stop her before she does somethin' stupid." Milly runs off, tossing the second bag of cotton candy to Nevill. Her flip-flops slap as she chases down her sister.

Nevill looks to the kids, and since he doesn't know what to do with the three of them, he just shrugs and tosses them the bag.

Just as the cotton candy hits the triplets' waiting arms, cut to: Rocky's butt pounding the dirt outside the front gates. Mack makes sure to put a little oomph into the hurl, so Rocky really feels the crack.

"Fuck you!" Rocky spits. "You coulda broke somethin'!"

"There's still time, shit-bird." Mack rolls his arms.

"Funny," Rocky sneers and sniffs his jacket dramatically. "I don't think it's me that stinks of shit..."

Mack's about to shut Rocky up with a kick when a scream from behind interrupts him, making Mack turn to watch as two of his colleagues drag Leigh through the front gates.

"Mack, come on, man, cut me a break!" Leigh begs.

"I wish, Leigh, but you just had to get into a fight right in front of my boss. She sees your ass back in the park today, and it's mine that'll be out in the dirt, not shit-for-brains here."

"Would it help if I said I'm sorry?" Leigh flutters her eyes. It's more insulting than cute but gets a smile out of Mack anyway.

"Are you?"

"No, but I'll fake it," she winks.

"Sorry, kid." He pats her shoulder as the other two guards let go. "Come back another time." Mack then turns to Rocky. "You, you're banned for life," then to the staff at the ticket booth, "Make a note of that."

"The hell!" Rocky slaps some dirt. "She started it!"

The guards make their way back inside, and Mack warns Leigh to "behave" on his way.

Rocky climbs to his feet and dusts himself off. "How the hell do you know that man-ape? He your new boyfriend or something?"

"Nah." Leigh flips him off. "He's too busy banging yo momma."

"Watch what you say about my mom," Rocky warns her.

"Why? Are you making out with her too?" Leigh taunts, and the pair of them prepare for round two.

The bathroom door clangs open, rebounding off the wall with tremendous force as Sully barges through. There are a few people in there, but one look at the bedraggled girl, covered in tears and greasepaint, and they filter out quietly.

She plonks herself down in the corner, next to a freestanding bin with a clown hugging the swing-lid, and sobs with her head against the wall. She hates how this day has gone, how she's failed once again. How she's never leaving this town, how her stupid sister thought some cotton candy would fix things, and worst of all, she hates how she's tearing open the bag, desperate to get at the junk within.

THAT'S 'CAUSE YOU'RE JUST A FATTY-FAT GOOBER-GOBBLER.

"I'm just a fat goober," Sully agrees.

EAT IT, FATTY! EAT IT!

127

Sully plunges her hand into the bag and tears out a chuck—pretty much half the bag. She feels it begin to crystalize against her sweaty fingers, turning them sticky, and then she shoves it all in her mouth at once. It melts on her tongue instantly, her body absorbing the sugar and... something else.

YES! EAT IT! EAT IT FATTY-FAT GOOBER-GOBB—

Sully begins to giggle, silencing her inner thoughts, much to their surprise. She doesn't even know why she's laughing, or if it's even her. There's no one else in the bathroom, and yet the sound's coming from her mouth. It doesn't feel like her at all, and she keeps doing it while she takes another scoop of the black cotton candy. It sticks to her teeth, coating them like tar as her mouth pulls into a smile of its own volition.

WHAT'S SO FUNNY!?

Tittering like a schoolgirl on helium, Sully climbs to her feet using the sink and stares at herself in the mirror. Whatever she sees must be highly amusing.

I SAID, WHAT'S SO FUNNY!?

The Sully in the mirror screams.

"You!" Sully cracks up, pointing at her own reflection. Her hands find their way to her face, to the top of her forehead. Even as her nails sink deep into her flesh, Sully continues to chuckle. She only laughs harder, more high-pitched, as she begins to peel away her flesh, rolling the skin down her forehead like a banana.

The one in the mirror watches with disgust and horror as Sully holds a flap of skin, looks at it for a second, then puts it in her mouth. Saliva gurgling and lips smacking as

128

she open-mouth chews, letting the girl in the mirror watch as Sully devours her old self. As something new, something true, begins to come alive within.

"Tasty," Sully says, and though the voice comes from her lips, it doesn't sound like the timid, broken girl from moments ago; no, this Sully's nothing but happy, deliriously so. "Tasty-tasty!" She bounces and giddily peels more skin from her face.

Beneath, instead of meat and muscles, there's a perfect rendition of the clown face she tried to paint earlier. The inverted tear drops coming down from her eyes are the blue of a summer sky, and the smears of red across her nose and mouth are the thick red of dried blood—the white sections spotted with artful speckles of crimson—and strands of purple, yellow, and orange snake through her hair.

"Hi," Sully the Clown titters, as Sully the put-down and the downtrodden girl dies. The one in the mirror backs away as the clown reaches through the glass, shattering it and taking her own reflection by the neck. Sully drags her inner self through, slams her to the ground, and chokes the life out of her.

On a dirty bathroom floor covered in shards of broken mirrors and blood, Sully the Clown kills both versions of her past self with the biggest smile on her face. She couldn't be happier, she thinks, till she hears Milly's voice call out from outside the bathroom.

"Sully!?"

Cut to: Ruth polishes the Zephyr with her sleeve.
"There, there, hope those nasty kids didn't upset you," she smiles adoringly, admiring the macabre lovechild of P.T. Barnum and H.H. Holmes.

A glint of light in the drum catches her eye, and Ruth feels her finger drawn to it. She reaches in, inches from the wicked, curved blades when the Zephyr rattles. Ruth jumps back, eyes flicking to the switch, and though it says off, she wonders. It was built by a serial killing cannibal, after all.

"What other tricks can you do?"

She watches as it moves again, somehow rocking around on its four fixed legs. Her beady black eyes gleam as a broad smile cracks her face.

"Can you hear me?"

The Zephyr whirs to life, all by itself, but there's something else. Another sound, hidden beneath the buzz and whirling. Ruth leans in, puts her ear to the drum, and listens. A moment passes, then an awestruck breathy gasp escapes her lips. Chest heaving, goosebumps rising, Ruth asks the Zephyr one more question.

"Daddy?"

Chapter Eleven
TASTY TASTY SWEET BANANAS

Mari hears the flaps of her tent ruffle and the chimes above tinkle.

"Just moment," she calls from the back in her faux European accent.

"It's just me, Mari," Reese says and drags his club foot across the tent, taking a seat with his bad leg stretched out.

"Heya Reesey," Mari clucks, dropping the Marianna accent, and joins him at the table. "How's you doin'?"

"Eh," Reese shrugs, "boss is makin' me work for it."

"Don't they all." Mari looks at Reese's foot and shakes her head. "You all good, though? Right? That," she nods to the foot.

"Yeah, yeah," Reese waves away her concern, "it is what it is."

"How you been livin'? Ain't see you since the old days."

"Eh, so-so," Resse shrugs. "Quit the carnival game for a while."

"You did? Thought ya said somethin' about another show out west? Montague? Somethin' like that? They not want a Monkey Boy?"

"Nah." Reese lays a hand flat on the table. "Didn't have the teeth for it no more. 'Sides, didn't want to be a

131

sideshow freak no more. Even if folks still gawp like I am one. Say, you hungry?"

"I could eat," Mari shrugs. "Sure."

Reese lifts a bag of jet black cotton candy.

"Ew, what the heck is that?" Mari recoils, screwing her face up. "Looks like somethin' yous scooped out from under the Wild Cat."

"This, right here, is cotton candy from the machine what did in Bonko."

"Shut up!" Mari snatches the bag and looks at it closely. She flips it over to get a better look at the contents without having to stare at the cartoon of Bonko's face. "Why's it black?"

"Dunno," Reese shrugs. "Just came out that way. Ruth's charging ten bucks a bag."

Mari snorts. "Yeah, I bet she is."

"Anyway, I snagged some for us old-timers. Figured the folks who used to have to work for the half pint would like a taste of the stuff."

"It's a step up from pissin' on his grave, that's for damn sure." Mari puts the bag on the table. "Gimme a second; I don't wanna ruin these." She reaches into her mouth, tugs, and then pulls out a set of false teeth. Reese looks at her face, still so beautiful even after everything she's been through, and the pain he feels on her behalf shows. "'S'OK," she says and looks to Reese's foot. "We all gots scars."

"Yeah," Reese agrees, "I suppose we do." He opens the bag and offers it to Mari. She takes a small piece and holds it by her lips demurely as Reese tears off his own. "To Bonko," he says and raises a toast.

"To Bonko!" Then Reese and Mari both add, "May he rot in hell!" before they partake of the black cotton candy.

As Mari and Reese lift the black cotton candy to their lips, cut in: a split screen as Ruth, shark eyes gleaming with wicked delight, lifts a fresh scoop of the stuff on a stick from the Zephyr's drum. Add in three more splits as the triplets tear into their bag of cotton candy and shove tiny fistfuls of it into their eager, piranha mouths. The chef and cooks at Burnt Ends nibble pieces as they flame grill some meat. A couple more—showing us a dozen or so different guests buying the black cotton candy, pulling open the bags, and reaching in. One more split slides in from below, a fullscreen bar of Stacey slipping her stolen cotton candy from her pocket and as her eyes light up, the black fluff seems to reach for her mouth—

Cliff slaps the black cotton candy from his sister's hand, and their frame fills the screen. "Don't eat that!"

"Ouch!" Stacey yelps and grabs her slapped hand. The cotton candy flies free, taken by a light breeze, and it's snapped out of the air by a small bird. "I'll tell Mom you hit me!"

"And I'll tell Mom you nearly put yourself in the hospital! You any idea how much sugar there is in that shit?"

Stacey sticks her tongue out and screws up her face in protest. She then licks the remnants of sugary crystals stuck to her fingers.

"Hey," Clark says as he walks out from The House of Bonko and rubs the back of his head.

"Hey, dude," Cliff says back.

"You didn't happen to see where Leigh went, did you?"

"Sorry, dude," Cliff shrugs. Unlike Stacey, who Leigh always seemed to like more than her boyfriend, Cliff's always found it hard to make a conversation with his now ex-girlfriend's stepbrother.

"Guess I'll just look for the biggest commotion in the whole carnival." Clark fixes his glasses.

"For sure," Cliff smiles. "Leigh does not do subtle."

"I'm sorry about you guys, you know?"

"Aw, dude, it's cool—Stacey go to hell!" Cliff cuts his sister off before she can wiggle her pinky again. "Wasn't like we were..." Cliff trails off when he realizes his smartmouth little sister is suspiciously quiet. "Stacey?"

The little girl holds her stomach, her chest races as she struggles to breathe, and when she finds the strength to look at her brother, there's no trace of the honeysuckle-hellion left. Stacey looks pale and desperate as she says, meekly, "I don't feel so good."

"Sully?" Milly cracks open the door to the bathroom and listens. "Sully girl, you in there?" She doesn't get an answer, but Milly recognizes something in the strange, high-toned tittering bouncing off the tiled walls within. It sure sounds like her sister, but also not. "You OK?" Milly slips in through the door and steps around the line of cubicles. "Ohmygod! Sully!?"

The girl sits on the floor, her back to Milly. Her hair is different; it shines with streaks of yellow, purple, and orange with a rough handmade bow sitting on her head—white cloth damp with something sticky and red—but it's Sully. Milly knows.

Shards of broken mirrors lie all around the girl as though moved to form a fractured web of reflections. Milly spots blues, red, and a dozen refractions of something like a smile, only it feels wrong—off,

134

somehow, like it's laughing at a joke yet to be told. Then she spots where it all came from, above a sink that sparkles with glass and blood—a space on the wall where the mirror once hung, now a ragged void covered in red smears and sticky handprints.

"Sully! Are you OK?" Milly panics. She wants to rush and check on her sister—it wouldn't be the first time she's found the girl bleeding on a bathroom floor, after all—but Sully doesn't seem upset. Not at all; the giggles coming from the girl feel real. It's like she's high or something.

"*Peel bananas,*" Sully begins to sing, "*peel, peel bananas!*" She giggles, and her whole body shudders with giddy euphoria. Milly steps around the carnage, careful not to step on any large shards in her cheap plastic flip-flops. "*Peel bananas,*" Sully continues to sing with the enthusiasm of a child; she's doing something with her hands. "*Peel, peel, bananas!*"

As her eyes land on Sully's hands, Milly's own race to her mouth in an attempt to block the surge of hot vomit racing up her throat. She's not fast enough, and chunks of watery bile slip between her fingers, pushing out the gaps as a second wave gushes through. Milly turns to the sink and lets it all out, heaving till there's nothing left inside.

"Sully," Milly ralphs again, "what've you done!?"

"*Peel bananas,*" Sully sings as she pulls back the limp, flaccid flesh of her index finger. "*Peel, peel, bananas.*" The rest of her right hand hangs in tatters to the wrist—she's one finger away from fully degloving herself. Sully's bare fingers are pale white with only trickles of spotty blood where tendons, veins, and wet muscle should be. "*Peel bananas—*"

"The fuck have you done, Sully!?"

The singing stops. Sully's head slowly turns and she cranes her neck up. Hungry, red eyes sparkle as they land on Milly. Her shoulders quiver as Sully brings a pale, white finger to her mouth, licking the blood off with a grin. "I'm peeling the bananas," she says with a coy, sweet smile. A laugh follows, and Sully flashes bloody teeth sticky with black cotton candy.

"You're bleeding! Fuck! Shit! I'll go get help. Just stop!" Milly turns to run and makes it a step.

"Nu-huh!" Sully singsongs and slices the back of Milly's ankle with a large piece of broken mirror, cutting a deep gouge that releases an ooze of thick blood. Milly's heel goes slick with red, and before the pain even registers, the wetness and the poor traction of the Dollar Store flip-flops send her to the floor, face first, jaw cracking on the tile.

Milly tries to push herself up, and though she gets her torso off the ground, her wounded leg won't respond; it's only when she looks down at it and sees the spreading puddle of blood on the tile that it really hits her how badly she's hurt. "What the fuck, Sully!?"

The clown skips across the floor, quickly stopping beside Milly. She leans down, both hands behind her back, delighted like it's her birthday, like her sister on the ground is her cake. Her tasty-tasty cake...

"Help me!" Milly demands, raising an outstretched hand.

Sully squeezes her shoulders up and giggles.

"*Chop bananas*"—a shard of bloodied mirror glass slices through the air—"*chop, chop, bananas*"—then another two times. Milly yanks her hand back, three fresh cuts forming a crude S across her palm, beads of blood spilling like runny jam. Her hand trembles as Milly looks at the damage.

136

"Sully," she whimpers.

"*Chop bananas.*" Sully swishes the glass across Milly's back. "*Chop, chop bananas!*"

Milly's body arcs in shock as she cries out, her sobbing accompanied by Sully's singsong humming. She doesn't cry for help. Milly knows it's pointless; this isn't her sister anymore. It can't be. She sobs as Sully steps around to her head, then looks up, eyes following the bottom of Sully's mismatched thrift store red and blue Docs up to her big red smile and gleeful eyes.

"*Smash bananas,*" Sully sings as she brings a boot down on Milly's head—her skull and jaw crack against the tile, but it doesn't kill her. "*Smash, smash bananas!*" Two more stomps, one of Milly's eyes popping out of the socket, still attached, still moving, and even that doesn't finish the girl off.

No, Milly's still alive, barely hanging in there, as Sully plops to the ground, right into a cross-legged position with the shard still in hand. Milly gurgles something indecipherable through her crushed jaw and shattered teeth. She keeps up the garbled pleas as Sully takes the detached eye, picking it up between two fingers and severs the optic nerves like cutting a piece of fruit free from a branch. Though you can't tell from Milly's warbled wailing, the lifting hurts more than the cutting.

"*Eat bananas,*" Sully sings as she plops the eyeball in her mouth—her face immediately takes on the look of a kid forced to eat vegetables, and Sully spits it back out, whole, into her hand. "Yucky!" Sully declares though she pockets it for later all the same.

Milly's body shuts down; random spasms fire, making her twitch as though electricity runs through her. Sully sits on the floor, cross-legged, and strokes Milly's exposed skin with the ragged edge of the mirror. She sings. "*Eat bananas... eat, eat, bananas!*"

"What's wrong with her?"

Cut to: Clark panics as Cliff races to catch his little sister before she faints. Stacey's eyes flicker like she's falling asleep.

"Stacey, no." Cliff supports her weight with one arm as he rummages in her pockets. "Fuck! Where is it!?"

"Here." Clark draws attention to a bench as he sweeps leftover junk food off it. Cliff lifts his little sister and carries her over, putting her down gently.

"My tummy," Stacey moans, and her hands grasp at her midsection.

"Fuck!" Cliff smashes his hands to his forehead, panic taking over. "Fuck, fuck, fuck!"

"Cliff, what's happening?" Clark asks, but Cliff's too jammed up with worry to even hear him. "Cliff!" Clark grabs the other boy by the shoulder and gets his attention. "Talk to me!"

"My sister"—tears well up in Cliff's eyes—"she's diabetic. Stupid brat must've eaten too much sugar. Stacey, if you die, I'm gonna give all your Barbies to that kid who starts fires!" Cliff kneels beside his sister. "You hear me? You still there!?"

Stacey meekly raises her hand and wiggles her pinky.

"OK," Cliff wipes his eyes, "stay with us. I'll get some water and... Stacey!" Her eyes flicker and close. "Stacey!?"

"Does she have one of those things? Like a shot!?"

"Yeah," Cliff says, "she's supposed to keep in on her, but it's not there. She must've lost it."

"Any idea where?"

"No, she's been on her own since—shit! The car!" A sudden realization sparks hope. "The little brat snuck here in the trunk of my car. Maybe it fell out there!?"

"You sure?"

"No, but maybe—"

"You go get it; I'll take her to first aid. Maybe they have what she needs?"

"Good. Yeah. That's a plan!" Cliff hugs Clark out of nowhere, and the other boy doesn't know what to do besides awkwardly accept it. "She's type 1, dude, going hyper. That's important."

"Type 1," Clark repeats, "hyper. Got it." And stoops to take Stacey in his arms. The kid feels as light as cotton candy in Clark's arms. Her eyes, closed tight, flicker behind her lids, and her lips are turning black. A faint smell, like apples and licorice, comes with each of her sharp, short breaths.

Cliff takes her hand, wet with cold sweat, and makes a promise. "You're gonna be OK, Stacey, I swear."

"I've got her," Clark reassures him. Both boys give one another a look, then a nod, before breaking for it. Clark jogs gently across the throughway, heading towards the hospitality area near the entrance, carefully keeping pace while doing all he can to keep Stacey safe and comfortable.

Cliff watches them go and then races off towards the back of the park, moving faster than he ever did on the track team. Faster, even, than Rocky.

Cut to: the Zephyr waits at The House of Bonko. Add in a split screen of Milly's blood flowing across the floor of the bathroom where she lays dying. As her life flows into the ground of Bonkin's Bonanza, the antique cotton

139

candy machine whirs to life once more, taking over the shot.

Something rattles around inside the machine as the blades spin; something within the dark, cherry wood giggles as clouds of cotton candy whir into existence.

There's a trail of blood on the ground. It starts off in drips and spatters and thickens to globs and smudges as it approaches the house. Red streaks and handprints on colorful walls accompany the trail as it leads inside, up and around the spiral staircase, along an off-kilter hallway to an office.

Inside, Ruth Hardstack stands with her back to the room, palms braced against a wall-spanning picture window looking down into the Big Top Circle. Her body rocks with a throaty chuckle and on the desk, like a damp, saggy meat towel, there's her face. It still grins like a hungry shark that's just caught the scent of blood.

Chapter Twelve
BALLYHOO BLITZ

Giggling. Mari can hear him giggling.

Bonko—every time she looks in the mirror and sees nothing but exposed gums, she hears the little bastard's cackle in her head. Even as she sat on the ground, blood pouring through her fingers, all she could hear was his laugh.

Fade in: she sits before a light bulb-run mirror in the back of her tent, cross-legged and despondent. Her tongue runs across her gums, picking out the final traces of that black cotton candy before she puts her false teeth back in. The taste, unusually rich even for something designed purely to rot teeth, lingers even after the rush of victory passes. Sure, it felt great to toast the death of Bonko with Reese, two of the old guards giving the dead king the finger, but the moment's passed, and here she is. Try as she might, Mari can't get past what Bonko took from her. Not her dignity, no: the one person who truly loved her, whose entire existence was centered on making her happy.

Chet's been gone for years, and she still can't bring herself to share her bed with another man. Not out of any sense of loyalty or devotion, but because every time she feels a hand on her thigh, it's Bonko's. Every pair of eyes that wanders down her chest are his sleazy little peepers. It's why she covers herself up in flowing, shapeless robes all these years later, still hiding from him, from herself.

The thought makes her laugh in her head. Then out loud. Before she knows it, Mari slaps the table and rubs teary eyes as the hilarity takes over.

Cut away: to another place, another time, where a younger Mari in a loose dress hanging provocatively off her shoulder laughs wildly with a near-empty glass of gin in her hand.

The bar is packed full of roust-a-bouts and performers—a dive somewhere off the beaten track in some one-horse town in the middle of God knows where. Two townies, locals in dirty coveralls, flank her, competing to see who's going back to her tent that night—neither of them caring one whit about the ring on her finger. One of them a brawny, older man with greying slicked-back hair, and the other a young man, wet behind the ears, thin with an air of foolish hopefulness around him. Both the types of men she likes for entirely different purposes.

"Listen, doll," the older one leans in and whispers loudly, "you don't want nothin' to do with that bum. You don't know where he's been. String o' broken hearts as long as your arm!"

"Oh." Mari raises an eyebrow as she downs the last of her gin. She doesn't need to ask; her suitors fill it up again right away. "Is that true?" She turns to the younger one. "You got girls lining up, big boy?"

"Well, uh—"

"That's good." Mari hooks a finger over his collar. "You must know howta please 'em!" Her smile and the

142

boldness accompanying it puts the younger man on the back foot.

"Sure, daft wee things with no sense," the older one comes back into play. "Something tells me you're a woman who appreciates a man with experience?" He puts a hand on Mari's leg and winks.

Mari lets him squeeze; the strength of his grip sends a shudder through her, and she follows his arm up to his thick body, to his eager eyes, and she snorts with laughter. "What makes you boys think I'm going home with either one of you!?" She claps and finds the whole thing so funny she almost falls off her bar stool. Both men seethe for a moment, calculating just how many days' pay they've wasted on gin for this woman, when she places one hand on each of their inner thighs. She runs her fingers up and takes a few squeezes of her own. "I mean, I have a very big bed after all..."

"That so?" The voice comes from behind. All three crane their necks up to behold the mountain of a man that fills the bar behind them. Chet Redwood smirks, "How big?"

Both suitors shoot a look to one another, to the days' worth of empty bottles on the counter, and do the math—both conclude it's not worth competing against Chet, and that's not even factoring in the way Mari looks at the giant man like he's for dinner. They quietly slip away as Mari crosses her legs over, leans back on the counter, and bites her lip. "Big enough." She raises her eyebrows and laughs.

Chet smiles bashfully, like a schoolboy at his first dance, then turns to the men scarpering away. "Where ya goin', boys?" The two of them pretend Chet's not talking to them, like they never laid eyes on Mari before. "You're missing out." He looks back to his wife, to the wickedly playful smirk she wears. "Trust me."

"I'm a bad wife, aren't I?" she teases.

"So bad!" Chet sweeps her up, much to her amusement. Mari laughs, too loud, and she doesn't care. "You're so beautiful when you laugh," he says as he tosses her through the air, launching and catching Mari as she giggles, delighted.

Then she lands all alone. In a seat in a dark room, the hand bearing her wedding band trembling. She watches as correctional officers strap her husband down and wishes she could at least be in the room with him.

"Promise me you'll find someone who makes you laugh," Chet says through the one-way mirror as the executioner asks him for his last words. "You're so beautiful when you laugh..."

"Am I still so fucking beautiful when I laugh?" Mari slams her palms down on the vanity. "Well!?" She grabs her crystal ball and hurls it across the tent, smashing it to pieces against one of the heavy supports. "Well!?" Still not satisfied, she tears at her gown, ripping a strip free, exposing half her chest.

Mari catches sight of herself in the mirror and stops for a moment. She likes what she sees, the way the torn garment sits across her body—it makes her want to explore it with her hands, and as she does, Mari pulls the rest free and ruffles her hair. Laughing with the beauty in the mirror, Mari begins to tease herself, threatening to expose her breasts with a burlesque gasp and naughty shoulder twist. She winks at herself and lets it all fall free, raising her arms to accentuate her nudity.

"Where have you been, Mrs. Marianna?" she purrs at herself. She puts her hands on her hips, raising one into an S pose that lets the rest of her clothes slip to the floor like a rehearsed routine. She turns, switching her dominant hip, to get a look at her behind in the mirror. "Nice butt," she laughs gracefully. She looks good, so good, and Mari can't help but laugh. It seems so silly to keep herself hidden like she's been doing. It feels good to be naked. So good she can't help but peel back more layers, starting with the skin above her collarbone. It comes away like peeling off lace gloves, unveiling alabaster skin, flawless and as smooth as poured paint. With the shreds of flesh goes the shame, the doubts, the trauma—Mari lets free what's been beneath, what's always been there, what she's kept repressed for so long, and it feels like coming home.

"I don't think this is a good idea." Candy lets Kat pull her hand and though she protests, she feels her spirits rise just a little.

"No, listen, you've been here all day and not had one bit of fun!" Kat beams. "This will be cool!" She leads Candy towards the 'Round The World ride. Just ahead of them, the family of three board the ride. "Come on!"

Kat's like this bouncing ball of positivity—she just realized that the boy she's loved forever doesn't want her back and instead of hating the subject of his affection, Kat's trying to cheer her up. It makes it hard for Candy to hate, hold what she did against her and, really, that's just Candy. As mad as she is at Leigh, she misses her already.

"Maybe I should go look for Leigh and Clark," Candy stalls.

"Bet you can spot them from up there!" Kat points up, full of energy, with her free hand.

145

Candy has to admit she has a point, and it beats wandering the park aimlessly, listening for Leigh's distinct brand of verbal battery.

"Oh! After, we can go on the Wild Cat!" Candy hides a laugh with her other hand, but Kat notices. "What's funny?"

"I'm too little to go on the Wild Cat." Candy makes herself even smaller, pursing her lips as she flashes doe eyes.

Kat doesn't laugh or so much as snicker; instead, she takes her rabbit ears off and pops them on Candy's head. "There, bet that does the trick."

"I don't think that's very safe," Candy squints.

Kat covers her mouth with the side of her hand and whispers, "Nothing here is."

That sets them off again, and Kat pulls Candy across the midway; Reese stumbles towards them, not looking where he's going. He barges between them, forcing the two girls to drop hands. "Hey!" Kat yells. "Watch where—"

Reese shoots them a look, like a small animal trying to scare a predator. He looks ill, his skin pale, bruised and flaking. Snarling, he pushes on, dragging his club foot.

"That was weird," Candy stares.

"Uh-huh." Kat rubs her arm where Reese just bumped her. "He looked kinda sick."

"Hope it's not catching." Candy looks to Kat, and the two head over to the ride, with considerably less enthusiasm.

"Hello?" Not-Stu leans in through the flaps of the fortune teller's tent; there's no one there. "You open?"

"In a minute, darling," Mari coos from the back, her breathy voice giving every syllable a spritz of perfume, a dose of wicked implication. "Sit, please."

"OK," Not-Stu smirks and nods his head. "Sounds like things are finally going my way," he mutters.

"What was that, darling?" Mari calls.

"Oh, uh, nothing! Just looking forward to hearing my fortune." Not-Stu shifts awkwardly and then takes his seat.

"I can tell you right now, darling, that it's going to be delightful."

Not-Stu bounces on his seat. "Oh, shit!" he mouths. He's heard about these kinds of places at carnivals. Fortune tellers and such sometimes being fronts for hookers. "Hot damn." He can't believe he's stumbled right into one. He's old enough to remember when all the stories about this place came out. Old Buster B. Bonkin running girls out of the trailers in back, and all the other stuff. They did say something about being "authentic," after all.

Well, goddamn, this is just the kind of realism Not-Stu can get behind. And hopefully in front of, too.

He switches between different sitting positions, trying to work out what looks best—leaning on the table with one arm, chin on his fist, making his forearm and bicep pop. That's too obvious and try hard, Not-Stu reckons, so he leans back, one arm over the back of the chair with his legs as wide as possible; thinking this is a more inviting pose, he sticks with that.

She sure seems to be taking her sweet time back there, Not-Stu thinks as he begins to lose feeling in his dangling arm. "Come on," he mutters under his breath. Or so he thinks.

"Patience, darling," Mari's voice lilts suggestively.

147

Not-Stu doesn't have much of that, so he figures he'll go for it. "You, uh, need a hand back there? Or two?"

Deep ringing laughter fills the tent. "I'm just getting dressed," Mari teases. "One minute."

Not-Stu nearly chokes; he can't believe his luck. If this is how his day's gonna end, then it makes up for getting booted to the back of the line because of that trashmouth, tall bitch.

The curtains part. Mari steps into the threshold, holding back the sheets with two outstretched arms. "Well, hello there."

Not-Stu gulps. "Fuck me..."

Mari clucks. "Naughty boy." But she stands there and lets Not-Stu admire her anyway. He doesn't know where to look. At the torn pantyhose fashioned into makeshift thigh highs? The shred of torn skirt that hangs down between her thighs, leaving her hips completely exposed—hips so pale and yet somehow vivid all at once? No, it's the dangling strips of silk used not so much to obscure her impressive cleavage as they are to accentuate it, the only mark on her perfect skin a tiny black love heart on her left breast.

"What're you lookin' at?" She slithers into the room, making every part of her body jiggle in a way that shuts Not-Stu down completely. She crosses to him and leans over, placing one hand on each of his knees. His heart's in his mouth as he stares down her cleavage; her perfume smells like candy and blood, and he wants to lick it off her skin. Her long black curls spill down across half her face, a face almost all white save for lips painted so red they're practically black and black streaks that run down from her eye like painted-on mascara tears that stop just short of faint pink blushes.

148

"The best damn pair of tits I ever saw, that's what!" Not-Stu declares. He's too mesmerized by them to notice the look Mari gives him, to notice the cold, dead light that shines in her almost white eye, the subtle twitch of the drawn black outline of her crimson lips. He reaches out, both hands eager to grab a handful, and Mari bats them away with a giggle.

"Not so fast"—she looks at his crotch—"big boy."

"Oh, you like that?" Not-Stu gestures to the tent in his pants.

"Mm-hmm," Mari nods enthusiastically. "Show me."

Not-Stu does not need to be told even once—his hands are on his buckle in a second, and he pulls at it so hard it takes him longer than it should. He curses, fumbles, but eventually, Not-Stu gets there, whipping it out and gesturing like it's something Mari should be impressed with. "Whatcha think?"

Mari bites her lip with a strangely dark tooth, it's a little weird, but Not-Stu's far too horned up to give two fucks about that, or the fresh blood the bite leaves behind on Mari's lip. She lowers herself, her one uncovered eye never leaving Not-Stu's as she purses her lips, opens her mouth, and unveils a ragged line of shiny blue-black teeth that sparkle like a beach under a full moon. Only they're not teeth; they're the fractured shards of a broken crystal ball forced so deep into Mari's gums they don't so much as wobble as she stretches her mouth wide. Blood wells around them, running down her chin.

"Wait—" Not-Stu finally protests, but it's too late. Mari takes his dick in her mouth and chomps down. "Fuck!" Shards of broken crystal ball gouge deeper into her gums as they cut through Not-Stu's shaft, not enough to sever it—but they sure leave it in tatters, and it's easy

149

enough for Mari to rip it free. "Oh-shit-oh-shit-oh-shit-oh-shit—" Not-Stu breathes like he's giving birth as all the blood that rushed to his dick, all the semen he was about to shoot into Mari's mouth, squirts and spurts all over the giggling clown. She cavorts in the spray, rubbing it over her face in ecstasy.

"See! This is fun," Kat says as the caged carriage begins the climb. Candy doesn't like the way it rocks with even the slightest breeze or the way the bolts securing them to the wheel creak. Worse, they keep stopping the ride, letting people on and off; each time, the sudden jerk and roll of the carriage makes her want to throw up.

"I don't think I like it up here." Candy grips the side of the carriage with one hand, Kat with the other. "I think I'm gonna ralph."

"Oh, but we're not even halfway to the top..."

"I—" The ride jumps to a start again, and their carriage resumes its painfully slow, creaking climb to a height Candy knows she was never meant to reach. "What, five feet?" Leigh completes the joke in Candy's head, and she realizes she wants nothing more than to find her friend and make things up. Well, almost anything; she'll settle for getting off this death trap for now.

"Hey, what's that?" Kat leans across to the other side of the carriage. She looks down towards the back of the park as they rise.

"I don't wanna know," Candy insists.

"I think somebody's hurt..." Kat watches as a man runs out of Marianna the Magnificent's tent. Some people approach him, then back away, dropping stuffed toys and snacks. He sinks to his knees, then down to the ground as a dark puddle spreads from his midsection.

150

Screams follow, audible even this high up and over the groan of metal on metal.

"What's happening?" Candy asks; against her better judgment, she wants to know but can't bring herself to cross the carriage and look.

"Some man's fainted," Kat explains, "and people are running towards him. Oh, there's Mari—" Kat's thrown back, across the carriage and into Candy as the ride comes to a sudden stop.

Candy begins to hyperventilate as she verges on a full-blown panic attack.

"It's OK." Kat takes Candy's free hand and squeezes it tightly as she takes a seat beside the girl. "It's gonna be OK. It's just stopped to let people off, that's all."

"Yeah," Candy manages to say, "so why's it not moving again?"

Kat doesn't have an answer. One doesn't come, either as their carriage rocks back and forth, almost at the apex of the wheel, far longer than it should.

Chapter Thirteen

YOU SCREAM, I SCREAM WE ALL SCREAM FOR...

Cut to: Reese shoving park guests aside as he barges his way along the midway, elbowing one kid so sharply he lets go of his balloon.

"Hey!" the kid's father protests and Reese only grunts in response—not stopping, he drags his foot behind him as the balloon floats up to the sky, followed by the kid's piercing wail.

Reese mutters and slaps himself—hard. Those around him, in his way, edge back carefully as Reese beats himself again, this time with his fist. He does it once more, this time a full-on punch, but instead of recoiling or crying out, Reese laughs. He hits himself again. And again. Each pound, each bash feels better than the last, gets closer to the true Reese within, making that Reese bray to be set free.

Parents pull children close, sweethearts squeeze hands tighter, and everyone gets out of the strange hunched man's way as he gives himself a right hook, then a left. Each blow brings near orgasmic joy to him; the greater the damage, the greater the pleasure. Soon his face is a pulpy mess, his mutton chops clumped, and Reese just smiles through bloody teeth—teeth still sticky with traces of jet black cotton candy.

"It hurts!" he chuckles. "It hurts so bad!"

A young woman, who wishes she'd gotten more out of the way, cringes as Reese comes within spitting distance; she flinches and tenses as Reese sets upon her, getting right in her face.

"D-don't hurt me," she pleads, "p-please?"

"Hurt you?" Reese's head twists like a confused animal. "Why would I hurt you?" He smiles at her, rank air washing over bloody and black gums. "You"—Reese points to her with a trembling hand, then taps his chest with it—"hurt me?"

"No! No, I wouldn't!?" the girl insists.

"No!" Reese slaps his face with both hands—the girl yelps.

"I wouldn't, mister, I swear—"

"No! Hurt me." Reese leans in till his nose touches hers, their eyes locked in an unblinking embrace. Hers shiver with anxiety, his with sadistic delight. "Hurt me, please!"

The scared girl raises one hand, her whole arm shaking, and holds it palm first, in a half-hearted slap-ready position. Reese snaps back, excited.

"Do it!" he grins. "Do-it-do-it-do-it!" She slaps, feebly, fingers barely brushing Reese's sweaty, flaky skin. "No!" Reese grabs her wrist, making the girl flinch. "Hurt me!" He forces the girl to slap him, this time with more force. "Again!"

"Hey! The fuck you doin' with my girl!?" a well-built young man yells from along the midway, marching towards the scene at a clipped place.

"She won't hurt me!" Reese moans, profoundly disappointed.

"You want hurt!?"

"Yes!" Reese cheers, shoulders hunched over as he chuckles. "Hurt me!"

"Oh, you got it, buddy." The young man picks up the pace, pulls his arm back, and decks Reese with a half-running punch. Reese goes flat on his back, cackling on the floor.

"Oh, yeah!" His head snaps up, grinning. "Do it again!"

The young man shrugs and grabs a fistful of the vest Reese wears below his Bonkin's Bonanza waistcoat. The young man lifts Reese, punches him again, cracking bone, and sends Reese's head bouncing off the cobblestones.

For a moment, the roust-a-bout is quiet, and the young man worries he's gone too far. Then a slow cackle creaks from Reese's turned head - "Ha-ha-ha-ha"—and he slowly turns with a face-wide smirk, eyes alive with sadistic excitement.

"Again!?" Reese insists, and the young man obliges.

"OK, shit," Cliff pumps himself up, "here we go again."

The same guard from this morning, the chunky metalhead, sits in the booth, and if Cliff didn't know for a fact he got up to chase Rocky earlier, he would swear the guy hasn't moved since this morning.

"It's cool; he never saw you. You got this." Cliff fixes his jacket, wipes the sweat from his forehead, and then strolls up to the gate as casually as he can. In the back of his head, he's screaming, move your damn ass, Stacey needs you, but Cliff keeps it together. He's good at that, after all; acting like nothing bothers him, putting others first even when he's hurting.

"Hey, dude," Cliff waves, "do me a solid and get the gate? Left my"—Cliff mimes using a lighter—"in my car."

154

"Oh, man, no worries," the metalhead says, and Cliff can't believe his luck. He shouldn't; the guard takes a Zippo out of his pocket and tosses it to Cliff. Grabbing it out of the air, Cliff thinks fast.

"Oh, you know what"—Cliff pats his pockets like he can't find something—"left my smokes out there too, my dude. I'll just—"

"No can do, buddy," the guard gets up, hefting a sagging belt. "Boss lady was just on the horn. Gates gotta stay closed."

"Say what?"

"Yeah, somethin' about somethin', I dunno. Wasn't listenin'. Just do as I'm told. Hey, where's your badge?" The guard looks at Cliff like he's slowly adding things up.

"Y'know," Cliff shrugs, "must have left it back at the old um, Wiener Wagon."

"Oh, shit, you work at the WW?" the guard nods. "Right on, how's Willie doin'?"

"Oh, he's cool, my dude," Cliff nods along, matching the guard's smile.

"Yeah, 'cept his name's not Willie." The guard drops the act and rests a hand on his nightstick.

"Now that's just not right. I mean, why's it called Willie's Wiener Wagon then?" Cliff acts indignant. "Do you even work here!? Huh!?"

"Do I"—the guard taps his chest with both hands and then gets out "the fuck—" as Cliff rushes past him, feinting and then making a line for the gate. "Come back here!" The metalhead gets his arms around Cliff, lifting him off his feet.

"Come on, dude," Cliff pleads, "be cool! Look, my sister needs her shot, and we left it in the car!"

"Yeah, tell me another one, let's see what Mack makes of you—"

155

"I'm not kidding! She could die!"

"Yeah, what's wrong with her, then!?"

"Diabetes, dude!"

"You made that up."

"You've seriously never heard of diabetes!?"

"Sounds made up to me—stop wriggling, you little shit!"

"Fuck this!" Cliff gives up. "Sorry, dude," and he elbows the guard in the face.

"Son of a bitch." The metalhead drops Cliff, letting him scuttle through the dirt towards the gate. He leans into the booth and slaps the button to release the electric lock—the gate buzzes, and Cliff makes a mad dash for it. He's not thinking about how he's gonna get back in; all his mental energy's focused on getting the insulin right now. Cliff makes it halfway through the gate when the metalhead grabs hold of his jacket.

"Just let me go!" Cliff begs.

"Not after that cheap shot, ya little punk-"

Cliff groans at the end of his patience and slips out of his jacket. He falls through the gate, leaving behind one pissed-off security guard holding his denim jacket.

"Got your jacket—"

"Keep it, burnout," Cliff yells as he sprints on. In his haste to get his sister's medication, he forgets one important thing—the keys to his car, now sitting in the metalhead guard's open palm as he watches the dumb kid blitz like hell.

"Candy!" Sully stands at the entrance to Candy Alley, sparkling red eyes exploring all the dangling candies and treats with entranced wonder. Her fingers, soaked in red like she's wearing splotchy red gloves, twiddle erratically as the excitement flows through her. Sully grins and can almost taste the sugar in the air.

She skips along through the crowd, lifting her mismatched blue and red thrift store Docs high as she swings her arms wildly. Park guests and staff only give her cursory looks, most assuming she's an actor, one of the numerous entertainers milling around the park. It's only when she snatches a churro from someone do things begin to turn.

"That's mine!" the annoyed guest yells as Sully crams it in her mouth.

"Yum!" Sully declares, then snatches a half-eaten candy apple from a small child. Before the little one can cry out, Sully takes a bite, nearly finishing the whole thing, and those close enough to see her teeth get the sense something's very wrong—the sticky black moss coating what looks like fangs is deeply unsettling.

"Ooh!" Sully tosses away the candy apple with a smile and prances across to an ice cream station.

She leans down, grinning as she licks her lips, inches from a boy holding a cone stacked with strawberry, chocolate, and vanilla scoops. Sully giggles and bites her finger, licking the tip—the boy gulps. She scares him, sure, but she's also kinda pretty, he thinks, in a scary clown girl kind of way, so out of both fear and the desire to be nice to a cute girl, the boy offers Sully his ice cream cone.

"For me?" Sully appears genuinely blown away by the boy's offer, though she doesn't hesitate to snatch the cone from his hand. She smiles, and it's only then the boy notices that the red of her smile, which curves asymmetrically up both cheeks, is different from the color of her lips, from the spot of paint on her nose. Darker, with crusty, dark flakes stuck here and there.

Sully licks the ice cream, mouth open wide, and a sickly sweetness wafts over the boy.

"You like ice cream?" Sully asks, already chortling at the joke she's about to pull.

"Y-yeah," the boy answers.

"What about"—Sully reaches into her pocket and then plops Milly's severed eye onto the top of the cone, like sticking in a chocolate flake—"eye scream!"

For a second, the boy thinks it's just one of these Halloween candies that look like eyeballs, and then it dawns on him that it's too wet, too slimy, too real.

The boy screams.

Sully screams.

They all scream, for eye scream!

"Help!"

Cut to: Clark screams as he bashes the door open with his back, turning into the room with an unconscious Stacey in his arms. He doesn't like the dark circles forming under her eyes or the way her lips are turning so blue they're black.

"Somebody help us, please!"

The first aid room leaves a lot to be desired. Posters hang on the wall for basic rescue procedures, guides to the recovery position, how to treat a burn—all things you would hope a medical professional, or at least a trained first-aider, wouldn't need help with. The bed in the corner looks dirtier than the floor.

"Help—"

"Settle down," a moan comes from behind a closed partition curtain, and a second later, it's pulled open, revealing a very sleepy balding man with a minimal effort spattering of white face paint and a cheap pop-on round red nose.

158

Clark's glasses sit askew, blurring half his vision, so for a second, he thinks this is just another injured park guest till he spots the Red Cross sign on the clown's t-shirt.

"Are you a doctor or a nurse?"

"Neither," the clown yawns. "I'm, and I can't fuckin' believe I gotta say this," he mutters, "Boohoo the First Aid Clown!" He pushes himself off the bed, waves his hands, and proclaims, "Ta-da! Now, what is it? I've got a hangover like you wouldn't believe."

"My friend's sister! She's," Clark takes a second to carefully recall what Cliff said, "going hyper!"

"So?" Boohoo rubs his temples. "Give her a time out."

"No! She's diabetic—"

"Why the fuck didn't you say so, kid?" Boohoo jumps to action, helping Clark lay Stacey down on the other bed. "You got her injector?"

"Her brother's gone to get it from the car."

"Shit, you better hope he's kept it cool, or she's fucked." Boohoo places the back of his hand on Stacey's head, shaking his head at what he feels.

"Don't you have any here?"

"Look around, kid! Does this shit hole look like it keeps expensive drugs with fuck all shelf life around? We got bandages and cold compresses. That's about it."

"What can we do!?" Clark grabs his head as the panic sets in.

"I'm gonna try and keep her hydrated." Boohoo folds pillows and slides them in under Stacey's head. "For all the good that'll do. There's a phone on the desk. Call 911."

"Right." Clark dashes over, picks up the handset, and rattles the receiver. "It's dead..."

"Now that ain't right—" Boohoo turns, looks over his shoulder, and as soon as his attention is elsewhere, Stacey's eyes pop open. That firestarter grin of hers spreads wide, too wide, as she grabs Boohoo's arm and sinks her teeth in. "Fuuuuuck!"

Stacey backs up on the bed until she's sitting with her knees to her chest. She shoots sunken puppy dog eyes and flashes an innocent smile ringed with black lips.

"Wasn't me!" she shrugs like butter wouldn't melt and giggles.

"Little bitch bit me!" Boohoo holds his wounded arm up. "That ain't hyperglycemia. The fuck is she on!?"

"She's not on—"

Stacey leaps from the bed onto Boohoo's shoulders, covering his eyes with her hands. "Guess who!? Hehe!"

"Get her off me!" Boohoo reaches up, and each grab he makes for Stacey's hands is met with a slap. She lets go of his eyes and grabs ahold of the tufts of hair jutting from his temples.

"Wheee!" Stacey cheers. "Go, horsey, go!"

"Stacey! Stop that!" Clark yells as the little girl yanks Boohoo this way and that, careening him across the room. The man rages as he swats at her. Losing his footing, Boohoo stumbles face-first into a wall and roars on impact.

"Yay! Again!" Stacey cheers, hanging on like a champion bull rider.

"Fuck this." Boohoo grabs a pair of bandage shears from the nearest table and tries to stab Stacey with them.

"Don't!" Clark protests, but it's for nothing anyway; Stacey wiggles out of his reach, and as Boohoo loses his balance again, the little girl snatches the scissors from him. "Stacey! No!" Clark shouts as she drives the slightly rounded points of the blades through Boohoo's neck, his

160

leathery skin offering some resistance at first before the impetus pierces his flesh, boring through in a round glut of dark red.

Boohoo grunts and gurgles, reaching for the wound as blood spills from his mouth. Stacey yanks the scissors out, letting free a sharp jet that hisses as it patters against the wall. Boohoo drops to his knees, then the floor, and Stacey hops off him like he was just one of the many f-f-f-fun rides at Bonkin's Bonanza!

She giggles and swishes her side ponytail as she turns to Clark. "You wanna play with me?"

Clark stands, frozen on the spot. There's blood across his face, spittles covering one side of his glasses.

"Play with me, Clarky!?" Stacey spins the scissors in her hands like an old-school gangster twirling a butterfly knife.

Clark doesn't want to hurt her or take the chance of ending up like Boohoo, but she's between him and the door. He looks around, and his only options are a barred window and a single steel grey locker. Clark goes for the latter, yanking the door open and slipping inside as Stacey lunges across the room.

"Play with me!" she demands as she flits between beating on the door and tugging at the handle.

Not for the first time in his life, Clark finds himself stuffed in a locker, hoping against hope this is as bad as it gets, though this time he holds the door shut from within, using all the strength he has to keep the door shut tight.

"You're no fun!" Stacey complains as she rattles the door.

"Damnit!"

Cut to: Cliff curses as he rattles the door to his car. He knows he had his keys in his jacket pocket—always keeps them in the buttoned-up chest pocket—but he's desperate, and desperation breeds hope.

He can see the pouch through the rear window, lying in the trunk with the blanket Stacey must have hidden under. He's gotta get that, and bring it to her five minutes ago, otherwise—

"Fuck it." Cliff looks around and grabs the biggest rock he can find. Without another thought, he smashes it through the rear window of his car, then uses it to clear away enough glass to safely reach in.

Cliff lifts the pouch out gently and opens the velcro latch, checking the contents. Wrapped up inside a keep-cool bag, two preprepared shots complete with their injectors. "Yes!" Cliff allows a brief celebration and then sets off towards the front side of Bonkin's Bonanza—the back gate is now most assuredly off-limits. He only hopes they'll let him in with no money or ticket on him, though the way he's feeling right now, they won't have much choice.

Since time is not on his side, Cliff breaks for it.

Time to roll up and take a gandering pan across Bonkin's Bonanza, as carnival-goers all over scatter and scream.

Cut to: the crowd surrounding Not-Stu's twitching body backs away as Mari the Clown emerges from the flaps of her tent, resplendent in all her gruesome glamour. She walks on poised balletic tiptoes—not caring about dipping her toes in Not-Stu's blood or bothering to go around him. She leaves a bloody footprint on his back as she steps on him, pausing with

162

one leg on him, knee pointed. She arches her back, lets her head roll, and winks at the slowly retreating crowd.

"Hello, boys," Mari moans, an elegant smile besmirched with blood and gore.

One runs, which breaks the dam, sending the circling crowd off in every direction.

Cut to: feet scattering through Candy Alley, too; panic spreads as Sully tra-la-la-las her way between the stalls. She holds up her eye scream like a trophy, stopping every now and then to pinch a piece of candy or popcorn, to add to the impossibly mounting pile of sugar and blood.

A stall worker cowers between two booths, hoping Sully will just pass by, but no such luck. The cutesy killer clown spots them and hops over.

"Hiya! Name's Sully!" she titters. "Sully the Clown! Pleased to meetcha! Want a lick!" She holds out the cone, and the poor worker's eyes can't get past the severed ear with a chewed lobe sticking out of the melting vanilla. The blood seeping from it stains the off-white cream like spilled raspberry sauce. "I ear it's really nice!"

"P-p-please—" the worker begs, holding their palm to Sully.

The clown sulks, offended. "Well, that's just rude!" She snatches the cone away, dramatically hiding it from sight. Her sad face flits between the concealed ice cream and the quivering worker like she's pondering some unintelligible point.

Sully squints at the worker as she takes a lick of the cone. "Bleh!" she spits. "You're right!" And grins. "It's missin' something... Oh, I know!"

"Please—" the worker screams as Sully bites down on his finger, teeth tearing through to the bone. He grabs his wrist with his other arm for all the good that'll do and watches as Sully pulls half of his finger free, as the skin tears, leaving behind a raw stump of pulsating blood and gnawed bone. The worker doesn't lower his outstretched hand—the shock's locked him in place—though he does throw up in his mouth as Sully sticks his severed finger into the top of her cone.

"You're right!" She jumps to her feet. "All it was missin' was a finger-flake! Thanks!" Sully clicks her heels and continues on her way down Candy Alley, leaving the worker to faint in the dirt.

Cut to: Reese laughing madly as the young man beats him bloody. His face is a smushed mess of teeth and torn sags of skin. His eyes gleam with frenzied delight, something about him compelling the young man to hit harder, faster. But for all the damage his blows do, Reese just begs for more.

"Hurt me! HURT! ME!"

Reese fuels his rage, goading him, and the young man puts all he has into it; he punches so hard the reverb of the impact forces the bones of his forearms to rip free, tearing through his skin below the elbow, causing him to fall to the dirt on his knees. He screams in agony as Reese squirms with pleasure beside him.

And then, sitting up as though the beating was nothing at all, Reese rearranges the mashed, mangled remains of his face, shaping it like putty. With one hand, Reese stretches his mouth into a wide half-circle that occupies half his face, shoving his nose and eyes higher up to make room; when his hand comes away, there's more gum than black-stained teeth. Both hands go to his ears, pulling on them till they stick out from his head, and his mutton chops droop like dirty little whiskers.

"Who-who-who-who's next?" Reese leers.

Chapter Fourteen

CHILDREN OF THE CANDY

Nevill flicks his cigarette away just before it reaches the filter; it's still smoking on the ground as he pops the packet out of his shirt pocket, tapping another into his hand. He lights up and leans back, right beside an adult-sized tin clown holding a no smoking sign—a too-big-to-be-real gloved hand points with an "aw shucks" look on his weirdly egg-shaped head.

Countless kids yell and parents scream behind him—you'd think someone was getting murdered the way they go on, the way they're rushing around like someone just lost their head.

"Hurry up, babydoll," Nevill mutters. He figured taking Milly and her brats to the park would be a quick way to get in her pants—not like it's all that hard, but he likes when she's grateful. And besides, couldn't do any harm to plant some seeds with that sister of hers. Sure, she's a grade-a weirdo, but that body—it's like God gave all the curves in that family to Sully. She can even keep the makeup on. Just for once, he'd like to stick it in someone that's not as thin as a twig. As his buddy down in Texas used to say, the bigger the cushion, the better the—

"Stop that right now!" Some shrill mother wrecks Nevill's dirty little daydream. "You! Yes! You in the hat!"

"Oh, you gotta be kiddin' me," Nevill groans. He turns around, cigarette bobbing between his lips. "Yeah?"

"Your three—" the furious mother shakes her head, knocking loose all the inappropriate names she wants to use and goes with, "children just hit my daughter!"

"Look, lady, those ain't my kids, so why don't you sit on this"—he flips her the finger—"and spin."

"Why you, urgh!" The mother stomps her feet as Nevill turns his back again. He lifts his Skidds Bay Sharks hat, runs fingers through greasy hair, and does his best to ignore all the clamor going on behind him.

The woman mutters something about "trailer trash" and tries to break up the fight herself. Two of the triplets play tug-o-war with another child, each yanking one arm as hard as they can. The kid in the middle cries out as the third triplet clings to their back, slapping at their face. It's a fair distance from where Nevill chills, so slightly out of focus, but even so, something's up with the triplets. They didn't have blue, green, and red hair last time Nevill looked, not that he would notice if he bothered to pay attention right now anyway.

Nah, Nevill just smokes and thinks about what he's gonna do with Milly later, maybe even with both sisters at the same time—while behind him, the triplets tear the arms from their little piggy in the middle.

Small Wood's Soft Play fills with screams, though that's par for the course, and Nevill doesn't take any more notice than he did before. The mother tries desperately to get to her child as the triplets turn on her, battering her with the severed arms like she's a piñata. Even when they get her to the ground, they don't stop.

All around the scene, parents run, scooping up their kids, flowing in all directions like a tsunami in a sippy cup.

Nevill stays oblivious. He checks out the short skirt on the neon yellow dress of a girl that walks by—a bright purple belt, an arm full of bangles, and the kind of hair Nevill can just imagine himself getting a hold of from behind.

"God—" He begins to smirk as the triplets set upon him, using the surprise to pull him over the barrier into the soft play. "Damn!"

The girl in yellow looks back at the sound, ready to flip off whatever creep was catcalling her, only to see nothing but a lit cigarette smoking away in the dirt.

Sitting in the dirt, sulking outside the front gates of Bonkin's Bonanza a few meters apart, Rocky and Leigh do their best to ignore one another. Neither are very good at it.

"I gotta know, did you take lessons, or are you just naturally such a bitch?" Rocky kicks an empty soda cup into the road.

"Nah, yo momma gives lessons down the YMCA. You get a free blow job with them too."

"Wow, two mom jokes already. And people say you're dumb."

"Me! Dumb!" Leigh gets to her feet, dusting off her torn tartan pants. "You know what, you gotta be the dumbest piece of shit on the planet! Steppin' out on the best girl you'll ever meet!"

"Yeah, that so?" Rocky rises too, ready for another go around.

"Yup! Need me to spell it out, Rock-For-Brains?"

"Call me whatever; where I'm standing, you done fucked up just as bad." Rocky throws his arms out, ramming his point home. "I'd never pull that shit with Cliff. I actually give two fucks about my friends."

"Yeah? You better hope nothin' happens to your little Cliff," Leigh snarls. "Otherwise, you'll wind up the loneliest little turd in the bowl."

"You watch what you're saying about Cliff—"

"Somebody say," Cliff comes running up, out of breath, and almost collapses before them, "my name?"

"Cliff, bro, shit!" Rocky races in and takes his friend's weight, helping the sweaty kid sit down. "The hell happened to you!?"

"No," Cliff pants. "Time," he huffs. "Stacey needs"— he holds out the injection kit— "her insulin."

"Shit," Leigh snaps. She couldn't care less about Cliff and Rocky, but Stacey's all right. "We gotta get our asses back in there. Now!"

Rocky, uneasy about agreeing with Leigh, nods. "We got banned, though—"

Screams erupt from behind the gates to Bonkin's Bonanza—and not the go faster, faster! kind. Not like wow, isn't this awesome? kind. No, these are the pure horror kind, the panic and run for your damn life kind; the screams proceed a stampeding horde racing for the gates. Terrified guests stream through the gates, forcing them open as they push and shove each other to safety.

Cliff, Leigh, and Rocky see their chance and with just a quick look at one another, they race into the crowd.

"Move it!" Leigh yells, driving a path through with her elbows, while Rocky helps Cliff follow in her wake. Just as Leigh makes it to the gate, one huge woman in a huge sun hat barges through, knocking Leigh on her ass. "Hey!"

"Run for your lives! They're killing everyone!" the woman bellows and charges on; she clips Cliff on the shoulder, making him drop the insulin kit. The black bag skids across the ground, getting lost in the bramble of moving legs.

"Shit!" Cliff curses and dives to the ground, crawling desperately through the chaos in the direction the kit went. "Please-please-please—" His eyes land on it just as he spots a pair of boots coming down right on top. "No!" He dives for it, but he's too slow.

Leigh's hands cover the kit just as the boot stomps down. She yells through gritted teeth and bears the pain as she protects the bag. The boot passes, leaving behind a dirty print embedded across the back of Leigh's hands. Cliff reaches for the bag; his fingers graze Leigh's for just a second, and at that moment, all is forgiven between them. Whatever animosity he held against her, the hidden resentment and suppressed longing to still be with her forgotten, replaced by unmitigated gratitude.

"Thanks—"

"Move it!"

"Guys!" Rocky yells, holding open one of the gates. "Let's go."

Cliff and Leigh get to their feet and push through. The three of them make it back inside and stumble over to the side, catching their breath against the wall.

"The fuck's going on?" Leigh wheezes.

"Aliens?" Cliff jokes.

"You and your damn aliens—" Leigh goes to tease him when the slam and rattle of metal interrupts her. Heavy shutters come crashing down on both sides of the rainbow arch, below the giant bug-eyed fiberglass Clownzilla version of Bonko. Some trapped park guests batter their fists against it; others try with no success to

169

pry them up from the bottom, while two others drag a man away, someone unlucky enough to have been just at the gate as it came down, slamming down on his arm and severing it as it hit the ground. Blood pumps from his stump, splattering across the spray-painted face of Bonko on the shutters.

"Shit," all three of them say at once.

"Shoot," Kat says without meaning to. She doesn't want to worry Candy anymore than she already has.

"What is it!?" Candy's little fingers are white from her grip on the carriage's bars. Even the gentle swaying it's lulled to makes her want to ralph, but since there's nowhere to hurl, she's doing all she can to keep it down.

"It's probably nothing," Kat tries to placate her unsuccessfully.

"Don't lie to me, Kat, please."

"Well." Kat tries to think of the least alarming way to phrase things. "There's a lot of people running to the exit. I think something's happened."

"Fire?" Candy sniffs the air; she thinks she can detect the faint trace of something burning, like someone burning trash in their backyard.

"I don't know..." Kat trails off. "Something is going on over at Marianna's tent," she adds as she watches the distinctly alluring, even from a distance, woman walk across the body of some man, lying face down on the ground. "And at Small Wood," Kat adds, watching the tiny forms of parents carrying children as they race to the exit. "And, oh no!"

"What!?" Candy panics.

"The front gates just came down."

"What does that mean!?"

"It's—" A buzzing from the door to their carriage cuts Kat off and draws both girls' attention. The lock clicks audibly.

"Kat—"

"It's OK." Kat comes over, making the carriage sway, and retakes Candy's hand. "It's gotta be like an emergency lockdown thing. You know, stop people panicking and climbing out the ride?"

"I really don't like this." Candy turns green.

"No, it's a good thing. They're just keeping us safe till everything's up and running again." Kat hesitates, then adds, "I'm sure."

Candy's whole body quivers. "Do you smell that?"

Kat sniffs the air. "Smells like a backyard barbecue, but"—Kat looks through the railings behind them, down to the bottom of the Balloon Wheel—"oh no..."

"Oh, god, what is it now!? Are we on fire?" Kat doesn't respond. "Kat!? Don't kid around with me!" Candy's heart can't take it. She risks turning her head, joining Kat's stare as they both look down to several people with colorful clown-like hair, throwing trash and whatever else they can onto a makeshift bonfire. The cut-out photo stand Candy saw the family take a picture at sticks out from the growing blaze, and another clown dances over, red canisters in both hands.

"What the hell are they doing?" Candy shrieks as the ride comes back to life and they climb higher, only to stop one space away from the apex.

"Please! Please! No!" the girls hear someone beg from below, and then the screams start—screams punctuated by maniacal laughter.

"Clark was taking her to the first aid station," Cliff finishes catching Rocky up. Leigh stands on top of a balloon cart, hand shielding her eyes as she searches for any signs of Candy.

"Right, so let's go." Rocky gets pumped.

"No, you guys find Candy," Cliff insists. "I'll get Clark and Stacey, then we'll all get the hell out of Dodge."

"Nuts to that, bro." Rocky puts a hand on Cliff's shoulder. "We're sticking together. Rocky 'n' Cliff—"

"Listen! Only you 'n' me know the way out back, and something's really fucked around here." Cliff nods to the crowd trying to force the shutters open. "I'd rather not find out what, you get me?"

"Damnit," Rocky relents. "Fine."

"Hey." Cliff raises a fist. "Rocky 'n' Cliff?"

"To the edge!" Rocky fist bumps his friend. A tear forms in the corner of his eye. "Now go get your sister." Rocky shoves him on, watching his best friend go, and can't shake a sense of lingering sadness. Like it's the last time he'll see him.

"Don't forget my stupid stepbrother!" Leigh yells as she jumps down from the stand.

"Any sign of her?" Rocky asks, hands in the pockets of his jacket.

"No," Leigh grunts. "Why does she have to be so freakin' tiny!"

Rocky can't help it; he snickers. "You know I once asked, in all seriousness, if she was a leprechaun?"

"No shit?" Leigh says. "I always suspected, but—"

A screech and hum interrupts them, piercingly shrill; it wavers and crackles through speakers mounted around the midway, in every corner of the park.

Cut to: Ruth's office inside The House of Bonko, as the red curves of her smile curl up her cheeks, the

172

bottom point reaching down her chin. Ruth coos into the microphone, sharp teeth coated in black sugar.

"Roll up! Roll Up! Ladies and gentlemen, boys and girls—"

Cut to: one speaker, mounted inside a plastic hybrid nightmare of a duck and a clown as Ruth continues: "—and welcome to Bonkin's Bonanza!"

The speaker looks down on a High Striker machine with a man tied to it, legs forced open and bound behind him. He begs the clowns to stop, but his pleas fall on giggling ears.

One clown, black and red diamond eyes blazing with mischief, wedges the neck end of a broken bottle into the puck. He pings it, making sure it's stable, and does a little jig as the glass rings. Hopping over to join another, a big, bearded clown with a sad-sack face and a mallet over his shoulder, Diamond Eyes gestures for his cohort to take the first turn.

"Jerry! Mike! Stop, guys, this ain't funny!" the man tied to the High Striker begs.

Sad-Sack takes three big, sideways waddling steps over and sidles up in line with the mallet ready to go. His tongue sticks out the corner of his mouth, all sticky and black, as he focuses on the target, taking a few practice swings to get his aim right.

"Jerry!"

There's no way this big, meaty bastard's not ringing the bell, so the poor guy strapped to the High Striker can't do anything but clench his eyes shut tight as Sad-Sack swings the mallet overhead. The pad clinks, and the machine goes ***BOP-BOP-BOP-BOP*** as the puck rises, fast, only to slow to a crawl as it reaches the bound man's crotch. The serrated edges of the broken bottle only tickle the bottom of his pants, plucking threads, and he laughs with nervous tension.

Sad-Sack blows a raspberry and sulks as he passes the mallet to Diamond Eyes. The man on the High Striker breathes a sigh of relief; if big Jerry couldn't ring the bell, then there's no way—Diamond Eyes arcs the mallet overhead, no messing around, and drives it down onto the pad. The puck races up, *BOPBOPBOPBOPBOP*, and forces the broken bottle right into the split in the bound man's legs; his cries of pain ring out to the accompaniment of Diamond Eye's and Sad-Sack's laughter and the High Striker's chimes.

A steady stream of blood pours through the neck of the bottle, spilling over the puck while Diamond Eyes goes for another bottle.

Cut to: a speaker on a high pole in the middle of Small Wood's Soft Play. "Have fun, Children of the Candy; enjoy yourselves!" Ruth commands.

"Heehee!" goes one of the triplets, the one who used to be called Trixie, her white face dominated by a large pink star over one eye. "Faster! Faster!" she demands, and the two boys oblige.

Tommy tips from side to side as he spins his arm and Tyler tinkles with laughter as he picks up the pace.

Heehee hops with sheer delight, pigtails fluttering in the air, as Tinkle and Haha make the wet rope go faster and faster. At first, Heehee was upset that there wasn't any jump rope to be found at the park, but when they dug inside Mommy's boyfriend, they found some. They found a lot! It's a bit slimy and stinky, but that just makes it more fun.

Nevill lies on the ground, a short distance from the triplets, his gouged open and disemboweled stomach stuffed full of balls from the pit.

"But don't have too much fun," Ruth calls through the speaker. Rocky and Leigh stare up at it. "After all, we don't want to spoil the big Blow Out!" Ruth's cackling proceeds more ear-piercing static, and the speaker cuts back to playing a never-ending loop of carnival music.

"What the fuck is a Blow Out?" Rocky looks to Leigh.

"If you have to ask," she shrugs.

"Ha, fuckin' ha, no seriously?"

"Nothing good," Leigh says. "We gotta find Candy, like right now."

"Yeah but, how? Split up and—"

"Hey, wait a minute." Leigh squints and blocks the sun as she looks to the far end of the park. Something catches her eye at the top of the big wheel. "No way?"

"What is it?"

"I think my Candy senses are tingling," Leigh says. "This way; I need a closer look."

Candy cries as the carriage jerks up another spot— they're now at the very tip of the wheel. The screams and smell of burning from below have only gotten worse, and now thick, greasy black smoke flows up around the carriage.

"It's no good; they've locked us in." Kat rattles the lock on their door with no success, any ideas of jumping out and making a run for it when their carriage got close enough to the ground dashed.

"Why are they doing this?" Candy panics.

"I think it's happening all over," Kat says. She can see Diamond Eyes and Sad-Sack at the High Striker from her side, though she doesn't tell Candy what they're doing to the poor man bound to it. Then she spots something odd. Two distant figures moving away from the mob gathered by the shuttered entrance, two crazy souls moving into the chaotic, carnival carnage of Bonkin's Bonanza, and from the way they move, the urgency, they don't feel like the crazy people to Kat.

"Candy, come here and look."

"I don't wanna." Candy grips the bars with two hands.

"No, seriously, I think... is that Rocky? And Leigh?"

Hearing their names makes Candy jump to action. She crawls across the carriage, fighting against the overwhelming dizziness and urge to puke.

"It is!" Candy yells with a sudden burst of hope. In her head, she knows she can't be sure, not from this distance, but she's not listening to that. No, her heart's telling her that it's Leigh, and she's split between the relief the sight brings, the idea that Leigh can get her out of this trap, while at the same time it sinks with worry that her best friend's wading into unspeakable danger and it's all her fault.

"Rocky!" Kat puts an arm through the bars and yells his name. "Rocky, over here!"

"Leigh!" Candy joins in, bracing herself tightly against the bars. Even though there's no way she could fit between them, she feels exposed and in danger of teetering over the edge with just her arm outside the carriage—but what choice does she have? "Up here! Leigh!"

The two distant figures stop for a second; one of them seems to point towards the big wheel, and then both start moving towards it.

For a second, Candy and Kat think they're going to be alright. Then the wheel jerks on, moving them down

176

one spot, and fresh screams erupt below as the smoke thickens.

Chapter Fifteen
CREAMING BLOODY MURDER

The camera centers on Brock Hauser as he fixes his hair in a compact mirror.

"We're not live?" Brock checks.

"Yeah, no worries, we're off the air," the camera operator assures him.

"You're sure?" Brock shoots a threatening sideways glance right down the camera. "I can have you fired for that fuck up earlier."

"I gotcha, Mr. H."

"All right, kid." Brock puts his mirror away, straightens his lapels, and faces the camera straight on.

The House of Bonko stands tall behind him, a little distance away, looking like someone rammed a carnival train car into the sort of place a Vincent Price character would scheme to murder his wife in.

"Don't see the point in them letting us on the ride and not allowing us to film it."

"Don't worry, Mr. H, I got some shots."

"You sneaky little bastard." Brock's mustache twitches like an excited caterpillar as he smiles. "Show me that after. You get the shark?"

"Oh, totally," the camera operator says, and Brock pumps his fists.

"I can smell another award coming, kid, now start rolling on three—"

"Uh, we've been rolling for five minutes Mr. H."

"You said we weren't." Brock shakes his head. "Nevermind, my fault for not being specific." He takes some deep breaths, a moment to focus, and then like flicking on a light, Brock puts on his newscaster's face.

"Hi, folks. Brock Hauser here at Bonkin's Bonanza, where I have just been granted the privilege to ride the park's new signature Murder Train—an exciting and educational concoction of ghost train thrills and true crime chills!" Brock's eyes gleam as he counts up the cash he'll get from Hardstack each time that line airs. "The very same crimes covered by yours truly for Channel Five News in the award-winning documentary Blood and Greasepaint: The Crimes of Buster B. Bonkin and, folks, I have to tell you... what a ride! As you can see, folks are just lining up for it!"

Brock gestures towards the line, and the camera pans to show a packed mob of park guests waiting their turn. As the camera pans back toward Brock, it catches just a glimpse of something - people dressed like clowns pulling guests out, throwing them to the ground.

"And that's not all, folks." Brock flashes a bright, white grin. "There's a special treat at the end for those brave enough." Brock reaches into his suit jacket pocket and slips out a bag of black cotton candy. "Bonkin's Bonanza proprietor Ruth Hardstack assures me that this bag of cotton candy comes from the very same machine that Chet Redwood used to murder Buster B. Bonkin, allowing the more adventurous among us to not only live history, but to taste it, too." Brock opens the bag, takes a small piece out, and holds it to his lips. "Care to join me?" He maintains that pose for around thirty seconds.

179

"And, cut," the camera operator says, and Brock puts the cotton candy back in the bag. "You're not gonna try it?"

"Oh, God no." Brock dusts his shirt then taps his teeth. "These veneers cost a grand, kid."

"Mind if I?"

Brock shrugs and holds the bag out for the camera operator. His hand comes into shot just as panic takes over Brock's face. "Watch out!"

The camera shakes as something impacts the operator; a grunt, a crack, and the sound of something wet follow, and the camera topples to the ground. It lands askew, facing the nearby carousel that Brock runs towards, a small crack in the corner of the screen.

The operator's hand falls into the shot, blood running across his fingers.

His mic must still be on, because we can hear Brock's desperate panting as he runs.

"What's the meaning of this!"

He tries to run around the carousel, but a mean-looking clown, hulking and gormless, with a tiny tuft of green hair on his egg-shaped head, blocks him. Brock runs the other way, but something out of shot stops him dead. "Oh, god, no, why are you doing this?"

"Because it's fun!" The mic picks up a squeaky, chortling voice as its owner comes into the frame—a girl in a short Day-Glo blue dress, pale white face with spiraling lipstick and a massive cloud of sky-blue hair.

Nowhere to go, Brock climbs the barrier to the carousel, and the two clowns leap over, moving to corner him. They back the newscaster towards one of the rising and lowering horses and give him no choice but to hop on it. He kicks out at them like a cowboy giving some would-be horse thieves the boot as the ride rotates them

180

all around, out of shot. Brock's mic picks up his screams, broken with static and maniacal laughter, before it cuts out.

When the ride rotates back around into shot, there's no sign of any of them.

"Clarky! Come out and play!" Stacey pulls on the locker door, and though she's not particularly strong, the kid has boundless energy. Clark's fingers are red where they grasp the inside of the lock, the rough edge of the rattling metal biting into his skin.

He loses his grip momentarily, and the door jerks open an inch; as quickly as Clark pulls it closed, Stacey's quicker, and she gets the tip of the scissors in through the gap. They scrape through, going as far as the crack will allow, reaching the top of Clark's curled fingers.

Stacey's sunken black eye appears in the gap. "Hiya!" Her lips curl.

"Why are you doing this!?" Clark pleads.

Through the crack, he sees Stacey's genuinely taken aback by his question, as though it makes no sense to her. "It's fun, duh!" She grins and rattles the scissors. "Come out and play!" Stacey pushes the tip of the scissors down toward Clark's fingers—the edge isn't sharp enough to break the skin, but he's already at a breaking point without the added pressure. Clark bears his teeth and squeezes his eyes tight, but it's no good. His fingers slip, and Stacey seizes the opportunity, yanking the locker door open.

"There you are, Clark-in-the-Box!" Stacey's grin spreads across her pallid face, and even beyond the limits of her mouth, the black smile continues, zig-zagging as though etched on her skin by some unseen chaotic artist. Her eyes roll white as she giggles, and her hair flows with

181

blue streaks as Stacey waves the bloody scissors around like a toy.

Clark attempts to protect himself as best he can, crossing his arms with his palms outstretched in a last-second bid for mercy. "Please, Stacey—"

He's cut off and so are Stacey's wild chortles as a needle lands in the little girl's bare shoulder. Stacey's head whips around, her side ponytail swishing the new color away as the black lipstick smile retreats across her face. Her eyes meet Cliff's, his whole face shiny with sweat that pools around the collar of his t-shirt. "Huh?" Stacey says as she faints into her brother's arms.

Catching the girl, Cliff looks at Clark. "You OK, dude?"

"Uh." Clark's in shock, still holding his defensive pose. He jerks when Cliff steps closer. His eyes look past Cliff and his unconscious sister, to the bloody corpse of Boohoo on the floor. Hand quivering, Clark points to the body. "Sh-she did that..."

Cliff follows Clark's finger, looks to Boohoo, but doesn't follow. "Your sister k-killed him!"

"Clark, dude, that makes no sense. Shit, look, we gotta book—we're meeting Rocky and the others—"

"No!" Clark slips out of the locker, keeping his back pressed to the wall. "I'm not going anywhere with her!"

"Dude! Listen!"

"No!" Clark slides along to the door, never taking his eyes off the oddly sweet and peaceful face of Stacey as she sleeps, tiny bubbles blowing from her lips. His hand grabs the handle, fumbles, and then throws the door open.

"Clark, look, we need to stick together—"

"I'm outta here, and if you had any sense, you'd get away from her while you still can!" Clark slips through

182

the door and takes off before Cliff can even take two steps in his direction.

By the time Cliff emerges in the hall, Stacey snug in his arms, there's no sign of which way Clark went, and as much as he doesn't want to abandon Leigh's brother, he's got his own family to look after.

"C'mon, brat," Cliff says to his sleeping sister and even gives her a gentle kiss on the forehead. "Let's get you home."

"Shoulda stayed at home!"

Cut to: Clark panting as he takes off, running through the strangely deserted Arcade Alley. Deserted arcade machines trill and buzz with unfinished street fights and abandoned space invasions, while games of chance lay hauntingly empty. There's something decidedly not right about a vacant carnival, but Clark has more pressing things in mind.

"Never should have let Leigh talk me into—shit!" Clark comes to a dead halt as he rounds a corner, seeing that he's not entirely as alone as he thought.

A few yards in front of him, blocking the path, some clowns have rearranged a bunch of the cut-out photo standees, lining them all up in a row like a shooting gallery. From where Clark stands, he can see close to half a dozen park guests on their knees, bound in colorful rope and ribbons to the railing behind the makeshift photo shoot—only there's no camera in sight.

A big clown—at least, it looks like one even though it's dressed in a Hawaiian shirt, board shorts, and the classic socks with sandals combo—mucks around with the gagged hostages, chuckling as he tightens their bonds. Clark spots a Polaroid Instant dangling from his neck—so there's the camera, but what is he doing?

183

Something laughing like a slide whistle rings out behind him, and Clark turns in time to see two more clowns sauntering along the alley.

They haven't seen him yet, and he's quick enough to duck behind a Grandmother Truth Fortune Telling Machine. The wizened animatronic of an older woman within waves her arms robotically as two clowns strut past. Only it's just one of them that looks like a clown to Clark, and it's the damn creepy one from earlier—Mr. Pies, the one who waved at the three of them from what feels like a whole year ago but was only just this morning. The other one looks like somebody's mom, only she fell asleep, and the kids covered her face with everything in her makeup bag.

Clark watches as these two meet up with Hawaiian Shirt Clown and exchange some strange giggling greeting that makes no sense to him. It's like they're laughing in some weird, secret code.

One of the hostages makes a run for it, somehow breaking free; they scarper away, but their legs are still bound and they don't get far. The Mom Clown drags the poor guy back over, clips him behind the head, and then forces his face through one of the holes, muffled pleas for mercy blocked by a gag made from brightly colored handkerchiefs.

Hawaiian Clown takes a ready stance on the other side of the cut-outs, legs wide and braced. He holds the camera one-handed, throwing an exaggerated thumbs up sign with the other.

Mr. Pies takes one of his namesakes from the tray and waves it around as though basking in the freshly baked aroma, despite the cake looking rancid, slapdash and lumpy. Layers of whipped cream have been applied on top, though Clark thinks he can spot something jutting

184

out through the cream—something dull and gray. Mr. Pies pulls back, lifting one leg as his back arches, as a malicious grin breaks out.

The unwilling subject struggles like he knows he's about to get much worse than a pie to the face, but Mom Clown holds him tight. Mr. Pies winds up, then fakes out—sending the other two clowns into fits of giggles as the man at the cut-out loses control of his bladder. A dark spot appears on his pants, running down and pooling on the cobblestones by his knees.

While the other clowns are laughing, Mr. Pies quickly pulls back and hurls the pie; it splats hard against the man at the cut-out, flush to his face as the flash of Hawaiian Clown's camera goes off.

Clark winces, though really, it's a pie—how bad can it be? He notices streaks of pink in the cream, and more of the white fluffiness turns red as the pie slides down the man's face.

"Oh, fuck," Clark mutters when he sees what the big deal is.

As the pie slides, it leaves behind streaks of darkening pink, rivulets of red trickling down like runny raspberry sauce. The cream covers his face, but not the holler of stomach-churning agony that makes no sense to Clark, not till the base of the pie slops to the ground and leaves behind a ring of razor wire embedded in the man's face, half-inch long strawberry gashes seeping red as he wails.

Mom Clown runs a finger through the cream and blood, pulling back a flap of skin that oozes a thick glob. She brings the pink fluff to her mouth and licks it clean, running her tongue all over just to make sure she gets it all.

Mr. Pies then chooses another pie from his tray—a flat, gelatinous yellow one. He winks to the others as he

185

picks up a halved lemon with his other hand and squeezes the juice all over the pie.

Clark's seen more than enough; there's nothing he can do to help, and if he tried, he'd end up in line for the same treatment. No, he has to find his stepsister and get out of this nuthouse of a carnival before it's too late. As he slinks away between a narrow gap in the arcade stands, he tries his best to shut out the agonized moans that follow another splat.

The door to the hospitality suite clatters open as Cliff barges through it backward, Stacey drooped in his arms. He turns and takes a few steps when something odd causes him to pause—a red wheelbarrow with two unconscious bodies, arms and legs hanging limply out the sides. The strange and unexpected sight steals his focus, and he overlooks the hunched clown on the awning above him. It perches in a squat, like a monkey, grinning at the boy below.

"Fuck is going on?" Cliff mutters as the little monkey clown leaps, landing on Cliff's back. Stacey flops to the ground, conking her head on the cobbles but stays out cold all the same. The monkey clown clings to Cliff's back.

"Get off me!" Cliff manages to break free as he slams his back against the wall.

Cliff turns, ready to fight, and his stomach turns at the face before him. It kinda looks like that dude from the trailer, the one he tricked into thinking he worked at the park, only his face is all messed up. His whole face is so pulped up Cliff can't make out any details—bold colors merge with bruised, swollen flesh. His big, gummy grin takes up most of what's there, warping the proportions into something vaguely chimp-like.

186

"Naughty boy!" Reese the Clown chuckles. "Naughty-naughty-Ruth-no-likey!"

"Dude! The fuck!?" Cliff makes fists and puts himself between the clown and his little sister. "Looks like somebody already fucked you up, but I'll go round two if you don't back off."

Reese the Clown reaches into the pocket of his vest and Cliff tenses up, expecting a knife, and then confusion sets in as Reese removes a torn scrap of paper. "Tickets! You're invited! You're all invited!" Reese scoots over on his haunches and holds the invite out for Cliff, the other hand hidden behind his back.

"Invited to what?" Cliff doesn't take it, nor does he take his eyes off the shifty little clown.

"Why, for"—Reese flashes all the gum he has—"the Big Blow Out, of course!"

The answer makes no sense to Cliff, but it's too late. The clown drops the paper as his hand snatches Cliff's. He pulls the boy in toward him as he swings the other arm around, bringing a lead pipe in a quick arc towards Cliff's head.

Cliff leans back just in time as the pipe whistles by mere inches from his face, but his foot stumbles against Stacey's body, causing him to fall on his backside on top of the girl. He grunts as he lands and looks up as Reese leaps. The clown brings the pipe down on Cliff's forehead with enough force to make everything instantly blur. Still conscious, Cliff clambers away, blood trickling from his scalp, down his nose. He has no coordination, not after that blow, and he collapses after a short crawl.

Things start to fade to black as he's dragged towards the wheelbarrow, as he's lifted and dumped on the other two bodies. Stacey's added on top, and with his thoughts all fuzzy, that's a comfort to him. At least they're together.

"Oh, yes-yes-yes, the Big Blow Out!" Reese chatters to himself as he pushes the wheelbarrow. It's the last thing Cliff hears before he fades out completely.

That and, "Bonko's gonna love it!"

Chapter Sixteen
CLOWNS JUST WANNA HAVE FUN

"You sure about this?"

Cut to: Leigh panting as she struggles to keep up with Rocky. Even with longer legs, it's a challenge. Whatever else she thinks of the guy, he sure can move.

"Yeah, trust me," Rocky says, "fastest way's right through Candy Alley."

Leigh snorts and comes to a halt as she tries to contain herself. She can't and leans against a popcorn stall to keep from falling over—partly from exertion, mostly from the hilarity.

"What's so funny?" Rocky slows and rocks on his heels, barely even a bead of sweat messing up his fluffy parted curtains.

"I just need to"—Leigh holds her stomach and focuses on breathing—"catch my—nope!" She doubles over again, giggling. Finally, wiping a tear from her eye, she looks at Rocky and says, "I mean, right through Candy Alley? Jeez, buy her dinner first, dude!"

It takes Rocky a second to click, and when he does, the stupid absurdity of the coincidence and innuendo acts like a much-needed pressure relief. He's been on the go so much today he didn't even have time to think, and now he takes a moment for the intrusive thoughts that were lagging behind all day to have a chance to catch up.

She doesn't want you back.

You'll never find another girl like her.

And in the eerie quiet that rests upon the deserted snack stands, wagons, and picnic tables made from barrels, Rocky realizes how pathetic those thoughts are, how utterly selfish, and the truth follows hot on that revelation.

You don't deserve her.

"Come on." Rocky's ready to go, to leave those thoughts in the dust. "Let's move." His eyes lead Leigh's above the stalls, at the stream of thick black smoke bleeding into the sky. "I don't like that smoke."

"Yeah, me neither." Leigh looks around at the nearby stalls. "Hang on a second." She leans over one booth and pulls on a baseball bat-sized lollipop; it's hooked into the back wall of the stall and refuses to budge.

"What're you doing?"

"I have this bad feeling we're gonna have to fuck some fools up and—urgh!" The giant lollipop comes away, but it's heavier than Leigh thought, and it falls behind the counter. "Shit," she complains and hops over. "Shit!" she yells when she finds the body on the floor.

Rocky races over and nearly hurls when he looks behind the counter. The body must have once been someone who worked in Candy Alley; that's the only thing they can discern. Anything recognizable about the person, their face, their hands—it's all torn, mangled, chewed beyond recognition. "The fuck happened to them!?" Rocky blocks his mouth with his fist and refuses to throw up.

"I dunno," Leigh prods the corpse with her boot, "but looks like whoever did it called for more paramedics."

Rocky stares at Leigh, no clue what that means.

"Seriously?" Leigh, likewise, stares at Rocky as though she can't believe he doesn't get it. "Send. More. Paramedics," Leigh says again, this time dropping her voice into a guttural moan as she lets her body sag and rolls her eyes to the whites. She shakes her head; it's incredulous to her. "That's from Candy's favorite scary movie."

"Really?" Rocky shrugs. "I didn't even know she liked those things."

Leigh climbs back over the counter, the giant lollipop in hand. "Well, you can find out an awful lot about a girl when you're down her alley."

"You'd know about that," Rocky mutters under his breath, though not quite enough for Leigh to miss.

"What's that, Rock-For-Brains?" Leigh tests the heft of the lollipop—it slaps on her waiting hand very satisfyingly. "Me 'n' my sweet slugger here didn't catch that."

"Nothin'." Rocky heads on. "Let's go."

"Pretty, pretty boy." Sully sits cross-legged on the roof of a frozen banana stand, watching the tall girl and the handsome boy walk through the scattered chaos of her playhouse. "Tasty, tasty, pretty boy." She chews on a rainbow sucker and wonders if the beautiful boy will taste half as sweet.

"The hell did you mean by that?" the girl yells. She's yucky; Sully doesn't like her, doesn't look like she tastes good at all.

"I didn't mean anything." The pretty boy marches on, stepping around some more leftovers. "And keep it down! Whatever did all this might still be creeping around."

"Yeah, better be careful. You might make out with them, too."

Sully giggles and dances in her seat.

"You know what." The pretty boy stops, turns, and gets right in the tall girl's face. "Fuck you! Yeah, I'm a piece of shit, got no excuse, but don't walk around like you got nothing to do with this whole shit show! You're just as selfish as I am, so get down off that fucking high horse! None of us would be here, trapped in a carnival with a fucking cannibal, if it wasn't for you!"

The tall girl looks like she's about to hit the pretty boy with the big sucker she holds like a hammer; her arm twitches and then drops to her side. She looks away from the boy, angry and hurt, though at who, exactly, Sully can't tell.

"Figure out why you felt you had to tear us apart another time," the pretty boy says and storms away. "I'm done with this shit. Candy needs us."

"Candy?" Sully's head tilts like a puppy that's just heard its name.

The tall girl looks like she's about to cry, and all Sully can think about is this candy-girl.

"Candy." Sully rubs her hands together gleefully. "Tasty, tasty candy-girl!" She sounds so sweet, and Sully just has to taste her, but the pretty boy's right here, right now.

Sully hops to her feet and skips from roof to roof, creeping a few steps behind the pretty boy, biting her lip to hide the giggles. She's about to pounce when the boy leaves Candy Alley and comes to a stop by the purple tent. He puts his head in his hand, kicks a bench, and yells, "Fuck!"

"No-no-no-no." Sully crouches down behind a marquee and peers over. "No, pretty boy," her voice quivers, "not the Bazoomba Lady." Scared, childlike whimpers escape her smeared lips as Sully watches a shapely silhouette appear from the darkness at the mouth of the tent. "Run, pretty boy, run," Sully pleads.

He doesn't hear her. Rocky doesn't hear anything, not once elegant, plaster-like naked arms wrap around him, covering his mouth with one hand and pulling him into the dark.

"Oh, poo," Sully pouts on the roof.

"Rocky!" The tall girl emerges from Candy Alley, looking around for any sign of the pretty boy. "Rocky!?"

Sully slinks back along the roofs of Candy Alley as the tall girl searches in vain for the kidnapped boy. She wanted to taste him, but the Bazoomba Lady has him now, so that's that.

"No fair." Sully plops her butt down on the roof of the frozen banana stand once again and blows her hair out of her face. She feels a bad mood coming on, though it doesn't last long.

A shriek from the entrance to Candy Alley makes her pop her head up like a jack-in-the-box. Sully crawls along the roof on her hands and knees and peers through the marquee. She sees a cutie of a boy on his hands and knees, searching for something in the dirt.

"Yay," Sully smiles, "more bananas!"

Rocky can't see a thing; all he can hear are his own muffled pleas to be let go. He struggles against a body that's both invitingly soft and yet as strong as iron. His nose fills with an intoxicating scent, a perfume, but not anything like Candy would wear. No, something more mature, more dangerous. It almost makes Rocky want to stop fighting.

Music fades in now, something old playing on a scratchy record player, but Rocky recognizes it all the same. Billy Paul singing about meeting someone at a café. All Rocky can think about is how his parents put this song on, full volume, thinking it covers the sounds of them getting it on.

His captor stumbles, and Rocky manages to slip free. The room is dark, lit by a single silk-covered lamp and a scattering of candles, but he can see the door. He makes it two steps before something wallops him over the head—not knocking him out cold, but it's enough to stun him, make him stagger back into this woman's arms. There's two, or maybe three, versions of the room before his eyes, and they spin in concentric circles as he's lifted off his feet and laid down. The woman fusses over his wrists, and Rocky's vision only realigns as he realizes she's bound him to the arm of a chaise lounge.

The woman slithers back into the shadows like some elegant predator.

"Lemme go!" Rocky demands. He tries to undo his binds, but she knows her way around a knot, whoever this woman is.

"Hush, pretty baby," she toys from the dark, and a sultry laugh follows.

Rocky searches for the source and can't find her, but he does lay eyes on a large framed photo of some incredibly buff man that looks right at him. She emerges from the gloom beside the candle-strewn vanity that holds the picture, hourglass body draped in torn silks and shadows. They reveal everything and nothing as she strides forward on pointed toes.

It's gotta be the lighting, but it looks to Rocky like her skin is white, pure white like she's been dipped in paint.

194

He tries not to look at her body, but his eyes do their own thing, and the more he fights it, the more he stares.

She closes the gap between them and then crawls up the chaise, her eyes locked on his except when he can't fight the urge to stare down her cleavage anymore, spotting a small black love heart on one of her breasts. When he manages to tear his eyes away and meet hers again, her porcelain face erupts in laughter, starkly contrasting with the black mascara tears that run down from one eye.

"You see something you like?" She bites her lip, and Rocky doesn't know what to say. Her hands find their way to his groin, and she has her answer. "Well, hello there, big boy."

"Hello!?"

Cut to: Clark calling out, though he doesn't quite raise his voice after what he just saw by the arcade. He's sure he could hear Leigh, though. There's no mistaking her verbal beatdowns, and somebody around here sure was on the receiving end of one.

There's an eerie stillness to Candy Alley, only broken by the hum of fridges and the churning of soda machines. As Clark walks between the deserted stalls, he turns, checking his back and blind spots as he goes, doing what he can to keep an eye out for more crazy-ass clowns, and misses the body on the floor. He trips across it and goes down to the dirt with his glasses landing some distance away. Clark slaps around for them, and his hand comes down on a dead body, on the half-chewed mess of its face, and even with blurred vision, he can tell what it is.

Clark shrieks and backs away on his butt. He clambers to his feet. He takes a few running steps and stops dead as his sneakers crunch on something fragile.

"Oh no," he says too late and hopes he hasn't just stood on his glasses. It takes him a second to focus his eyes, straining to make things clear, and he wishes he hadn't; right between his feet, the shattered remains of his glasses. "Shit."

"Hi!" The voice makes Clark jump and shriek again even though it's all pep, no threat. "Oh, that's no good. You broke your peepers!" She's cute, at least she sounds so to Clark, so he switches from being terrified to embarrassingly mortified.

"Y-yeah." Clark tries and fails to act cool. "Clumsy me."

The girl laughs, too loud, too fast, and slaps Clark on the arm.

"I know all about that! My sister's always like"—the girl puts her hands on her hips and does the kind of impression a child would do of an adult—"Sully, you're a clumsy little bitch! You got blood all over this bathroom!" The girl rolls her finger by her head. "I know, crazy, right?"

Sully, that's... "Hey, I know you! I think! From Mrs. Leaf's art class?"

"You know me? You're a liar!" The girl switches from bouncy to bestial in a heartbeat. "Nobody knows Sully! You're a liar!" She starts to cry, full waterworks.

"No, please don't cry," Clark begs, for her sake and because it's so loud, she's bound to draw one of the psycho clowns toward them. "There's some real bad clowns around here," Clark lowers his voice, "doing crazy shit."

He narrows his eyes, trying to focus his vision enough to make out what's wrong with Sully. Her face is a mash-up of colors, only too many to be normal—lots of blue and far too much red. Boisterous giggling accompanies his attempts and only heightens as he finally sees the bloody smear smile and light blue inverted teardrop eyes of Sully the Clown. Giggling that merges with—

Mari's saucy tittering, accompanying the tinkling metal of Rocky's belt as she unbuckles it, expertly and with ease. She never breaks eye contact with him for a second.

"What are you doing?" Rocky wants to resist, but his body's got other ideas.

"Don't tell me this is your first time?" Mari punctuates her tease with the release of Rocky's belt. "Handsome young man like you, betcha got ladies lining up all day and night?"

"I, uh, I got a girlfriend," Rocky gulps as Mari's fingers tease the elastic waistband of his Calvins.

Mari looks over one shoulder, then the other, before meeting Rocky's eyes again and shrugging. "Not in here, you don't." Mari slides a hand inside his shorts, and Rocky's whole body shudders at her touch. "Oops." She pulls her hand back. "Better slow down a bit."

Mari hops off Rocky and stands to the side, curves slipping in and out of dancing shadows. She begins to move in time to the music, rolling her shoulders and rocking her hips. It's not so much that she takes her clothes off but that they fall away, melting into the shadows as she sways. "Chet hates it when the show's over too fast." Mari's swinging arms draw Rocky's attention to the framed photo.

"W-who's Chet?" Rocky asks, though he doesn't want to know.

"Silly boy, he's my husband." Mari looks over her shoulder, winks at the framed picture of Chet, and blows it a kiss. "He loves to watch."

Well, this just got a fuck-ton crazier, Rocky thinks, but maybe...

"How does he like it? To watch, I mean?"

"Well—" Mari frolics and lays down, half beside, half on top of Rocky. She strokes his face and bites her lip before leaning in and whispering, "He loves it when handsome young men fuck me from behind. He likes to see in my eyes how much fun I'm having." She purrs and licks Rocky's ear.

Every inch of Rocky from the neck down wants to give in, and he fights for control. Candy, he needs to get the fuck out of here and find Candy. But damn, she's so hot, maybe—no! No, he's got to get away, but the only way seems to be if he plays along.

"How can I do that if I'm tied up?" Rocky tilts his head, drawing Mari's attention to the binds. "Untie me, and I'll give your husband one hell of a show?"

"Oh?" Mari raises an eyebrow.

"Chet likes it when you're naughty, right?" Rocky leans in, his lips inches from her. Mari doesn't answer; the moan and smile she gives say enough. "Have you been naughty?" Mari only purrs at that suggestion. "Naughty girls get spanked, don't they?"

"Oh, they do?" Mari looks to the side with a wanton smirk. As though she has no clue whatsoever, as though this isn't exactly what she wants.

"You have been naughty, haven't you?"

Mari looks Rocky in the eye. "Oh, you have no idea."

"I think you need to be spanked."

"Yes," Mari nods, "yes, sir," and she reaches for the silk binding Rocky's hands. Her breast comes up against his face, and it's almost enough to make Rocky forget the plan altogether. He closes his eyes, sees the heartbroken face of Candy, tears flowing down her cheek, and forces himself to have the conviction to stay on task. It would be so easy to give this woman what she wants, though...

And would Candy ever even know?

The second his hands are free, Rocky freezes. His heart screams for Candy, but his body wants Mari. She's here, right now, and—Candy's face flashes before his eyes. Her small, vulnerable features, her tears, and Rocky feels the shame.

You don't deserve her...

You're right, he says to himself, and it's damn time you did something about that.

Rocky shoves Mari aside with all his strength and rushes to the door.

"No!" Mari shrieks. "Bastard!" She bounds off the chaise and through the air, landing on Rocky's back and forcing him to the ground. "How dare you embarrass me in front of my husband!" She grabs a fistful of Rocky's curtains, lifts his head, then slams it down on the ground.

"Liar!"

Cut to: Sully smashes her palm down on the cotton candy stall next to her, and Clark flinches, throwing his arms up to protect himself.

"No! It's true! I-I know you! You always h-had this little banana pencil case. Everyone used to make fun of it, but not me! I thought it was cute! I thought you were cute!"

"You... thought Sully was cute?" The clown girl acts as though none of those words make sense.

199

"I did. They all called you The Banana Queen, but I never did! I wanted to ask you on a date, but I got scared every time. Honest!"

"You wanna date Sully?" She touches her chest with two fingers as though barely able to comprehend the concept.

"Y-yeah!" Clark nods enthusiastically, both because it's true and it seems to placate her. She's not as violent as the other clowns he saw, or at least she doesn't seem to be, so maybe he can talk his way out of this.

"Where would we go?" She asks it so innocently, lips covered in blood.

"Maybe just get a bite to eat?"

Sully's eyes burst with delight. "Oh, goody!" She jumps on the spot and snatches Clark's hand. Sully pulls him along as she skips down Candy Alley, singing joyous gibberish.

"Where are we going?" Clark lets himself be pulled along; not much else he can do.

"Going on a date, duh!" Sully laughs and then comes to a sudden halt. Clark crashes right into her. "Hey!" She shoves him back playfully. "No getting fresh now." And she wags her finger at him. They're right in front of the frozen banana stand, and Sully plucks something from the counter, from the body slumped over it, blood-streaked arm hanging limply. She holds the cold lump of torn flesh up to Clark's lips. "Want some?"

"What is it?" Clark asks, blinking and trying to focus.

Sully blows a raspberry. "It's a banana, duh," and she shoves the ripped piece of flesh into Clark's mouth. The second the cold, wet flavor of iron and salt hits his tongue, Clark spits it back out, then spits some more to get rid of the taste.

"That wasn't a banana!"

Sully stands there, heartbroken, watching in silence as her date spits out the treat she chose to share with him. It was all a lie; she knew it. He's a liar. Just like everyone else, always lying about Sully, telling stories.

"Liar!" Sully shrieks.

"Wait!" Clark pleads, still spitting.

"LIAR!" Sully grabs a tray from the frozen banana stand and clocks Clark over the head with it. "LIAR!" He goes flat against the shack, ears ringing. "LIAR-LIAR-LIAR!" Sully bashes Clark with each screech. He slumps and falls flat on his ass.

"No," Clark pleads in the wrong direction, dazed; he crawls backward, one hand up as he begs Sully to stop.

Split-screen: Rocky, crawling on his back away from Mari, slides in, and both boys scoot away in tandem; Sully cries hysterically, "You never liked me! Nobody likes Sully!"; Mari snarls, "How dare you turn me down in front of my husband! Is his woman not good enough for you!?" Both women close in on their prey. Rocky backs up against the vanity, crashing hard enough to knock over the framed portrait and some candles. The fire spreads quickly, and a wicked orange glow highlights Mari's terrifying beauty; Clark backs up against another stall, and Sully stands over him, legs apart as she wails.

"Hey!" Leigh calls, and Rocky's side takes over just as Sully lifts her banana high. Mari turns in time to see the girl swing her sweet slugger right at her head. It hits, dead on, and something cracks. Mari twirls as she falls, landing on the ground between Rocky and the picture of her husband.

"Thanks," is all Rocky can say as he looks up at Leigh.

Her eyes flicker down to his pants, sitting around his ankles. "Why do I keep catching you with your pants down?"

Rocky climbs to his feet, pulling his jeans up. "Don't tell me you set this up, too?" He looks down at the unconscious clown, her hand inches from her husband's picture. The fire spreads across the rest of the tent, whooshing as it devours silk and canvas.

"Nope, Romeo. Booby the Clown here's all you. Now let's get the hell outta here before we get too hot under the collar."

The kids run for it, ducking under the door to the collapsing tent while Mari lies on the floor. Flames spread to her hair, and her eye shoots open, filled with scorn.

Clark lies flat on his back with Sully cross-legged beside him; her head bobs as she hums. "*Come, Mister Glasses Man, tally me banana.*" Sully giggles. "*Date night comes*"—her voice wavers as her whole body slumps— "*and he wants to go home...*" Sully breaks down into tears, wailing at the sky. "Nobody wants Sully!" Wiping tears and snot on her chocolate- and blood-smeared arm, Sully climbs to her feet. She walks down Candy Alley, no longer interested in all the sweets and treats.

Behind her, in the dirt, Clark's face is a mess of melted chocolate, yogurt, sprinkles, and blood-laced spittle. His jaw, broken open, hangs loosely to the side. Smushed and crushed frozen bananas spill out of his still mouth like rainbow-colored flowers.

All this candy tastes like poop to Sully now; none of it's cheering her up. Maybe this candy-girl? She has to be sweet if she's made of the stuff, right? Sully takes some consolation in that and sets off in search of some tasty, tasty candy.

Chapter Seventeen

FULL METAL BARBEQUE

"Stop this!" The demand comes from someone who sounds like she's used to being obeyed. "Stop this right now!"

The clown securing the face painting boss to the front carriage of the Wild Cat's not listening. He doesn't seem to care at all, no matter how much she wriggles and threatens him—her words go over his bald, white head. "I mean it! Stop this, or I'm telling Ruth!"

At the mention of that name, the bald clown freezes. In his stillness, there's perhaps a hint of fear. He slowly meets the woman's gaze, one of his thin, squiggly eyebrows arcing as he raises one finger lazily to his lips.

"Shhhhh." His lips turn up, incrementally, into an off-kilter smile but the amusement doesn't reach his dour eyes.

The patch of black hair under his chin doesn't even wobble—everything about this clown seems low energy. Like he just doesn't care to put in any effort. Yet he's bound her firmly to the front carriage effectively, tied down across the front like a starfish.

"This is dangerous!" the woman complains. "You hear me! I said—"

The Bored Clown turns around, looks to the ride control booth, and gives a lazy thumbs up. The rest of the boss lady's words go with the wind as the roller coaster car launches; released from its braking mechanism, it hurtles along wooden tracks with the rhythm of a machine gun as the clown waves her off with a lazy salute.

All she can do is scream, the wind force pushing her eyes open wide, catching her mouth and making her cheeks flutter like sails as she bobs up and down each rise. Her teeth rattle so hard it feels like they might fall out. The only respite comes when the car reaches the bottom of The Wild Cat's main incline.

It clunks and clicks its way to the top, and each second that passes pushes the woman towards a breaking point. She grows lightheaded, but remains aware and alert nevertheless. For a brief moment, she's offered the most incredible view in the whole carnival, rivaled only by the apex point of the adjacent 'Round the World big wheel.

The woman doesn't have time to enjoy the respite or view. She doesn't see the bizarre fire at the base of the big wheel. Before catching her breath, her car tips over the peak and races down with unbridled speed.

She barrels into the final section, her screams echoing as she momentarily vanishes into the gaping fiberglass maw of a weather-cracked, giant blue cat. Coming out the other side, she makes some jarringly sharp twists, the momentum of the drop still pushing the car on. It hurtles around the last bend, and she barely has time to register the back of a parked carriage, sticky and dark red like a slaughterhouse hammer, before it's too late.

She becomes pulp on impact—leaving behind intact hands, feet, and a head locked in a forever scream as the car drifts back from the crash. Bits of her insides collapse onto the wooden rails, slopping through the slats and raining down to the grass below like mushy, clumpy hail.

Kat watches as the two Wild Cat cars collide and winces at the impact. She can hear the crash even over the panicked screams from below. The stench of burning flesh and trash is everywhere, making her think the poor woman on the Wild Cat got out easy. Their carriage jumps to life, and they rotate one more spot—now at three o'clock, just a few more stops from the ramshackle tailgate clown barbeque below.

For once, no fresh screams follow the move; perhaps the car was empty or—

"Leigh once told me more people die from smoke than from the fire," Candy says, eyes staring a million miles away. "Maybe we should—"

"No!" Kat wraps Candy in her arms. "Don't even say that!"

"It's gotta be better than the alternative." Candy gives up. She thinks about how broken she was this morning, wishing she was dead because of a boy, and now it looks like she's about to get her wish.

"Let's talk about something else." Kat guides Candy's head onto her shoulder.

"Sure. Seen any good movies?" Candy asks, deadpan.

"Casual Sex?" Kat answers without realizing how it sounds.

"Really, Kat?" Candy gives out a single chuckle. "I mean..."

"Oh, God!" Kat covers her face as it flushes with embarrassment. "I didn't mean that! It's a movie with the girl from Back to the Future!"

"Oh." Candy smiles nervously and shrugs. "There's probably worse things you can do before you die, though."

Kat doesn't want to let Candy slide back into vacant depression, so she flips it. "What about you? Seen any good ones?"

"The Blob was kinda cool." Candy half-smiles and brings her knuckle to her mouth. "I like the old one better."

"So..." Kat thinks of something else. "What college are you going to?"

"I, um, didn't get into any." Candy shrugs.

"Oh," Kat says, "sorry. I thought you and Rocky—"

"He got into UCLA, track scholarship, so..."

Despite her impending death and everything that's come between them, the idea of Rocky going away to college while she's stuck at home still doesn't sit right with her. She doesn't know why, though.

No, that's not true.

The truth is the second Rocky told her the news, Candy knew they were over. She just couldn't bring herself to accept that and so she carried on, waiting for fate to do the hard part for her. Except fate's a fickle bitch, as Leigh always said, and found the most unexpected and painful way.

"I'm really sorry, Candy," Kat apologizes again, "for everything."

Candy doesn't answer; she rolls around in her mental rut, letting self-pity and her inevitable demise immobilize her. And then another thought pops up in her head, not her own but part of her all the same.

"Bitch, get off your cute little butt and stop feeling sorry for yourself," Leigh speaks up from somewhere

206

deep inside Candy, her best friend's relentless attitude kicking her into action even when she's not around.

Candy gets to her feet, shaky but determined. "There's gotta be something we can do?" She rattles the lock, but nothing gives. "What would Leigh do?"

"Swear and kick something?" Kat offers.

"Yeah." Candy nods. "Yeah!" She kicks the door—it shakes but holds firm. "Fuck you, you fucking fuck door!" Candy screams and kicks again. It's probably pointless; both Candy and Kat know this. All the same, Candy would rather go down raging against the world like Leigh than cowering away like a child. "Fucking—"

"Move, Alex, honey, we're moving again," says a mother, round glasses magnifying the hopeless terror in her eyes.

"Just look at Daddy, you hear me?" Alex, the milkshake-scented mustached dad, says to a small child clinging to his mother. "Just keep looking at Daddy." And not the inferno behind you, he adds to himself.

The little boy shifts to take a peek.

"No!" Alex snaps. "Come on, now, look!" He sticks his tongue out and wiggles his fingers behind his ears. "Daddy's doing silly faces!"

That makes the child giggle for a second, then the carriage moves.

"No-no-no-no!" the people in the next one beg. "No!" and then their anguished screams burn hotter than the flames.

Alex gulps; they're next. It doesn't feel possible; this stuff doesn't happen to families like them, yet as the screams below turn to ash, he knows it's time. Alex looks to his wife, and they both share a solemn, resigned nod.

No discussion needs to happen. Her hands move from the top of the child's head to his soft, pudgy face.

"Wait," Alex says. He can't watch this, can't let the mother of his child do this. He puts all his love for his family into one big, fake smile and says, "Come give Daddy a hug."

Their mother urges the boy on, silently mouthing, "Thank you."

The boy crosses the carriage and tucks himself under his father's arms. Alex holds him tight, then closes his hands across his mouth. It's so tiny he has no trouble covering the boy's lips and pinching his nose closed.

He struggles for a minute. Small arms slap against his father's chest, and tiny legs kick off little shoes, but Alex holds firm. His face red, eyes wet, teeth clenched hard, so hard he tastes blood. This brutal mercy's the single hardest thing he's ever done, and the one saving grace is it'll be the last.

He doesn't let go even after the boy stops moving. Even as their carriage begins, its final descent into the flames. Even as the woman he loves, the mother of his child, begins to burn.

"I love you both so much," she says as the heat blisters her skin, using that love to push down on the fear.

"I love you too, Maranda," Alex says and lets that love give him the strength to meet his end, chin held high— at least, till the screaming starts.

Candy kicks, then Kat, then Candy again, in almost perfect rhythm.

"Come"—kick—"on"—kick—"you"—kick— "bitch!"

Something breaks. Not the lock, not the door, but something. Enough to make the door hang at an odd angle—to create a small gap. Not enough to get through, but enough to let in some semblance of hope.

If only there was enough time to keep at it, maybe they could force it open after all—but they're next, and the screaming from the family below has stopped. They know this means there are only moments left.

"It's no good," Candy growls. "We need more time." She feels the urge to shut down again, to go away to a happy place in her head. To just shut her eyes and pretend she's at Leigh's, on a sleepover, their stomaches hurting from too much junk food as they lie, foreheads kissing, sharing secrets while some dumb scary movie plays on TV.

"Don't give up. What would Leigh say?" Kat tries to spark Candy's spirits again.

"She'd say—"

"Fuck you, you trashy ass clown bitches!"

For a second, Candy thinks she imagines the voice. Only Kat also turns toward it, and as they look through the bars of their carriage, they see something more impossible than a gaggle of clowns turning a big wheel into a rotisserie of death. They see Leigh and Rocky working together as they charge in like Saturday-morning cartoon heroes.

Leigh comes at the one by the ride's gate—a Carnie Clown with a slapdash, greasy smile, and she whams him over the head with the sweet slugger. Candy can hear the crack up in the carriage and watches as the clown folds over the guardrail like a cheap, poorly stuffed prize teddy. She's not surprised when he doesn't get up.

Rocky leaps the fences gracefully like they're hurdles and he's putting on a show for some college scouts. His speed lets him catch one more clown by surprise. The clown goes down hard with the momentum Rocky puts into the punch. He gives it a few kicks while it's on the ground, not letting that thing have a chance to get back up.

Leigh catches up with him, holding the blood-smeared giant lollipop club like she's posing for the cover of Conan in Candyland. Three more clowns turn from the fire pit, putting down the trash they were using for kindling and cans of cooking oil. Each of them wears a matching apron, the logo a fiery truck with the words "Burnt Ends" scrawled below.

"Candy!" Leigh yells, keeping an eye on the clowns while scanning the ride.

"Leigh!" Candy's tiny arm shoots out through the bars of her carriage.

"Candy! I'm so sorry!"

"Look out!" Candy calls, but it's too late.

A massive clown so tall he even towers over Leigh steps out from the booth. Most of his skin is blisters and burns with a coating of black soot, while the bottom half of his face is smeared with black, red, and white, like he was huffing paint fumes. He doesn't wear an apron, but a muscle-fitting t-shirt bearing the same emblem as the three Cook Clowns. He grabs Leigh by the hair, yanks her away, and throws her aside like she was a doll. Rocky reacts quick enough to get out of the way as the Burnt Clown swings for him.

"Fuck you going, Freddy?" Leigh snaps and kicks the Burnt Clown's foot out from under him as he moves after Rocky. He comes tumbling down as Leigh gets to her feet and rolls over as she swings her sweet slugger overhead.

"Smashy-smash," she smirks and brings it down fast, aiming to crush the Burnt Clown's skull, only for him to catch it in one hand. "Oh, shit," Leigh curses as the clown rips the lollipop from her, hurling it away; it lands somewhere near the firepit.

The three Cook Clowns come after Rocky, scuttling around the fire and across the frame of the big wheel, moving to block him off. They don't realize just how fast he is; that's exactly what he wants. He's gotta keep them away from the fire, from the controls long enough. Buy time for Leigh to get Candy and Kat out of there. It looks like she's got her hands full with the giant burnt-up clown neither of them noticed, though, and the whole plan's coming apart faster than it came together.

"There's too many of them." Candy bites down on her knuckle and feels her heartbeat through it. "We have to get this open. Now!" Candy takes a running start from the back of the carriage and puts her sneaker into the door. "Come on!"

Kat joins her, the two of them backing up together, then charge, kicking the door as one. They go again and this time throw their combined weight into it, making the door shift. The gap widens at the bottom, and with some gritted teeth prying, Kat's able to force it open some more. It's not enough for her to fit, though, but: "Candy! I think you can get through here. If I hold it."

"I'm not leaving you!" Candy protests; the idea of abandoning Kat makes her feel sick, the same kind of sickness as seeing those rejection letters in the trash. That dread that comes with denying the inevitable.

"You don't have a choice! Leigh needs you."

Candy looks through the bars, watching as Leigh tries to dodge the Burnt Clown's swings, not realizing he's backing her up against a fence.

Kat's right. She needs to go, so Candy lies on her stomach and goes through the gap backward. She puts her legs through first; broken metal edges scrape along her exposed thighs, peeling skin like pencil shavings and leaving behind thin streaks of dotted red lines. Candy squishes her eyes closed and bites through the pain. She sucks in her gut as she wiggles her body through till her neck catches on the metal.

"I'm not leaving you," Candy promises and slips out the hole, hanging on with both hands as she dangles. It's a steep drop below and onto hard metal. It's gonna suck, for sure, but she's not going yet.

Candy pulls herself higher, clambering up till she's gripping the squinty door with both hands.

"Candy, what are you doing!?"

"I said"—Candy throws all her weight back while clinging on—"I'm not"—she does it again, grunting and throwing all the force she can—"leaving you!

The door comes away, and Candy with it, both flying backward and both landing, thankfully, on the grass. The impact knocks the wind out of her, but the soft ground cushions some of the fall.

She looks up at Kat, standing in the open door of the carriage, the wind making her white lace dress flutter. "Leigh!" Kat points.

Candy turns, watching as the Burnt Clown grabs Leigh by the head and slams her against the fence. She gets up, takes one step, and falls over in agony. Candy looks down at her foot; it's already swelling and turning red. It's not broken; she'd feel that for sure, but putting any weight on it at all is gonna suck.

"Fuck you!" Leigh curses, but the fight's gone from her.

No time for pity or pain. Candy bites down. Leigh needs her. She forces herself to her feet and into a hobbling, awkward run, scooping up the giant lollipop on the way. The thing's nearly half the size of her, and Candy has to drag it like a sledgehammer. Building momentum and rage, Candy screams as she hefts the lollipop overhead. The weight of it carries her along for the ride as she hurls it hammer throw-style at the Burnt Clown.

The lollipop connects with his head, sending him against the fence with a clunk. As he collapses to the side, Leigh spots Candy hobbling towards her with a pair of rabbit ears on her head. Not the strangest thing she's seen all day, but still.

"Candy!" Leigh yells, unable to contain her joy, and she rushes to her friend, catching the girl in her arms.

"Leigh," Candy sighs as she goes limp, letting Leigh take her weight.

They hold each other so tight it hurts, and before they part, they kiss foreheads once more. "You came back." Candy smiles.

"Yeah, well, some dumb bitch once said: Candy and Leigh, together forever—"

"You'll see," Candy giggles, her wide smile flashing adorable little raccoon fang teeth.

Leigh pings one of the bunny ears. "So what's up, Doc?" she teases.

"Gee, this don't look like Albuquerque," Candy finishes the joke, and then they hug again.

"Need a hand?" Rocky yells up to Kat and glances away as the wind lifts her skirt. He didn't need to know she wears Zoozie the Space Pirate underoos, but now he does.

Kat dangles one foot over the edge and suddenly loses all courage. She knows staying there, in the carriage, is certain death when those clowns come back, but still, her mind refuses to let her make the jump.

"I'll catch you. I swear," Rocky promises, and those words, spoken by the boy she loves, overpower all sense of logic and control. She believes she'll be OK because she wants to. "Come on. I gave those weirdos the slip, but they'll be back." Rocky holds his arms out and readies himself to catch her.

Kat closes her eyes, puts a hand to her chest, and takes a leap of faith. She flutters through the air and lands safely in Rocky's arms. He spins with the force of her impact and doesn't let go even when they come to a stop. Her fingers grip the leather of his jacket, the softness of his hair, and she never wants to let go. Even though Kat knows she doesn't belong there, Kat can't help but feel at home in Rocky's arms.

"We have to go," he says, lips tickling her ears.

"I know," Kat sniffs, "but I don't want to."

"Kat—"

"Shh. I know," Kat sighs. "I know. Just let me have this moment. Just this once, please?"

Rocky holds her tight. "Sure," he says.

The four of them regroup by the entrance, exhausted, beaten, but alive.

"OK, so, plan?" Candy asks, looking from Rocky to Leigh.

"Cliff's getting Clark and Stacey; he's gonna meet us by the back door, and we'll get the fuck out of here."

"And we fuck up any bozos who get in our way," Leigh adds as she rests the sweet slugger on her shoulder.

"OK, lead the way," Candy says to Rocky, and he nods. It feels good, her talking to him that way. Sure, it's because they need to stick together to get out of this giggling apocalypse, but all the same, it beats where they were an hour or so ago.

As the four of them head out to the midway, Kat stops. "Wait," she yells and runs back through the path toward the ride.

"Where you going!?" Rocky yells and makes to go after her.

"I can't leave the rest of them!" Kat points at the remaining carriages full of trapped riders. "There's gotta be a release in there." Kat slips into the booth. A second later, all the doors on the big wheel open. "Gotcha!" She poses with pride, watching as people clamber out the carriages, climbing down carefully.

"Kat!" Rocky yells, too late.

Her smile turns to horror as the Burnt Clown swoops her up in his arms, lifting the girl off her feet with no effort.

Kat's hair, arms, and legs flutter through the air as the Burnt Clown spins her around, releases his grip, and sends Kat hurtling toward the firepit. It all happens in slow motion for the rest of them. There's nothing they can do.

"Rocky!" she begs as she soars through the air, and then she's gone.

The world catches up with the others as Kat's screams reach out from within the fire. A second later, a burned, hairless charred mess of a girl falls out of the flames, arm out for help, only to go facedown on the ground.

"Rocky," she pleads. Skin ruptures as she lifts agonized eyes to Rocky.

It's a small mercy that she can't see the Burnt Clown's boot as it comes down on her head, crushing her like a barbequed melon.

Chapter Eighteen

I THINK WE'RE ALONE NOW

"No!" Ruth stamps her shiny black high-heeled boots down in the dirt. "Stop that!"

She marches across the ring, puffing her chest out, eyes fierce, towards a clown sitting on the ground beside a scattering of unconscious bodies. He feeds a long balloon tube into the mouth of an unconscious boy.

"Right. Now!" Ruth commands, towering over the other clown.

The clown looks up, a big goofy grin on his face, cheeks sticking out like a hamster that's swallowed some marbles, and his expression doesn't change as Ruth backhands him.

"Hurt him!" Reese chitters as he skitters across the ring on all fours, sidling up against Ruth and holding onto her leg. "Hurt him real bad!"

The Smiley Clown just looks up as blood runs down his nose, holding up more new balloons as though that explains anything.

"Listen up!" Ruth turns, raising her arms to the rest of the Big Top, and declares, "Nobody kills any more of our guests! You hear me?"

Other clowns work diligently, assembling something inside the ring while human guests are herded and corralled.

Ruth leans down, blocking the stage lights above with her significant bulk, and sneers in the Smiley Clown's face as she says, "Not till the show begins."

The threat of another backhander makes him crawl away like a kicked puppy.

It's then Ruth notices something about the boy; she recognizes him. Kneeling, she takes the boy's face in her hand, brushing aside a mop of unruly hair. Her too-white fingers trace his slightly chubby cheeks. "This boy was on the inaugural tour of the House," Ruth recalls as she turns Cliff's unconscious face in her hands. Her attention flits to the next body, the small, sickly face of Stacey.

"Oh, child." Ruth drops Cliff and strokes the little girl's face. "What did they do to you? You were one of us, and now... no. No, Daddy's not gonna like this, not one bit." She stands, turns to Reese, and points to the brother and sister. "These two, I've something special in mind for them. Yes, oh, yes, they'll be part of the show. Put them somewhere safe." Reese hobbles to it only for Ruth to grab his vest and pull him in close. "Then see if you can find the others." She spits the words into his doughy, battered face. "If they're alive, I want them in my show, you understand?"

"Yes, boss!" Reese grins and gets excited, thinking about how much Ruth's going to hurt them. It's enough to make him feel jealous. He grabs Cliff by the arms and drags the boy away.

Leigh pulls Rocky back as he steps towards the big wheel, fingers looped around the collar of his jacket.

Kat's dead.

She was gone before he even lifted his feet, but it's still not sunk in. He held her in his arms a few moments ago, and without uttering a word, told her he'd never love her, not like he loves Candy, and after seeing her die doing something impossibly heroic, he feels wrong. It can't possibly be his fault; Rocky didn't bring her to the carnival, he didn't make her go back to save the others, and yet he feels responsible all the same.

You didn't deserve her love either.

He knows: he should be the one set aflame and crushed under boot, not Kat. He deserves it.

"Kat..." Rocky still makes for her, hoping there's something he can do.

"Come on, Rock-For-Brains," Leigh growls, "we gotta move it."

"But, we, she, I mean—"

"She's gone, and so are we if we keep fuckin' around here."

"Rocky," Candy pleads, and when his eyes land on her, taking in the torn-up legs, the swollen and red inflammation around one ankle, his heart shatters. She always seemed so delicate to him, as brittle as her namesake, but here she is covered in wounds and still standing. She's tougher than he thinks, and it puts him to shame. Kat's gone, but Candy isn't. He swears, at that moment, even if he has to crawl back from hell, he'll keep her safe.

"OK, shit, yeah, OK," Rocky agrees and heads over to Candy. She uses the giant lollipop as a crutch, but it's too heavy to use as a walking stick, so Candy hands it back to Leigh, and Rocky moves in, taking her weight on his shoulder. She feels lighter than she ever did, and it makes him ache, the awareness of her vulnerability.

"Which way?" Leigh asks, twisting the weapon in her hands.

"There"—Rocky points back toward Candy Alley—"I came through there when I snuck in; the gate's on the other side."

"I'm not going back through that particular hell hole." Leigh shudders.

"What's back there? Like, it can't be worse than a revolving barbecue?" Candy asks and hopes there's not an answer that proves her wrong.

"Let's just say at least the Burny Bozos were cooking the meat before chowing down."

"Oh," Candy says, and when it sinks in, "Oh..." and she bites back the urge to ralph.

"Let's go around, then," Rocky says, and the three set off. They round the corner of Mari's smoldering tent, the flames spreading to a nearby souvenir stand.

"Shit, get down!" Rocky pulls Candy to the side, ducking down behind a bench, and Leigh follows.

Two clowns waddle up, carrying large drum buckets. The first one stands, legs wide apart, as he swings the barrel underarm, warming up and putting more energy into the throw with each swing.

"Are they really gonna put the fire out?" Candy asks.

The first clown tosses the bucket; a clear liquid soars through the air, and before it even touches the flames, it ignites, a gout of fire ripping through the air like a dragon's breath. It scorches the clown's spiky green mop, leaving behind singed ends and the scent of burning hair.

"Guess not," Leigh whispers. "Where did they even get that?"

"I think we need to stop asking why and just accept this whole carnival's fucked up beyond all recognition," Rocky adds.

The first clown stomps his feet and dramatically pats at his body, pretending as though he's on fire—the second one points and laughs. Just as the first clown stops his pantomime act, the second hurls his bucket—not at the fire but at the first clown, drenching him; the first clown sulks, his clothes and remaining hair sagging from the dampness.

"Wait, don't," Rocky mutters as the first clown takes a step back, closer to the burning tent, and the flames make the jump. The clown runs around, arms waving, his whole body consumed by fire as the second clown points and laughs, holding onto his gut, he finds the entire debacle that funny. Even when the first clown falls to the ground and stops moving, the second one keeps mocking him—even squats by the burning corpse and rubs his eyes dramatically.

"That's so wrong. They don't even care about each other," Candy whispers. "It's all a joke to them."

"Should we take him?" Leigh grips the sweet slugger tight. "It's just one. We can—"

"I don't think we're in any position to fight." Rocky draws Leigh's eye to Candy.

"There they are!" The shout comes from behind, and the three kids turn to see the Burnt Clown, pointing towards them.

His three fellow Cook Clowns take off like a pack of dogs, snarling and whooping.

The Hysterical Clown comes at them from the other side, forcing Rocky to head in the total opposite direction from the backyard. Leigh follows his lead, lollipop at the ready, and as one of the Cook Clowns gets close, she takes a swing. It misses, but the clown goes on its ass, trying to dodge the blow.

Candy does all she can to keep up with Rocky, but with her fucked up foot, it's only a matter of time before more of the clowns catch up. Rocky realizes this too, and before Candy can even suggest leaving her behind, he swoops her up into her arms.

"Hold on," Rocky states, and Candy wraps her arms around his neck. She really doesn't weigh all that much, and for the second time in so many minutes, Candy's tiny frame, her diminutive figure that she always cursed, works in her favor.

Rocky picks up speed, and Candy feels her hair whip in the wind.

"We gotta lose them!" Leigh yells from behind, swinging her lollipop at another pursuer.

More clowns join the chase, laughing wildly with the thrill of the hunt.

"Through there!" Rocky yells, and though he can't point, Leigh gets it.

Across the midway: the Mirror Maze. She hates those things, has traumatic childhood memories of thinking she saw the way out only to give herself a concussion running flat into a glass wall, but it's better than being run down by a pack of rainbow-colored maniacs.

Leigh leaps the fence, but Rocky takes the long way around with Candy in his arms. She waits by the door, weapon at the ready, and as soon as Rocky catches up, the three of them barge through.

"See if you can lock it," Rocky says as he leans over, setting Candy down on the floor in front of a wall-spanning mirror.

"Yeah, there's bolts! Quick!" Leigh shoves the door closed just as one clown rams it from outside—a too-white hand reaches through the gap, and more join it. "Little help!"

Rocky bashes his shoulder into the door, causing it to slam closed to delighted yelps of pain and squeaking from the clowns outside. Leigh pushes the top bolts up as Rocky kicks the lower ones into place, securing the door as the clowns outside beat against the metal with a furious frenzy.

In time they give up. Perhaps looking for another way in, or their attention span's so erratic they're already distracted by something, or someone else, to torment.

"I think we're alone now," Rocky says, and for a second, all the three of them can hear is the beating of their own hearts.

Candy laughs, breaking the silence, a deliciously delirious little titter, and for a second, Leigh and Rocky worry she's become one of them.

"The hell's so funny, Short Stack?" Leigh wants to know.

"Nothin'." Candy wipes away a tear of exhaustion. "It's just funny. You two make a pretty good team."

Rocky and Leigh look at each other, then turn away, both insulted at the suggestion and the unspoken truth behind it.

Candy's teasing pokes at the greatest vulnerability in their alliance. Rocky and Leigh are more similar than not, more so than either would care to acknowledge, yet the one thing that unites also divides them. Candy's safe, as much as she can be for now, and once they make it out of the carnival, both know the truce will not hold. Rocky wants Candy back, while Leigh wants to keep Candy safe from a handsome boy with heartbreak written all over his face.

They look to the large, warped mirror that Candy rests her back against; the twisted and deformed glass alters their reflections drastically, swapping places and proportions. The only thing unchanged is the girl between them on the floor.

Ruth leans closer till she's almost head to head with her reflection in the ring-side window to the aquarium. She grins back at herself, tapping the glass to no avail.

"Come now, Brucey. Momma has a treat for you."

She climbs a stepladder and stops a few rungs from the top, waiting for the shark to appear. In all the stories about Bonko, it's said he could summon the beast with a whistle, and yet Bruce ignores her. Unless blood is involved, that is. So be it; Ruth shrugs and climbs the last few steps. Standing over the open top, she bites down on a finger hard enough to draw blood—she spits it in the water, and a sudden flurry of waves responds.

In seconds, the bull shark bashes against the window with so much force it nearly knocks Ruth's ladder back.

"There's my boy!" Ruth calls, arms held out as though the shark could leap out of the water and embrace her. And soon, he will. Ruth reaches into her ringmaster's coat pocket and takes out a bag of black cotton candy.

"Daddy's missed you," Ruth coos and sprinkles the cotton candy over the aquarium as though it was fish food.

Bruce ignores it.

"Rude," Ruth scowls and then snaps her fingers. "Of course! Reese! Monkey Boy! I need a hand!" She holds her own out, waiting for her lackey to oblige. Moments later, Reese clambers over and places a freshly severed hand in Ruth's; blood still leaks from where it was torn free.

"Good boy." Ruth smiles at him and gives Reese his reward, a full-face slap with the hand. He falls to the ground, writhing in ecstasy, rubbing himself all over.

224

Ruth places the rest of the black cotton candy on the severed hand, closes the fingers around it, and tosses it into the water. It lands with a plop, tendrils of red slithering through the blue, and in a flurry of bubbles, Bruce races to swallow the hand whole.

The red haze of the water floods with other colors, with purple and orange and green, as the change comes upon the shark quickly.

"Welcome back to the family," Ruth grins. "Daddy's missed you, sweet baby."

"Sweet baby Jesus, the fuck happened here?" Leigh says as she looks at a dozen funhouse mirrors, all broken into thousands of shards that litter the floor like a twinkling night sky.

"I dunno, but somebody's gonna have about a hundred years of bad luck," Candy replies.

"Least it ain't us." Leigh's joke earns a "please don't" stare from both Candy and Rocky.

They head down a tight corridor, Leigh out front with her weapon ready to go.

"Fuck!" she yells and swings the sweet slugger at the wall to her right, making Candy and Rocky shuffle back.

"What is it!?" Rocky instinctively puts himself between the threat and Candy.

"Fucking clowns!" Leigh growls and punches a life-size clown mannequin mounted inside a hidden alcove. Three of the clowns line each side of the corridor, invisible till you step into it—all six posed like they're making faces in a mirror.

"Are they real?" Candy panics.

"They're dummies." Leigh smacks the closest one again.

"You sure?" Candy eyes the next clown warily. "Would be the perfect place for one of them to hide."

"Say no more, sister." Leigh tosses her weapon to Rocky and then punches each mannequin in the nuts. None of them react, apart from wobbling slightly on their base.

"You look like you enjoyed that," Rocky gulps.

"The little things make life worth living," Leigh smirks.

"Here." Rocky holds out the giant lollipop.

"Wait." Leigh holds a hand up to silence the other.

"What?" Rocky whispers.

"Missed one." She fake-outs, pretending to whack Rocky in the nuts, and he leaps back.

"Not cool," Rocky says with his heart and other things in his mouth.

Leigh snickers and snatches her weapon back and they head on, keeping watchful eyes on the stuffed clowns, just in case.

Their sneakers crunch on broken shards as they head down a winding corridor, more mirrors cracked and shattered lining the way. Whoever came through the halls didn't like what they saw in the mirror.

"You think they're still here?" Candy looks up at Leigh.

"They better fuckin' hope not." Leigh cracks her neck and tightens her grip on the lollipop mace.

"How is that thing still in one piece?" Rocky wonders.

"I know, right? Imagine what this sweet slugger would do to some kid's teeth. Dentist's wet dream."

"I'd have gone with Lolli-bop," Candy smirks.

"Shit." Leigh's in shock. "That's so much better..."

"He's looking at me; they're looking at me." Singing from the next hall makes the three of them stop and hush up.

"Shit." Rocky steps in front of the girls. Using his arm to hold them back, he creeps along to the end of the hall, carefully placing each step to avoid making a sound on the carpet of glass. The singing picks up, if you could call it that. It reminds Rocky of one of those wind-up dolls, but a broken one that's either too fast or too slow—always just off tempo.

The girl sits on the floor, her back to the door, legs open wide, and Rocky thinks he recognizes her. The beaten-to-hell blue and red Docs with mismatched leggings and a tutu skirt. It's that weird art chick, he realizes, only her hair is now full of blue, orange, and purple streaks. Fuck, what was her name? Rocky can't recall, but from the hair, the creepy singing, and the dark smears all over her arms, he sure as hell knows she's one of those crazy-ass killer clowns now.

Creeping back to the others, Rocky crouches down with them and whispers, "It's one of them. She's just sitting there, singing."

"Good." Leigh grips the lollipop. "We can take her."

"Wait." Rocky puts a hand on the weapon as something sits uneasily on his mind. Cliff said she was into him, just like Kat. "I have an idea. Maybe we don't have to hurt her."

"What!?" Leigh can't believe it; she's about ready to smash some clown ass.

"Let's hear him out." Candy, once again, bridges the gap between them.

"I think if we play along with them, they won't hurt us. One of them tried to." Rocky looks into Candy's eyes and realizes if he explains what he did with Mari, even if

227

it was the only way to survive, it's not gonna go over well given his recent mistakes. "Look, I played along before and it bought me time to escape. I think if we just humor her, we might have a chance to get through without anyone else dying."

"Fuck that." Leigh tenses up.

"Leigh"—Candy sees the guilt in Rocky's eyes, the weight of Kat's death weighing him down—"let's give it a shot."

"Urgh! Fine!" Leigh stands up. "But if Bozodonna out there tries anything, I'm gonna whack her so hard she'll think she's a virgin again."

They enter the hall together—Rocky out front, with Candy close behind him and Leigh at the rear, keeping the newly renamed lolli-bop low but ready all the same.

"He's looking at me, they're looking at me," Sully sings. "STOP LOOKING AT ME!" an entirely different person growls from within the clown.

The sudden change in tone makes the three jump, and Candy yelps. She covers her mouth, too late, as Sully snaps her head around and stares at the three of them.

Candy, Leigh, and Rocky hold their poses, not even wanting to breathe out of fear it might trigger the clown.

Sully raises a hand slowly and waves gently. "Hi."

"H-hi." Rocky returns her wave. "Um, I'm—"

"You're Pretty Boy." Sully tilts her head as she smiles. She then looks to the side, biting her lip, and whispers to nobody like she's telling them some scandalous secret. "I know. How did he get away from the Bazoomba Lady?"

"Who's—" Candy asks, and Sully interrupts.

"Sully thought you were dead, Pretty Boy." Her giggles and hair twirl says she's glad he's not.

"Um, this is cute 'n' all, but we really need to be going." Leigh takes a sideways step toward the exit, bringing Candy with her.

"Bleh!" Sully spits at them. "You're the Mean Girl, yucky."

"Huh," Leigh sneers. "Bitch—"

"Leigh, don't." Rocky stops Leigh from making a move. "Sully, right?" He steps towards the girl, leaning down to give her the eyes. "Can we go through? Is that OK?"

"Friends? Friends-friends-friends." Sully shuffles around, and then her eyes land on Candy. She gasps, "Your friend is hurt!"

Sully pads on her hands and knees across the floor, crawling past Rocky, and takes Candy's hand. She trembles but keeps her cool as Sully hovers dirty, bloody fingers over the cuts and scrapes. "Tiny Girl is hurt, no-no-no, no good." Sully fusses over the wounds but doesn't actually do anything to them.

Leigh catches Rocky's eye and tilts her head toward the exit, but neither are going anywhere while Sully's so fixated on Candy.

"Tiny Girl, Sully will help, yes!"

"Thank you, um, Sully." Candy looks to the others, and they shrug. Play along, she remembers, and does just that. "It's nice to meet you, Sully. My name's Candy."

"Candy?" Sully's red eyes dilate, and her lips pull black, sharp little fangs gleaming.

"We should—" Candy screams as Sully sinks her teeth into her hand, latching on like a junkyard dog.

"Fuck!" Rocky yells.

Leigh's already on the way, giant lollipop swinging overhead, but as she brings it down, Sully slips away, dodging the blow and leaving Candy holding a badly wounded hand, blood pumping between her fingers.

Sully cowers in the corner, but she's anything but afraid. She smiles as she chews on a piece of Candy's torn skin. "Tasty, tasty, Candy Girl." Sully's whole body shudders with delight.

Rocky swoops in and gets hold of Candy. He helps her over to the exit as Leigh gets between them and the clown.

"You like candy?" Leigh twirls the lollipop.

"Oh, yes!" Sully nods enthusiastically. "Yes-yes-yes!"

"Have some then!" Leigh goes at the clown with another swing, but she's just as fast, only this time a hidden knife flicks out, cutting up and catching Leigh on the arm. "Fuck!" Leigh drops the lollipop and only just manages to dodge a second swipe. This little bitch is faster than she looks, Leigh realizes, and she's backed halfway to the exit before she knows it.

"Come on!" Rocky yells by the back door.

Leigh doesn't like leaving the weapon behind; it's served them well, but that freaky bitch already has it, holding it up like she's that dude from Thundercats.

"Fuck." Leigh gives in, joins the others, and they bash through the exit together—coming face-to-face with the barrel of a sawn-off shotgun. All three hold their collective breath; the sudden shift from darkness to the bright lights of day temporarily blinds them, but as their vision returns, they see that it's Mack pointing the gun at them.

"Get down!" Mack orders, and all three kids hit the deck.

"Oh, poo," Sully gulps as Mack pulls the trigger.

KRAKA-BOOM!

The muzzle flashes. A wave of pellets blasts at such point-blank range they completely disintegrate the giant lollipop, spattering Sully's face and hair with sugary dust. "Whoops." She flashes a smile, then zips away as Mack breaks the gun, shakes the empty shells out, and pops two more in from his vest pocket.

Candy, Rocky, and Leigh stay down, ears ringing. Mack reaches down with one hand, offering it to Rocky.

He accepts, and Rocky lets Mack pull him to his feet with slight hesitation. Before the big guy lets go of Rocky's hand, he sneers at the boy, telling him the war isn't over, but he'll call it a truce for now. There's a lot of that going on, and Rocky's grateful either way. He helps Candy to her feet as Mack does the same for Leigh.

"You kids OK?" Mack checks, and he doesn't need an answer. Leigh keeps the pressure on her cut. Candy does the same, leaning awkwardly to keep the pressure off her wounded foot, and though Rocky looks a little rough, it's not nearly as bad as the girls. Figures, Mack snorts. "Nevermind. Come on, let's get y'all dumb shits the fuck outta here."

Chapter Nineteen
DOWN AND OUT IN CANDY ALLEY

KRAKA-BOOM!

The shotgun thunders and blasts a clown clean off its feet—blood and rainbow confetti explode from the creep's chest like a popped balloon. Still grinning, it flops on its back as Mack and the others hurry past.

"Keep up," Mack orders and doesn't look back.

He turns the gun on another clown; this one looks like a hobo with a cigarette dangling from his lips. "Wait!" Hobo the Clown says as he throws his arms up and—*BOOM!* Mack takes him out; this one's head explodes into clumps of meat with no sparkles.

"Fuck! Mack! I think that was just a dude!" Leigh yells.

As Candy hobbles past the first dead clown, leaning more on Rocky than before, she tries not to look at the thing's exposed innards. Tries, but she can't help but stare at the vibrant blue and pink organs, at the spiderweb of black cotton candy that seems to be alive somehow. They're long gone before it begins to knit the wound back together.

"How the shit am I supposed to tell?" he yells. "This way." Mack nods toward a narrow path that leads to some bathrooms. All four skid to a halt as soon as they round the corner.

"You want some?" another clown giggles as it shuffles forward, hand held out.

The stink hits them, and they screw their faces up in disgust; Leigh dry retches, and Candy bites on her fist.

The clown's gormless, under-biting face is mostly smeared in brown, with only speckles of red poking through the filth. It shuffles towards them with sagging pants around its ankles, dragging them through the dirt. Whatever's in them's pretty weighty and keeps the clown pretty much to a crawl. It shakes the offered hand, clumpy brown contents slopping around.

"It's the go-o-o-od stuff." The clown smiles and shoves a handful of shit into its mouth, hungry tongue licking at the remaining nuggets stuck to his hand. The joy on its face gives a whole new meaning to the phrase shit-eating grin.

"Fuck this." Mack retches but stops himself from throwing up. "I dunno, Leigh, does Shiggles here look like a regular old clown?"

"Here you go." Shiggles shuffles forward.

"Doesn't matter." Leigh throws up in her mouth, then spits it on the ground. "Shoot the bozo either way."

Mack levels the sawn-off with one hand, breathes in, and squeezes the trigger. ***BOOM***—the blast paints the wall behind Shiggles the Clown with red, pink, and blue spatter like someone blew up a bag of meat in a crayon factory.

Evidently, the shit in the clown's pants wasn't just his own, as it voids its bowels—fresh steaming clumps clop into the pile as it takes one more step and topples over.

"Come on." Mack takes a step towards the corpse.

"Fuck no," Leigh says as she covers her mouth.

"Gotta be another way," Rocky agrees.

"You dumb shits wanna go back out there with more of those whackos?" Mack breaks the shotgun open and lets the spent shell clink to the ground.

"Fair point." Rocky nods.

Each of them holds their nose and tiptoes through the butt tulips. They come out back in Candy Alley, and for a second, Rocky and Leigh are about to tell Mack to stop. Warn him about the all-you-can-eat cannibal buffet. The smoking remains of the shit-eating clowns and the confident way he reloads the sawn-off, flipping it shut with a flick of his thick wrist, says they'll be all right.

"Keep up," he orders and heads on through a sugar cane gate into Candy Alley.

"Wake up!"

Cut to: Stacey taps on Cliff's sleeping, chubby cheeks, and when that doesn't do the trick, she winds up and slaps him hard.

Cliff scatters to life, scooting back, confused. "I swear I wasn't—Stacey?" He backs up to the bars of a carriage, thick metal ones closing off an archway of red and yellow wood. It's dark inside, with a musty, moth-eaten canvas covering much of the bars, letting only slivers of lights filter through. "What's going on, Stacey? Last thing I remember—" Cliff rubs his head, and his hand comes away with rusty, dried bits of scab.

"You've been snoring and farting. That's what's been happening," Stacey pouts. "And scratching your little—" She wiggles her pinky to elaborate.

Ordinarily, Cliff would explode with some hyperbolic threat against his sister—it's his love language—but after thinking she was gone, he scrambles across the floor of the lion cage and takes her up into his arms.

234

"Ew! Gross!" Stacey protests but doesn't stop her brother from hugging her nearly to death. Her eyes begin to water. "Lemme go! Your B.O.'s making me cry."

Cliff pulls back and looks at his little sister, keeping a hand on both of her shoulders. She's pale but normal pale, not the white-faced clown kind, and though there are dark circles under her eyes, they're marks of exhaustion, nothing more.

"You're back to normal!"

"No doy! You're such a spaz!" Stacey tries to poke fun, but Cliff's outpouring of love wears her down.

"I swear, we're getting outta here, and then I'm gonna buy you all the Barbies they have at the mall!"

"I—" Stacey doesn't know what to say. "You better!"

"Aw, well ain't this cute!" A hysterical laugh follows, and Cliff looks behind his sister to see a hunched-up, knotted mess of a man clinging to the bars. A debased semicircle of a mouth grins below twinkling beady eyes, making the stringy sideburns twitch as it chuckles. The thing looks more monkey than human to Cliff. Like someone loaded face paint into a shotgun and let off both barrels below their chin, and yet it speaks. "Ruth's gonna love this!"

Cliff's head's still spinning, and it's only then he realizes it's the same freaky monkey clown who jumped him earlier. "The hell do you want with us!?" Cliff pulls Stacey in close, holding her head to his chest so that she doesn't have to look at the twisted thing.

Reese limps away, chittering excitedly, calling Ruth's name over and over.

He can hear her approach, footsteps striding through the dirt with bold confidence, and Cliff winces as one side of the canvas sheet flies up. Searing stage lights burn

Cliff's eyes briefly before an out of proportion silhouette moves in like an eclipse.

"Ah, you're awake at last," she says, and as Cliff's eyes adjust, he makes out the wide, spiraling smile that extends down the chin and shark-like eyes of Ruth Hardstack. "Good!"

"—thing you came along when you did, Mack."

Cut to: Leigh and Mack as they take the lead down Candy Alley. Mack keeps his head on a swivel as he checks the booths and blind spots between them, but they haven't seen any living clowns since the two Mack blasted before.

"Yeah, well, I saw your scrawny ass headin' into the Mirror House with Footloose over there." Mack nods back, over his shoulder, to Rocky and Candy, following a few yards behind. "Shoulda known you wouldn't do what you're told. You're worse than a kid, you know?"

"Speaking of, how's Sally-Jo?"

"Ha! She'd give you a run for your money," Mack smirks. "Just turned nine last week. Sure as shit glad I didn't let her come today." He shoots another look back, this one at the tiny, bloody, and beaten-up blonde girl, and doesn't feel he needs to point out she's lost an awful lot of blood.

"How's the leg?" Rocky asks as Candy grunts, accidentally putting more weight on it than she meant to.

"Not as bad as the hand."

"You always get hurt at the fair." Rocky smiles at a memory from a happier time. "Remember the school fair? When the Whirler got you all dizzy."

"Yeah, I stood up and—"

"Clunk!" they say together. "Bar comes right down on your head."

"Ouch, don't remind me." Candy also smiles at the memory, despite the pain and the bruise she had to cover in her yearbook photo. "You stayed with me in the nurse's office till my parents got me."

"Of course," Rocky says and feels, not unjustly, insulted that she'd be surprised he'd do that.

"I've really fucked things up, haven't I?" Rocky sighs.

"I think all things considered, you get a pass." Candy winces.

"You mean—?"

"No." Candy shakes her head. "No."

"I still love you. I never stopped. I—"

"I love you, Rocky." Candy frees herself from his support and leans against a stand. The other two ahead notice and give her a moment to rest without a word, Mack scanning their surroundings with the gun at the ready. "I do," Candy continues.

"Yeah?" Rocky takes a rest beside her. "Then, why?"

"Because you're going places. You've got this amazing life ahead of you, just waiting, and I can't just tag along, watching from the sidelines like a cheerleader, you know?"

"I don't care about that. I'll never run again if it means I can be with you, Candy. I—"

"I know, Rocky, I know, and that's why I can't let you stay. I can't be the thing that holds you back. Might make us both happy today, eventually..." Candy puts a hand on his cheek. "You were born to run, and I'm just a small-town girl." Her eyes tear up. "But despite current events, I wouldn't have had things any other way."

"For sure?"

"Yeah." Candy pats his face, and Rocky savors her touch, drinks in the last few precious tingles of love between them. He'd stay there all day, surrounded by the dead, if only to drag out what little time they still have together.

"So"—thinking of something to distract himself from his breaking heart—"so, how does Leigh know Roadhouse over there?" Rocky nods to Mack and Leigh.

"Oh, Mack was Leigh's mom's boyfriend when Leigh was little. Her dad, you know he died, right?"

"I didn't." Rocky feels like a shitheel for that. He never liked Leigh all that much, but she's Candy's best friend, and he should have made an effort for her, at least.

"Yeah, Mack was kinda like her dad for a while, till high school. Even though they split up, he still checks in on Leigh, especially after her mom..."

"Jesus," Rocky sighs. "She's not had it easy." And just like that, it all makes sense, all the bad attitude and bullshit.

"She's amazing."

"Yeah," Rocky has to admit. "I couldn't—I mean, I don't think I'd be half as strong as she is if I went through all that." He watches Mack say something to Leigh; he can't hear it, but he sees the fatherly concern on his furrowed face. A love that survived a breakup and death. That's something of a bittersweet comfort to him, that even breaking up with Candy doesn't mean he has to stop loving her because honestly, he doesn't think that's even a possibility.

"You guys came back for your friend?" Mack asks, wiping his mouth with the back of his hand.

"Well, duh." Leigh winces as she pokes at her cut.

"She's lucky to have you two morons," Mack snorts.

I'm lucky to have her, Leigh says to herself, the words rising from a place deep inside her chest. It's a thought that fills her with foolish optimism as they go on the move again and reach the bend in Candy Alley. The roof of the frozen banana stand looms over on the far side. They round the corner, and the goofy smile on Leigh's face turns to sickening disgust as she feels her heart drop to her stomach.

"Clark!" Leigh races to the boy, skidding down on her knees like she's playing ball, kicking up a cloud of dust. "Clark!" She grabs hold of the kid's cold, dead body and shakes it to no avail. He lies on his back, jaw broken open and stuffed full of yellow and brown tentacles, sprinkled with rainbow droplets, chocolate sauce, and blood dried hard against his skin. "Clark!" Leigh yells again like it's going to do any good. The boy's colder than the frozen bananas rammed down his throat.

Candy and Rocky race to catch up and skid to a halt as they see her stepbrother's corpse.

"Oh, no." Candy's response is weak, the fight sapped out of her by the shock, but it's sincere nevertheless. She limps over and kneels with Leigh, wrapping her arms around her. "I'm so sorry, Leigh, I'm so sorry!"

"He's not dead." Leigh trembles, a coldness flowing through her veins, dulling all sensation. "No, not Clark, not him too." Something inside her breaks. "Mom. Dad. Clark? Not, not him too, not him, no—"

"Shit," Mack curses as he spots some figures cavorting at the far end of Candy Alley. They haven't seen Mack and the kids yet, but it's only a matter of time if Leigh keeps on like she is. "We gotta move."

Rocky sides up with Mack and they share a nod. Mack heads on, sawn-off at the ready, to deal with the clowns.

239

Leigh's hand hovers over Clark's face, shaking as she's unable to bring herself to touch him. "Where are your glasses?" Leigh asks like it's the most normal thing in the world. "Your mom's gonna kick your ass if you've lost another pair, doofus."

Rocky drops to his knees on the other side of Leigh. "Guys, we gotta book, like yesterday—" The **_BOOM-BOOM_** of both barrels going off interrupts him. "We can't stay here."

"Clark can't go anywhere without his glasses," Leigh says and starts searching the ground in vain for them. "He—"

"You can't do anything for him anymore, Leigh! Shit, look, I know it sucks—" And another thought intrudes. Cliff was going back for Clark, so what happened to his best friend and Stacey? "Leigh, we have to go. Now."

"I'm not going anywhere without my brother," Leigh insists.

"He's right." Candy tries to talk some sense into Leigh, but that was a tall order under normal circumstances. "I'm sorry, but we have to—"

"I'm not leaving him!" That snaps something inside Leigh; the dam breaks. She yells so loud it draws wild calls, hoots, and giggles from beyond the shacks and stalls of Candy Alley.

"Fuck, they're coming. We don't have time for this." Rocky catches Candy's eye, and she gets it. Rocky slips his arms under Leigh's from behind and pulls her away from Clark.

"No!" she screams, digging her heels in as Candy follows, taking one of Leigh's hands and trying to both guide and calm her. "Clark!"

Two more **BOOMS** reverb through the stalls, and a curse follows. "You dumbass kids better move y'all's asses. I only got five of these left."

Rocky can barely keep Leigh restrained, and just as she slips free, Mack swoops in, picking her up in his massive arms.

"Clark!" Leigh reaches out, kicking wildly as Mack pins her to his chest with one hand, the sawn-off gripped tight in the other, and carries the wailing girl away from her dead brother, trying to keep his focus and cool all the while her pain, her suffering, tears him up inside.

Rocky pauses at the exit and gives one look back at the body on the ground. "Shit, Cliff. Bro, where the hell are you?"

Chapter Twenty
ROCKY'S GIRL

Cut to: Cliff takes two steps through the door before Reese shoves him, hard, and sends the kid down on his face. With his hands bound behind him, there's nothing he can do to break the fall. He groans and feels his lip burst against his teeth.

"Watch where you're goin', ya little shit!" Reese hollers, enjoying the cruelty while also seething with envy.

"That's enough, Monkey Boy," Ruth declares, though she doesn't turn away from the large picture window overlooking the ring.

Reese hops over, squatting by Cliff's side, and attempts to help the boy sit up.

"Get the fuck away from me!" Cliff bashes the clown with his shoulder and gets to his feet on his own. "Where's my sister?" The question answers itself when he looks over the desk and sees her, held tight by Ruth's side. Stacey shivers, too terrified to even cry. "Stacey! I swear to God, hurt her, and I'll rip your fucking throat out with my teeth!"

"Calm yourself down," Ruth half turns and sneers, "dude. I'm not going to do a thing to her. You are."

"The fuck you say!?"

"Reese! Monkey Boy, fetch!"

Reese slinks out of the office, shooting Cliff a disgruntled eye.

"You're fortunate, you know that, boy?" Ruth returns her attention to the work going on below. She buzzes on the inside with anticipation but remains in control of her calm yet domineering composition.

"Sure, tell you what, let me and my sister go, and I'll pick some lottery numbers for you."

Ruth laughs, a single chortle. "Do I look like a woman concerned with something as vulgar as money?"

"Lady, no offense, but you look like you're batshit fucking crazy."

"Spectacle!" Ruth pumps and clenches a fist, drawing it down across her body. "Grandeur." She turns around, bringing Stacey with her, and grins at Cliff, painted lips spiraling up in line with her eyes. "Family."

Reese clangs in through the door again, sulking as he shuffles across the room. He slams down a bag of the black cotton candy on the desk and waddles back out, sneering at Cliff again on the way.

"What's his problem? Nobody eat the lice outta his hair today?"

"Reese doesn't approve of what I'm about to offer you, boy. You see, somehow, you took this child away from us." Ruth rubs her meaty, too-white fingers across Stacey's face, and it's all Cliff can do to keep himself from leaping over that desk. "She was chosen."

"Yeah, by who?"

"By Bonko, of course." Ruth says the name of the dead clown as though it makes perfect sense. "Of all those present at his return, some were chosen to join the carnival. Drawn to the taste of blood, destined to be a Child of the Candy. Like this precious little one." Ruth's finger pushes its way into Stacey's mouth. "And you took her from us!" Stacey screams as Ruth lifts her by the neck.

243

"Please! Don't!" Cliff begs, dropping to his knees. "Don't hurt my sister."

"I already told you, that's up to you." Ruth tosses the girl across the room; she lands on a carpet, thankfully, and scurries into the corner. Cliff puts himself between her and the Ringmaster Clown.

Ruth picks up the bag of cotton candy, holding it in her palm like something precious. She takes a few powerful strides across the room, and Cliff steels himself for whatever she's about to do.

"How did you do it?" Ruth gets right in Cliff's face. He can taste the rancid sugar on her breath.

The insulin, Cliff realizes. It helps the body break down sugars. Whatever's in that cotton candy that's turning people into freaky ass clowns must work like sugar and insulin fucks with it. He's not about to tell her that, though.

"She never ate the whole thing," Cliff says, and it's the truth. "I smacked it out of her hands before she could. It must not have been enough of whatever that shit is to make her stay all Ronald McMurder."

"Hmm." Ruth squints like she doesn't quite buy it, but it's believable enough for her to entertain the possibility.

Cliff's fingers find their way to his back pocket, but the kit's missing. Shit, he curses to himself, it must have fallen out in the cage or the wheelbarrow.

"If that's the case." Ruth takes out a knife, and Cliff gulps as she brings it in close. She reaches around and slices his bonds—Cliff immediately begins trying to rub some sensation back into his wrists. He stops when he notices Ruth holding out the bag of black cotton candy. "Take some," she orders, shark eyes gleaming.

Cliff reaches into the bag, tearing off a small piece of the jet-black fluff.

"That's enough for either you or her," Ruth smiles. "One of you will join us for the Grand Blow-Off! The other likely won't live to see the morning." Ruth stands up, pocketing the cotton candy, and strides across to the door, leaving Cliff on his knees with a small patch of the stuff crystalizing between his fingers.

"Wait? What?" Cliff turns to the big clown. "What are you saying—"

"You know exactly what I'm saying, boy!" Ruth half turns, grins, and as she closes the door, she makes things very simple. "Choose."

Rocky and Candy reach the back gate first, and as they look around for how to open it from this side, Mack whistles. Turning, Rocky reacts quickly enough to catch the keys Mack tosses him, and he fiddles with the door as the security guard sets Leigh down.

"You cool now?" Mack leans in, waiting for Leigh to meet his eyes. He reaches out to place a comforting hand on her shoulder, and Leigh swats it away.

"No! How the fuck could I be?! Clark's dead." Finally admitting it hits Leigh like a sudden wave of cold from an open freezer. "My brother's dead, and it's my fault."

"No, kid, it's not," Mack tries, but Leigh's already sunk too deep into the freshly uncovered well of pain within.

"Everyone I love dies. Dad, Mom, Clark..." Leigh's eyes turn to Candy as she and Rocky pull the gate open. It's only a matter of time, she thinks.

"None of that was your fault, kid," Mack says.

"Yeah?" Leigh's defiance breaks through the sorrow. "Who made Clark camp out overnight so we could skip the queue? Who was the screaming baby Dad went to the store to get formula for in the middle of the night? Well? Who was throwing a goddamn tantrum in the car

245

when Mom lost control?" Leigh slaps her chest. "This bitch, that's who!"

Mack doesn't know what to say to that. He sees Leigh's logic and that because of the way she feels right now, there's no way to make her realize how twisted it is. The way her head is right now, she's never going to accept that a baby isn't accountable for a hold-up gone bad, for a patch of black ice, for a damn carnival full of killer psycho clowns.

"Doesn't feel right, leaving him there." Leigh resigns herself to moving on, physically at least.

"We get out, get help, the cops will get him."

Leigh thinks about the crazy little cannibal bitch who bit Candy. "If there's anything left."

As the four of them creep through the trailer lot, everyone except Leigh watches the corners and shadows. She, however, can't take her eyes off Candy. Specifically, the way she seems all close with Rock-For-Brains again. She's over his bullshit, it appears, letting him hold her like that, putting her arm around his shoulder like she does. They're awfully close, and it burns Leigh up seeing that. Why couldn't it have been him... She doesn't finish that thought, stops herself, but it's in her all the same.

"Shit!" Mack curses as Candy turns, hiding her face in Rocky's chest. Only Leigh misses it at first, but as she snaps out of her mental descent, she sees what's up.

Someone's gone and wrapped an obscene amount of padlocked chains across the back exit gates; they criss-cross the fence like banners on the Fourth of July. That's not the most fucked up part, though; no, that's the former metalhead guard who's tied to the gate, arms and legs stretched wide though neither appendages nor his head, for that matter, are attached to his torso. It reminds Leigh of a dissection diorama from biology class.

"Jesus shat the bed," Mack curses while Rocky shields Candy's head.

"What do we do now? We're supposed to meet Cliff and"—he shoots Leigh an awkward glance—"Stacey back here." Rocky's silently glad there's no sign of Cliff and tries not to think about what that could mean.

Your friend's dead.

The thought pops into Leigh's head, uninvited, as does the next.

Or he better be, if he got Clark killed...

"Is there any other way out of here?" Candy feels faint. "I can't keep going. I'm gonna—" She doesn't finish. Everything goes woozy and she falls into Rocky's arms.

"Candy! Candy, stay with us." Rocky helps her maintain balance.

"Come on." Mack heads back toward the trailer lot. "We need to figure this out, and we sure as shit can't stay out here."

"Where we going?" Rocky asks, lifting Candy up into his arms.

"My trailer, patch your girl—"

His girl, Leigh snarls silently.

"—up, restock Betsy here"—Mack waves the sawn-off—"and see if we can't think up a way outta this shithole."

Rocky nods and follows. Leigh, too, though with her eyes burning a hole in the back of Rocky's leather jacket.

Cliff stares at the black cotton candy, and his eyes flit from the fluff to his sister. There really is only one choice he can make, but that doesn't mean he's in any kind of rush to go through with this.

"I don't want it," Stacey says as though she can read Cliff's mind. "I don't wanna be one of those things again. It's scary."

"I know," Cliff sighs. "I know. But you gotta."

"No—"

"Stacey, listen." Cliff approaches his sister and gets in close. He lowers his voice, just in case the clowns are listening. "I cured you once. I can do it again; you just gotta play along long enough for me to find a way outta this."

Stacey wipes away a tear. "How?"

"Rocky," Cliff says with absolute certainty. "When he sees we're not at the gate, he'll come looking. I know he will."

"And," Stacey sniffs, "Leigh too?"

Cliff nods. "Her too. Believe it."

"Even though all you gots is a—" Stacey waggles her pinky, sadly.

"Even so." Cliff smiles. It's good to see a bit of the old Stacey still in there. He keeps that smile as he holds out the piece of black cotton candy. "I'll see you on the other side, 'kay?"

Stacey's lips tremble as she opens her mouth and lets her brother place the cotton candy on her tongue like a carnivalesque communion wafer.

The change is quicker with a full dose of the cursed sugar this time. Stacey's body twitches erratically, her head snapping at random angles as her teeth gnash.

"I'm scared!" Stacey cries, and Cliff pulls her in close, wrapping his arms around the girl. He holds her tight to his chest as she thrashes, as her cries turn to cackles.

"Me too, brat." Cliff squeezes his eyes shut. "Me too."

He stays like that, even as Stacey begins to scratch and bite at him as the clown takes over. It takes Ruth yanking

248

him away to separate the two, and before Cliff can get to his feet, he feels the pinching grip of Reese's paws pinning him to the floor. The sniveling clown digs his black ringed nails in, savoring the flicker of pain that Cliff bites down on.

"Welcome back to the carnival!" Ruth greets Stacey the Clown with wide, open arms.

"I wanna play!" Stacey titters, bouncing on her heels like she's on a sugar high.

"Oh, sweet child, you will." Ruth takes a knee and lovingly strokes Stacey's hair. She looks into the child's black-ringed eyes and says, "But first, how did the boy change you back?"

"Dinky-Winky didn't say!" Stacey pouts, and then her eyes light up with wicked delight. "Buuuuuut, I know where his friends are gonna be!"

"Stacey! No!" Cliff pleads, and his lights go out as Reese whacks him over the head again.

"She's alive. Unconscious, but alive."

Cut to: Mack laying Candy on his bed at the back of his trailer. "Bleeding stopped, but I'm gonna be surprised if she doesn't need a transfusion."

Leigh stands by the threshold, arms crossed, a silent guardian. Mack reaches to take her wounded arm, and Leigh refuses. "I'm fine," she declares and pushes past him, going over to the bed and sitting down beside Candy.

"Suit yourself," Mack says and heads over to the sink to wash up.

In the bedroom, Leigh takes Candy's hand. It's cold and so much smaller than she ever realized. Her free hand very much wants to reach up and stroke the girl's face, so that's just what it does. Keeping their fingers

249

entwined, Leigh lies down and places her forehead against Candy's.

"You're so pretty when you sleep," Leigh whispers and closes her eyes.

Flashback to: Leigh's house, sometime in the middle of the night, to a room lit by the glow from a TV.

It shines on the two girls, tangled up in a mess of blankets and pillows on the floor, and a voluptuous woman with big hair, a punk rock attitude, and a valley girl accent talking about some old British horror movie. The volume's low; Leigh doesn't want to wake Candy as she lies on her side, her mouth slightly parted and snoring gently, but the temptation to sneak off, get her camera and capture Little Miss Barton in all her un-glory bites at her. The desire to just be there, to lie beside the girl, to sink into the warmth of this moment is even more powerful, so that's just what Leigh does.

Some of Candy's hair slides down, unfurls across her face, and curls into her nose. Leigh watches her face twitch like a rabbit sniffing the air. Leigh tries not to laugh as she brushes the stray hair aside, and her fingers linger there, just behind those cute elf ears.

Leigh's eyes wander, down the dangling cleft of Candy's nightie, into the shadows below, and her lips feel so incredibly dry all of a sudden. As she raises her eyes, Leigh jumps as they meet Candy's. The girl's mouth opens to speak and—

"Leigh?" Candy says. "Leigh, you OK?"

"Shit!" Leigh's eyes jerk open. She must have fallen asleep. What the hell, she thinks, I wasn't even tired. "Did I—"

"It's OK." Candy strokes her arm. "You must have just crashed out. You were smiling; nice dream?"

Leigh's eyes flick from Candy to her chest, then away, to anywhere else but the girl. "Yeah," is all the answer she gives and then climbs out of bed. Candy follows, and Leigh halts her. "I'm just gonna see what Wingus and Dingus are up to. You should rest till we need to go."

Candy can't argue with that; she feels like she weighs ten times her weight, so she flops back down with a lazy salute. "Yes, sir!"

Something about that gives Leigh pause, then she shakes it off as she heads out front.

Rocky's at one of the windows, peering through the blinds as discreetly as possible. Mack sits at the kitchenette table, shells lined up in rows as he cleans the gun. The lights are low, with just a small overhead one on to let Mack see what he's doing.

"Fuck me, how long's it been?" Leigh asks, noting the distinct lack of light filtering around Rocky.

"Thirty, forty minutes, maybe," Mack says without looking up.

"You're shitting me. The hell are we still doing here!?"

"Keep it down," Mack warns her.

"Yeah, couple of those fuckers went heeheeing past here about five minutes ago," Rocky adds.

"All the more fuel to the *why the fuck are we still here* fire then!?"

Mack puts his cleaning kit down. "There's no other way out," he says with grim resignation.

"What do you mean? There's no way they built a whole carnival with just the front and back gate. That's nowhere near up to code? Right?"

"Yeah, except this one happened to be built by a four-foot-tall Tony Montana," Rocky explains.

251

"It's true," Mack clarifies. "Front gate for the mooches, back for the real business. Hookers, blow, all that shit. Bonkin' didn't want any narcs or rivals sneaking into his kingdom. Sealed this place up tighter than a nun's asshole."

"Thanks for that mental image. Well then, Saint Mack of the Midway, what's the plan?"

"You're looking at it." Mack loads two shells into Betsy. "Way I figure it, bunch of folks got out before Hardstack slammed the gates. Been maybe two hours. Can't be more than another before the staties show up. We lay low, keep our cool"—he cocks the sawn-off—"and blow the fuck out of anything with a red nose that comes through that door."

"It's not a plan," Leigh sighs and looks back to Candy, wounded and resting on the bed. "But fuck else can we do?"

"Yeah, well, I can't sit on my ass doing nothing." Rocky steps back from the window. "Cliff's out there; Stacey too. I gotta—"

"Stay away from that door, kid," Mack warns. "You go out there, you might let all those honkers know where we are."

"Try and stop me." Rocky heads for the door, and Leigh blocks him. "Out of my way," he warns her. "Cliff's—"

"What? Gonna end up like my brother?"

"Leigh... shit, we don't know—"

"You're friend"—Leigh pokes Rocky's chest—"was supposed to get my brother, keep him safe, and how did that end!? Huh!? You want Candy to end up like that, too!?"

"Watch it." Rocky glares at her.

252

"You don't give a fuck about her," Leigh scoffs, "not really. She's just a thing to you. You don't love her—"

"Like you do?" Rocky takes Leigh's finger and shoves it away. It's his words that stun her more than the gesture, though.

"Wh-what do you mean?"

"Oh come on, Leigh. Jesus Christ, how can you not know? It's so fucking obvious."

"Oh, go fuck yourself; no, actually, go fuck your tiny-dicked friend. I mean, you're all fired up to go get him while Candy's out of it back there!" Leigh looks to Mack for help, and he smartly avoids her eyes. "If anyone's—"

"No, you hate me because you wish you were me! You want Candy, everyone knows it 'cept you."

"I-I-I-don't." Leigh's face flushes red, and she spins without moving. "I'm not... Candy—"

"Guys?" Candy asks from the bedroom door. "What's going on?"

No one knows how to answer that, nor do they have to. The lights go out just as the moment grows awkward, and static erupts from speakers outside the trailer.

"Ladies and gentlemen, boys and girls," Ruth's worryingly cheery voice echoes, "you're all invited to Bonkin's Bontastic Blow-Off!"

Chapter Twenty-One
ATTACK OF
THE WERECLOWNS

Ruth's lips curl into a sinister snarl, bearing sugar-blackened teeth as she speaks into the microphone mounted to her desk.

"Roll up, roll up! Come one, come all, to the biggest show in town!"

She throws her arms back, making a grand gesture for an audience of none. Ruth's alone in her office, and yet her ears ring with applause and praise, gasps of delight and horror.

Behind her, through the picture window, clowns march and prod unwilling audience members into seats around the ring, some of them bound in brightly-colored rope, holding fresh wounds and flinching at every cavorting clown.

"It's almost showtime!" Ruth's glee borders on hysteria. "We're just waiting for the guests of honor..."

"They're coming," Leigh says, somewhat glad for the distraction. So many confusing thoughts are swirling around in her head. It's almost a relief to deal with the psycho clowns again.

"Relax." Mack gets up from the table and heads to the front of the trailer. "They don't know where we are." He puts his side to the wall and peeks through the curtain with no reaction. "Cut the power to the whole backyard, by the looks of it. Keep quiet, and we're good."

"Till they start going trailer to trailer," Rocky points out.

"Rock-For-Brains has a point," Leigh relents. "What if the bozos go all Balloonnacht on us?"

"Then my point about blasting those red-nosed shits stands," Mack snaps. "Now keep it down."

A tense moment of silence passes.

"I can't. Cliff—" Rocky makes for the door, and Mack moves to block it. "Let me past."

"Ain't nothin' doin', Ferris. Now sit your ass down 'fore I make you."

For a second, Rocky contemplates sucker-punching Mack, but the idea passes. He doubts he could hit the guy hard enough even to tickle him. The dude looks like his muscles have muscles, after all. Besides, he knows from experience there's more than one way out of these trailers.

The touch of a tiny hand on his stops him dead. He looks down to see Candy holding his hand with both of hers.

"If you go back out there, you could get yourself killed," Candy says, like it would be the worst thing in the world. Knowing that they're over, and he'll never share another quiet moment of intimacy with her, that he'll never hold her little head against his chest as she wraps her arms around his waist, Rocky wholeheartedly disagrees with that sentiment. Without her, he's bound to wither and die, so he might as well do that trying to help his friend.

"Look, guys, Cliff wouldn't be here if it wasn't for me. Stacey either." Rocky takes a deep breath and then kneels upon unstable ground with one last plea. "Leigh, you gotta know where I'm coming from. If it was—"

"Don't you fucking say it—"

"You know you'd be right back out there, kicking seven shades of shit out of everything that honks just to find him."

"Fuck you," Leigh spits. It's a low blow, and Rocky's a dick for taking that shot, but he's not wrong. "Let him go," she says to Mack.

"Who the shit put you in charge, kid?" Mack snorts.

"Fine," Leigh sighs. "Tillman's Roadhouse, Valentine's Day last year."

"You wouldn't?"

"Try me."

Mack locks his eyes with Leigh and grunts when she refuses to back down.

"We're square now." Mack slides away from the door. "Yeah?"

"Eh," Leigh shrugs, "squarish."

Candy and Rocky stare on with complete confusion, no idea what any of this means.

"Keep your head down and stick to the shadows, shit bird," Mack warns Rocky as he heads to the door. "Once you're out that door, don't come back; you find your friends and lay low till the cops get here, got me?"

Rocky nods then says to Leigh, "Keep her safe?"

"You know I will." Leigh crosses her arms.

Rocky wants to wish Leigh luck. First for making it through the night and then for what will come after. He shouldn't have said what he did, but it's out there, and he can see it in her face, Leigh's feelings for Candy coming at her like a tsunami.

"Please don't," Candy pleads for Rocky to stay. "I..."

256

"Hey." Rocky lifts Candy's chin to meet her sad, watery eyes. "No way any of these clowns can keep up. I'll be fine."

His farewells said, Rocky heads to the door and pumps himself up on the spot. "OK, ready."

Mack pulls the door open, holding it ajar for the kid, and he only takes two steps before his eyes bulge and jaw drops.

"Hiya, Pretty Boy!" Sully waves from the bottom of the steps. She lunges toward them with a high-toned snarl just as Rocky leaps back. Her arm doesn't make it through before Mack can slam the door closed; only the tip of her knife does. It's flushed tight against the jam and snaps in two. "Rude!" Sully yells from outside. "You broke Mr. Stabby!" She cries like a child confronted with the death of a beloved hamster.

Mack braces his back to the door as angry fists and mismatched boots beat against it.

"How many are there!?"

Rocky, frozen in panic, doesn't answer.

"Shit bird! How many—"

"Just her!" Rocky snaps to attention. "Just the one I—"

The window on the other side smashes, and Candy screams as scrawny arms burst through the blinds. Unfazed by raw gashes carved open by the broken glass, they grab ahold of her hair and pull her up onto the table.

Mack and Leigh snap into action at the same time. She grabs a knife from the sink and brings it down into the too-white, hairy arm that looks like a bleached cactus. Even though Leigh sticks it right in, the clown doesn't let go. If anything, it holds on tighter. It does back off when Mack swoops up the sawn-off and blind fires out the window, the whole trailer flashing with brilliant light and filling with gunsmoke.

Rocky takes Mack's place by the door, flattening his back against it and digging his heels in.

"D'you get him?" Leigh asks as she pulls Candy into her arms, shielding her.

"I dunno." Mack cracks the sawn-off and replaces the single spent shell.

Candy trembles in Leigh's arms; the proximity to the shot has knocked her hearing out temporarily, and everything's just a buzzing drone that seems to jump around at random.

"You got any more of them?" Rocky nods to the gun as Sully takes a running kick at the door. Mack shakes his head.

"Preeeeeeety Boy!" Sully sings from outside. "The Big Lady says you gotta come and play with us! Stop! Being! Mean!"

"Somethin' tells me Sparkle Farts ain't meanin' Twister," Mack says.

"There's seriously no other way outta here?" Leigh asks. "Like, how did Bonko get away with half the shit he did with everything out in the open?"

"Maybe"—Mack thinks for a second—"Shit, it's gotta be. Folks used to say there was an old bootlegger tunnel. But—"

"Worth a shot, right!?" Rocky grunts as Sully throws her whole body against the door.

"Owie-owie-owie-ouch!"

"It's just a legend, and even if it's real, it's under the old Bonkin's House. Under the fuckin' Big Top."

"We—"

A crash and shattering of glass in the back cuts them off. They turn to see a heavyset clown standing in the

258

doorway like he's trying to stop them from getting to home base. Sagging pudgy cheeks with two off-balance red blush circles wobble as it chuckles and takes steady steps forward, hands waving with lustful cheer in time with a protruding, swishing gut.

"Shit, Leigh, your date's here," Mack says and then blasts the chubby clown in the gut, sending him sprawling back in a haze of red dust and sprinkles.

As soon as the big clown hits the floor, three things come scampering across its body. None of them can believe their eyes; it's three tittering toddler-sized clowns chuckling like a pack of hyenas. The fact that they're just little kids—fucked up clown kids, but children, all the same—stops Mack from unloading another round into one of them.

Leigh has no such compunction, and she gives Heehee a swift boot, sending the kid hurtling back through the bedroom window like a giggling football. Haha and Tinkle get past her and Candy—Haha climbs up onto the sofa and springs through the air, landing on Mack's face, while Tinkle runs at Rocky, latching onto his leg and biting down.

Candy's hearing and focus return, and she breaks with Leigh, going for the tiny terror nipping at Rocky's knee while Leigh dances around, avoiding Mack's swinging arms.

"Stand still!" Leigh orders.

"Get the little fucker off me! It's drooling everywhere!"

Leigh grabs the kid clown and pulls it off, spinning it around before she hurls it out the smashed window. It soars through the air with a "Wheeeee!"

Candy crosses the trailer, arms at full extension, with Tinkle snapping like an angry turtle. She drops the child

259

clown through the window, wincing at the sound it makes hitting the ground below.

Mack wipes moistness from his chin with the back of his arm. "Fuckin' gross ass kindergartener spit," he complains.

Leigh's eyes pop as she thinks about the warm yellow stains all over the kiddie clown's front. Best not to tell Mack that it's not just drool...

"Come on!" Sully begs at the door. "Pretty Boy! Candy Girl! I only wanna play witcha! I won't bite... OK, maybe a little!"

Chunky Clown sits up as much as he can with half his lower body looking like it's been through a blender. He takes a handful of brightly-colored innards—blue intestines and pink muscle tissue in his too-white hands—and examines them with curious awe. His blasted gut reeks, but not of bile and shit; it's more like over-sweetened cookies and spilled syrup.

"We gotta get out of here before one of these fuckers thinks to set the trailer on fire," Rocky says through gritted teeth. The very mention of fire makes Candy's eyes go wide, and he instantly regrets saying it.

"I think they want us alive," Candy gulps.

"So what?" Rocky doesn't get it. "Go with them? Play a round or two of Monopoly and call it a night?"

"Look what happened last time we tried that shit," Leigh points out. She doesn't need to remind him that that idea nearly cost Candy her hand.

"I wouldn't trust these fuckin' clowns as far as—"

"Hey there!" the monkey-like clown at the window interrupts and then zips down like some ratcheted-up whack-a-mole as Mack lets off another round. "Truce!" His head slowly rises to peek over the shattered glass and torn blinds. He grins, though it's more like someone drew a smile in a bowl of cold mashed potatoes. "Your friend is right; come along and play some games. That's all we want!"

"That so," Mack says with serious doubts.

"Uh, not you, Muscles," Reese chitters. "Only those three."

"You sayin' these kids will be safe if we let y'all in? What happens to me?"

Reese shrugs as he tries to act innocent and fails miserably.

Leigh can see him doing the math, working out this deal, and knows he's the kind of man who'll take it, lay down his ass for the three of them, and she's had enough of people she loves dying to let that happen. She shoves into Mack, taking him by surprise, and snags the gun from his hand.

"Leigh!" Mack protests as she takes aim and fires the last round at Reese.

The hunched, contorted clown shrieks and drops from sight as the spray rips the last of the blinds to shreds.

"There's no way we're trusting these bozos, and nobody's making some dumb heroic sacrifice. That shit's just for bad movies and Saturday-morning cartoons." Leigh stomps to the window. "You hear me, Bozo!? Get fucked—" She ducks down as something comes hurtling through the window, a blue blur that sails over her head and collides into Mack with a wet pop.

Mack shakes his suddenly soaked hair and beard; it's just a water balloon, only—

"Man, that stinks. Oh, fuck." Mack closes his eyes and tries to will away his disgust.

"Ew." Candy reels with instant shame, covering her mouth and nose.

261

"This can't be the first time you've gotten pee on you," Leigh sniggers. "Didn't you roadie for the Crue?"

"This ain't even the first time today!" Mack wipes his face with a dish towel and shoots a glare at Rocky.

"Sorry." Rocky flashes his best attempt at an innocent smile as Sully rams the door again.

A sudden blast of light fills the trailer, and Rocky thinks about those dumb alien books Cliff loves for the briefest of seconds. Shit about little towns disappearing overnight, people floating out of their bedrooms under intense light. That's all they need now, a goddamn UFO. The reality is so much stranger and worse.

"Guys, look!" Candy points through the main window at a pair of high beams blasting from a truck. "I think they're gonna—"

The truck revs forward, crashing into the trailer and sending the occupants scattering around like it's an earthquake. Rocky falls away from the door, and it flies open with Sully on the threshold.

Leigh stumbles, keeps her balance, and swings the sawn-off towards the clown girl and—click. Empty.

"Whoopsie!" Sully tilts her head, then grabs Rocky by the sneakers and drags him.

"Rocky!" Candy screams and clutches his outstretched hands, starting a game of tug-o-war with the crazy clown girl.

"Candy Girl," Sully grins and forgets all about Rocky. She clambers over him, oblivious to his grunts of pain as her mismatched Docs leave filthy prints across his back.

Candy shrieks, lets go of Rocky and crawls back away as Sully closes in, her rabid grin drooling with anticipation.

"Not so fuckin' fast, Bitey." Leigh steps over Sully, hooks an arm around her neck, and lifts the clown to her feet. Sully wiggles, giggling like she loves it, but can't get free. Leigh's bigger, tougher, and way too pissed off.

"Oh, poo!" Sully pouts. "You guys are no fun!"

Mack, sliding more rounds into the sawn-off, nods towards the dropped kitchen knife. Candy scoops it up and holds it to Sully's throat. The clown's eyes go wide, but she doesn't seem all that scared. If anything, the blade excites her.

"Oh, boy!" Sully smiles.

"Listen up, bozos!" Leigh yells out the open door. "We got your little sweet tooth bitch in here, so back the fuck off, or we'll turn her into a Pez dispenser."

"Yay!" Sully buzzes. "I love Pez!"

There's a bunch of murmuring and whispering from outside, done loudly enough to let the four of them know it's going on. None of them can pick out any words; it sounds like just a bunch of chittering gibberish done for effect.

"OK!" Reese calls. "We'll let you guys go if you let her go. Deal?"

"Do we trust them?" Leigh looks to Mack as he readies the sawn-off.

"Nope," he says and shoves the rest of the shells into his pockets. "You two"—he nods to Candy and Rocky— "over there"—then nods to the kitchen. Both of them grab a knife of their own. "OK," Mack yells out the window, "we're coming out. Any of you fuckers try shit, and your girl gets it first."

"Sure, sure," Reese snickers.

"They're gonna try something," Rocky warns.

"Oh, definitely." Mack looks to Candy. "So don't hesitate. One of those clowns makes a grab, you stick that knife in their neck. You hear me, kid?"

Candy nods nervously.

263

"Listen to me, kid, you shit your pants out there, and it's your pal or your boyfriend that'll get it, you hear me?"

Candy tenses up, grits her teeth, and nods, firmer this time. "I won't mess around."

"OK." Mack gives the kids one last look and hopes to God he's doing the right thing by them. "Let's do this."

They step out into the light, Mack first with the sawn-off resting on his forearm. The others follow, one at a time, starting with Leigh; she keeps Sully in a tight arm lock that does nothing to stop the clown's tittering.

"Fuck me, it's bright." Leigh squeezes her eyes shut; it's the best she can do. The others at least have a hand free to block some of the glare. "Now I know how Carol-Anne felt."

"You fuckers wanna dim those lights?"

"Oh, our bad," Reese giggles. "Kill the lights, boys!"

The high beams clunk out, and as their eyes adjust, they can see Reese squatting on the front of a pickup truck, hunched over like an oversized monkey-themed hood ornament. He taps the hood twice, and then both doors of the car open.

They spill out, one by one, two then four then six then eight then... too many to count in the gloom, with eyes still burning with dots of light. Too many clowns to fit even inside a big old pickup.

"Oh, fuck me," Leigh sighs as the clowns fan out, forming a barrier blocking the exit to this lot of trailers. More slink in from the shadows beside and behind them, around a dozen at least. The sun's gone down, and the full moon's out with the whole damn freakshow gathered beneath.

There's nowhere to go; they're entirely surrounded.

264

"I mean it. I'll pop this little bitch and watch her buzz around like a fuckin' balloon," Leigh warns the entire congregation of smiling, chuckling clowns.

"Do it." Reese bounces on his haunches. "Do it, do it, do it!"

"Mack," Leigh says out the side of her mouth, "I have a very fucked up idea." She lets go of Sully, kicking the girl in the butt as she staggers forward.

"Owie!" Sully complains, rubbing her backside as she stomps over to her fellow clowns. "You wasn't gonna really let them hurt Sully, was you, Mr. Monkey Man?"

Reese doesn't answer; he just grins.

"Oh," Sully sulks.

"Come along now," Reese nods to some hefty-looking clowns nearby, and they begin to approach. "Ruthie's waiting for ya!"

"Put the gun to my head," Leigh says.

"The fuck!?"

"Leigh!?"

"What!?"

"Just fuckin' do it before it's too late!"

Mack does what she asks, his hand trembling as he points both barrels at her. He makes sure his fingers are nowhere near the trigger, though.

The approaching clown heaves to a stop, grumbles, and looks back to Reese for instruction.

"Tell them you'll execute each of us before you let them take us," Leigh quietly instructs Mack.

"Leigh, shit, that's dark," Mack hushes back and then steels himself to put on a show. "Listen up, you red-nosed shit fuckers. I'll blast these kids before I let you get your pasty ass hands on them, you hear!?"

Reese raises a hand to the others, halting them for a moment while Mack's threat dances around his

265

misshapen head. He locks eyes with Mack across the lot, staring the big man down, and when he doesn't back off, Reese slams both hands down on the hood, making Mack jump.

"Shit!" Mack curses, and the other three wince as one. No shot rings out.

"Thought so," Resse laughs. "Get 'em!"

The horde of clowns surges forth, coming from everywhere all at once. Candy shrieks as one grabs her arm, trying to pull her away only for Rocky to cold clock him. Another one comes at them and doesn't even flinch as Candy slashes at it with her knife.

Reese hops down off the car's hood and holds out his hand. One of his fellow clowns puts a tire iron in it, and Reese hobbles forward, testing the weapon's weight.

Mack fires the sawn-off, taking off three-quarters of one clown's head, spraying Leigh with a spattering of blood and glitter. She spits.

"Tastes like sour candy!"

Mack is training the shotgun on another approaching clown when Reese swings the iron into his knee.

"Fuck!"

Mack loses control of that leg; he wobbles forward as it gives out and as soon as he's low enough, Reese whams him so hard over the head Mack feels it in his teeth. For a second, he forgets who he is and where he is, then goes face down in the dirt.

"Mack!" Leigh screams and reaches out for the man, and two clowns take hold, dragging her down to her knees and then to the ground.

Rocky keeps Candy behind him as a group of four clowns close in. The Burnt Clown's one of them, and he looks royally pissed at Rocky for spoiling his barbeque.

"Wonder if you'll burn like your little girlie friend!" the Burnt Clown teases, and Rocky snaps.

Launching himself at the clown, Rocky takes a stab and misses. Others flood into the gap between him and Candy, dragging her away as she swipes at them.

Burnt Clown grabs Rocky by his parted curtains and lifts him off the ground. He bites down, swallowing the pain as he feels his hair slowly rip from his scalp.

"If the boss didn't have somethin' real fun in mind for you, you'd be dinner."

"Shame you're gonna miss dessert." Rocky stabs the knife into Burnt Clown's throat, so quick and deep it stays in all on its own as the big clown staggers back, reaching for the handle. "That's for Kat!" Rocky spits as another clown grabs him from behind. He doesn't care; right now, all he wants is to watch the Burnt Clown pull the knife out and marvel at the spigot of blood gushing like a broken water fountain.

All of them are thrown to the dirt, lined up in a row as several clowns go about tying up Candy, Rocky, and Leigh with colorful handkerchief ropes. None of them bother securing Mack.

Reese crouches down by the big man's head, lifting it to check he's still alive. He spots Sully pulling Candy's head aside, licking her face with delight, and drops Mack back in the dirt.

"No!" Reese threatens Sully with a tire iron backhand, and the girl scurries away.

"I just wanted a taste is all." Sully pulls her knees to her chin and cries.

"Ruth wants these three, so Ruth gets these three, understand?"

Sully nods like she knows she's in trouble.

"You, though." Reese turns back to Mack as the man begins to regain focus. "We don't want you."

One clown scurries over, holding out the sawn-off for Reese to take. The little monkey clown picks up the gun, grinning as his beady eyes explore the short, brutal barrel.

"Get-get you're fuckin' hands off my Betsy." Mack spits blood.

Reese aims the barrel at Mack's upturned forehead, pushes the ragged metal circles up against the man's skin and then, instead of firing, flips the gun around and bashes Mack over the head with the stock.

"Leave him alone!" Leigh begs.

"Stop!" Candy joins her.

"Shut them the fuck up!" Reese commands, and the other clowns comply, stuffing the kids' mouths with brightly-colored handkerchiefs. "Where was I? Oh, yeah." Reese cackles like a hyena as he brings the stock down again on Mack's head, this time hard enough to hear something crack. He doesn't stop there; Reese swings the gun up in giant arcs, bringing it down with wild hoots and wet cracks as he pounds Mack's skull into the dust. Betsy's handle comes away sticky, dark, and with clumps of hair stuck to it.

"Urgh." Reese sniffs the gore and then hurls the gun away, over the trailers, and into the dark.

Leigh sobs, screaming against her gag, her face red with fury. Her muffled threats are drowned out by an out-of-tune chorus of clown laughter.

Candy, Leigh, and Rocky march along the midway, surrounded by a cavalcade of capering clowns; they parade between lit-up rides pumping rock and metal riffs with no lines while corpses ride the Electro Wheel and the Vulture's Drop, as they have for the past several hours.

Candy tries to get to Leigh, to comfort her somehow, but the clowns won't let her close. One shoves Candy forward, sparking Rocky to try and make a move, but it's all for naught. There's nothing they can do but follow the dancing, cheering procession of clowns and carnage to their doom.

Bonko's Big Top looms ahead, lit with dancing spotlights that race in time to a garish fanfare. Fireworks erupt above the tent, painting the sky with every color of the rainbow as blood soaks into the midway below.

Chapter Twenty-Two
THE STRANGEST SHOW ON EARTH

Stray clowns hop and dance towards the Big Top as a buzz of music and anticipation flows into the night. They plod through puddles of blood, skipping over scattered, twisted corpses still clutching cameras and spilled bags of popcorn.

Inside the tent, accordions warm up and spotlights weave a figure eight across the darkened ring, briefly allowing glimpses of structures and shapes in the gloom—hints of a figure, standing ready in the dead center.

The audience shifts in their seats, more fearful of the clown guards brandishing spiked baseball bats and bloodied cleavers than whatever waits in the ring. The fools. Silence strikes as the spotlights cut out, plunging the entire tent into darkness.

Two blasts of light come down on the figure in the ring. A bloodred cropped ringmaster's coat with golden tassels dangling from the lapels. A matching bodysuit, fishnet stockings, and thigh-high leather stiletto boots. A top hat sits jauntily, obscuring her bowed head. Her hands beat a rhythm on a cane while her shoes tap it out in the dirt, bullwhip on her hip bouncing along. A wicked grin, full of prideful pleasure, peeks out below the brim of the hat.

"Ladies and gents, this is what you've been dyin' for," Ruth hisses in song, her voice carried through speakers mounted around the tent.

"Don't cha-don't cha-don't cha-don't cha," a chorus of unseen clowns chants along, keeping beat with Ruth's almost violently confident tempo.

"Choking on your blood, you can't wait for it anymore." Ruth's voice shifts to a growl.

"Don't cha-don't cha-don't cha-don't cha," the chorus continues.

"Crawlin' on broken bones, dirt soakin' in open sores."

"Don't cha-don't cha-don't cha-don't cha."

"You'll beg, you'll plead." Ruth throws her arms wide as more lights hit her. Throwing her head back, hat somehow staying on: *"You'll lie, you'll bleed—"*

The tempo picks up as Ruth starts running around the ring, spotlights keeping up with her, offering fleeting hints at the structures in the dark.

"Don't cha wanna run with the carnie crowd." Ruth takes high running steps up onto the roof of a shack, the spotlights unveiling a Balloon Pop Game.

"Let your freak flag fly, loud and proud?" She leaps to the next stall, chorus keeping the beat and filling the gap.

"Hehe-haha-hehe-haha."

"Don't cha feel it, somethin' wicked this way comes." Ruth sweeps her arms at the crowd from the top of a Rope Ladder Game. *"Don't cha need it? Aren't you sick of crumbs?"*

"Hehe-haha-hehe-haha."

She jumps to the ground and takes off at a sprint; the lights race to keep up and shoot across more booths, more crooked games of chance.

"It's chaos, it's carnage, it's lust, it's life," Ruth sings. *"It's a smile in the dark, grinning with a knife."*

The lights cut out again, and the music halts. It's just Ruth's voice, hissing through the dark as the captive audience squirms. "*Sayin' don't cha want it, don't cha wanna pay the price? Don't cha need it, don't cha dare think twice!*"

The whole ring erupts with light; sparklers flicker to life atop the stalls and twirl through the air as the chorus of clowns run erratically, dodging in and out each other's path.

"*Run them over your sweet tooth!*" Ruth skips towards one booth, where Sully sits with her legs crossed on the counter, bobbing along enthusiastically with a lollipop in her mouth.

"*Whisper them like dirty truths.*" Ruth goes back-to-back with Mari, half her formerly flawless body covered in burns, bald on one side now. They both writhe down to a squat and back up like exotic dancers. Mari throws what hair she has left to the side and smiles with a mouth full of glittering shards, reveling in her grotesque glamor.

"*Get on your knees, say the words.*" Ruth points to the audience with her cane, daring and inviting them. "*Don't cha wanna be One of Us!*"

"*Gooble-gobble-gooble-gobble,*" the chorus chants.

"*Come on, enjoy the ride.*" Ruth books it alongside the Triplets. Haha, Heehee and Tinkle each sit on a saddle strapped to the back of three crawling adults, one with a horse mask, another an elephant, and the third a raccoon mask stapled to their heads. Pathetic sobs simmer below the music and yelps ring out as the Triplets whip their "horsies."

"*Stop fightin', it's only gonna hurt worse.*" Ruth twirls her cane, then lashes Reese across his backside with all the force she can muster. The hunkered monkey clown skitters forth, squealing with joy.

"*Start beggin', start sayin' the words.*" Stacey swerves in and out of Ruth's path on a colorful trike.

Ruth circles back to the middle of the ring, and all the spotlights weave through the amusements, following the other clowns as they join her, lining up like backup dancers.

"*Hehe-haha.*" Reese spanks his own backside over and over.

"*Don't cha-don't cha.*" Sully bounces from foot to foot, running her tongue over her lollipop both innocently and perversely at the same time.

"*Hehe-haha.*" Mari va-va-vooms as she wiggles her shoulders, winking at the audience while she jiggles, twirling tassels like helicopter blades.

"*Don't cha-don't cha.*" The Triplets giggle and snort as their rides carry them around the others in a circle, leaving trails from bloody knees in the dirt. Stacey races by on her three-wheel bike, waving at the audience.

"*Don't cha wanna be One of Us!*"

Ruth reaches to the sky as the music hits a crescendo.

In her head, she hears the audience whoop and cheer. They stand up, applauding so hard it sounds like hail, like thunder and the sky falling. In reality, they sit in their seats, horrified and confused about the tuneless cacophony they actually saw, not the all-singing, all-dancing extravaganza Ruth thought she performed.

Ruth takes a moment to drink in the imagined adoration of her public before taking a bow, doffing her hat. She snaps back with a stomp, bringing her legs together and the chorus to attention as one.

Inside the lion cage, Rocky slaps at Cliff's cold cheeks. "Come on, bro, wake up," Rocky pleads. "Wake up."

273

Leigh's backed into the far corner, legs pulled up to her chin with her arms around her knees. She didn't watch the show; in fact, she's a million miles away, still reeling from the loss of Mack and Clark. Candy leans against her friend, feeling her body tremble, and knows there's not much she can do besides just be there.

Cliff's head shakes and his eyes open. He blinks with confusion, and as the memories of the last few hours kick back in, he jerks up. "Stacey!"

"Cliff!" Rocky's so happy he throws his arms around the boy, tears running down his face, and he just doesn't care. "Bro!"

"Rocky!" Cliff hugs his best friend back. "Dude! Where's Stacey?"

"Oh, man, I dunno how to say it. Stacey's—"

"One of those fuckin' bozos," Leigh growls, broken beyond even her limited level of tact.

"Jesus, Leigh, I know things are fucked, but can you reel the bitch in? That's his sister—"

"No, it's cool." Cliff tries to stand but can't quite get his balance. It still looks like there are two of everything. "I can cure her."

"How?" Candy asks, eyes wandering to the nightmarish ensemble cast posing out in the spotlight.

Cliff blinks rapidly as he scans the floor of the cage, and his eyes land on the insulin kit. "There." He scrambles over, falling to one side, and picks it up. "Thank fuck it's still here."

"Is that Stacey's shots?" Leigh comes out of herself. "How's that shit gonna help?"

"I dunno." Cliff checks that there's still one shot ready to go in the padded case. It feels warm, so it's probably expired, but it's all he has. "But she was all clowny back at the nurse's station with Clark." Noticing he's not there

274

with them and then Leigh's sudden body rocking sobs, it clicks. "Oh no, oh fuck no." Cliff crawls over and puts his hands on Leigh's knees. "I'm so sorry, Leigh, I'm… Jesus, Clark was such a nice guy. I dunno what to say." And Cliff breaks down into tears.

Leigh does something unexpected. She holds her arms open and lets Cliff come in for a hug. Holding the other arm out, Candy comes in at the side, and the three of them embrace as one sobbing mess of teenage misery.

"Get your stupid ass in here before I change my mind, Rock-For-Brains," Leigh sniffs, and Rocky doesn't need to be asked twice. The four of them huddle in the corner, wrapped in each other's arms, scraping the only shred of comfort they can from the fucked up carnival nightmare they're trapped in. It's too much for Leigh, and she breaks the moment. "I swear to God if one of you farts—" and that sets them off laughing, the desperate, raw laughter of the soon-to-be-hanged.

"Listen, if I don't make it," Cliff begins.

"Shut up. Nobody else is dying!" Leigh insists.

"Just promise me one of you'll get to Stacey with this?" Cliff holds out the insulin kit.

"How does it work?" Rocky asks.

"Fuck knows, dude, but I think it's got something to do with that black cotton candy. There's something in the sugar, I think, turns them into—shit, man, are wereclowns even a thing?"

"Maybe they're aliens?" Candy suggests. "Like *Killer Klowns from Outer Space*?"

"That's as dumb as that hippie dude on the radio sayin' alien zombies burned that town down," Leigh points out. "So, maybe?"

The four of them look through the bars to see a cavorting, twirling pageant of pale painted faces and brightly colored hair.

"How about the honking dead?" Leigh offers.

"Yeah... fuck that noise," Cliff sighs. "So I think the insulin helps the body break down the sugar faster. It made Stacey normal—well not normal. I mean it made her Stacey again."

"This is startin' to make some sense," Leigh says, and the other three shoot her incredulous glances. "In a fucked up horror movie kinda way."

"This ain't a movie, Leigh," Rocky points out.

"Maybe it's the God of the Reels—"

"I don't think I've seen that one." Candy shakes her head.

"It's not a movie, just a dumb urban legend," Cliff explains. "About this old movie guy from the forties—"

"Anyway, you rude bitches," Leigh complains, "that's the machine old Bonko got slam dunked in, right?"

"That's what that woman said," Candy agrees and wishes dearly they could just go back to dumb teenage drama like this morning when the worst thing that happened to her was Rocky kissing another girl. A girl who died saving others while Candy just stood there, watching. That doesn't sit easily with her—all day, everyone's been looking after her, coming to her rescue. Too many have paid too steep a price for her worthless rear...

"OK, so if this is a shitty horror movie, that makes it a cursed object, right, Candy?"

"Right," Candy agrees. "Kinda like *Christine*."

"Who's Christine?" Rocky is confused.

"It's a car, just, never mind. Here's what I'm thinking. That"—Leigh points at the Zephyr—"is the heart of this shit. Maybe if we can fuck it up, it all ends."

"Big if," Rocky says, "though even if all it does is piss those pasty-faced fuck-wits off, I'm game."

"Sometimes you say things that make me want to tolerate you, Rock-For-Brains."

"Yeah, I dunno if we wanna follow this horror movie bullshit to the logical conclusion," Cliff points out. "Isn't it usually just one chick who makes it out of those things?"

"There can only be one final girl," Candy agrees solemnly.

"Since when do I play by the rules?" Leigh takes Candy's hand, and it brings some small comfort to Candy for a brief moment.

"Guys, they're doing something," Rocky points out, and the rest clamber to watch.

Ruth runs a loving finger across the surface of the Zephyr, smiling as though tracing the outline of a loved one's naked body. A ring of tiki torches surrounds it, marking the machine like an altar.

"Ladies and Gentlemen," her voice booms through the speakers. "It's time I introduced the man who, without his vision, none of this wonderful extravaganza could come to pass."

Ruth clicks her fingers, and Reese scurries over with a crowbar, jamming it into the side of the Zephyr. The wood panel at the front of the machine cracks; it's about to fall free when Ruth gives Reese the signal to hold it for a second.

"It is my greatest pleasure and privilege to welcome back to the Bonkin's Bonanza Family, the man who started it all!"

Reese cracks the rest of the wood and pops the front panel free. What audience members remain sane gasp in disgusted horror at the sight within. All the machine's mechanical components are coated in strings and sheets of weaving cotton candy, stretched and spread about like a thousand pink spider webs. At the center, a still and unmoving face. A familiar and yet unbelievable one. It bears the same markings as Ruth, the same as the late Buster B. Bonkin, as Bonko the Clown. It's like someone carved the face from cotton candy, a perfect still likeness of the notorious underworld terror—then its eyes open.

Darting around with excited fury, the impossibly human eyes roll as though their owner is just figuring out how to use them. They land on a poor audience member in the circle-side seats.

"Hiya f-f-f-fucker!" Bonko chirps. "I'm back!"

Ruth nods to one of the clowns guarding the audience and drags the one Bonko locked onto over the barrier, forcing him to march towards Bonko with a hand on the back of his neck. He tosses the man down to his knees before Ruth.

"P-p-please," the man begs. "I have a family!"

"That's so sweet," Ruth grins. "Me too. And Daddy's hungry!" Ruth grabs the man and hurls him against the Zephyr. Tendrils of cotton candy shoot out, sticking to the man and binding him to the machine. He screams and struggles, tearing at the webs, but they spread too fast, crawling and enveloping him as Bonko laughs madly. The cotton candy reaches the man's face, creeping around his open mouth and holding it open in a forever scream. He becomes a still, cocooned statue of

278

a man frozen in the throes of utter agony—faint twitches show he's still alive in there as Bonko's delirious groans of pleasure ring out across the Big Top.

"Oh man, that's nasty." Rocky feels like throwing up.

Candy dry heaves. "Do you think she means he's really her dad?"

"I, um, think she means the naughty-naughty spank me kind," Cliff says with a slow shake of his head that says he firmly disagrees with the idea.

"I think it's both." Leigh bites her lip.

It takes the other three half a second to click, which sets them all off again.

"I didn't think you could make psycho wereclowns any worse, but there ya go," Cliff groans. "Incest for the win, I guess."

"Pfft, incest, more like wincest," Leigh jokes. The other three just stare at her. As disgusting as it is, Leigh's borderline wrong humor is exactly what they need to keep their minds in one piece after what they've just seen. If only it was enough to save them from what happens next.

"Shit, they're coming."

Reese and another clown, a huge one, make their way over to the cage, and the kids find the grim reality of their situation crashing back down on them.

"That one." Reese points to Cliff. "That little shit's first!"

Cliff turns to the others, thrusting the insulin kit into Rocky's hands. "Whatever happens—"

"Don't, bro, it's gonna be—"

"Just promise me, dude." Cliff makes a fist. "Promise me!"

Rocky bites down, shaking his head, but makes a fist back.

"Rocky," he says through gritted teeth.

"And Cliff." The boys fist bump. "To the—"

He doesn't get to finish. The giant clown pulls Cliff through the cage door, shoving Rocky back with a meaty fist.

Rocky lands on his ass, on the boards of the cage with the insulin kit in one hand and the other held out, desperately reaching for his friend being dragged through the dirt towards the center of the ring where Ruth and Bonko wait.

Chapter Twenty-Three
SPLISH-SPLASH

Spotlights criss-cross, and then all come to rest on Ruth's outstretched arms as a disembodied drum roll fills the Big Top. The face of Bonko leers, cackling as blood seeps through the web of cotton candy, snaking through vein-like strings.

"Ladies and gentlemen, boys and girls"—Ruth shoots a wicked eye to Bonko—"and everything else, what's a carnival without games of chance?"

Reese shoves Cliff down to his knees and hisses in the boy's ear, "Don't try anythin' funny, or you'll get the Bonko treatment."

"Gee and I thought you clowns like funny." Cliff's small act of verbal defiance earns him a clip around the back of his head.

Ruth, ignoring this interaction like a true showman, continues.

"Why, who among you hasn't rolled up their sleeves and gone at it, trying to win a prize for that special someone!? It's a rite of passage! A genuine, homegrown tradition! Picture the scene—"

Ruth waves her hand as though playing a magic trick, and with a flick of her wrist, one spotlight descends on the nearby Balloon Pop Game. A sign reads *Pop three! Win a prize!*

Sully stands acting all cute and coy by the counter, hands clasped with one heel up, fluttering her blue teardrop painted eyes at the clown next to her. He's in a letter jacket, with slightly too-long slicked-back hair that curls at the neck with a black diamond over one eye. A dart twirls through the air, sharp point glinting, and he catches it with ease.

"You're on a date with your honey"—Ruth drops into a cutesy impression, and Sully mimes along over-dramatically—"and you spot the darndest prize!"

Another spotlight hits the target board, only instead of a simple wall of underinflated rubber balloons, there's a gagged man bound up, arms and legs as wide as possible, with multi-colored balloons stuck across his knees, elbows, hands, waist, and ears.

"I want it! I want it!" Ruth squeals, grabbing her knees and shaking her hips as Sully jumps on the spot, pointing at a dirty, stained teddy bear stuck to the wall above the human target's head. "Win it for me, honey-bunny!"

Another clown in a Bonkin's Bonanza vest appears behind the Balloon Pop counter like a jack-in-the-box. He slams five darts down on the counter.

Sully's boy picks them up, puffing his chest and moving his shoulders with an exaggerated swagger. With a smarmy air of unfortunate cockiness, Sully's boy aims with one dart, his arm flowing back and forth smoothly as he lines up the shot. He lets the dart fly; it sails through the air, misses the balloon, and lands squarely in the middle of the man's hand—a pained groan gets through his gag, and the balloons tied to his body bop around.

"Oh, that's a shame. Better try harder with your next one!" Ruth continues. Then, with the back of her hand to her mouth, she not so subtly adds, "There's one born every minute, after all!"

Sully sulks, stamping her feet and crossing her arms with a cartoonish frown.

Sully's boy takes heart, works himself up, and fires off another two darts right away. One pops the balloon by the man's left ear, but the other goes right in his open eye—the poor man's body arcs as a red line runs down like a tear. He can't blink, and his other eye races around in search of help.

"Oh, that's gotta hurt," Ruth jeers. "Two shots left, and he's gotta make them both if he wants to keep his sweetheart sweet!"

Two other clowns sidle up, taking posts casually beside Sully as though chatting her up at the bar. Her boy looks flustered, and he slaps himself to gain some focus.

"Don't hesitate, young man!" Ruth raises a fist to the sky. "Or some bolder hand will reach out and grab your prize!"

The other two clowns begin pawing at Sully, and she giggles as though she's having a great time, flicking her hair and leaning into them as she laughs.

Sully's boy puts on a show of priming himself and tries to get the audience to clap along. No one joins in, so Ruth throws a quick hand signal to the clowns in the crowd. Prods with the tips of blades, the business ends of bats, get them clapping, awkwardly and out of sync. In time with the applause, the hopeful clown jumps up and down and then takes his next shot—pop! The balloon tied to the man's left knee pops with a yelp and a rapidly spreading dark patch along his leg.

"Yes!" Ruth cheers as Sully suddenly finds the clown with the darts interesting again, shoving through the other two suitors and cozying up with him. The clown pumps his fist, celebrating, and then all acting stops with a sharp hand wave from Ruth. A weighted hush descended upon the Big Top, a silent blanket of dread. "This is it, Boys and Girls! It all comes down..."

283

Sully's boy closes his eyes, bringing the tip of the last dart to his red nose in prayer. Everyone holds their collective breath; all that breaks the calm is the desperate whimpers of the man on the board.

The dart flies in slow motion. Spinning through the air, catching glints of light as it twirls. Dozens of eyes follow it, including the only one the man on the board has left. He watches as the sharp metal point heads right for him, misses the balloon, and sinks so deep into his cheek it scrapes his teeth, gouging into his gums. A pained gasp escapes and blood follows, trailing from the hole and the corner of his mouth.

"Oh, well, there you go," Ruth sighs as Sully's boy stomps on the spot. "Can't win 'em all, I guess."

The light goes out on the bound man, but not the loser clown. Sully struts away, shaking her hips as she passes between the other two boys.

"Life is a game, ladies and gentlemen." Ruth's voice takes on something approximating solemnity. "There are winners and losers, prizes"—and now creeping cruelty slithers in—"and prices."

The other two clowns quickly pounce and grab hold of the loser, wrestling him to the ground, and it doesn't seem like an act anymore — he's really struggling.

"What's that saying, folks?" Ruth asks the audience

The Balloon Clown dances into the spotlight, dozens of uninflated balloons dangling from his belt and suspenders. He takes out one long, thick-looking balloon and presents it to the audience for approval, then the two clowns holding the loser down. They nod excitedly.

Dropping to his knees, the Balloon Clown feeds the balloon up the loser's nose till only the bottom sticks out, then produces an oversized, candy cane-colored pump from the pouch on his belt. He shows it off for all to see with immense pride before connecting the tube to the end of the balloon sticking out of the loser's nose. The loser tries to refuse, fight the others off, but they hold him down harder.

Turning to the audience, the Balloon Clown teases, pushing the pump, giggling and nodding furiously. Music starts up, a steady one-two-three beat, and on each third, the Balloon Clown plunges the pump down, sending a shot of air to the balloon inside the loser's nasal cavity. The skin below his eye begins to bulge as though swelling up from a sting. As the music picks up speed, so does the Balloon Clown, and the bulge grows bigger, redder, till finally the pressure is too much, and the loser's eye pops right out of the socket like a ping pong ball on a string.

"An eye for an eye," Ruth concludes. The spotlight on the clowns goes out as the Balloon Clown takes a bow.

"Now, to the main event!" A light blasts on Cliff, forcing him to shield his eyes. "This young man here has twice offended the Bonkin's Bonanza Family." Ruth holds for boos, and when they don't come, she hardly signals her clowns to make the audience react. Half-hearted boos follow. Ruth acts like it's an overwhelming wave of condemnation. "I know, I know! Can you believe he turned down an invitation to join the Family? And then had the gall to try and steal our most precious, adorable little sister!" Ruth holds an arm out, and Stacey cartwheels into the spotlight, coming to a rest against Ruth's thigh as the big woman places a hand on the child's head.

"Fuck you! She's *my* sister, you bi—"

Ruth silences Cliff with a slap.

"Now, I know what you're all thinking! To the shark tank with him!" Spotlights come on by Bruce's tank as jets of blood squirt into the water from hidden spigots, making Bruce ram the window in a flurry of foam that masks something vibrantly terrifying.

Stacey gnashes her teeth while making a shark fin with her palms.

"But here at Bonkin's Bonanza, we are not about that! No, no, sirs and madams, we are not! We are going to let this young rapscallion take a shot at the grand prize—his life—because what's a carnival without a little peril and paste!"

Ruth crosses over to a large object covered in tarpaulin, and the spotlights follow her. Clutching the edge of the sheet, she pulls and reveals a massive Wheel of Fortune with a flurry of fabric and fanfare.

"Come, boy, time to play." Ruth gestures for Cliff to follow, and when he refuses, an unseen clown pushes him on, nipping at his heels from the shadows. "Spin the wheel and let fate decide your game."

"Yeah? And if I refuse?" Cliff tries to put a brave front on.

Ruth covers her microphone so that only Cliff can hear. "Then I'll make your sister play instead..."

"Fuck," Cliff curses and puts his hand on the wheel. He takes a deep breath then spins it. A drum roll beats from the speakers as the wheel clacks, spinning like a mesmerizing rainbow whirlpool. Cliff's, Stacey's, and Ruth's eyes follow the wheel, round and round, till it slows to a crawl then clacks to a stop on—

"The Dunk Tank!" Ruth declares with delight. Fireworks shoot from behind the wheel, and lights descend upon the chosen game—a simple metal container full of some transparent liquid with a caged seat resting precariously above. Attached to the side is a single wall featuring the painting of a clown, his nose the bright red target button.

"The Dunk Tank, that's good," Leigh says as she holds the bars of their cage, face pressed between them, watching Cliff march across to the game.

"How is any of this good?" Rocky asks.

"'Cause, Rock-For-Brains, all these games are rigged as shit; that's why nobody ever wins."

"That's not true," Candy points out. "Is it? I mean, people do win?"

"Yeah, for show. Over-inflated basketballs and oval hoops; rings the same size as the bottles; half-inflated balloons—they make it look easy to hide the trick. There's not much you can do with a Dunk Tank to fuck with it, though."

"So?" Rocky wonders.

"So Cliff's got a decent shot at winning."

"Yeah?" Rocky looks at his friend. "But why does that still feel like a bad idea?"

Five bean bags, each a different color, sit on the Dunk Tank's counter as Cliff's shoved up to it.

"Hit the target three times, that's three out of five shots, to drown the clown and win the crown!" Ruth explains with flair.

"Clown?" Cliff wonders aloud and then spots Stacey clambering up the side ladder and watches as she climbs through the cage, sealing it closed behind herself. She plonks down on the plank, swishing her side ponytail and kicking her feet.

Cliff turns to Ruth. "You sayin' I just gotta dunk my sister, and I win?"

"Of course!" Ruth turns to the audience. "We play fair and square here at Bonkin's Bonanza!"

"Really? That's it? I hit that nose three times, Stacey takes a bath, and I walk? What's the catch?"

"No catch, my boy!" Ruth claims. "Now, it's showtime!"

Ruth backs away into the shadows, leaving all eyes on Cliff. He doesn't trust any of this, but it's not like he has any choice, so Cliff picks up the first bean bag. It feels heavy enough to do the job, but not so that he'll have any trouble throwing it the distance. There's gotta be some other trick then.

Cliff pulls back with a wind-up and hurls the bean bag, whamming the clown's big button nose dead in the middle. Light bulbs inside the eyes glow for a second, and the game buzzes.

On the tank underneath Stacey, one of three lights comes on.

"One down, folks, two to go!" Ruth's cheer echoes through the shadows.

"Can't be this easy," Cliff says to himself as he lifts the second bean bag and throws it. He misses, and the bag thunks against the wall just to the side of the target. "Shit!"

"Oh, a near miss," Ruth comments. "But you know what they say. A miss by an inch is as good as a mile!"

"Fuck this!" Cliff picks up the third and hits the target, dead on, so hard the whole thing shakes. It buzzes, the eyes flash, and the second of three lights below Stacey comes on. "Yes!" Cliff arm pumps and cheers.

"One hit left, two shots to go, things are looking pretty good for our boy here, huh folks?"

Cliff takes the fourth bean bag in hand and juggles it, testing the weight. It seems good, like the others, but there's gotta be something.

"Hey, Looooooser," Stacey taunts from the cage. "Betcha, this is the only time you'll ever get to dump a girl!" She cackles, laughing so hard she almost falls off her perch.

"Don't," Cliff tells himself. "Keep it cool." And he takes another deep breath.

"Miss!" Stacey hisses, rolling around on her plank.

Cliff pulls back, aims and—

"Miss!" Stacey yells as Cliff throws, causing the bean bag to go way off target.

"Fuck!" Cliff curses.

"It's down to one, folks," Ruth's voice almost whispers.

Stacey's legs kick wildly with joy as she applauds herself. One of her sneakers comes flying off; it rebounds off the window and sinks into the vat below.

Cliff picks up the last bean bag, and his eye catches the slowly spiraling sneaker through the slightly off-color liquid. A fury of bubbles surrounds it, and he watches as the black fabric turns yellowish-white. Bits of it begin to flake off as though eaten away by something unseen.

"That's not water..."

"Correct!" Ruth declares. "Here at Bonkin's Bonanza, we don't do things by half measures, no sir, we don't. Why settle for a couple of gallons of boring old water when sulphuric acid makes it"—she blows a chef's kiss— "caliente!"

"Come on, loser!" Stacey sticks her tongue out. "You gonna make out with that bean bag, or throw it?"

Cliff can't dunk his little sister in a vat of acid, no matter how much of a brat she is, and so he throws the last bean bag to the floor, staring into the dark with resolute defiance. Whatever they'll do to him, at least Stacey's safe.

289

"You're no fun!" Stacey pouts as the cage door opens and she climbs out.

The two Bouncer Clowns appear on either side of Cliff as Ruth calls, "Time for round two!"

"Wait, what!?"

Both clowns grab Cliff and drag him by the shoulder across to the vat. They force him onto the ladder and push him up with such force that he almost falls off the plank inside the cage. He rattles the door, but it refuses to open. He's too busy trying to get out that he almost falls off the plank with shock as the buzzer goes off and the first light comes on.

"Stacey!"

The little clown girl giggles and flicks her hair, already picking up the second bean bag.

"Stacey, please don't!"

BUZZ! The second light comes on.

This is it, then; a moment of cold clarity settles upon Cliff—he's not getting out of this cage. He has faith, though. Rocky has the insulin, and the others will save Stacey. He knows this. He has to.

"Stacey, I'm sorry I said I'd melt your Barbies and shave your eyebrows off! I'm sorry I made you eat cricket tacos and locked you in Honey Monster's dog crate! You're the best little sister in the world, and I lo—"

BUZZ!

Cliff falls in slow motion.

Split-screen: Rocky and Candy can't bear to watch, while Leigh can't make herself look away; Cliff splashes into the vat of acid.

The single merciful thing is that it burns so deep, so fast, his nerve endings are gone before the pain has time to register. The blue denim of his jeans fades to white, as does his skin. Crusty yellow rinds crack across exposed flesh like rapidly growing, cantankerous barnacles. The color is ripped from his eyes, sapping his humanity and hiding the horror in them as parts of his scalp drift off, the hair vanishing as it's burned away almost instantly. Yellowing hands, skin peeling off with threads of red, beat against the window till they don't anymore.

Silence fills the Big Top, only broken when Ruth speaks up.

"Well folks, wasn't that touching? I dunno about you, but my heart just about melted!"

Chapter Twenty-Four
SIDESHOW REJECTS

"Cliff..."

It isn't possible; Rocky simply can't accept what's just happened. The cavalier, cartoonish cruelty.

"Cliff? Come on, bro..."

"Rocky, I'm so sorry." Candy crawls across the cage, arm outstretched.

"Cliff!" Rocky screams, grabbing the bars and rattling the cage with such violence that Candy is thrown back, landing in the corner with a high-tone yelp. "Cliff!" Rocky's oblivious to the others, to the way Candy recoils from his searing rage. Rocky's face burns red, his eyes narrow into focal points of pure fury. "I'll kill you! I'll kill you all!" The whole cage rattles.

Leigh approaches him calmly and gets shoved back for her efforts without recognition.

"You bastards! I'll kill you all!"

One of the bars gives ever so slightly as a bolt clatters free, but Rocky doesn't even notice as fire and spit fly from his ragged, raw throat.

Center stage, Ruth holds court as the lights dim on the Dunk Tank. "Well, ladies and gentle—"

"I'll fucking kill you all!" Rocky's hate-filled promise rings out louder than Ruth's amplified voice. She tries to compose herself, striking a confident pose only for the boy to interrupt again. "You're dead! All you fucking clowns!"

Ruth holds a finger in the air and flashes a fake smile. "We'll be right back, folks!" Then signals to cut the lights.

Storming over towards the cage, Reese and the two heavy clowns flank her, all semblance of stage charm gone. This is Ruth, the boss, and she's not about to let some teenage twerp ruin her big moment.

"Shut him up, but make sure he can still play," Ruth instructs, and the two heavies approach the cage.

One of them unlocks the door but doesn't get to open it—Rocky explodes through, knocking the first clown down and launching himself at the second. Despite the clown being nearly twice Rocky's size, he gets him to the ground, and his knuckles are a bloody blur of punches in seconds.

"I'll kill you! I'll kill you!" Rocky roars through ravaged vocal cords. "I'll kill you!"

Reese leaps on his back, throwing the tire iron around Rocky's neck and reining him in like a bucking bronco.

"Get the fuck off me!" Rocky grabs the iron with both hands and hurls Reese overhead, sending the hunched clown right past Ruth and more of her laughing minions. It takes three of them to wrestle Rocky to his knees but even then, he fights, and it's a challenge to keep him under control.

"Well, you're a feisty one," Ruth sneers, and Rocky spits in her face. For a second, it looks like she'll take that on the chin, a facade of good humor, and then she backhands Rocky with enough force to send him to the dirt.

"Stop!" Candy pleads from the cage. "Just stop!" And it's not clear if she means Rocky, Ruth, or both.

"Whatcha wanna do with him, boss?" one of the clowns says in an *aw, shucks* kind of voice.

Ruth mulls it over for a minute, her tongue poking at her cheek from within, tasting Rocky's rage. With a wicked smile, she says, "Let's take him to see Daddy."

"No!" Candy reaches through the bars. "Please don't!"

"Bitch," Leigh joins in. "Don't you fucking dare!"

Ruth blows both girls a kiss as she walks backward, beside Rocky as he's dragged across to the Zephyr.

He's dumped on his knees, and before Rocky can even think about going at them again, Ruth grabs his hair, a thick handful from the roots, and yanks back with enough force to make the boy crane his neck to a breaking point. She forces Rocky to go face-to-face with the pink, paradoxically fluffy and crusty face of Bonko. The cotton candy clown laughs, spewing air both foul and sickeningly sweet.

"What should we do with this one, Daddy?" Ruth coos.

"Well, ain't he a f-f-f-fine lookin' boy! I'll say, I'll say Bonko ain't no queer, no sir, that's the toot-tootin' truth... but you sure is pretty enough to nibble my pickle like a girlie!" Bonko's eyes roll around. "If I still had one! Ay-yup!"

The other clowns laugh, thinking it's a joke.

"That's not f-f-f-funny!" Bonko flares up. "Y'all think it's f-f-f-fuckin' f-f-f-funny!"

"N-no, Daddy," Ruth quivers and looks to the other clowns with a demand for silence.

"I think it's f-f-f-fuckin' f-f-f-funny." Rocky does an impersonation. "I mean, how are you gonna go f-f-f-fuck your f-f-f-fat bitch daughter now you f-f-f-fucked up backwoods sideshow reject!"

"Hey!" Bonko's face folds into a mask of rage, like a baby with too much skin frowning. "I ain't gonna sit here an' take that f-f-f-from a boy who ain't old enough to lose his pussy f-f-f-fuck cherry!"

"Is it true your momma treated you like a baby till you were, shit, I don't wanna say grown up, 'cause, you know..."

"Do you wanna know what it's like to be drained, slowly, for hours on end?" Bonko's candy tendril flutters, drawing Rocky's attention to the man encased in the cotton cocoon. His fingers still twitch, still alive inside his pink tomb. "Have the life sucked outta ya?"

"Sure, but isn't your momma dead!?"

Bonko trembles with fury, sugar-spun lips curling into a savage sneer, and then a glint of evil sparks in his eye. "Mari! Marianna! Get your ass over here!"

The burlesque clown slips from the shadows, body maintaining her s-shape as she struts over.

"Boy, I was gonna let you plow Mari right in f-f-f-fronta me." He flicks a sick approximation of a tongue at the half-burned beauty. "Ain't that how your mister used ta like it?" For the briefest of moments, something passes over Mari's poised smile, a fleeting flashback to another place, another time. It's gone, just like that, and the preening pinup performance resumes. "But you had to be a wiseass, so you know whatcha gonna do? You're gonna watch your girlie over there take her turn."

All of Rocky's defiance and outrage dissipate at those words.

"No, it's my turn!" Rocky yells. "It's my turn, you cowards! Let me play, not her!"

Bonko looks at Mari. "Go get me his bitch! Ay-yup!"

"Fuuuuck!" Leigh curses and kicks the inside of the cage. "Shit, they're coming for you next."

"I don't know what to do; I've never won anything in my life!" Candy's overcome with a cold sweat.

"Look." Leigh puts her forehead to Candy's, the tips of their noses touching. Her hands find their way to Candy's cheeks, those slightly pudgy cheeks tickled by flickers of messy blonde hair. "Whatever it is, it's rigged. These games trick you into thinking they're easy, so look for what they want you to do, then flip it. And hope to fuck it's not the Rope Ladder."

"What," Candy sniffs, "what's wrong with the Rope Ladder?"

"It's just fuckin' evil, nearly impossible."

Mari dances over to the cage; flicking her hair, she raises a hand and points.

"I'm scared, Leigh." Candy's whole body shakes. "I don't wanna die—"

"And you're not!" Leigh makes Candy look her in the eye. "Remember. It's you and me..."

The cage door opens.

"T-together forever," Candy sobs.

Arms reach in, grasping.

"You'll see—" Leigh just finishes as Mari grabs her by the collar. "Wait, what?" Leigh's so taken aback she barely puts up a fight as Mari drags her out of the cage.

"Leigh!" Candy rushes, flattening her tiny body against the bars. They give, slightly, but Candy doesn't notice.

"Candy!" Leigh finds her fight and slams herself against the cage, locking fingers with the girl she's only just come to accept she's madly in love with. It's more than just a final farewell, though; Leigh pushes the bar, not saying a word but making sure Candy notices the way it wobbles.

Leigh's thrown down next to Rocky before the warped face of Bonko.

Rocky looks to her, confused, expecting Candy and shamefully relieved that it's Leigh they're making play their fucked up game this time. She shakes her head, urging him not to say anything. Mari only saw them together. She must have just assumed they were a couple. The idea revolts her and yet brings a certain comfort, knowing it keeps Candy out of the spotlight—for now, at least.

"Say, she's a bit tall for ya, ain't she bucko?" Bonko titters. "Y'all's like a cat climbing a tree!"

"Yeah? Well, a kindergartener's tall for you, and from what I hear, that never stopped you!" Leigh bites back.

"Lies! I didn't never bonk no kids!" Bonko growls. "You got a sassy mouth on ya, don't cha girlie? You ever get bored of standin' over Pretty Boy here, I got a seat for ya—right on my f-f-f-face!" Bonko's eyes swirl as his fluffy tongue bats from side to side, casting off flakes of crystallized cotton candy. His wheezy laughter subsides, and then Bonko gives the order. "Take her to the Wheel!"

The other clowns resume control of Rocky as Ruth pulls Leigh up and marches her away.

"You know you would make an excellent clown, my dear," Ruth whispers in Leigh's ear.

"And I was gonna say you'd make one hell of a bitch, but, I mean, redundant."

Ruth leans in and sniffs Leigh's hair, letting out a perverse moan. "Oh, there are secrets inside you that so desperately want out. That's all Daddy wants, you see?

297

For everyone to be their true selves. You could join us, be who you've always wanted to be." Ruth smiles. "With who you've always wanted to be with."

"Are you saying we could, my friends and I, live if we buy into your whole Barnum and Manson Family vibe?"

"Perhaps." Ruth shoves Leigh towards the Wheel of Fortune as the spotlights blast down, and the music resumes. "But first, the show must go on!"

"Shit," Leigh mutters as she looks at the options on the Wheel. There's stuff on there she knows she could stand a fighting chance at, but so many of the games are just sheer dumb luck, and while she knows she's got plenty of the former, Leigh's always been lacking on the latter. "Fuck me, here goes," she says and spins the Wheel.

Clackclackclackclackclack-clackclackclack-clack-clack... clack.

"Fuuuuuuuuck." She slaps her forehead as the wheel lands on her game. The Rope Ladder Challenge.

"All right, where is this bitch?" Leigh looks to Ruth, and the big woman nods with a grin towards the far end of the ring. Spotlights come to life, illuminating the shark tank and two tall poles with ladders bolted to them — a hewn rope ladder sagging between both above the momentarily still waters of Bruce's tank. "Oh, you gotta be shittin' me..."

"Damnit!"

Cut to: Candy digs the nail of her thumb into the one remaining screw holding the bar in place, pushing into decades of filth. Shards of rust flutter away as she blows on the screw, leaving an all but imperceptible gap between the spotted metal and hard wooden floor. This cage may have never been cleaned, from the volume her hot-pink nail scoops up.

Rocky's assault on the cage loosened it enough to give her a shot. Candy hopes he's OK; after the turn this day's taken, everything from this morning seems almost quaint and innocent in comparison. She squints into the dark but can't see any sign of him; all lights are on Leigh at the Wheel and the giant fish tank all the way across the Big Top.

"OK, here goes." Candy pushes her nail into the cleared groove and tries to work it like a screwdriver. There's some resistance, and then Candy's nail comes clean off. Blood quickly fills the space with thick globs before Candy can even recoil. She cries out in pain, clutching the wound as more blood wells between her fingers.

Though it stings and the pain only intensifies as the raw skin below is irritated, that's not what makes Candy break down into tears. She feels completely and utterly useless. Before she can even counter her own intrusive thoughts with the fact that she saved Leigh back at the big wheel, they snap back—Leigh never would have been there if not for you. Neither would Cliff...

I'm just a useless waste of space. If this was a movie, I'd be dead before the title card, Candy says to herself. But here I am, just sitting around while more people get killed. I'm—

"Shut up! Bitch!" Candy shouts, slapping herself out of the funk. You can have a goddamn pity party when you get your tiny ass outta here and save us, Leigh's voice rings through her head. Like when you botched your nose piercing, you mean, Candy answers the thought back and then clicks—that's it.

Rolling up her t-shirt, Candy reveals a metallic purple belly button ring.

Flashback to: Candy lying on Leigh's bed in jeans and a neon-pink sports bra, t-shirt on the floor, biting down on her thumb as Leigh cradles a bowl of ice beside her.

"You sure you want me to do this?" Leigh asks.

"Uh-huh," Candy moans, and she sounds anything but sure. She almost screams the house down a second later. "Stop-stop-stop, it hurts!"

Leigh gives Candy a "you gotta be kidding look" and holds up an ice cube as she says, "Bitch, it's just the ice."

Candy, embarrassed, sinks into her shoulders and looks away. "I don't like the cold."

"Oh, yeah?" Leigh nods with a wicked smirk. "Tell you what. If you can keep quiet while I put this ice cube on you, I'll... do whatever you want."

"Anything?" Candy perks up.

"Anything," Leigh says and tries not to look at the way Candy's loose blonde hair sits across her chest. Tries not to let something unspoken linger with that word.

"Will you go on a date with Cliff?"

"Urgh!" Leigh moans, frustrated in ways she doesn't understand. "Fine, but you can't move or make a single noise!"

"Deal!" Candy lies back down and tries to control her breathing. Leigh watches the way her stomach quivers, the downy, almost invisible hairs trembling.

"Ready," Candy says, and when Leigh doesn't respond: "I said, ready."

"OK." Leigh snaps to it, taking a fresh ice cube from the bowl. She starts below Candy's belly, just above the top of her jeans. Candy trembles, her fingers digging into the bedsheets, but doesn't utter a single word as Leigh slowly slides the ice cube across her tanned skin. It leaves behind a clear trail of wetness as Leigh brings it to Candy's belly button, as she circles it almost dreamily. The cube's practically melted—it's a hot night, after all—and Leigh finds herself staring again.

"You ready?" Leigh checks as she picks up the needle.

"Yeah-h Shiiiii-ooot!" Candy yells as Leigh drives the needle through. She nearly blacks out, and when she looks down, Candy sees a shiny new metallic purple ring and one very smug best friend.

Candy takes the piercing out in the lion's cage and carefully examines it. This just might do, she hopes, and goes back to the bar's last screw. She digs the tip of the piercing into the groove, and, with some effort, Candy's face lights up as the metal begins to turn.

Leigh places one hand on the ladder and begins the climb.

"Of all the fucking bitch games in this shitty carnival, you had to get this one." She reaches the top and steps out onto the plank; the spotlights blind her as she looks for Candy. She can't see anything, but every second she wastes buys Candy more time to escape. And it delays the inevitable — there's no way she can win this game.

Months worth of allowances wasted as a kid at state fairs, and it wasn't till Mack explained how damn difficult the game was and the only viable strategy that she even got halfway up a regular one. Never mind all the way across a shark tank-spanning monstrosity like the one before her.

Leigh gets on her hands and knees and crawls to where the plank ends and the rope ladder begins. Most people would assume the correct way to win this game is to place your hands and feet on the wooden rungs, strewn so invitingly along the rope ladder—but that's a mistake. Like she said to Candy, look for the obvious, then do the opposite. Using the handles focuses your body weight into a focal point, causing the rope to swing like a pendulum—it's not much help but putting your hands and feet on the outside distributes the weight more evenly.

She makes slow progress, trying to ignore the continuous drum roll droning from uncomfortably close speakers.

Though Leigh tries not to look down, the spinning lights and sparklers by the tank constantly draw her eye, making her think there's movement in the dark blue.

"Guess Candy was right when she insisted *Jaws* was a horror movie," Leigh mutters to try and distract herself. "And *Vertigo*." It seems to work; she makes it about a quarter of the way across.

Of course, it's not going to be that easy.

A shape scuttling up the far side pole catches Leigh's eye, and she groans as Reese hobbles onto the opposite platform. He prances up and down, twiddling his little hands like monkey paws, chewed up face contorted with perverse delight.

"I don't suppose you're here to hold it steady for me?" Leigh yells.

Reese's shoulders jerk up and down as he grabs the rope and shakes it.

"Fuck off! This is bullshit enough without—" Leigh's right hand slips, bringing the matching leg with it; she just manages to hold on with her left side, and the rope spins, flipping her upside down. "You su-uu-uu-ck!"

"Well, folks, looks like our foul-mouthed contestant's in a bit of a pickle," Ruth's voice booms from the

302

speakers. "Between you and me, there's not much you can do once you slip but, you know, fall..."

"Yeah, yeah, yeah," Leigh curses. "Bitch."

Ruth's correct, though, and Leigh knows it. The force it would take to climb back up would only make the ladder spin more and most likely propel her into the pool below. The thing is, though, Leigh never planned on winning this game, just dragging it out as long as possible. She can hang on there for a good while, and Leigh plans on making Ruth fully aware that she's just too stubborn to die.

"I can hang around here all day," Leigh taunts. "It's kinda nice. Bit breezy—" she gulps down her joke as the rope ladder begins to shake.

Reese crawls along the ladder, quickly, confidently like a scampering monkey.

"Of fucking course," Leigh groans.

Reese crawls right up to Leigh's face, grinning as his scraggly sideburn whiskers tickle her. He starts shaking the ladder like he's humping it.

"Quit it!" Leigh yells and feels her grip slip.

Reese grins as he opens his mouth and lunges in to bite down on Leigh's white-knuckled hand. She manages to get her other hand in the way, though, and howls as the dumb little monkey clown sinks his teeth in, gnashing like a hungry pug. When she pulls free, blood flicks across both their faces, the rope, and splatters down to the waters below.

A sudden flurry beneath the surface sparks possibly the dumbest, craziest idea she's ever had.

Leigh slaps Reese with her bloody hand, smearing a red palm print across his mangled face, and she takes hold of his long, lank hair.

"Bath time, Monkey Boy," she sneers and lets go of the rope. Reese comes with her, both of them falling through the air towards blue water speckled with red spots. The drum roll stops, and the Big Top fills with silence broken first by Leigh splashing into the tank, then Reese.

Leigh breaks water a second later, gasping for breath and pushing her hair out of her face. She's not far from the edge, and as she takes a stroke towards her escape; Reese surfaces right on her back, grabbing a fistful of her hair.

He's about to say something about bitches and hair pulling when a third presence breaks the surface. In stunned awe, Leigh looks over her shoulder as a massive pure white bull shark with purple and green cow-like patches lunges. Hunger gleams in its single, orange diamond-covered eye as it lurches through the air. It takes Reese inside its gaping maw and crunches down, severing the monkey clown's hand at the wrist, swallowing the rest whole.

Leigh's over the edge, on her back on the ground, before she flicks the severed hand away like a gross bug, before it hits her that she was a hand's reach away from certain death. It's cold comfort, however, as she's surrounded by clowns within seconds, including one very pissed-off Ruth.

"Uh, technically, I didn't lose." Leigh raises an eyebrow, figuring if this is it, she's going out how she lived—pissing everyone around her off.

"You didn't win, either," Ruth sneers. "Take her back to the cage; she'll go again after the others."

Leigh very much enjoys that pissed-off look on Ruth's face as she's lifted and carried back to the lion's cage.

Even more when they find it's empty, and the ringmaster bitch just about explodes.

Chapter Twenty-Five

RETURN TO THE HOUSE OF A THOUSAND GIGGLES

Candy slinks through the dark; the stage lights focusing on the shark tank provide not only the perfect cover, but distraction, too. She darts silently from booth to booth, weaving through the eerie ghost town of carnival games. That crazy clown woman in red sure went to some lengths for this show of hers, and Candy's grateful for the maniac's hubris. The ring is massive, and someone would have surely spotted her sprinting across it, dark or not, without this maze to hide in.

Ducking behind a hoop toss game, Candy holds her breath as two clowns walk past, giggling and shoving each other like boys who've found an older brother's porn stash.

She waits for them to move on before making the dash to the backstage curtain. It doesn't even occur to Candy that she could make a run for it, head out the main exit and get the hell away from this twisted game show. Even if the back gate weren't chained tight, if there was a way out of the carnival grounds, she wouldn't take it. Leigh and Rocky need her.

There's a window overlooking the ring, and it sure looks important to Candy. Maybe up there, she can find something, she hopes. She might not be able to kick ass like Leigh or fly like Rocky, but she's little and sneaky and going to find a way to get her friends out of here—even if she has to burn the whole damn place down.

306

Sure she's made a clean break, Candy slips backstage just as the drum roll stops, as two heavy splashes sound from the shark tank. Candy doesn't notice that or the single clown who watches her go.

"Hehehe." The clown checks to make sure the boss isn't watching and giggles when she sees the big woman at the shark tank. It's naughty, and she's not allowed, which just makes her want it more. The boss lady won't like it, nor will her mean old daddy, but what they don't know... She licks her lips—"Tasty, tasty Candy Girl"—and follows.

Cut to: Ruth holds her hands behind her neck, fingers interlocked as she both pushes and pulls against herself. A steady growl vibrates through her whole body, and the clowns around her slowly back off. First, this smart-mouthed bitch makes a fool of her, openly mocks the show, Ruth's crowning achievement. Now the last contestant escapes from right under their big red noses.

Ruth strikes like a viper, snatches the closest clown, and hurls the unfortunate bastard to the ground. His green curly head barely hits the dirt before Ruth's heel comes down, hard. The pointed tip of her laced-up thigh-high leather boot goes in through the clown's ear as the rest of her foot cracks his skull. Blood and glitter spurt like an egg packed with jam and confetti.

"Find her," Ruth snarls. "Find her before the next game, or every single one of you will pay." The clowns slowly creep away. "Now!" And they take off, all but the ones keeping Leigh hostage.

"Aw, that's gotta suck," Leigh smirks. "You got somethin' on your shoes, by the way."

Ruth kicks away chunks of dead clown clinging to the leather, leaving greasy smears. She fixes her outfit, brushing dust off her lapels.

"I don't know why you're smiling, my dear"—some composure returns—"If your friend doesn't take her turn, then it'll be yours again."

"Oh, goody!" Leigh acts all giddy. "Wonder how many of your lackeys I can get killed this time? I mean, the monkey man was your friend, right?"

Ruth glowers, eye twitching.

"Pet?" Leigh plays around. "Boyfriend?" She shrugs. "Both?"

Ruth places a hand on Leigh's cheek, forcing the girl to look her in the eye. "You knew how to play the Rope Ladder Game?"

"Not like it's science," Leigh laughs. "Oh, wait, it is."

"You think you're smart? Think you know our tricks? So you know the games are rigged?" And then, right in Leigh's ear, she whispers, "Then you know there's no way you're ever going to win."

Mari poses by the Wheel of Fortune, half-Freddy Kruger, half-Farrah Fawcett, oozing with the charm of both. She holds the Wheel like a perverse game show assistant, teasing the handles provocatively while staring right at Rocky.

"You wanna take me for a spin, handsome?" Mari winks and giggles, throwing her head back and flashing her broken glass smile.

"No, I'm good," Rocky says from his knees, looking to the side and wondering what the hell the commotion is.

Ruth strides over, and before she puts the stage smile on, Rocky catches the anger and frustration. So Leigh's

308

still alive; no one else he knows is capable of pissing someone off quite like that. She swirls her hand, signaling for the show to resume, and the music picks back up.

Ruth turns to her audience and holds her arms wide with a stapled-on grin. "Ladies, gentlemen, it's time for Round Three! Meet our contestant!" A light hits Rocky, making him duck his head to shield his eyes. "Aw, look, he's shy! Don't worry though"—Ruth nods to Mari—"our very own mystical bombshell, the gorgeous, the glamorous Marianna'll keep him company while his lady friend gets dried off, won't cha, dollface?"

Mari slithers from the Wheel and saunters across the ring on pointed toes, lights going out behind her and shining down before her as she moves. As she passes Ruth, the ringmaster leans in, whispering in Mari's ear, "Make it a good show, or I'll give you to Daddy."

Again, that flicker—

Remember!

Mari's seductive smile reasserts itself, ignoring the doubts. She approaches Rocky as the boy's lifted to his feet, and Mari wraps her arms around him, locking fingers behind his neck. Swaying her hips, she grinds up and down, winking with an open-mouthed smile.

"Time to play, handsome," she purrs and walks Rocky to the Wheel of Fortune, her arm in his and her head on his shoulder. "Do you want me to do it for you?" she says with a husky breath, eyes wandering down his body.

"I got this," Rocky says and shrugs free.

"Yes, you do," Mari giggles and bites her lip. "Say, is that a gun in your pocket or are you glad to see me again?"

Shit. Rocky only realizes as Mari leers at him that he has the insulin kit stuffed in his pocket. It's not like he planned on losing whatever fucked up game these clowns are gonna make him play, but Rocky has to make it through now. For Stacey, for Cliff...

"Here goes," he sighs and spins the Wheel, the colors and words becoming a whirling blur.

Cut to: Candy finds herself in a corridor where the line between carnival and mansion blurs and colorful brickwork meshes awkwardly with ancient masonry before more garish paintwork takes over.

She finds herself in the same grand and bizarre vestibule from earlier. The disorientating black and white zig-zag tiles below her sneakers almost instill a sense of vertigo. That, added to the blood loss and exhaustion, makes Candy stagger. Dazed, dizzy, there's nothing in her stomach, but still, she wants to throw it up.

Candy reaches the striped spiral staircase leading up to the next floor, flanked by the garish elephant statues with diminutive clown riders on the back of each. If Candy didn't need to hold on to the railing with both hands just to stay on her feet, she might do something about those stupid, grinning Bonkos.

She heads up the stairs, figuring that has to be the way to the office she could make out looming over the ring. If there's a way to shut this place down, it will be up there.

The ascent feels like an optical illusion; the more Candy climbs, the farther away the second floor feels, and when she finally steps on it, Candy has to pause to let the strange dizziness pass.

A jittery giggle bounces off the walls as Candy leans against a railing. She looks around, down both corridors that seem to get smaller and smaller dramatically, ducking in case the owner is nearby. There's no sign of anyone else and yet it continues, liltingly menacingly, teetering between a low chuckle and high-pitched titter.

Glancing down the spiral staircase, blinking rapidly to offset vertigo, Candy spots a hand slap down on the railing at the bottom. Bloody streaks and smears cover the fingers like torn gloves, starkly contrasting with too-white skin.

A head pops out, bright red eyes framed with bright blue inverted teardrops, purple, yellow, and green hair tamed by an oversized bow, a wide painted smile extended across her face with bloody streaks.

"Hiya Candy Girl!" Sully calls out ecstatically. "Where you goin'?" Her voice sinks as she frowns. "You no wanna play with Sully?"

Candy feels the bite mark on her hand flare up, and, vertigo or not, she runs for it, picking the closest corridor at random.

"Wait up!" Sully calls as she stomps up the stairs, laughter spinning and bouncing in her wake.

Cut to: Mari plays with a pair of balls in her hands, spinning them around with her thumb, never taking her eye from Rocky's.

"You done with them or what?" Rocky says, standing before a covered booth, three barrels at the far end with pyramids of milk bottles stacked on top. Crooked, painted bullseyes cross them, with bold dots on the central bottle of each stack.

Mari blows on the balls, then winks with a kiss as she drops them in Rocky's open palm. Three more balls sit on the counter, but she leaves those alone. Instead, she lifts her butt, sliding gracefully onto the counter, and crosses her leg. One bare foot slides up Rocky's jeans, and he steps away as her toe rises.

311

"Three targets!" Ruth booms. "Five shots! Can our young contestant make it? Can he resist Mari's darling charms long enough to even take them? Let's see!" The droning, steady drum roll kicks in.

"I know where you could put those balls," Mari pouts and smiles through her hair.

"Just shut up, will you?" It's going to be hard enough to win this damn game without her purring in his ear, without spending all his focus resisting the urge to do exactly what she wants. He throws the first ball, putting some spin on it, but at the last second, Mari casually drawing a hand across her cleavage catches his eye, and the shot goes wide.

"Oops," Mari giggles.

"Damnit!" Rocky slams a fist down on the counter. "Will you fuck off!?"

"Oh." Mari shivers. "I love a man who plays a little rough."

"That's a miss, folks! Our contestant can only afford one more slip up!"

Rocky shuts his eyes, takes a deep breath, and takes his second shot, hitting the target dead in the middle, and... Nothing happens. The bottles remain standing.

"Hey! That's cheating! I hit it!"

"It's OK, honey; I'll show you how to hit the right spot."

Rocky slaps the counter, losing his cool. "Eventually, you're gonna go too far, and it won't be sexy anymore. It'll just be sad," Rocky snaps.

Mari spreads her legs and licks her lips. "You think I'm sexy?" she smirks, and Rocky blushes. She revels in proving him wrong.

"Oh, tough luck," Ruth comments. "Our boy's gotta hit three for three or..." She descends into maniacal laughter.

Or Stacey's done for, stuck as one of these damn clowns, Rocky continues the thought. Candy's next, and, shit, even Leigh; they never got along, but she doesn't deserve this. Luck isn't on his side, though... Wait! Rocky remembers what Leigh said. It's not about luck; these games are rigged. They make it look easy... His eyes focus on the glaringly apparent bullseyes, and he realizes that's exactly where these clown fucks want him to aim.

"Gotcha." Rocky takes the third ball from the counter and doesn't give Mari the time to make another obscene comment; he whips it through the air, taking out a bottle right in the bottom middle row. The rest tumble and fall, clinking in a cascade of dirty, painted glass. "Yeah." Rocky grins. He's got this.

"Oh my." Mari applauds. "Nice arm." She leans in, rubbing her hands over Rocky's muscles, and he yanks it away.

Rocky can't see where Ruth lurks in the darkness, but he points in what he hopes is her direction anyway. "I got this, you face painted freaks."

He winds up, pulls back, and doesn't even notice as Mari lies back on the counter, arching her back as she plays with her hair, one leg raised with her toe pointed high. The ball rips through the air, taking out two bottles this time, and the rest clatter like dominoes.

Mari applauds, bicycling her legs in the air as Rocky celebrates with a fist pump.

"One more to go!" Ruth's voice thunders, and Rocky echoes the sentiment.

He looks to the counter for the last ball, only to see Mari has it. She rolls it back and forth, her cleavage feigning coy innocence.

Rocky reaches for it, and she pulls it away, holding the ball at arm's length—forcing Rocky to lean over her. Her lips brush his ear as she whispers, "Kiss me handsome, and you won't need to play. Let me taste you, and we can be together forever and ever, two lovers laughing in the dark."

In his head, he hears, "Kiss me, Rocky, I've always loved you," the words spoken by a girl no longer with them. If he showed some restraint, then maybe... It's too late for that. But he can take control, here and now.

"No," Rocky states, plain and simple. "I won't." And he snatches the ball from her.

Mari snarls as Rocky winds up and takes his last shot.

Candy's long shot pays off; as she peels down a hall, the pattern on the carpet making her feel like she's on a treadmill, she spots a door marked "office."

Sully's taunting follows her, but as yet, there's no sign of the maniacal, hyper-active pixie cannibal. Candy slips in through the door before that changes.

There's a snib on the handle within, and though Candy clicks it on, she doubts that it would hold for very long, especially with the erratic energy that clown seems to possess. She finds herself in a room lined with ornate framed posters for old Bonkin's Bonanza acts, along with news clippings focusing on Buster B. Bonkin's Carnival of Crime. While downstairs was like a museum, this feels more like a shrine. Ruth Hardstack worships Bonko, that's clear; whether she is or isn't his daughter, Candy couldn't care less.

She crosses the office to a grand desk, thick velvet curtains closed behind a high back leather chair, and tugs on a gilded rope cord. That kicks off a hidden mechanism that pulls the curtains back, revealing a massive picture window looking down on the ring below.

All light and focus are on Rocky at one of the booths. That slutty clown rolls around on the counter, but Candy can see Rocky's ignoring her even from this distance. She's relieved, not because of any jealousy though that's there—they can break up, put a whole country between them, but he'll always have been her Rocky. She'll always love him, in a way. That's just how it is; the people we love stay with us, even if it hurts, carved into our hearts like names on a tree. No, it feels like he's grown up, and it fills her with faith and confidence that he'll pull through. Now, it's her turn.

There's no sign of Leigh anywhere, and Candy tries to push that from her mind as she searches the desk. There's a solid-looking microphone bolted to it and switches marked for different parts of the carnival. That would really ruin that big woman's show if she took over the music. Now if only she could find something to—

"Knock-knock!" Sully interrupts from the other side of the door, and the handle rattles. "Hehe, I know you're in there, Candy Girl," Sully sings. "I'm hungry! Let me in!" she growls.

The door shakes but holds.

Candy's eyes dart around the room, looking for ideas, and they land on a record player, two hefty speakers mounted to the wall above it.

The highback chair skids across the room, crashing into the wall. Candy's on top of it before it even comes to a rest. She pulls on one of the speakers, and the second it comes away, the weight of it nearly flattens her. It's all

315

she can do to hold on as it pushes her down into the seat, and the momentum sends her back across the room. Wire rips from the wall and yanks the record player half off the counter. It reaches, though, and Candy carefully balances the speaker on its side by the microphone, the bulk of the thing nearly half her size.

"Lemme in!" Sully rages like a maniac against the door, hungry like she's never been before. "You guys keep doing this to me! No fair!" Sully kicks the door.

"Records, records, records..." Candy looks around but can't spot any. There has to be, though. She drops to her knees and opens the cupboards below the record player. "Yes!" Vinyl covers fly out, this way and that, as Candy tears through Ruth's collection, looking for the right one, and her eyes light up as she holds a pink record sleeve with a stomach-down nude woman on the cover.

Rocky's eyes glint with victory as he spins, both fists in the air. The last of the bottles clang to the floor behind him.

"Got ya!"

"You sure did," Mari smirks and springs to action. She wraps her legs and arms around him from behind, pulling Rocky back against the counter.

"The hell you doing!?"

Her ankles lock around his waist, pinning Rocky's arms to his side. One hand explores his chest while the other strokes his face.

"Let me go!"

As Ruth approaches, spotlights pave her way. A kazoo fanfare blasts to raining confetti and cartwheeling, backflipping clowns. Ruth slowly applauds, a sinister grin spreading across her face. "Bravo, my boy, bravo!"

316

"I won! Played your dumb game! Beat you clown fucks at your own shit."

"Indeed you did," Ruth snaps her fingers, "and now for your prize..." A clown lackey hurries over with a bag of the black cotton candy.

Rocky goes cold. "Get that shit away from me."

"Mari, dear?" Ruth nods, and the burlesque clown grabs a fist full of Rocky's hair, pulling his head back as her other hand holds his jaw open. Rocky gargles for them to stop, but there's nothing he can do as—

Split-screen: Candy flips a record over, places the needle at the start, and the office fills with a racing drumbeat; Leigh eyes the missing pole from the lion cage, sitting in the dirt unseen by her captors; Rocky twists his face to the side, trying to avoid the black cotton candy; Candy flips all the buttons at once, and the fanfare is instantly replaced by jaunty guitar riffs; Ruth snaps around, raging at the interruption to her show; Leigh takes advantage of the distraction to elbow one guard in the gut, knee the other, and make a grab for the iron bar; Rocky's face turns red as Ruth slams the black cotton candy in his mouth—Mari pulls him into a kiss; Candy goes to the window, pumped and ready to witness the Big Top Blitz below and all three screens become her, staring with abject horror as she sees what's happening to Rocky.

"No." Candy's stomach turns. "No..."

The door behind her smashes open, the handle breaking away and crashing to the floor. Sully stands in the doorway, grinning from ear to ear. "*I want Candy,*" she sings.

Chapter Twenty-Six

I WANT CANDY

"You! You! And you!"

Cut to: Ruth points to three clowns. "Shut that damn noise up! It's ruining my show!" She's distraught, and on the verge of tears as poppy, upbeat riffs fill the Big Top.

For a second, it looks like they might disobey, as though questioning her authority, but the snarl she shoots them gets them running.

"And bring me the little runaway!" The noise rattles her. It makes Ruth bite her lips with nervous energy. "They're not gonna ruin my big moment, no they're not, they're not!"

Mari lets Rocky slip away as the music picks up. She rubs her hands with delight as the boy falls to his knees.

Bow Wow Wow sings about a guy who's tough but sweet to a Bo Diddley beat. Rocky claws at his heart, eyes bulging and lips pulling into a mad, lustful grin.

They sing about a boy so fine as Rocky rips his shirt, and the skin below flushes pale white.

Bow Wow Wow says he's got everything they desire as two thin dark lines cut through his eyes, matching two razor-like red ticks extending Rocky's lips into a permanent smile.

Rocky runs his hands through his hair, and the curtains stay up, quaffed into sharply dramatic devil horns. His hair flushes deep red as Bow Wow Wow sings about the boy who sets the summer sun on fire.

"I want—"

The song continues, and Rocky screams through black-stained teeth along with it.

"—*candy!*"

"*I want Candy.*" Sully jiggles her hips and sings along, throwing in her own cute but creepy flair. "*A-doo-do-da-doo-da-do! Bum-bum!*" She jumps from side to side, blocking all attempts Candy makes at getting past her.

Candy needs to get past this damn clown, get to Rocky, while Bow Wow Wow sings about going to see a boy as the sun goes down. Her eyes dart around as she looks for something to use as a weapon, and they land on an ornate letter opener on the desk.

Her eyes light up as the record continues spinning about there being no finer boy in town.

Candy dashes for the blade, and it's in her hands in less than a second, pointed right at Sully, who doesn't seem to care. The clown dances along to the music as she closes in.

Candy backs up till she's flat against the picture window.

"*So sweet,*" Sully sings. "Makin' my mouth water, Candy Girl." She grins wide, showing Candy her black candy-coated teeth.

"*I want candy,*" the song continues ringside. "*I want—*"

"Candy!" Rocky the Clown roars, his voice almost demonic, dark ringed eyes staring up at the picture window with predatory intensity.

"Get him under control," Ruth snaps.

Mari purses her lips; whatever control Ruth had over the other clowns is slipping as the big woman sweats.

Remember!

Mari shakes it off again and obeys. Or, she tries to. As soon as she places one hand on Rocky, he elbows her, sending the burlesque clown flying as he stands up.

"Enough!" Ruth cracks her whip, then with a flick of her wrist snaps it taut around Rocky's neck. She yanks him in close, lifting him onto his toes to meet her eyes. "This is MY show! You will NOT upstage me! Not in front of Da—"

"Hey, bitch!" a voice cuts in, and Ruth turns to see an iron bar heading right for her face.

Sully leaps up onto the desk, mismatched boots kicking the speaker, causing it to clatter to the floor. The cord pulls tight, yanking the record player across the room, and the needle skips.

The song repeats "*wrapped in a sweater*"—scratch— "*wrapped in a sweater,*" over and over.

"Aww," Sully complains, "why'd you hafta go and ruin the music!?"

"I don't wanna hurt you." Candy holds the letter opener at Sully, tip pointed and arms at full extension.

"I don't wanna hurt you either, Candy Girl!" Sully plops down on the desk, kicking her boots. "I just wanna taste ya!"

Boots clatter in the hallway, and seconds later, the three clowns Ruth sent arrive. They cluster at the doorway, not sure what's going on in the office.

"The boss says we hafta bring her—"

"No!" Sully snaps and pushes herself off the table. She lands less than an inch from the tip of Candy's letter opener; the girl yelps, and the point quivers in line with the clown's painted red nose. Sully smiles, almost kittenish, as she licks her lips and leans in, the blade passing so close to her skin it moves through Sully's soft rainbow hair.

Candy's heart races, air whistling in and out of her parted lips as her breathing becomes erratically panicked. Sully reaches Candy's ear, and she can feel the clown's warm breath brush it.

"She's mine," Sully says and runs her tongue slowly across Candy's ear.

"But da boss said we gots ta bring her!" one of the lackeys by the door says.

Sully grunts, harrumphs, and spins on her heels, but before she storms over to deal with the clowns, she pauses to pluck the letter opener from Candy's quaking hands. Even after Sully skips away, Candy can't bring herself to lower her arms.

"Da boss is gunna be real mad—"

"Oh, poo to the boss." Sully rolls her eyes as she brings the blade across the first clown's throat. She giggles and lets the glittery blood spray all over her face.

One of the other clowns finds his companion's demise utterly hilarious right up until Sully rams the blade into his temple. He makes a noise that sounds something like, "Oh-doy," as his eyes flutter like a sputtering projector. He wavers for a moment even after Sully yanks the letter opener free, crumpling after a short delay.

The death of the second clown snaps Candy into action; she needs to get the hell out of there, but the problem is the only door's become a Three Stooges spatterfest. There's nothing but displays and shelves to either side, so that only leaves...

Candy turns around and swallows hard as she looks through the window. Something is going on down in the ring; it's chaos, but she doesn't have time for that. Her eyes settle on the intersecting catwalks just below the window. Sure it's only a short hop down to it, but it's a multi-story fall to the ground below.

It's that or the clown, and as much as Candy hates heights, a psychotic clown girl with a knife and a taste for human flesh is slightly less preferable.

Candy kicks the window as grunts and wet stabs hit out in tandem behind her. She cries out, forgetting her foot's still banged up from when she leaped off the big wheel. She's not breaking this thing herself; no, Candy needs something heavy, with heft, and a quick look to the floor gives her the answer—the speaker.

The thing's half her size and feels like it's ten times as heavy. It takes all her strength and a roar that's adorably ferocious for Candy to hurl the thing. It crashes through the window, breaking a hole not much larger than the speaker, sending spiderwebs across what remains. The fractured glass, though, is easy enough for Candy to kick free as the sounds of slaughter behind her fade.

"Hey!" Sully yells. "Where you goin', Candy Girl?"

Biting down on her knuckle, Candy shuts her eyes and leaps through the window.

"Oh f—"

"—uck you!" The pole connects with Ruth's head, and the big woman spins almost three times with the impact before staggering away, not quite falling, but barely able to keep on her feet.

The whip around Rocky's neck slackens, and the clown hits the dirt.

"My show," Ruth growls, falling from foot to foot as the Big Top spins around her. "My show!" She roars and launches herself at Leigh. "You ruined it!"

Leigh doesn't fuck around; she swings the bar again, and this clunk sends Ruth to the floor. The ringmaster goes flat on her back in a cloud of dust.

A piercing tone whines through the speakers as the music cuts out, the Big Top descending into a stunned silence. Leigh can feel countless eyes on her from the stands and stalls—terrified hostages and confused clowns, no longer sure what to do now that the ringleader is out of commission. Whatever mockery of order and control Ruth Hardstack asserted over the rabid wereclowns falters as she writhes in the dust. Sporadic screams ring out as renegade clowns set upon the captive audience, but for most, they stare as though this is part of the show, as though waiting to be told what to do.

"The hell is wrong with you people." Leigh spots the mic pinned to Ruth's lapel. It might make her a bitch, but Leigh feels almost no pity. If she and Candy can fight back, so can they; shit, maybe things would never have gotten so out of hand if they all fought instead of cowering, willing to keep quiet as others died just in the chance they'd be OK.

Snatching the mic, Leigh snarls, "You bitches just gonna sit there and let these bozos get away with this shit?"

A few cowering faces in the audience glance up.

"There's more of you than these pasty-faced fuckwits!"

Painted smiles snarl, bearing black-stained teeth in warning.

"You're probably gonna die anyway; might as well punch some fuckin' bozos on your way out!"

"Fuck, yeah!" A big guy rises to his feet, decks the nearest clown, and takes a cleaver to the neck as he cheers.

323

"No!" a woman screams and bounds over the man, wrestling that clown out of sight behind the seats. She emerges, a moment later, splattered in sparkly blood.

Leigh's words, brazen and confrontational, spark an insurrection. Her eyes light up as the world descends into a *Big Top Blitz*.

One man rises from his seat and lunges for the clown holding a spiked baseball bat. Wrestling it free, he brings it around and whacks the clown over the head with it. He lets go, but the bat stays where it is.

A woman stands, making fists as two clowns close in on her, blocking a crying child with her body. Just as the clown reaches her, another kid hurls themself on its back. Together they beat on the clown, laying into it like it's a blue-haired piñata.

Leigh basks in the blitz, in the glorious chaos for a moment. Then her eyes land on Rocky, face down in the dirt, Mari squatting by his side, pawing at him.

"You want some too, skank?" Leigh threatens Mari, and the burlesque clown slips away, no longer quite so poised, her movements more natural and less deliberate.

Rocky rises to his knees, and it's only then that Leigh sees what's going on. That his transformation into a clown is complete.

"Shit!" Leigh drops the weapon and goes to him, fear, horror, and concern that surprises her drawn across her face. "No, Rocky, shit!" True, she never liked him, but that doesn't mean she enjoys seeing him become one of those honking nightmares.

"Candy?" Rocky says with a faraway stare, seemingly unaware Leigh's even there.

"No, Rock-For-Brains, it's me." Leigh doesn't want to get too close but can't quite bring herself to back away either.

"Candy!?" Rocky looks around like a confused dog searching for its missing owner.

A yelp from above snaps both his and Leigh's attention. They look up to see Candy crawling across a catwalk. She's on her hands and knees, paralyzed with fear, a short distance from the broken office window. That creepy little cannibal clown drops through the window, landing on the catwalk with a jaunty bounce.

"Oh, fuck," Leigh curses.

"Candy!?" Rocky yells, ripping his shirt fully open with raw, untapped rage.

"Easy there, Horny the Clown." Leigh backs away, carefully stepping toward the backstage curtain while trying not to spook the clown. She'll put him down if she has to, but even if he's one of those things, he's still Rocky and he still means something to Candy.

Rocky stares with jutted teeth, like some simpleminded animal trying to track its elusive prey. His eyes bulge as they follow Candy's slow crawl and Sully's joyful approach. They follow the catwalk to the far side, to a post at the edge of the ring. It reaches from the ground to the top, with a ladder fixed to the side, one that goes right to the catwalk.

"Candy!" Rocky the Clown roars and sets off, on all fours at first and then rising to his feet, barely able to contain the beast within.

"Shit," Leigh cusses as Rocky kicks up dust. She breaks backstage, hoping to hell she can make it to Candy before either of the clowns do.

"Hey, Toots! You just gonna leave me here!?" Bonko calls to Mari, smacking his crusty, flaky lips.

Mari doesn't hear him. She wanders through the chaos of the ring, listening to ghosts whispering in her ear.

Remember our love.

That boy, the handsome one, his love for that girl, the way he cried her name, awoke a dormant part of her—the Mari buried below the desire, decadence, and debauchery.

"Chet?" Mari asks the ghosts in her head.

"Hey! I'm talking to ya, toots! Scoot that pretty ass over here!"

Mari hears him this time and turns to the oversized face of Bonko, leering from within the gunked-up mechanism of an antique machine. She follows his voice nervously, her movements devoid of her usual glitz.

"Yeah, that's the shit! You f-f-f-fancy a little head? Or a big one, ay-yup!" Bonko laughs so hard the front wheels of his machine lift off the ground, clattering back down.

Mari doesn't see what's so funny.

"Say, how's your husband?" Bonko winks. "Whoops! Silly me, I forgot they f-f-f-fried his ass, right? Or did they stick a coupla pricks in him? That's what he wanted, right?"

Mari grabs her head as flashes of memories strobe. The image of a man strong enough in body to break another in two, gentle enough at heart to only care for his love's joy. Wicked smiles across candlelit rooms, lips biting on red silk sheets, lust and love intertwined like no other.

"What kinda f-f-f-fag gets off on his squeeze sucking another man's f-f-f-flagpole!? If you were mine, honey, I'd never share ya! That's the toot-tootin' truth!"

That's supposed to be a compliment? Preferable? No, it's not, and Mari remembers who she truly is, what she's lost, and what this monster before her has taken.

"Yeah, you get me so f-f-f-fuckin' f-f-f-fired up, toots! Come to Bonko!" She stands before him. "Take it off! Take it all off!"

Mari obliges, letting the loose slip that barely hangs from her shoulder fall to the dirt. She kneels, scoops it up, and just as Bonko runs that tongue-like monstrosity over his lips, she crams the cloth into his mouth.

"Kinky," Bonko mumbles. "I love it, ay-yup!"

He doesn't love it when Mari grabs a nearby tiki torch and lights the silk on fire.

"Wait!" Bonko protests and tries to spit the clothes out, but Mari holds them in place with the torch. She could have just set him on fire, but she wants the bastard to see it coming first. Let him feel what it's like to have something violate his body. He doesn't love that, but then again, Bonko never could understand that it's not always about you. Chet could. His joy was Mari's, wherever and however she found it, and she hopes the memory of that remarkable man is watching her fuck this disgusting one's mouth with a tiki pole, because this is making her happier than she's been in years.

"F-f-f-fuck!"

"Die for real this time, you sick little freak!"

Mari laughs madly in the flickering glow as the vile sugar-caked and shunted Bonko pops and crackles, as he cries out in helpless agony.

This whole nightmare started with him years ago, and no matter the depraved cruelty perpetrated by the cursed clowns on this day, all of them, the Children of the Candy, are victims of this man. This creature clinging to a twisted mockery of life, held together by spilled blood and evil machinery, corrupting this place and all those he touches.

Maybe it's finally ending Bonko, finishing what her husband started, that's released her from his influence. Or the twisted magic in that cursed cotton candy backfiring, waking up the true Mari—a woman unafraid to take what she wants, which just so happens to be brutal, agonizing vengeance—but Mari finally feels herself again.

It began with Bonko and Mari, and so it ends with them. One of them wailing in anguish, the other embracing the flames like a long-lost lover.

Above the snapping flames of the Zephyr, Candy clings onto the edges of the catwalk. Her knuckles are white, and her knees tremble as she inches along. If she could get to her feet and run, she'd already be at the other side, despite the swollen ankle. Even the thought of that, though, makes the red and white of the Big Top swirl.

Sully scrapes the letter opener along the handrail, the screeching so sour Candy can feel it in her teeth.

"Candy Girl, whatcha doin'?" Sully calls. "You're gonna fall!" She jumps and slams her mismatched boots down, making the walkway sway and Candy cling on for dear life. Sully chuckles, skipping and kicking her unlaced boots to the side, delighting in how Candy curls against the railing. "You look like a little kitty who thinks she's gonna—" Sully shakes the walkway and laughs.

A thud and a rattle from the far side stop her in mid-guffaw.

"Hey! Whatcha doin' up here?" Sully shakes the letter opener at the interloper like they're a naughty child. "Ain't nobody invited you, Pretty Boy!"

"Candy," Rocky snarls, drool dripping from bared fangs.

"She's mine," Sully snaps, snorting like a dog protecting its bone.

Rocky runs, pounding along the catwalk, racing like thunder, larger than life. The swaying, rattling metal doesn't slow his momentum for a second, and though he has more ground to cover than Sully, that's not going to be a problem for him.

"No!" Sully takes off too, her strides off-kilter, stumbling but effective all the same.

Candy, caught between two maniacal clowns and with nowhere to go but down, does the only thing she can—closes her eyes, tenses up, and holds out hope that whichever one gets her makes it quick. She expects the sharp tip of a blade and instead feels sudden weightlessness, and her hands slip from their white-knuckle grip on the rail. Her body lifted, swept off her feet like—Candy dares to open her eyes on the frightening and beautiful face of Rocky. Even through warped clown eyes, he looks at her with nothing less than pure, undying love, cradling her in his arms.

"Rocky?" Candy gasps.

"Candy," he says like it's the only word he knows. Even if it is, it's the only one that matters.

She looks upon his too-white face, the flicked razor-slash lips, wild matted horns of hair, and Candy sees only the boy. She feels no fear. Till the blade cuts across her view, plunging into Rocky's chest.

Rocky howls and shoves Sully away, keeping Candy safe while the giggling clown pulls her wet weapon back.

Sully licks the edge of the blade; it slices her tongue, and she savors the taste of their mixed blood.

"Tasty, tasty—" Rocky doesn't let her finish; he barges past, carrying Candy like she was Fay Wray to his King Kong—a wild midnight movie fantasy come to twisted life.

"Rude!" Sully yells and leaps on his back, wrapping her legs around him and holding onto his hair with one hand. Rocky doesn't let her slow him down; he pounds along the catwalk toward the office, the girl he loves tucked in his arms as the one on his back plunges the blade into him, over and over. Blood runs down the tatters of his leather jacket.

They're almost at the window, and Sully changes tack. She lifts the red knife and flicks it around and down into the side of Rocky's neck. This brings him to a stop, and his mouth opens, a thick glut of blood pouring forth.

"Rocky!" Candy screams, the blade buried to the handle inches from her face. "No!"

For a second, it looks like the fight's gone from him, that Sully's won, but the girl in his arms gives him the strength to keep up the fight. He thrusts himself back, spitting blood with a roar, and slams Sully into the railing.

"Oh, poo!" Sully yelps as she tumbles backward over the rail, disappearing into the dark below.

Rocky continues on, each step slower, heavier than the one before. He uses the speaker as a step to climb up and through the window into the office. He makes it to the nearest wall before dropping Candy.

"Rocky, no, no, no." She immediately turns to try and help him, but Rocky holds her away gently. One hand reaches for the blade as he falls to his knees. "No, leave it!" Candy insists, but he's not listening. Rocky pulls the letter opener free, and the blood flows.

"Candy?" he says as he collapses.

"No-no-no—" Candy sinks to the floor to catch him. She sits with him, cradling the boy's head in her lap as his blood spreads across her thighs. Trembling, crimson spotted hands brush his hair as Rocky stares far away, the light fading from his eyes. "I'm so sorry..."

"Candy," Rocky manages as he reaches into his jacket, and with the last of his strength, takes out the insulin kit. "Candy," he groans as he offers it to her. "Cliff—" and then drops it as his arm flops to the floor. Rocky dies in the lap of the love he lost, failing the best friend he ever had. There's just enough of the boy left in there to feel that and not enough to see the way Candy stares at him, broken in awe.

She just stares in silence at him, unable to process what's happened, and brushes her fingers through his hair till Leigh finds them. The dead boy and the girl he loved, both soaked in his blood.

"Candy…"

Chapter Twenty-Seven

LITTLE MONSTERS

"Candy!"

Flashback to: Rocky yells down a sun-dappled woodland trail. Birds twitter a sweet woodland symphony. "You still there?"

"Hey!" Candy cries out. "This isn't," she grunts, "as easy—oh, wow, Rocky..." Candy reaches the top of the trail, and her eyes land on a pre-made picnic laid out on full display. A single red balloon floats, tied to the basket, bobbing in the high-altitude breeze. "Did you—?"

"Came up this morning, while you were still snoring, to set up." Rocky smiles as he dumps his rucksack. He stretches like the climb was barely a warmup.

"I don't snore." Candy squints, her nose scrunching. "You did this"—Candy shrugs her backpack off and just about falls to the ground with it—"twice? I'm totally outta shape."

Rocky shrugs. "I mean, with those legs, it's like four times the climb for you, so—"

"Hey!" Candy barks. "I didn't hear you complaining about these legs last night!" She pouts and holds her arms out. "Carry me!"

Rocky sweeps his curtain fringe back, heads over to his girl, and kneels by her side. He lifts her onto his back, holding her thighs on either side of his body.

"Master Luke, this way, yes, heeheehee." Candy does a Yoda impression as Rocky carries her to the blanket.

332

"You're such a nerd," Rocky says as he lays her down, and Candy giggles as she pulls him with her. They roll, in a tangle, and Rocky lands with his head in her lap.

"Hi," Candy smiles down at him.

"Hi," Rocky smiles up at her.

A sudden gust blows Rocky's hair over his face. Candy brushes it aside and looks deep into the eyes of the boy she loves. She saw the acceptance letter sitting on his kitchen table this morning and knows that things will never be the same after they come down this trail. Each step they take now carries them further apart, rather than closer together, but none of that matters at this moment.

The wind snaps the balloon free from its tether, and it races into the sky before either of them can make a grab for it.

"Oh no!" Candy gasps as she watches it rise and disappear, carried away by forces far beyond her control, and stares into the sky long after it's gone.

"We have to go!"

Cut to: Leigh shouting, Candy just staring at the ceiling, hand still stroking Rocky's matted, blood-clumped hair robotically.

"Candy!"

Blinking, coming back to herself, Candy suddenly realizes where she is, what's just happened, and her eyes meet Leigh's.

"Rocky's dead..." she says meekly like it wasn't evident.

"I know." Leigh squats and tries to take Candy's hands; she pulls away and keeps petting Rocky's head. "We need to go. Now!" she insists, but Candy ignores her, slipping away again. "What would Rocky want you to do?" Leigh doesn't want to go there, but she does.

"He... he'd tell me to run." Her hands freeze, and then she turns back to Leigh. "He'd tell me to run."

"So let's do it," Leigh nods and spots the insulin kit in Rocky's hand. She picks it up, stuffs it into the back pocket of her torn tartan pants, and then holds a hand out for her friend.

"OK," Candy nods, "OK," and takes Leigh's hand.

Before she leaves, Candy kneels and closes Rocky's eyes, brushes his hair aside one more time, and kisses him farewell.

Down in the ring, a jumble of incoherent mumbles calls out from a tangle of broken wood and canvas.

Haha, Heehee, and Tinkle clamber over the ruins, pulling at the debris and tossing chunks of cheap wood at each other. The collapsed awning flutters as a shape rises within, fighting against the sheet with violent frustration. It tosses aside the colored trap, revealing a very flustered, pissed-off Sully the Clown.

She pouts, and a chunk of wood plonks off her head. Sully slowly turns, a pained frown turning to a dangerous growl, as her eyes settle on the culprit—Tinkle, covering her mouth with both hands as her little clown body bounces with laughter.

"Dat's not very nice!"

"Sowee!" Tinkle giggles, and her brothers join in with a chorus. "Sowee-sowee-sowee!"

Sully climbs to her feet as the Triplets dance around her, chanting. She takes one step out from the carnage and falls flat on her face.

"Oh! Poo!" Sully looks down and sees her red Doc sitting at an impossibly twisted angle.

"Poo-poo-poo!" the Triplets chant.

Sully reaches for her damaged foot with a limp arm. It hangs in the wrong direction. The way it wiggles, almost lifelessly, amuses Sully and the Triplets greatly.

"Hehe, Sully's all brokey-broke!"

Tittering, as though delighted by the agony, she uses her one good arm to climb to her one good foot and drags herself toward the backstage curtain. Her one-track mind drives her on despite her broken, mangled body.

"Tasty," Sully grunts, "tasty," and coughs blood, "Candy Girl..."

The Triplets look to one another, repeating the word silently, like a bunch of dogs hearing the name of their favorite snack. Yipping excitedly, they follow on Sully's heel as she leans on the broken leg with a shotgun-like crack.

"There you are, you Goddamn townie bitches! I'm gonna ring your fuckin' necks so hard your eyes pop like motherfucking balloons!" Ruth snarls, and the crack of her whip resounds through the halls, bringing Candy and Leigh to a sudden halt. She seems gigantic in the warped perspective of the hall's decor, a hulking, snarling beast in a bodysuit and ripped fishnet stockings.

"Don't cha mean daddy-fucking?" Leigh can't hide her smirk.

"I'm gonna make you watch me split your little friend in two!"

Ruth comes at them, and with Candy's swollen ankle, she closes in fast.

The two of them barge through the nearest door, finding themselves in a sterile, grey cinder block staircase that's startlingly utilitarian after the Escheresque hall. Leigh takes Candy's weight as they blast down the stairs, skipping as many as they can. They're two flights down when Ruth crashes through the door, her furious roar pinging off the barren walls.

"You RUINED my SHOW!"

Candy and Leigh reach the bottom and push through the only door, coming out somewhere familiar. The loading bay for the Buster B. Bonkin Murder Ride.

"Candy Girl!" Sully squeals like a fangirl looking for an autograph at the entrance. "Do ya wanna play with my friends?"

"What the fuck are those!" Leigh snaps in disgust at the three pint-sized clowns dancing around Sully's feet.

"Hey, look!" Sully points to Candy's swollen ankle then to her one broken one, the boot resting on its side, almost facing backward. "Samesies!"

As the door clangs shut behind them, the sound of Ruth bounding down the stairs is shut off, but she's close. Left with little choice, Candy and Leigh jump down onto the track.

Candy lands with a grunt but doesn't let the pain stop her. They run into the dark together on foot. Behind them, Sully's squeals and singing becomes lost in the reverberations, drowned out by the tapped narrations being set off as Candy and Leigh race along the track. They trigger jump scares and prompts, the noises tripping over one another, but they ignore it all as they hurry through the gloom.

Ahead, the hall glows with the waving blue light that filters through this side of the shark tank.

"We're nearly there." Leigh almost smiles, and Candy bites down on the pain as she forces herself to keep up.

A dark form eclipses the light as Ruth blocks the track ahead.

"Fuck!" Leigh skids to a halt; Candy bites down on her lip.

Ruth wraps her whip around her hands, turning it onto a thick, knotted garotte.

Sully's cheery singing catches up as she hobbles into sight like a broken puppet dancing along with half its strings cut.

"I want the Candy Girl!" Sully yells; the Triplets chanting echoes her.

"No!" Ruth growls. "The skinny brat and the big bitch are mine!"

"OK, first"—Leigh holds up a hand—"fuck you all and, second, really? I mean, like, pot kettle, you fucking Clydesdale!" Leigh glances around, looking for anything that can save them, and it seems like their only option is a maintenance door off to the side. The problem is it's closer to Ruth than them, and though Leigh could probably make it, there's no way Candy, with that swollen ankle, can.

"Leigh, don't." Candy doesn't need to read her mind. Leigh's her best friend, and Candy knows what she's thinking. "Don't you dare!"

"Get that cute little butt of yours outta here!" Leigh shoves away from Candy and charges at Ruth. "Here I am, bitch!"

"Go get her!" Sully orders the Triplets. They scamper on, yipping and hooting.

Candy limps after Leigh as fast as possible, pushing back against the pains shooting through her leg. "No!"

Leigh swings for Ruth, and the large clown steps aside with alarming grace, allowing Leigh to sail past her. She hooks the whip over the girl's neck, yanking her back with enough force to lift Leigh off her feet and make her eyes almost pop. Ruth pulls the girl flat to her chest, turning her so Candy can see her friend's face as the whip bites deep enough into Leigh's neck to draw blood.

"This is what you get for ruining my show!" Ruth snarls and pulls back harder, lifting Leigh off her feet. The girl holds out one hand, waving for Candy to go.

"Leigh!" Candy yells as Haha jumps on her back, Tinkle wraps her arms and legs around Candy's, and Heehee grabs her hand.

"I'm coming for ya!" Sully drags herself along the tunnel, tittering in anguish.

"Go!" Leigh manages to rasp, and the command spurs Candy into action. She tears the kid off her back, kicks the one on her leg free, and slaps the last one away. Out of options and time, Candy hurries to the maintenance door; she looks back once more at Leigh as her friend's hand goes limp. Somehow, Leigh manages to smile as the life's choked out of her.

Candy slams the door shut inside the room, braces her back, and slides to the floor. The thick metal cuts most of the noise from outside, but she can still hear Sully's off-key singing and Ruth's roars of fury.

There's nowhere for her to go. No windows or other doors. Just dirty metal shelves stacked with pieces of machinery and boxes stacked haphazardly around, as though recently dumped there with no thought to organization.

Rocky's dead, and it's all her fault. Rocky, the boy she loved, turned into one of those things, stabbed to death because she couldn't find the willpower to move her ass. Even as one of those damn clowns he did more for her than she ever could.

Leigh's dying, and it's all her fault. Leigh, her best friend, fought her way through hell, only to willingly give

338

her life up for her. And for what? They'll get through the door eventually, and finally, the fate she's been dodging all day will catch up with her. They'll have died for nothing, for someone who doesn't deserve their love, their devotion—just a ditzy bimbette, sitting on her ass crying like a baby, as always.

She wishes there was some way to make their sacrifices worth it, something she could do to repay them. To be worthy of their love. She wishes she was somewhere else, anywhere else, like on the floor of Leigh's bedroom, the two of them snug inside the same sleeping bag, foreheads pressed together, tips of their noses touching.

"It's you and me," she sobs, "Candy and Leigh"—the tears flow—"together for-forever!" she cries and kicks out, knocking over one of the boxes. Its contents spill across the floor, landing inches from her. Candy's brow rises as a dangerously desperate thought crosses her mind, and she doesn't think twice. "You'll see..."

Everything goes white, and as Leigh fades away, she goes somewhere else.

To her balmy bedroom in the middle of the night, lit only by a blue and red lava lamp. Gentle snores break the heavy silence, but they're not what keeps Leigh wide awake, staring at the ceiling and doing all she can to keep her eyes off the t-shirt lying on the floor. The one that belongs to Candy, her best friend, and the girl she keeps thinking of when she closes her eyes. When she kisses her boyfriend. She shouldn't think about these things. It's not right. Yet when Cliff kisses her, Cherry Coke on his lips, Leigh can't help but wonder if that's what Candy's lip gloss tastes like. What Candy's lips...

Then they're tangled up in blankets on the floor at Candy's, and the girl leans against her, using Leigh's back as a pillow while they watch some cheesy black and white Vincent Price movie.

Then Leigh's running an ice cube across Candy's exposed navel and feeling a rush as she watches the way the girl shivers. The way her body moves. Eyes drawn to where her underwear shows through unbuttoned jeans, that thin line of fabric pressed against Candy's waist.

They're singing and dancing in the car.

They're throwing popcorn at each other in the theatre. Candy gets some down Leigh's top and acts grossed out when she plucks it up and shoves it in her mouth.

She's... fading now... she's...

Leigh falls to her knees, air flooding back into her lungs. She's alive, she's free, somehow...

A scream, like something a demonic pixie would make, rings out, and Leigh half-turns to see a small form attached to Ruth, its back to her with legs wrapped around the big clown's head.

"You little bitch!" Ruth snaps, punching at the girl with all her strength, and still, she clings on.

"Mine!" Sully growls from behind her, and that's when Leigh realizes it's not the cannibal clown attacking Ruth.

"Candy?" Leigh's confused.

"Candy Girl!" Sully groans, and Leigh's had it. She turns on the other clown, storms over, and kicks her broken leg out from under her. "Meanie!" Sully spits.

"Will you shut up!" Leigh stomps down on the broken leg, sending Sully into fits of utterly insane, agonized laughter. Leigh kicks her again, and the boot to Sully's head shuts her up.

The Triplets scarper, racing back through the tunnel like they just got caught with all their hands in the cookie jar.

"My eyes!" Ruth bellows and gets free of her attacker, bumbling back swatting at her face. Her eyes are gone; there's just two bleeding hollows with crimson mascara running down her face. She stumbles in the dark, bouncing off the walls.

The other girl lands on her feet, throwing away the eyes like discarding stale popcorn.

"Candy?" Leigh asks though she knows it's her. She'd recognize that cute little butt anywhere, but right here, right now, she wishes it was anyone else.

The little clown turns, tilting her head, flashing Leigh a wide smile laced with black stains. Her nose, a hot pink spot above bright red lips, with black stitchwork detailing, like it's sewn to her face. She only has one eyebrow, thick and curving like a cursive capital S above an inverted green triangle. The other eye circled in blue, with more painted on stitches.

"Oh, God, Candy, what have you done?"

Candy blows Leigh a kiss.

Flash-cut: Candy's hand trembles as she picks up one of the bags of black cotton candy.

"I just did what Rocky would do!" She bites her finger and giggles like a murderous chipmunk. "What you would do—"

Flash-cut: Candy holds a handful of the black cotton candy less than an inch from her lips. She hesitates for a second and closes her eyes. She sees Leigh kicking ass, flipping off the world with a rebel yell, and finds the strength to do what she must.

"No, you didn't, you shouldn't have." Leigh steps toward Candy. Even covered in blood, with the face of a mad clown, she's still the most important thing in the world to her.

Candy's eyes waver, confused.

Flash-cut: Candy's mouth twitches as the black cotton candy seeps into her blood, as it seeks out what's below, deep down, and brings it raging to the surface. She sobs, trying to stem the flood with bloody hands, but can't. Tears run down her face, leaving streaks of blue, green, and white in their wake. Candy wipes her face, spreading the tears and revealing another face—washing away her humanity and unveiling the clown within.

"I didn't do good?" Candy looks from side to side, fear twisting into soft, vivid features. "I did a bad?"

"I didn't want you to get hurt." Leigh's caught between horror and heartache, between revulsion for what she's become and the deep-rooted desire to wrap herself around Candy.

"Leigh's hurt?" Candy's head tilts as she reaches up to stroke the red welts on Leigh's neck. "Ouchies," Candy says and goes on her tiptoes, pulling Leigh down toward her with one hand; she kisses her on the neck.

Intense desire rushes through Leigh's body; she comes alive at the touch of Candy's lips on her skin. It's everything she's ever wanted and more. And it's wrong.

"No!" Leigh pushes Candy away. "Don't!"

"Candy, not good?" Candy looks at Leigh like a kicked puppy. "You don't want me?"

"I want you more than anything in the world! I spend nights thinking about you, your t-shirt on my floor, the way you laugh—the cuteness turning into belly rocking snorts. Pretending you mean it a different way when you say you love me, but not like this."

"Candy's... not worth it." Her eyes water, her lips tremble.

342

"Candy—"

"WORTHLESS CANDY!" She leaps at Leigh, slashing with sharp little nails. "WORTHLESS-WORTHLESS-WORTHLESS!"

"That's not true!"

"WORTHLESS!" Candy shrieks. "CANDY DOESN'T DESERVE LOVE!"

"You deserve all the love! You're sweet and caring, and everything I'm not!"

"NO! WORTH NOTHING!"

"You're worth everything to me," Leigh says, and she stops backing away. "I love you, Candy." She holds an arm out, the other behind her back, and waits for Candy to attack. "I do." Candy snarls, clawing at Leigh. As soon as she's close enough, Leigh wraps her arm around Candy, pinning her against her. "I love you more than you'll ever know," Leigh says through fresh tears as she sticks the needle in Candy's neck, and everything goes dark, the beating of their hearts the only sound in the cavernous silence.

Chapter Twenty-Eight
THE FINAL BITCH

Her eyes flicker, and visions of blankets bathed in the glow from a television fades, replaced by nondescript boxes and practical shelving. Despite the location, she feels safe, her head pressed against a chest that hides a racing heart.

"Leigh?" Candy smacks her lips, blinking away a gap in her memory.

"You know you snore, like real bad?" Leigh teases. Her back's up against a stack of boxes, packs of black cotton candy scattered on the floor around them.

"I don't snore," Candy protests and playfully slaps Leigh's thigh. She doesn't have the strength to lift it away, and Leigh's more than happy for her to leave it there.

"Looks like the bozos were planning on taking this show on the road," Leigh says, kicking the box of black cotton candy. It's more to distract herself from Candy's touch than anything.

"Maybe they were going to ship that junk out," Candy shudders. "Can you imagine?"

Leigh does, and it terrifies her. Despite that, she feels safe, like she could take them, as long as she has Candy. Things aren't quite as scary when you've got someone who loves you by your side, after all.

"What... what happened?" Candy struggles to recall how they ended up in this room together. The last thing she remembers was... "Oh, I, wait—"

"I got you," Leigh says. "You got me."

"That shot was for Stacey!"

"I know, but neither of us is in any condition to go looking for her." She's right. They're both too fucked up to move. "Took all I had to drag your tiny ass in here."

They sit in silence for a moment, both wishing this wasn't the case. Hoping the kid's okay, wherever she is.

"I miss Rocky," Candy sobs.

"Oh." It doesn't hurt Leigh to hear that as much as it would have just hours ago.

Rocky was a lot of things. He was Candy's first love, and though Leigh can't understand why he made Candy happy, maybe she's grown a little, and Leigh's grateful to him for giving her that. He was a dumb kid whose feet were faster than his brain and his heart even more so. A fool who made terrible mistakes and, in the end, a hero who saved the girl they both love. Leigh will always owe him a debt for that.

"Yeah, I guess Rock-For Brains wasn't so bad, all things considered."

Candy knows that's Leigh-speak for she'll miss him too, and cuddles in more.

"Too many people died today," Candy's voice quivers. "I'm glad you're still here."

"I can't believe you went all killer clown from Tiny Town just to save my ass."

"Yeah, well, I figured it was my turn to do something insanely stupid to help a friend. For a change. Did I do anything crazy?" Candy asks, trying to change the subject.

"Eh." Leigh shrugs. "You ripped the big bitch's eyes out—"

"Ew, that's so gross."

"Yeah, well it makes sense. Eyes are the groin of the face, after all."

"Still."

"Oh." Leigh hesitates to open this door, but since there's a chance neither of them are getting off this floor she figures why the hell not. "And then you tried to kiss me."

"I did what!?"

"I know, you were super horny—"

"Not! Funny!" Candy slaps Leigh's thigh again, weak as a kitten.

"It's true." Leigh's throat goes dry as she figures it's either now or never. "Candy, I..."

"I know."

"You... Did you hear? Back at the trailer?"

"No." Candy cuddles in. "I've known for a long time. I think before you did."

"Oh... well, shit, bitch, you coulda told me!"

"I figured you'd say when you were ready." Candy shrugs and then moans; even that slight movement hurts.

"It doesn't freak you out?"

"Does it freak you out?"

"Yeah!" Leigh scoffs. "Scares the shit out of me! Bad enough falling in love with your best friend, but she's a girl too; I kept feeling like something was wrong with me. Like a part of me was stuck or something, you know? Kept trying to force myself to like boys—"

"But you don't. You like girls, Leigh. It's OK."

"I don't... I don't know, but I got a bad case of loving this one, for sure."

"Yeah? I hope she's cute."

346

Leigh looks down at Candy, at the way her messy blonde hair falls across her little face, her doe eyes staring up and tiny raccoon teeth biting her lip.

"Yeah, she's pretty damn cute."

"Good." Candy snuggles in. "You deserve the cutest girlfriend there is."

"Yeah? Thing is, there's no way she's interested."

"I dunno." Candy shrugs. "I mean, I could get into it."

"Oh hell no!" Leigh snaps. "That's it! Screw this! We're getting our butts outta here right now!"

"Ouch! I thought you said—"

"Forget what I said." Leigh tries to lift herself up and can't manage it. "Damnit!"

"It's OK. This is nice. Kinda like a sleepover."

"Yeah," Leigh snorts, "only in a dusty murder basement."

"Just like in the movies."

Leigh looks at her again, at that messy hair and slightly pudgy face. "Doesn't it bug you having that hair in your face?"

"Yeah, but I'm too tired to fix it." Candy tries to blow it clear.

"Here, let me." Leigh reaches over to brush Candy's hair aside and halts. The strands flicker as though dancing in a breeze.

"What's the matter"?

"Your hair. It's..." Leigh doesn't finish the thought. Her eyes dart around the room, looking for the source of the draft. "Shh," she urges and listens carefully. There's a barely audible flutter of plastic, and now that she's listening for it, it's all Leigh can hear.

Carefully disentangling herself from Candy, Leigh forces herself to her feet and follows the sound. Atop one of the stacks of boxes, the edges of the black cotton

347

candy packaging crinkle in the breeze. Grunting, Leigh shoves the boxes aside and finds a small wooden door hidden behind them.

"No way." She can't help but smile as she pulls it open and stares into a long, dark tunnel. "Mack was right..."

"What is it?" Candy leans over to see.

"Bonko's secret bootlegger tunnel." Leigh goes to Candy and grimaces as she kneels. "Come on." She holds a hand out.

Candy tries to stand and falls back down, face scrunched up in pain. "I can't," she groans. "I feel like I'm getting sewn back together or something. It really hurts. You go—"

"Fuck that," Leigh grunts and takes Candy in her arms. "I'll carry you outta here if I have to, bitch."

Candy puts her arms around Leigh's neck and rests her head on her shoulders.

"You're the best, Leigh."

They're deep into the tunnel, the light far behind them, when the laughing starts. It bounds off rotten, old supports that don't look capable of supporting the tunnel much longer.

"Caaaaaandy Girl!" Sully's call rings out. "Oh, Caaaaaaandy Girl, where are you!?"

"Oh, you gotta be shitting me," Leigh curses. She half turns to see the silhouette of the clown in the light, jerking this way and that, like a broken doll moved by some invisible hand.

"Taaaaasty, Taaaaaasty," Sully giggles.

"I mean, she's got a point," Leigh teases and picks up the pace.

"That's not funny." Candy rubs her bite wound. "She tried to eat me."

"Tryin' to make me jealous now?"

"Not funny!"

Sully hobbles along behind them, the gap growing, but she doesn't seem to care. She drags her mangled body along, using the wall for support, the sweet taste of Candy pushing her on and on.

Leigh reaches a set of worm- and time-eaten wooden stairs, and though they sag under the combined weight of both girls, they hold as Leigh climbs them. Ahead of them, a thin stream of light breaks the darkness, shining down from high. They push through the door at the top, the old lock tearing free from the rotten wood with ease, and emerge outside what looks to be a faux outhouse, surrounded by overgrown foliage.

"Where are we?" Candy asks as Leigh puts her down. She can just about stand on her own legs but still needs to lean on Leigh for support.

Looking around, Leigh spots flickering lights and the glow of exploding fireworks roughly in the direction they came from. "There, that's Bonkin's Bonanza, so..." Through the trees, she spots something familiar. "That's Cliff's car! Come on!"

Candy and Leigh limp through the forest together towards the car. Leigh's boots crunch on broken glass and gravel as they reach it.

"Jesus, somebody smashed his window," Candy points out.

"That's nothing compared to... Actually, never mind, gimme a second." Leigh helps Candy lean on the car and climbs through the broken rear window. She clambers over to the front and puts herself down in the driver's seat. "Come on," she says as she leans over and opens the passenger door for Candy.

"You don't have the keys," Candy says as she hops along the side.

Leigh flips the sun visor down, and a key lands in her waiting palm. "Cliff was always losing them, so he kept a spare here."

Candy grunts as she sits down. "That's so... how did nobody steal it!?"

"Um." Leigh gestures around.

"Good point."

Leigh turns the key, the engine sputtering to life like it's coughing up a lung.

"Ready to get the fuck outta here?" Leigh says, taking the handbrake off.

"Yeah!" Candy cheers, then: "Look out!" as Sully throws herself on the hood.

"Hiya!" She shakes her shoulders, wide, red eyes full of demented glee.

"Fuck this!" Leigh floors it, swerving left and right, trying to shake the clown loose, but Sully just clings on, laughing like it's the best ride in the whole carnival.

"Hoo," she hoots. "Ha," she gasps.

"Leigh! Be careful!" Candy warns, too late. Unable to see where she's going, thanks to the rainbow-haired hood ornament, Leigh bumps a barrier, the car wigs out, and turns hard towards a tree. She—cut to black.

Everything is darkness
Sounds swirl around her.

Ruth staggers through the chaos of her carnival as clowns and customers fight, as delirious savagery meets indignant defiance. Screams, curses, the breaking of bones, and smashing of glass. She sees none of it and stumbles, arms held out, through the front of the Big Top.

350

The night is alive with carnival sounds: rocking riffs and wild screams ring out to the accompaniment of fireworks and gunfire, to wailing sirens and authoritative demands to desist.

"Freeze!" a voice commands, but Ruth doesn't listen. Why should she? This is her carnival, show, and the adoring public call for her presence. "Last warning!"

"Encore?" she smiles; of course! Ruth stumbles on.

"Lady, I mean it! Stop!"

"How could I say no to that!?" Ruth continues.

She doesn't hear the staccato of gunfire that follows, no that's applause! Roaring, ripping applause so profound, so emotional, it makes her shake and quiver. It floors her, and she feels the love pouring out, the rush of her fans' feet as they race towards her, and a smile spreads across Ruth's eyeless face, one that will never fade.

Leigh blinks awake to the sound of chewing. Her vision, blurry, shows her three Sullys with her back to her through a broken windshield. They spin around and around till they become one, till Leigh realizes what she's eating.

"No!" Leigh tries to open her door, rattling it, but it's been wrecked in the crash and won't budge. "Fuck!" she curses and climbs out the other side, broken body be damned. She races over to the clown, a shard of glass wedged in her thigh. "Get the fuck away from her!"

Candy lies on the ground, mercifully unconscious, as Sully holds her arm up. Blood flows down the girl's skin, streaming from three missing chunks of flesh.

Sully half-turns, looking at Leigh from the corner of her eye, a slab of Candy's flesh between her wide, smiling teeth. Vibrant, fresh splashes of crimson dot the soft blue below her eyes, spattering the whiteness of her forehead.

"You fucking little bitch!" Leigh rages.

Sully drops Candy's arm; it flops hard, lifelessly. She wipes away thick globs of blood and drool, smearing the sticky mess across her face and arms.

"I'll—" Leigh doesn't get to finish; Sully snaps around and propels herself at Leigh, sinking her teeth into her thigh. Leigh screams, and again as Sully puts her bloody paw on the shard of glass and pushes it in, deeper.

"Fuck you!" Leigh punches the clown, and it does nothing, so she does it again and again, hitting Sully with the edge, side, whichever part of her fist she can.

The clown bites down harder, her teeth almost locking.

Leigh howls, the pain agonizing, and Sully pushes the advantage—releasing the bite, she shoves, and Leigh goes down hard. Her back cracks on some rocks, and in seconds Sully's scurrying on top of her.

"Mean!" Sully growls and spits in Leigh's face. "Taste yucky!"

"Hope you fucking choke on it!" Leigh snarls and slaps at the clown while Sully takes the hits, flashing bloody, blackened teeth, and goes for Leigh's neck.

Leigh twists her shoulder at the last second, blocking Sully's lunge, and feels teeth sink into her shoulder instead.

Sully grabs a fistful of Leigh's hair and pulls hard, hoping to yank her head aside and expose the neck, but Leigh holds firm. The clown comes away with a fistful of hair instead.

Leigh's hand slaps in the grass, searching for a rock, something, anything to hit the clown with, and it lands on something cold, made of steel and wood.

No way, she thinks. Betsy. She remembers Reese hurling Mack's sawn-off away into the night, and shit, what're the odds? It's like Mack's still looking out for her somehow.

She gets her hand around the grip, and through blades of grass, Leigh can see it's open, with one shell left in the right barrel. Gotta make this count, then, she tells herself.

Sully pulls back, taking a hunk of Leigh's shoulder with her, spitting it away in disgust. Leigh, saying fuck you to the pain, headbutts the clown and, while she's dazed, Leigh flicks the sawn-off closed, brings it up, and shoves it right into the clown's mouth.

"Eat this you freaky clown bitch!"

"Oh, poo," the clown says with a mouth full of cold steel

KRAKA-BOOM!

Sully's head explodes like a balloon stuffed with meat and glitter. All that remains is the bottom half of a jaw, still gibbering as her body falls to the side.

Leigh kisses the shotgun, says a silent thank you to Mack, and detangles herself from the clown.

"Please be okay, please be okay, please be okay," Leigh begs as she scuttles over to Candy.

The girl lies still as blood pulses from open wounds.

"No." Leigh's heart sinks. "No Candy, please!" Leigh shakes her, lightly slaps her cheeks. "Don't do this to me! Don't make me the final bitch!" She feels nothing but pure, raw joy flood her heart as Candy's eyes flicker open. "Oh, thank fuck, you're—" Leigh can't finish. A tear runs down her cheek.

"Leigh? You're crying?"

"It's nothing." Leigh wipes it away and pulls Candy into the tightest hug she's ever given. "Just a single bitch tear."

They stumble out of the woods a few minutes later, onto a quiet stretch of highway. Candy's almost as pale as when she was a clown, the blood loss taking its toll. They need help, fast.

As though answering the call, a pair of headlights break the gloom in the distance.

Leigh helps Candy sit and then hobbles into the middle of the road herself. She's not giving the driver any option and waves her arms above her head while Candy slumps to the side.

The lights grow brighter, so intense Leigh has to shut her eyes and look away, but she holds her position, and it works—the truck slows to a crawl. Engine rumbling, the driver opens his door and jumps down. Leigh can't make much out, except he's a big guy.

"Please help us!" Leigh begs, pointing to Candy sitting on the grass, trying to keep pressure on her wounds.

"Jesus Christ," the driver says. "Get in." He gestures with his thumb and heads over to pick up Candy.

It takes all of Leigh's remaining strength to pull herself up into the cab and shuffle along to the middle. The passenger door opens, and the trucker places Candy down gently on the seat.

"There's a first aid kit under your seat," he nods, but Leigh doesn't have the energy. She pulls Candy in close and feels the girl's cold hand slip into hers. Tiny fingers coiling around hers without enough strength to grip.

"We're safe now," Leigh reassures her. "I got you."

Music comes through the radio, faint with low volume, but it's a song Leigh knows well, and she hums it like a lullaby.

"'Cause, girl, you were made for me." Leigh squeezes Candy's hand and feels the girl sink into her. Her whole body weight presses in, and it feels right. Like it's where she belongs. "Girl, I was made for you," she hums as tears race to her chin.

The trucker climbs behind the wheel and takes in the two blood-stained and chewed-up girls, eyebrows raising to the brim of his beaten and torn mesh cap.

"The hell happened to you two!?" he asks as flashing red and blue lights stream past, going in the opposite direction, sirens wailing into the night.

Leigh watches the lights disappear in the mirror. "Bonkin's..." is the only answer she gives.

"Clowns," the trucker shudders. He puts the truck in gear and hits the gas. "I fuckin' hate clowns."

Roll credits.

CREDITS

Well, everyone, I hope you had some f-f-f-fun and enjoyed your day at Bonkin's Bonanza. Even if you didn't, we got a strict no refunds policy around here. Complaints? Direct them to our hospitality department head, Bruce. Careful, though, he's had something funny to eat and isn't feeling himself.

This book would not exist without two incredible, talented, and inspiring women.

It started as a joke, a way to torment my good friend Casey, and quickly became my main obsession. Now, it may surprise you to find out that I am not, nor have I ever been, a teenage girl questioning her sexuality with an all-consuming crush on her best friend. Casey kept me right on that, and suggested one of the books nastiest kills—poor Not-Stu—and Shiggles the Clown was all her. Thank you for being awesome, kicking my ass, and keeping me productive on this one. You're the best.

For a long time now, I have admired the makeup effects and character work of Sully the Clown. That's right, folks, Sully's real, and she's amazing. You can find her on Instagram as @sully_the_clown, and I stress she is NOT a cannibal. At least, as far as I can tell. When I started this project, I approached her like a fanboy, saying how I wanted to create a character like one of hers. Sully graciously let me use her name and design for the book's Sully, and I only hope I've done her justice. You're an inspiration and thank you.

The artwork this time, including the interior illustrations, were by the immensely talented Matt Taylor with chapter titles by Derek Eubanks. Thank you both.

You may notice a certain level of polish to this one, and that's all down to editor extraordinaire Kelly Brocklehurst. Thank you for taking on *The Cotton Candy Massacre*.

Big thanks to my beta readers, Max and Rob, for suggesting some gnarly ideas, keeping me right, and lending me their time as always.

And now, an apology. Craig, the real-life Walker, I am deeply sorry for what I did to your character in the opening chapter. OK, no, I'm not; keep complaining and see what happens to you in the next one... Seriously, though, thank you as always for reading each draft, offering suggestions, and all your support despite you and your fictional counterpart both holding the same opinion on clowns. So—

MID-CREDITS SCENE:

"You!" Brock calls, and the camera shakes as he runs. "You! Yes, you? Wanna make ten bucks? Hold this." The camera whirls, and hands clatter across the plastic near the mic. "Like that!"

The camera settles on Brock Hauser in a poorly framed, shaking shot. His hair is a riot, suit torn and covered in dirt, but he's alive.

"This is Brock Hauser reporting exclusively from inside Bonkin's Bonanza where scenes of unspeakable carnage have occurred."

Behind him, EMTs see to the wounded carnival patrons; bodies are carried away on stretchers.

"I can't even begin to describe the horror and bloodshed, my own cameraman murdered before my eyes, people torn apart on carousels, games of chance turned into instruments of torture. I—Look out!"

The camera clatters to the ground. In the poorly angled shot, the Triplets jump, latching onto Brock. They scratch, bite, and—cut to black.

CREDITS (CONT'D)

Apologies. What happened there? Anyway...

Some shoutouts to those who keep me going.

Damien Casey — for your kind words and highly entertaining self.

Alana K. Drex — you always cheer me up with your youness and support.

Sam Hallam — thanks for always being such a huge supporter of indie horror.

Bret Laurie — for your friendship and feedback.

Jamie Stewart — whose talent is only rivaled by his kindness. Shine on, my book brother, shine on.

All the members of the Bookstagram Writer's Circle, who're always there for advice and to discuss vital topics such as hamster names and unconventional kinks.

And a special credit goes to Alex Quin — winner of the #isurvivedvirginnight contest. Alex won a death scene in *The Cotton Candy Massacre*, and he's just an awesome supporter of indie horror to boot. Thanks for playing; I feel a little bad I turned your whole family into a clown barbeque, though.

I wouldn't be able to do this without each and every one of you that's bought, read, and shared your thoughts on these books. They're only trashy horror novels, but I like them and I hope you do too. So, thank you.

And, as always, thank you Dexter for being a good boy.

Anyway, it's almost time. Soon the leaves will begin to fall, and the nights will grow long. And they'll gather, once more, somewhere in the static, lost between the channels. *The October Society Season Two*—coming soon...

POST-CREDIT SCENE:

A tricycle wheel creaks along the highway. Ahead of it sits a lonely gas station.

Stacey rides up to the first pump, and the bell dings as she crosses the sensor with the trike. No one emerges from within, so she reverses back and forth across the sensor, playing the chimes like a song.

"I'm coming, I'm coming," the voice grumbles from inside. "Keep your damn panties on..." Sully's dad trails off at the sight of a tiny clown sitting on a three-wheeled bike in front of a pump.

"Fill her up, please!" Stacey grins and flicks the bell on her trike.

"Fuck off, kid, I'm too hungover for this shit." He heads back in and slams the door.

Stacey scowls, and then her eyes flick as she smiles and hops off her trike. She flicks a knife out from her front pocket and skips over to the door.

"I said... Wait, what the fuck—" Things clang and smash inside the gas station. "The hell you doing!" Wet screams ring out and then silence.

Stacey emerges a few moments later, splattered in fresh blood, eating a bag of chips. A strangely-colored bird lands on her shoulder, and Stacey offers it one. The bird takes it, and Stacey puts another in her mouth, crunching down with a wide, bloody smile.

Matt Taylor Art Gallery

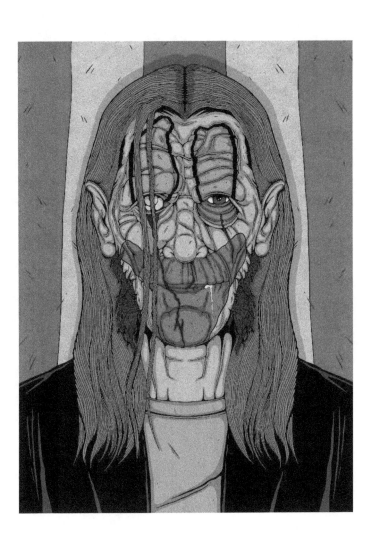

ABOUT THE DIRECTOR

Christopher Robertson has been called the "Ryan Reynolds of Indie Horror" and "some Scottish Dr. Frankenstein." He doesn't care that they were joking. His stories are popcorn features that have been described as wholesome and gruesome in the same sentence multiple times. They include the 50s teen rom-zom-com *My Zombie Sweetheart*, kid-centric throwback *The October Society*, and 90s teen-comedy meta-slasher *Virgin Night*. You can find him on Instagram as @kit_romero, and he'd love it if you stalked him there.

Also From

Once upon a time at a drive-in…

TERROR! From outer space comes crashing to Earth,
giving rise to creatures of pure—

HORROR! The likes of which the quiet little town has
never seen and the—

NIGHTMARE! That befalls two old friends as they
struggle to survive against impossible odds!

It's Friday night, date night, in the quiet little town of
Woodvale. For Suzie Palmer, this means hanging out at
the All-Night Diner and maybe cruising up to Make-
Out Point with her sweetheart. Little does she know
there's something on its way to Woodvale. Something
cruel and insidious. Something… out of this world…

MY ZOMBIE SWEETHEART is a love letter to 1950s
sci-fi movies like *The Blob* and *Invasion of the Body
Snatchers*. It's a tale of young love and alien invaders
coming soon to a drive-in near you!

The October Society

Halloween approaches, and The October Society gathers.

They come to share their stories.

Tales of dark magic and crooked lies.

Of tragic pasts and wicked cruelty.

Of misguided misadventure and sinister pranks...

Collected here are the first six episodes of the spookiest show that never was. A series only found in the static between channels, that can only be watched on broken TVs in dusty attics and damp basements. Tune in, if you can, because the author of *My Zombie Sweetheart* welcomes you to *The October Society*.

Before Valentine's Day, there is… VIRGIN NIGHT!

In the picturesque town of Cherry Lake, the kids aren't alright.

Neither is the centuries-old undead slasher that haunts the town.

Or the all-powerful megachurch with designs of the future.

On February 13th, 1998 — VIRGIN NIGHT — these will collide and the town of Cherry Lake will never be the same again.

For fans of self-aware 90s slashers — VIRGIN NIGHT will take you back to when low-rise jeans were cool, frosted tips were a thing, and getting laid was all that mattered.

I DO HOPE YOU'RE ENJOYING ALL OF MY
LITTLE PRODUCTIONS.
- Theodore Gorman.

CPSIA information can be obtained
at www.ICGtesting.com
Printed in the USA
LVHW050743040323
740925LV00013B/1022